Losing Christina
Collection

Losing Christina
Collection

CAROLINE B. COONEY

SCHOLASTIC INC.

New York   Toronto   London   Auckland   Sydney
Mexico City   New Delhi   Hong Kong   Buenos Aires

The Fog, ISBN 0-590-43806-9, Copyright © 1989 by Caroline B. Cooney.
The Snow, ISBN 0-590-41640-5, Copyright © 1990 by Caroline B. Cooney.
The Fire, ISBN 0-590-41641-3, Copyright © 1990 by Caroline B. Cooney.

12 11 10 9 8 7 6 5 4 3 2 1   6 7 8 9 10 11/0

Printed in the U.S.A.   23

This edition created exclusively for Barnes & Noble, Inc.
2006 Barnes & Noble Books

ISBN-13: 978-0-7607-9620-7
ISBN-10: 0-7607-9620-3

CONTENTS

FOG

Chapter 1

It was very hot the last week before school began: as though the wind from another world were crossing the island.

Christina packed her trunks, filling them with the heavy sweaters and thick socks she would need for a Maine winter.

Her mother kept handing her things like long underwear and pajamas with feet. Hand knit mittens with snowflakes and bathrobes with hoods. Christina would never wear such things in front of mainland children. She put them on the bottom layer of the trunk, planning never to touch them.

Burning Fog Isle had only three hundred year-round residents. Twenty-eight miles out to sea, it was Maine's most famous, most beautiful island. And it had only four children between the ages of thirteen and seventeen, so once they finished sixth grade, they were sent to the mainland for junior and senior high.

Christina knew the town on shore almost as well

as the island; her father's truck and her mother's car were kept in garages by the dock; they went into town on Frankie's boat a couple of times a month; they saw movies and shopped, went to the dentist, and got sneakers on sale just like everybody else.

It was only school that Christina had not done like everybody else. Christina had never been in a school with classrooms, a cafeteria, hallways, bells that rang, art, music, gym, and hundreds of kids. Now she would be in junior high; instead of four friends, she would have dozens.

Christina had been told that going to the mainland would be an Advantage. "You will have Advantages there," people said.

Advantages sounded rather dull and sturdy, like winter socks.

Christina did not want any part of that. She wanted love, adventure, and wild, fierce emotions that would batter her, as storms battered the island. I am thirteen, Christina thought, I am ready. I want it all.

Christina finished packing. She and her mother lugged the trunk to the front hall and locked it. Christina put the key in her purse. She had never had a purse before. She had never needed one. Now she had her first key, her first handbag, her first allowance.

Christina hurtled over the pink-flecked granite that was the symbol of Burning Fog Isle — huge, diagonally thrusting cliffs sparkling with silver mica. She ran past strangled fir trees growing out of cracks and leaped over the pink rock roses that dusted the rims.

She found the other children gathered on the hill above the village. The heat had worn them down; they looked collapsed and sunburned.

Benjamin, who would be a sophomore, regarded school as a state-mandated prison between fishing seasons. He ached for his sixteenth birthday, when he could quit school. He would turn sixteen around Thanksgiving, and he planned to stop school right then, that afternoon, and go home on Frankie's boat. Benj was rightfully a lobsterman.

His brother Michael was going into ninth grade, and he had explained several times to Christina that ninth-graders never spoke to or associated with seventh-graders. She must not expect Michael to talk to her in school. If Christina tried to hold his hand, Michael would flatten her.

Michael was fourteen. Christina had adored him all her life, and Michael had not noticed it all his life.

Boys were always difficult.

But Anya? A beautiful, brilliant star of a student? Why was Anya not excited? It was going to be her senior year. Christina had always thought of senior year as a sort of heaven, glistening and full of rainbows.

But Anya was as tense and fidgety today as she had been all summer.

"It shouldn't be so hot," said Anya. "The ocean

like glass? The morning sky free of fog? Everything is wrong."

The children squinted in the glare of sun off the smooth water.

"You nervous about school starting, Christina?" asked Benjamin. Benj was never nervous. He was fifteen and solid. He had had his own lobster boat for years. Benj got up at four every morning, started the outboard motor like his father and uncle and cousins, and went out to sea.

Christina had read many books and Benj did not fit into any of them. He was the only fifteen-year-old boy Christina knew, but he had nothing in common with fifteen-year-olds in books. Benj was more like parents in books, only stronger. Nothing frightened Benjamin Jaye.

"Seventh grade isn't so bad." Benj said.

Christina did not know why he was asking if *she* was nervous. It was so clearly Anya who was. Anya shook her head, as if the strange stillness of the Atlantic Ocean bothered her ears.

Christina had always wanted to be and look just like Anya. Anya was very fair, and unlike everybody else on the island, whether year-around, day tripper, or tourist, Anya never tanned. Like a princess in a fairy tale, Anya remained chalk white, with a frame of black hair so thick and heavy it seemed to weight her slender neck.

"We get to stay at the Schooner Inne," said Christina to the older girl. "Aren't you excited about that?"

Schooner Inne was a lovely sea captain's house,

now a bed and breakfast, which usually closed down for the winter season. This year the Inne had new owners — the high school principal and his wife. They wanted to try staying open during winter and had agreed to take the four island children who had to board in town through the school year.

"It'll be luxury," Christina reminded Anya. She knew that Anya adored rich things.

Anya's parents were real Maine, and that meant they were poor. Anya hated being poor. She hated her tiny house, its shingles curled from the salt air, white trim peeling, enormous piles of lobster traps filling the little yard. Anya dreamed of cities: sky-scrapers, escalators, high fashion, and taxis. She worked hard in school; striving, striving, striving to put Burning Fog Isle behind her and become somebody else.

Christina would be sharing a room at the sea captain's house with Anya. Christina was worried. What if she didn't please Anya? What if Anya grew angry with Christina for being younger, dumber, and duller? What if the town kids teased Anya for hanging around with a baby like Christina?

Mainland kids always teased island kids. Michael and Anya had given her instructions on how to handle the teasing. "Just laugh," they said. "No fists. It doesn't work. It gives the island a bad reputation."

Nobody was more "island" than Christina. Everybody who saw her called her "local color." She had had a thousand photographs taken of her, and been painted twice. "You are beautiful," the tourists and the artists would tell her, but they would ruin it by smiling slightly, as if it were a weird beauty or they were lying. She was as harsh and stern as the pink granite she stood on. This did not make Christina happy. She had never read anything in *Seventeen* about strength as beauty.

Christina was the only child she or the summer people had ever come across with tri-colored hair. Mostly dark brown, it was streaked with silver and gold. With every movement, Christina seemed to change color. She loved her hair and wore it just like Anya, but on Anya the mass of hair was magnificent, and on Christina it was a tangled thicket.

When Christina studied *Seventeen* magazine, analyzing models, make-overs, and teenage stars, she found no resemblance between herself and those girls — not hair, lips, eyes, cheekbones, posture — nothing.

If she did possess any beauty, Christina did not know what it consisted of.

The sea captain's house was beautiful. Symmetrical and graceful, high and white. Perhaps she would absorb some of that beauty just living there.

"The sea captain's wife," Anya said in a strange, glassy voice, "committed suicide."

"Oh, Anya," said Benj irritably. "That's just a legend, and anyway it was a hundred years ago and who cares?"

"It might have been weather like this when the sea captain's wife stepped off her roof," said Anya. She walked away from the other children to balance on a granite outcropping that rose from the Atlantic

Ocean like drowned rocks. She stared at the mirror of the sea as if reading her fortune in its seaweed-laden palm.

The sunshine poured out of the sky like liquid. The Atlantic did not move. Even though the tide was coming in, there was no sound of surf. No waves crashing against the rocks. No booming where air was slapped into rock pockets. The water just lay there, as if a personality stronger than the ocean itself had flattened it.

Below them, in the small, sheltered harbor of Burning Fog Isle, tourists gathered on the dock for the return boat to the mainland. Their baggage and suitcases littered the wharf. They crowded into the tiny souvenir shack, buying proof that they had visited the most famous island off the coast of Maine.

Christina thought, in a few days my island life will shut down. No longer one of the little children in the white schoolhouse, but off-island at last! Maybe I'll even have a boyfriend like Anya.

Anya's boyfriend was a very preppy townie named Blake. Blake had come out to the island once during the summer, as a surprise for Anya. Blake was dressed in what the children called Catalog Maine — a fine rugby shirt with wide stripes, high quality boat shoes without socks, and loose trousers made of imported cotton.

Christina was sure that what depressed Anya was not the strange weather, not the beginning of school, not having to room with somebody four years younger, and not even the oddity of boarding with the principal.

It was Blake. Her boyfriend had seen her as she really was — poor, island Maine. And would he, during their senior year, with SAT's, football season, college applications, prom, and graduation, still be interested in Anya Rothrock?

Frankie's boat nosed into the dock. The tourists jumped up and down with excitement. They got in the way, and their little children barely escaped falling into the water and getting crushed between boat and wharf. They abandoned the souvenir shack.

The souvenir shack was so dilapidated its roof had settled in a curve, and its door no longer closed. The shingles had fallen off the entire ocean side of the building. Winter weather would knock it down for good, and maybe the creature who ran it would never return.

The children called her a creature, rather than a woman.

She had skin like leather left out on the rocks — cracked and crusted. She wore fingernail polish as dark as dried blood, and several of her teeth were missing. She was the only person Christina had ever encountered who never went to the dentist.

The tourists clambered onto Frankie's boat. Frankie's dog, Rindge, snarled at all of them.

Frankie used to have a sweeter dog. Peg. How Christina had loved Peg! A soft Alaskan husky with eyes as blue as the sky. But Peg went overboard once to catch a hot dog a tourist tossed for her, and the sea was rough and Frankie couldn't get her back, even though she was a good swimmer.

Frankie tried so hard to reach Peg, and Peg tried even harder to swim back to him, but they didn't make it. Peg drowned.

Christina shivered, remembering.

She shook the memory away. "You know what we could get at the souvenir shop?" she said. "Posters for our bedroom walls! Let's all buy a poster."

Christina loved to imagine her room at the Schooner Inne. Would she have a bed with a lacy canopy? Wallpaper with sprigged flowers? Would there be a little desk beneath the window, so when she tired of doing homework, she could look out across the sea? She knew what she would have on her bed: the quilt her mother had made her. Each square on the quilt had a lovely name: falling star, bear's paw, flying geese. Dark reds, soft pinks, and rich blues tumbled together to make a work of art.

"I want a flower poster," announced Christina, jumping from rock to rock, reaching the top of a long slanted wooden stair with splintered handrails. "Manet or Monet, or whoever he is, or both."

But Anya did not want any posters in their room. "Let's not go down there," she said. "I'm afraid of that souvenir woman. Her eyes are too blue."

Benj and Michael took the steps two at a time, passing the girls. The entire stair swayed drunkenly under their feet.

"I don't know where the souvenir woman spends the night," Christina told Anya.

"She doesn't sleep," said Anya.

The door of the souvenir shop was flung open, and

banged hard against the wall. The souvenir woman stood in the doorway like a photograph of herself.

"Look at the hoods on those eyes," Anya whispered to Christina. "They aren't hinged for closing. Those eyes are following me, Christina. Lobster eyes on stalks. Don't they remind you of Peg? That woman took Peg's dead eyes out of the ocean and stuck them in her own head."

Christina felt sick, almost dizzy. "That's the most disgusting thing I ever heard, Anya," she said. "Don't talk like that." But the thought stayed with her: Peg, brown paws failing, slipping beneath the waves, only to have this creature seize her eyes. So that Peg swam on forever, without air, without sight.

The souvenir woman smiled, black holes where her teeth were missing, as if she had been shot. Slowly she pulled a poster out of the barrel. The woman moved toward the girls. Her layered skirts were long and thick, as leathery as her skin.

"If she touches me," said Anya, "I will turn to leather."

Christina swallowed. Already it seemed her throat had hardened, gotten thicker, turned leathery.

Anya stepped behind Christina, using her for a shield.

The souvenir woman rolled toward them, like a wave or a tire. The lobster eyes chose Anya. "I have a poster just for you." The poster in her claw-like hand was rolled picture side in, so it was only a plain white tube. "Come. Take it."

Christina shook her head. Anya laughed out of

tune. "Don't let her touch me, Chrissie," whispered Anya.

Christina could think of nothing to say, either to the souvenir woman or to Anya. Would she be like this at school? Speechless and stupid in front of the sophisticated mainland kids?

"Yours," said the woman, with her dreadful smile.

"No, thank you," said Christina.

The woman laughed. Each eye focused separately; one eye for Anya, one eye for Christina. "No charge," said the woman to Anya. "I want you to have it."

Christina shook her head for both of them.

The woman jabbed Christina in the stomach with the poster, as if it were a lance or a sword. Behind her, Anya whimpered.

It's paper, Christina told herself, it's nothing but a piece of paper. I can just stuff it in the garbage as soon as I'm home.

She took the poster. In her hand it felt strangely damp, as if it were not made of paper at all, but of sea water.

"Come on, come on," Michael was saying, "don't take all day, Chrissie. Have you got the one you want?" He and Benj were each holding posters; they had somehow finished paying for them.

Christina stared down at the poster in her hand.

The souvenir woman smiled, blue eyes lying in her face like jellyfish dying on the rocks.

The children abandoned the village and went to Christina's house.

Burning Fog Isle had three kinds of houses: real ones, like Anya's or the boys'; summer houses, built by vacationers; and summer cottages, built by millionaires generations ago.

To Christina the word "cottage" meant "castle." The cottage in which Christina and her family lived had thirty-two rooms. It had been built in 1905 by a family from Boston and was owned now by a family from Dallas who came up three weeks a summer, if they came at all.

Christina's family lived there year-round in the wing over the kitchens and pantries.

Christina's father could do anything: electricity, plumbing, carpentry, roof repair, gardening. It never bothered him that the Romneys didn't have a house of their own. He just slowly circled the cottage, year by year, painting and caulking his way around.

"What's your poster of?" Michael said to Christina.

"It's not my poster. I don't know what it's of," said Christina.

"You don't *know*?" said Michael. "What do you mean? You didn't look at it before you bought it? Christina, you are so strange."

Christina could not bear for Michael, whom she worshiped, to think her strange. "We didn't pick it out," said Christina. "She forced it on us."

"Who?" Michael asked.

"The woman who owns the shack," said Anya. "She made us take it."

"She was stabbing me with that poster," agreed Christina.

Michael was disgusted. "Christina, when you get to the mainland, you better not be yarning all the time. People don't make friends with people who yarn."

"I'm not yarning," protested Christina. "Weren't you watching? Didn't you see her, all wrinkled and evil, forcing me to take this?"

"Don't use that word, *yarn*," said Michael. "It's island. It's local. You have to behave right once you're in school, Christina, or you'll get picked on. You say dumb things like 'wrinkled and evil' about some pitiful old woman who can't even afford to go to the dentist and you won't make any friends. You want to have friends, don't you?"

Christina could think of nothing more hideous than not having friends. The boys made it sound as if they would not be her friends either, should she go yarning around. Michael and Benj rolled their eyes. "And we have to live with her for a whole year," said Michael.

Christina flushed.

"Let's see this famous poster," said Benj.

Christina pulled the rubber band off the tube. Anya took one corner of the poster and Christina the other, and together they held it open.

It was a poster of the sea.

The sea at its cruelest, the sea bringing destruction.

Green, blue, and black blended into a cauldron. Waves stretched up as if to rip a child off the rocks. White froth like beckoning fingers strangled little fish. Beneath the water blurry figures tried to swim up to the surface.

"Look," whispered Anya. Her long, thin fingers tightened convulsively on the paper. "You can see the drowned. Their bodies are floating at the bottom of the poster."

Christina found herself tipping forward, wanting to rescue everybody. It's paper, she reminded herself.

Anya stared into the poster. She swayed slightly, and her white skin grew even paler. "Look at the fingers of the dead," she whispered. "See them scrabbling at the surface?"

Michael inspected the poster. "Christina, you're so funny," he teased. "We live by the sea. It's eating the paint off our houses. It drowned our ancestors. Why do you want more of it? I can't believe you went and bought a poster of the sea."

Christina let go her corner. The poster folded up diagonally, so that a corner of sea stared from the long white tube.

"It drowned our ancestors," Anya repeated. "Perhaps it's been too long for the sea since it had a Romney. Or a Rothrock. Or a Jaye."

Christina rolled the poster sea side in and threw it in the grass. But then she picked it up again.

Chapter 2

There was shut-in fog the day they left: thick fog, like the inside of an envelope.

This was the fog for which the island was famous. A trick of atmosphere sometimes occurred, so that when the sun shone behind the fog, it looked like fire. Many times in the last three hundred years mainlanders had thought there was something burning at sea: a ship perhaps, in desperate need. But it had always been just the fog that hovered over the island.

Christina loved the fog. It hugged her and kept her secrets. It belonged to the sea and went back to the sea, and you could neither hold it nor summon it.

Anya hated fog. She insisted that her hair never looked good: She could work an hour setting her hair, walk out the door, and the fog would finger through her hair and ruin it.

The parents carried the children's trunks and boxes and suitcases on board Frankie's boat.

Dolly stood to one side and wept.

Dolly was Benj and Michael's little sister. She was also Christina's best friend. Only eight months younger than Christina, Dolly was in sixth grade, and, because they were the only girls anywhere near the same age, Christina and Dolly had always done everything together.

Dolly was small and wiry, with red hair in braids. "Christina gets to go to the mainland. Christina gets to go to real school. Christina gets to board at Schooner Inne. Have Anya for a roommate." Dolly ripped the top of her old white sneaker against the splinters of the dock. "Next year," said Dolly in grief, "when I get to board, Anya will have graduated. Benj will have quit school. It won't be the same! It's not fair. I want to go this year, too!" cried Dolly.

"Don't be silly," said her parents.

"Get lost," said her brothers.

Dolly had been born on Thanksgiving Day, and Mrs. Jaye let them use her for Baby Jesus in that year's Christmas pageant. She was only four weeks old and a ten-year-old Mary dropped Dolly headfirst into the manger, but there wasn't any brain damage, the doctor who was flown in told them. (Michael and Benj always said there was plenty, the worst kind.) Dolly wanted to be Baby Jesus every year. Dolly said it was pretty boring to have Jesus always either in diapers or dying on a cross, and why didn't we have a nice six-year-old Jesus (Dolly) or a really decent ten-year-old Jesus (Dolly), and now she said, "I'm almost as old as Christina, let me come to school, too!" But her parents hung onto her.

Christina was swept by panic. What if she didn't make friends? What if Dolly remained, forever, the only friend Christina ever had? What if Anya hated sharing a room with her and Michael and Benj hated sharing rooms with each other and everything was awful?

She hugged Dolly fiercely. Summer people laughed gently. Christina knew they thought of her as a pitiful little country girl who had never been off-island and was afraid of the Big Bad Mainland. Christina felt like spitting on them.

"Have a good time," whispered Dolly. "Send me tapes." She pressed into Christina's hand a beautifully wrapped present, which Christina knew, since they had mail-ordered it together, contained a half dozen new, blank cassette tapes on which Christina was to dictate all the news, tell Dolly every single detail, and on which, by return boat, Dolly would describe the island.

Frankie said, "Okay, now, we said our good-byes? We sure? We absolutely done here? Huh, Lady Christina?" Frankie was very tall and thin; just skin tightened over lanky bones. He wore a Red Sox baseball cap and chewed a pipe. He never bought tobacco and never smoked; he just liked the pipe in his mouth.

"Done," said Christina, and she felt horribly, terrifyingly, "done" — as if she would never return to Burning Fog Isle. She said nothing, letting Dolly do all the weeping good-bye. She waved calmly to her parents and spoke in a relaxed fashion to Anya. The wind fingered their hair, making Anya's a dark storm and Christina's a mass of glowing ribbons. The tourists said how beautiful they were.

Frankie took the boat out into the solid gray of the ocean. They headed into the fog, and the island vanished; the fog soaked it up.

"The island has drowned," said Anya. She trailed her fingers in the fog. "Or have we drowned?"

One tourist murmured to his wife, "Don't those two girls look like ancient island princesses? Marked out for sacrifice?"

The wife did not laugh. "Sent away for the sake of the islanders," she whispered, "to be given to the sea."

Anya accidentally jogged Christina's arm.

The silvery-paper package with its pink and lavender ribbons was knocked out of Christina's hand. She tried to catch it, but it fell overboard. Frankie's boat surged on. The present floated in the waves, only the ribbons above water.

"It's an omen," said the summer people, laughing.

The children did not laugh.

"It's only tapes," said Christina, although she felt sick and desperate, because now how would she exchange with Dolly? She had not even read Dolly's good-bye card yet. Christina let herself cry a moment, knowing that her face was so damp from the fog nobody would be able to tell.

The boys had seen. They came out of the cabin to commiserate. Benj said not to worry; he would buy Christina another tape. I'm such a hick I forgot I could buy more, she thought. I forgot about stores.

Christina thought of her allowance. Her mother had given her five dollars a week. It sounded like a fortune, but Anya said it was nothing; Anya said Christina would be island poor and laughed at.

It was low tide when they docked. The pilings that held up the dock were long and naked, like telephone poles. They weren't pretty. They weren't symmetrically placed. They were just there.

Out in the harbor were friendship sloops, lobster smacks, visiting yachts, and cabin cruisers, trawlers, and Boston Whalers. The rich, sick, sea smell of bait was everywhere, coming from the herring in the barrels in the bait house.

Before them the town rose in layers.

There were the docks, boathouses, and fishmarkets. Then came the tourist lanes — boutiques; antique shops; boat, moped, and bike rentals; real estate agents, and ocean view inns. Next came the real town — gas station, bank, laundromat, shoe store, discount appliance store. Up on the hills were the houses, jammed next to each other. Layers of green tree and hill poked between roofs. Scarlet geraniums bloomed in dooryards.

The summer people clambered off Frankie's boat first, the way summer people always do. Michael and Benj began shouldering the trunks and boxes.

A wave of excitement as wild and strong as the ocean gales swept over Christina.

She was crossing a frontier.

Childhood jumped rope on the isle, but now she would put away childhood, and be a teenager. She would fend for herself and answer to none.

"Anya, I'm grown up now," she whispered, but Anya neither agreed nor disagreed. Anya's eyes were searching for the Shevvingtons.

The children were all old Maine stock, with old names. Benj, Michael, and Dolly were Jayes; Anya was a Rothrock; and Christina, a Romney. The sea captain's wife, who stepped off the roof all those generations ago, had been born a Rothrock like Anya. She had married Captain Shevvington.

The principal's name was Shevvington. Christina's father said that was why the school board hired him — to have a Shevvington back in town, to match Shevvington Street, Shevvington House Restaurant, and the Shevvington Collection in the Maritime Museum.

At orientation back in July, the island parents and children had met Mr. Shevvington. He had strange eyes. Unblinking and hypnotic, like a dog's. Christina had wanted to stare right back, but the mad dog image frightened her, as if to stare wrongly would make Mr. Shevvington bite her, and she would be mortally wounded and die in agony.

How impressed all the parents were with the principal! He's such a caring man! they said to each other. He's so understanding and yet so well disciplined. He's gentle with the children, but strong and firm. He will be a perfect role model for the boys and a father figure for the girls.

Christina had been amazed to hear her own parents talking like this, as if they had all just read the same pop psychology book.

Christina, Anya, and the boys stood on the dock, surrounded by piles of possessions. Trunks, cardboard boxes, tennis rackets, suitcases, tote bags, backpacks. Christina felt like an immigrant who would probably have to get shots before she would be allowed to stay.

High on the cliffs to their left, on the other side of the Singing Bridge, perched on top of Candle Cove, sat the Schooner Inne.

Nobody in his right mind would build on Candle Cove. It was a fine place for warehouses or factories, but not for homes.

Tide at Candle Cove was twenty-eight feet — as high as the roof of a house! The sides of the cove were rocks, huge outcroppings with ledges and shelves that appealed to children and romantics.

A hundred years before, a couple on their honeymoon had picnicked on a granite outcropping that was twenty-five feet above the mud. How happy they must have been, sharing lemonade, perhaps nibbling at the same scarlet apple. How exciting the tide must have seemed, rumbling forward, the waves leaping and lashing. And suddenly the two lovers must have realized that twenty-five feet was not high enough to be safe from a twenty-eight foot tide. Christina imagined them trying to get off the ledge, the boy lifting the girl, her long skirts snagging, the water roaring around them, the boy thinking *No, no, no, no, please don't* —

Their bodies were never found. The sea took them to picnic forever and ever. The town had fenced off the cliff around Candle Cove, but still people went down there, climbing on the rocks, or worse, walking on the mud flats exposed at low tide.

If nobody in his right mind would build on Candle Cove, thought Christina, then the sea captain was not in his right mind when he built his house. Why did his bride step off the roof?

"If the Shevvingtons don't hurry up and get here," said Benj irritably, "we'll use your father's truck to haul this stuff to the Inne, Christina. You got keys?"

"Of course she doesn't have keys," said his brother. "She's only thirteen. She doesn't know how to drive."

A solid trunk of a woman appeared between them. She had no female shape at all. She was without curves: a large thick post with hair on top. Even her head had no curves. Her features were very flat, so that she had no profile, only a face. "There will be no bickering in my household," she said, laying a hand on the shoulders of the brothers. Her hands were fat, the flesh bulging over the many rings on her short fingers. The nails were long and hooked and had just been polished dark red, so that they seemed to bleed.

Michael and Benj, who, with their sister Dolly, had never done anything except bicker, pulled away from her hands.

"I am Mrs. Shevvington. Load your belongings into the van. Do not dillydally. There will be no dillydallying in my household."

Christina could not imagine this pie dough wed to Mr. Shevvington. Many years and many pounds separated them. Mr. Shevvington was so graceful, handsome, and silvery.

The creature closed her thick, curved palm over Christina's cheek. "Dillydallying?"

"No, no," said Christina, leaping away from the hand. It was sweaty. It had left a damp print on her cheek.

The boys began loading the mountain of possessions into a dark green utility van with rust along the bottom. A driver sat motionless behind the steering wheel.

Mrs. Shevvington commented that they had brought a considerable amount with them; she did not know where they thought they would store all these things. Certainly she, Mrs. Shevvington, did not propose to have her precious space given up to old tattered suitcases.

"You have an inn," protested Christina. "You must be able to store a million suitcases and trunks."

"When I state a fact, Christina, do not contradict me."

Christina flushed. The others looked embarrassed for her.

Their posters had been rolled into one cardboard shipping tube, which had fallen on the dock. "Is this garbage?" Mrs. Shevvington asked.

"No, I just didn't see it," said Benj.

"Sloppy," said Mrs. Shevvington. "There will be no sloppy thinking or acting in my household."

Benjamin's smile faltered and vanished. Christina's face would not even form a smile. She has flattened all our faces to match hers, thought Christina, and we have known her only for a minute.

Mrs. Shevvington waved the van away. It drove off without them.

"We will walk," said Mrs. Shevvington. "It is a brisk walk, straight up Breakneck Hill. Good for you."

Michael nodded. "There will be no laziness in your household, huh, Mrs. Shevvington?" he said, with his most charming smile, the smile that won all the summer visitors over and made them come back the next year.

Mrs. Shevvington smiled. Her teeth were as short as her fingernails: tiny yellowed stubs that hardly seemed like teeth at all. Michael's sweet smile vanished slowly, as if being erased. When Michael's smile was entirely gone, Mrs. Shevvington closed her own lips. Her face remained solid. "It is called Breakneck Hill," she said, "because a hundred years ago, when bicycles first came into fashion, a young boy — about your age, Christina — rode his bicycle down that hill. Of course it was too steep for the rudimentary brake his cycle possessed."

"What happened to him?" Michael asked.

Mrs. Shevvington raised thin wispy eyebrows. "He broke his neck, of course."

I don't want to live with her for a year, Christina thought. I can't bear to sit at breakfast with her, or sort laundry with her, or have her say good night.

Christina wanted to run back down Breakneck Hill and leap back on the boat with Frankie, where

Rindge would wag his tail and keep her safe, with his salty, doggy smell.

How could the others walk so calmly up Breakneck Hill?

Christina looked back. Frankie was already leaving. She clung to the safety fence, and it wobbled beneath her grip.

Breakneck Hill was very steep, and no effort had been made to terrace it. It hurt their feet to walk at such a tilt. The wind tore at them, alternately pushing them away from the edge and yanking them toward it. In winter, spray from the waves would glaze the sidewalk with ice.

It must have been a tragic time, a hundred years ago, she thought, what with the boy on the bike, the honeymooners, and the sea captain's wife.

Mrs. Shevvington handed Anya the poster tube to carry, and Anya went white and shivered, taking it.

Michael pointed down into the mud flats that spread on either side of the channel. Out on the flats walked a man in a wet suit. The wet suit was brown rather than the usual black, and it was hard to distinguish the man from the mud. He seemed bodyless. Skinless. Rubbery and slick.

"Idiot," said Mrs. Shevvington. She sounded rather pleased, as if she liked comparing herself favorably to idiots. She paused to watch the man.

They were directly over Candle Cove, with breathtaking views out to sea and into Maine.

The tide crept slowly in. Licking the barnacles,

inching toward the docks and the town, it slithered along like a great flat fish.

The man in the brown wet suit looked at the pancake of water and cocked his head, as if wondering whether to bother about it.

A queer, sickening whisper had begun.

Benj said, "It's the tide. It's coming." He ran to the edge of the cliff and leaned over the flimsy wire. "Get out!" he yelled at the wet suit. "Get out of the cove! Now!"

Christina, whose life was governed by tides, had never seen a tide like this. Although she had sat on the town docks a hundred times as this very tide came in, and from safety had laughed at its power, she had never seen the tide from above — the horror of the ocean coming home to Candle Cove.

The pancake of flat water that had crawled over the mud flats rippled, as if monsters were writhing in it.

The wet suit began running now, in a horrible slow pattern, like a man living out all Christina's nightmares: his feet caught, the mud sucking on him.

The wet suit reached one of the ladders that stuck down into the cove like trellises for roses.

The water at his feet buckled like a milkshake in a blender.

The wet suit ran up the ladder, and the water ran with him, eating his ankles.

The rest of the ocean hurtled into the narrow granite opening of the Cove. It was loud as thunder, loud as a rock concert when you're sitting next to the stage.

Tons of green water crashed toward the docks.

As the first wave passed beneath them, the children actually tasted it. The wind lifted salt up toward them, and the air was colder from the cold of the Atlantic, and it brushed their cheeks with ocean air.

Anya cried out, but her cry was drowned by the crash of the tide.

The wet suit made it.

He stood only inches above the waves that had tried to taste him, and delicately shook off his feet to get rid of clinging seaweed.

The wet suit did not seem like a person, but like brown rubber that moved. Christina wanted to say so but she was afraid to yarn in front of Mrs. Shevvington. When she looked around for comfort, Mrs. Shevvington's one-dimensional face horrified Christina as much as the wet suit.

Christina took Anya's arm for support.

Anya was smiling insanely. It was a weird, glowing smile, as if something fluorescent moved inside her. "You don't want to be here this year after all, do you?" whispered Anya. "For all your dreams of freedom, and first love, and sea captains' houses, you know it's wrong, don't you, Christina? The sea is wrong, the year is wrong, the — "

"Anya," said Benj, "stop making Chrissie nervous. She's got enough to worry about, starting junior high."

Chapter 3

The sea captain had built his house solidly — white clapboard with shutters in a green so dark it was almost black, like the sea in bad weather. There was no land around the Inne: The back steps opened onto the sea cliffs, and the front steps opened right to the street. Stapled to the cliff edge, high above the sea, the house loomed against an empty sky as if there were not one thing between the house and Europe.

Mrs. Shevvington slid her key into the gleaming brass handle of a green front door so large three people could walk in at once. The door swung silently open.

Inside, the hall was narrow, with narrow stairs going steeply up, as if the captain had forgotten this was a mansion he was building, not a crowded ship.

Christina looked up the stairwell. It was like looking up a lighthouse. The steps ran in ovals, curving at the landings. High, high above, the glass in the cupola glittered in the September sun. The cupola did not seem to have a floor. Christina was disappointed. "I thought you could sit up there," she said to Mrs. Shevvington. She had thought of herself with a book, binoculars, and a bag of potato chips, sitting tucked away in the cupola, with the best view in Maine all to herself.

"No. It is unsafe. It can be reached only by a ladder. Never go up there." Mrs. Shevvington made it sound as dangerous as picnicking on railroad tracks. "If I find I cannot trust you children to stay away from it," said Mrs. Shevvington, her voice slowing down and getting rougher, "I will have to take Steps."

In the dining room, black-and-gold willow trees arched over narrow bridges, while black peacocks strutted in stone-littered gardens. What strange wallpaper, thought Christina.

"The sea captain sailed to Japan a lot," said Mrs. Shevvington in explanation. "House has the original wallpaper. Very historic. Nothing children should ever be near," she added, glaring, as if they were already attacking the walls with crayons.

"Are there any guests right now?" Christina asked.

"No."

Michael started to walk into the dining room but Mrs. Shevvington caught his shoulder. What strength was in that grip. Michael froze like a child playing Stone Tag. His mobile face and laughing mouth became solid, his knees stiff; he was a tilted statue.

"These rooms are not for you," said Mrs. Shevvington. "These rooms are for paying guests." She let go of the statue and he turned back into Michael.

"We pay," Christina objected.

"A pittance from the town; it's hardly an income."

Michael rubbed his shoulder where her hand had been attached.

"And do not run down the stairs. It will bother the guests, and you might fall."

It was Christina's opinion that there was no way to get down a staircase except by running. And she had never fallen in her life.

Mrs. Shevvington showed them the formal living room. It too was Oriental in flavor, with shiny lacquered furniture and pearl inlaid flowers.

Christina was beginning to have sympathy for the bride who had hurled herself off the cliff. Who could be comfortable in rooms full of black-and-gold peacocks?

"For guests," said Mrs. Shevvington.

She showed them a library. Walls of shelves, but very few books. Big leather chairs and a bare desk. "For guests," said Mrs. Shevvington.

"But we're guests, too," Christina said.

Mrs. Shevvington led them into the kitchen, which was enormous. It must have been remodeled in the 1950s, because it had rows of white metal cabinets with curved edges. The countertops were green marbleized Formica with stainless steel rims. Near the sink tiny steel cabinets with little doors opened to reveal rolls of waxed paper and aluminum foil, waiting to be torn off. A very large table with a white surface and wooden legs as thick as thighs sat in the middle of the room.

Christina thought it was the ugliest kitchen she had ever seen in her life.

The Atlantic Ocean pounded outside. But even when Christina stood at the sink and drew up on her tiptoes to look out, she could not see the water.

Off the kitchen was a small, dark room, filled with old sagging furniture, the kind people left in beach houses rented out by the week. It had a small black-and-white television and a worn stack of last year's magazines. "You children will be using this room," said Mrs. Shevvington.

Christina waited for the others to object. She had spoken up several times; it was their turn — they were older.

But Anya merely stood with the poster of the sea in her hand as if she were glued to it. Michael was staring at his shoelaces. Benj was playing with his Swiss army knife.

Well, all right, if they wanted to be toads and get run over by a truck like Mrs. Shevvington, they could stay silent. Christina had never made a habit of staying silent. She had yelled at summer residents who dropped soda cans on the rocks and summer artists who abandoned paint tubes among the wildflowers. She had yelled at summer yachters who had the nerve to tie up at her father's slip, so that when he came into the harbor he had no place for his own boat on his own island.

Christina was more than capable of yelling at anyone.

She turned to yell at Mrs. Shevvington.

Mrs. Shevvington's eyes moved inside her flat

head. The eyes seemed to separate from her face, like movable eyes in an oil painting. "Yes, Christina?" she said very softly. She inclined her head toward Christina, like a guillotine in slow motion.

Christina looked at Michael and Benj and Anya for support. Surely this was not how mainland people normally treated island boarders.

Mrs. Shevvington smiled at Christina. Her horrid little teeth were like kernels of corn on a shriveled ear.

The poster of the sea fell out of Anya's hand.

"Our parents — " Christina began, leaning over to pick up the poster. But she got no further.

Mr. Shevvington entered the room.

Christina recognized him from the orientation of the previous July. How handsome he was! What fine features he had — not squashed and rubbery like his wife's, but sharp and defined. He wore a suit, which to Christina was very unusual. Nobody on the island ever wore one. The suit was soft gray, with the narrowest, most subtle pinstripes and in the breast pocket a dramatic red paisley silk handkerchief. Christina longed to touch the handkerchief. It was city fabric, city style.

She saw her parents suddenly as hicks, who would never own any handkerchief except Kleenex.

Christina looked into Mr. Shevvington's eyes. They were soft and gray, as welcome as spring rain.

"Children. What a pleasure. We've been getting ready for you all summer." With his fist he tilted Christina's chin up and kissed her forehead. She felt that if she were to ask for the silk hanky he would give it to her, that he would give her anything, and therefore she could not bear to ask him for a single thing. His height was perfect, the way he loomed over her was protection, his shadow was warmth.

"Christina," he said, "we don't want to worry our parents, now, do we? There are going to be adjustments we'll all have to make, learning how to live under one roof and get along."

He said he knew he could trust Christina never to be difficult or cause scenes. He said a child who loved her parents would write only cheerful letters, make only happy phone calls, because love meant never worrying your mother and father.

His smile moved across all four of the children, binding them, requiring smiles in return, like signatures on a contract, so they could never forget, never be bad. They would always adjust.

He said, "Christina, I can see already that you're going to be the spokeswoman of the group. I'm very impressed. A girl of your age, and already so articulate."

She felt as warm as if she had been toasting in front of a fire. Christina resolved never to tell her parents if she had any problems. A girl who was in junior high was old enough to take care of herself and protect her parents from worry.

Mr. Shevvington laughed and turned to his wife. "Candy, we're going to enjoy Christina, aren't we?" he said.

Candy? Her name is Candy? Christina thought. Impossible.

"Anya," Mr. Shevvington said now. He kissed

her in just the same way, fist under Anya's delicate chin, his lips planted on her forehead. "You are looking as beautiful as last year. We expect great things of you during your senior year, Anya." He surveyed her with the attention of a student learning the details of a piece of art.

Anya smiled up into Mr. Shevvington's eyes. "I won't let you down," she said, her voice full of emotion. "I'll do anything you say."

The principal smiled. It was a flat, bright smile, like the glassy sea on the day they got the posters. "I know," he said.

The Shevvingtons are sticky, Christina thought. Like the back of a stamp. I'm afraid of them.

Mrs. Shevvington's arm went around Christina's shoulder, and it tightened in what might have been a hug, or the first move of a strangle.

The principal spoke to Benj, saying he knew this school year was going to be so wonderful that Benj would never want to quit. Benj looked bored, but he didn't bother to argue, and just nodded.

Mr. Shevvington shook hands with Michael, saying that as a ninth-grader Michael was eligible for Junior Varsity and, with Michael on the teams, the school would have a splendid athletic year.

Anya turned her face toward the principal like a sunflower to the sky.

"I'm sorry I can't have lunch with you," Mr. Shevvington said, his handsome features drooping with distress. Anya's face mirrored his. "But I must run back to the high school to deal with some annoying odds and ends before we open in the morning." His face re-lit. "First day of class! You kids pretty excited?"

The boys remained bored.

Anya nodded joyfully. A puppy in a litter, thought Christina, wagging a tail for him.

"Upstairs," said Mrs. Shevvington, steering them through the halls. Christina was slow to obey. Mrs. Shevvington pushed her. It was like being touched by a jellyfish. Flesh soft and flaccid, as if there were no bones beneath the white surface.

The Jaye brothers were already racing upstairs. "Third floor," said Mrs. Shevvington. "Mr. Shevvington and I and the guests are on the second floor."

The boys' feet pounded on thick vermilion carpet up to the second floor and then sounded completely different — heavier, drummier.

There's no carpet on our stairs, thought Christina, and it seemed a metaphor for the year to come — there would be no carpet on this year.

"Your rooms are a bit bare," Mrs. Shevvington said. "But you may decorate any way you wish." She stayed at the bottom while the children circled the long, climbing stairs.

At the second floor a white-banistered balcony ran all the way around the open stairs, and numbered doors opened off it. One door was open. Inside, a white nubbly rug lay beside a shiny brass bed, and a puffy pink comforter matched balloon curtains. A delicate nightstand, white with gold trim, held a tiny hobnail glass lamp and a pretty little antique clock.

Let my room be like that! Christina thought.

The gentle curve of the stairs became tighter. The carpet stopped. The stairs were plain wood, and scuffing feet had worn hollows in the treads. The banisters needed dusting; the little knobs and whorls of the posts were black with grime.

The room that Anya and Christina were to share was at the top of the stairs. The door opened right onto the stairs. Christina thought, If we miss the bathroom at night, we'll fall all the way. Break every bone until we hit bottom.

Anya and Christina's room had a bare wood floor, white walls, no curtains, just paper shades yellow with age. Twin beds without headboards wore plain white sheets and old mustard-colored blankets tucked in hard, like a punishment. Unmatched chests of drawers stood next to each other. Under the eaves, two closets were lit by bare bulbs on pull strings.

Christina wanted to cry.

Anya took a deep breath. "Better than where I stayed before," she said, sliding her trunk with her knee toward the further bed.

"Better?" said Christina, shocked.

"I didn't tell you on the island, because you'd have told your parents and worried them. They don't like us here. The people in this town. They're against us. You'll see. That's why we're living with the Shevvingtons. Mr. Shevvington is so kind! He's so thoughtful. He knew how hard it was for Michael and Benj and me last year, separated, living in ugly places with mean people because nobody else would take us. Mr. Shevvington is the only one on our side, Christina. He's all we have."

"Side?" Christina repeated.

"It's them against us," Anya said. Anya chose a chest of drawers. She opened her trunk and took out lilac-scented, flowered liner paper for the drawers. Anya was so well organized she had packed her scissors right next to it, and calmly she began cutting lengths of paper and laying them in her drawers. A faint scent of lilac filled the room.

Christina could not bear to start unpacking in this gloomy attic. She crossed the balcony to check out the boys' room. It too was bare as bones. But the boys had had no dreams of lace and satin. They flung their stuff around, bounced on the beds, and seemed pleased. The boys' walls were the same blackish green as the outside shutters. "My Marilyn Monroe poster will look really great up here," Michael said to Christina. Then he shouted down the stairwell, "Can we scotch tape things right to the walls, Mrs. Shevvington?"

"Of course not," muttered Christina. "In a house where you can't run down the stairs and can't enter the living room and can't eat in the dining room, you think you're going to be allowed to put scotch tape on walls?"

Christina leaned over the balcony rail. Mrs. Shevvington was standing at the bottom. "Certainly," she called.

Christina went back into their bedroom.

"Here," said Anya. "I cut you drawer liners, too." Christina had never lined a drawer in her life. At least there was one pretty thing in here. Too bad it had to lie hidden by her clothing.

A single window filled the only dormer, making a tiny alcove. Far below, the surf boomed, and the spray tossed. Christina examined the view, down Breakneck Hill, over the rooftops, and beyond to the hills. She picked out the garage where her father's truck and her mother's car were locked up. "Where did you board last year, Anya?"

Anya squeezed into the dormer beside Christina. After a moment of searching she pointed to an ugly, squat building the color of fungus.

Christina shivered. "How could you stand it? Why didn't you say how awful it was?"

Anya shrugged. "I don't exactly live in a magnificent beach house myself, remember. And even if things are bad, you can't tell anybody. It just worries people back on the island. They can't do anything about it anyway."

Christina's parents had always been able to solve anything. But they were islanders, and still on the island. They did not wear silk paisley handkerchiefs in their suit pockets. Anya was right. Looking at the strength of the sea made Christina strong. She remembered she was granite. She thought, What's the big deal? We can make the room pretty. And I'll never tell the others that the Shevvingtons make me nervous, because that's yarning, and they won't be friends with me if I yarn.

Them against us. What did that mean? Did it mean — could it possibly mean — that Christina would have no friends in seventh grade — no allies but Michael and Benj and Anya — no one on her side but Mr. Shevvington?

The tide continued to rise rather gently, considering its first cannonade.

"It really sounds like somebody puffing out birthday candles, doesn't it?" Anya said. She pushed the window open. The two girls crammed themselves through the opening and leaned into the salty air. The window was tall for so small a dormer. The windowsill pressed just above Christina's knees. If somebody wanted to shove us out the window . . . , Christina thought.

She suddenly wondered where the poster of the sea was. The center of her back crawled, and Christina tried to turn in the small space, thinking —

Anya grabbed her. "Look!"

It was the man (woman?) in the wet suit. Still there. Still standing on the opposite cliff of Candle Cove.

He — it — waved at the girls.

Anya waved back.

Christina could not bring herself to make a human communication with a creature so lacking in human features. It was like Mrs. Shevvington, rubbery and flattened.

Anya jerked back into the room, yanking Christina with her, knocking both their skulls against the window frame. "What's the matter?" Christina asked. Her head hurt. She rubbed the dent.

Anya's white finger trembled, pointing. "There's your present from Dolly," she whispered.

It was borne in on the next wave, riding neatly on top, its metallic bow still gleaming.

"The ocean knows where you are," Anya said. She laughed madly. "It followed us here."

Mrs. Shevvington called them down for lunch. They ate in the kitchen.

Christina had been hoping for peanut butter and jelly sandwiches, chicken noodle soup, and potato chips, which was her idea of the perfect noon meal. Mrs. Shevvington had made red flannel hash with poached eggs laid on top of each helping.

Christina did not know what to do. She loathed soft eggs, and the sick horrid way the yellow spurted around, like blood. She hated onions, and she especially hated beets. As for leftover corned beef, it should be fed to the sea gulls, not gagged down by human beings. "Mrs. Shevvington," said Christina as courteously as she knew how, "may I make myself a sandwich instead?"

Mrs. Shevvington looked truly shocked, as if Christina had done something quite rude and socially unacceptable. "Christina, common courtesy requires you to eat what is put before you."

Christina flushed.

Michael and Benj, who were of the shovel school of eating, had already begun shoveling. Michael used the side of his fork to cut his helping into squares, which he put into his mouth as if he were laying tiles. Yellow egg yolk dripped off his fork.

Mrs. Shevvington smiled.

Christina swallowed to stop herself from gagging. She drank her milk.

It was whole milk. Christina hated whole milk; it was thick and disgusting. She drank only skim, which was like blue water, and thirst quenching. Her fingers tightened around the glass.

She said to herself, We are paying to be here. We are guests. Just like any other guests. And I hate egg yolks. I'll throw up. She said, "Mrs. Shevvington, I'm sorry, and if we were going to be visiting for one night, I would eat anything with a smile, but we're going to be here for a year. So we should get straight what we can and can't eat."

Mrs. Shevvington's eyes lay in her head like the poached eggs on the hash. Rounded and glossy and soft.

"I don't like corned beef and poached eggs," said Christina.

"Christina, one reason you are here is to learn civilized behavior, get along with other people."

"But I get along fine with other people," Christina said. "The tourists are always taking my photograph, and — "

"Christina! Boasting is the quickest way to make enemies. I hope you realize that island children, especially island girls, have a hard time getting along. You must try much harder than this, Christina. Your task is to make the island proud of you, not ashamed."

Michael and Benj and Anya did not speak up. Was she really being horribly rude? Would Anya scream at her tonight, in that soft hissing rage she could drum up, saying, "Christina, what is the matter with you? Why can't you behave?"

"Eat your eggs, Christina," Mrs. Shevvington said. "In this house you eat what is put before you or go hungry."

Christina looked at the yellow blood running over her plate. She set her fork back down on her napkin, linking her fingers together in her lap like chains. She felt as if they had just declared war, she and the principal's wife.

Christina was so hungry. Breakfast at home had been a long time before and a long sea trip away. What was so terrible about making a sandwich?

Nobody talked. They ate seriously, as if it were a chore.

Christina's mother never allowed silence, either at home or at her restaurant at mealtimes. If nobody talked Mrs. Romney interrogated them and made them contribute. I don't actually want to be at war with her, thought Christina. How can I come home to runny yellow eggs every night? So I shall make friends. "Is running the Inne your full-time job, Mrs. Shevvington?" she asked politely.

A tiny yellow smile curled on her pie dough face. "No," said Mrs. Shevvington. "This isn't my only job. I am also the seventh-grade English teacher, Christina."

They spent the afternoon unpacking. Anya hummed as she stacked neat little piles of bikini panties and lacy bras. Christina hated being neat.

It took so much effort and who cared? But obviously Anya cared, and they had to learn to live together. This was what being roommates was — stacking your panties if the other person stacked hers.

Christina finished first because she had fewer clothes, no accessories, and, according to Anya, lower standards of neatness. She sat cross-legged on her bed watching Anya. Anya finished. She too sat on her bed. But she rocked backwards, as if something were tipping her. "Christina, when did you put it up?" whispered Anya. "I thought — I thought you were going to throw it out."

The poster of the sea was fastened to the wall over Christina's bed.

"I didn't touch it," Christina said. She turned to look, but her neck felt stiff, it was hard to turn all the way. "Hey, Michael!" she yelled. "Benj! You come in here and put our poster up?"

"Why would we go in your room?" Michael yelled back.

Anya put her hands over her ears. "They're talking to me," she whispered, her eyes darting around like minnows. "I can hear them. Chrissie, can you hear them?"

The boys have the only roll of tape, Christina thought. They must have come in here to put it up. "Somebody put it up," she said irritably.

"Chrissie," whispered Anya, "it's wet in here."

Christina stared at her roommate. Anya's thin graceful hands were arched toward the ceiling like a ballerina stretching toward the sky.

"They're calling to me," Anya whispered. Her

breath came in spurts; she was panting. "Can you hear them, Chrissie?"

"No," Christina said. "Anya, hold my hand."

"I don't want to swim," Anya cried. "I hate the water, I hate boats, I hate the island." Her hands weren't graceful, they were frantic — pumping — reaching — struggling. "Pull me out, Chrissie, they're touching me, I can feel their fingers, they almost have me — they — "

Christina grabbed one of the wild arms. Anya stared past Christina's face, her eyes huge. "The fingers," she cried.

What fingers? Christina thought. She did not let go of Anya. Christina smelled mothballs as her face pressed into the blanket.

"All right!" Michael shouted. "Action!" The boys thudded into the room, jumped on top of Christina and Anya, and began wrestling, throwing pillows and lashing towels. Michael's towel flicked with loud snaps against walls and skin. Christina grabbed the end of his towel and jerked him to the floor, where Anya, giggling, rolled him under the bed. Benj bounced on the bed like a trampoline. They were shouting and laughing when Mrs. Shevvington's voice cut like a chain saw, buzzing and cruel.

"There will be no roughhousing here. There will be no fighting. You boys stay out of the girls' room, do you hear me? There will be decent behavior at all times. Christina, did you start this?"

Night fell.

Christina's first night away from her parents, her

first night at Schooner Inne, her first night with a roommate.

Outside, the town ceased to move. It slept, cars silent, lights off.

There was no sound on the earth but the sound of the sea.

Long after midnight they were still awake.

They learned why nobody had built houses on Candle Cove — nobody but the sea captain, whose wife threw herself to her death among the tons of green water that leaped up to meet her.

Noise.

The children had grown up with the battering drum of surf and storm; their island had inured them to all sounds of the sea.

Or so they had thought.

Every six hours and thirteen minutes, there is a tide: Two low and two high tides occur every twenty-four hours and fifty-two minutes.

Tide began at one A.M. with an eerie slushing sound, like tires caught in snow. It woke all four of them up — Michael and Benj in their room by the road, and Anya and Christina over the Cove.

The slushy sound became louder, like violins tuning up. Michael and Benj came into the girls' room. They sat on Christina's bed under the poster. Like engines revving for the Indianapolis 500, the fury of the tide increased. Like rockets, the sea burst in, attacking the harbor in a tidal wave of fury, hitting the cliff below Schooner Inne with a slap so great it blocked their minds to anything but sound. The sounds did not stay outside, but came into the room; they were swimming in noise.

In fifteen minutes it was over.

The waves were just the waves.

"How do we sleep through that?" Christina said. "And it will be different every night. Tomorrow it'll start at one-thirteen, and the night after that at one twenty-six."

Outside the window the ocean chuckled and slithered.

"Listen," whispered Anya.

They listened.

Anya stood in the moonlight, a long thin white nightgown draping her slender body, her hair ruffling like dark ribbons in the night wind. "The sea can smack the rocks like a hand smacking a cheek. It can hiss or gurgle or even kiss. But when it wants, it can go quiet. And then," said Anya Rothrock, "you can hear the voices of the drowned."

The waves had settled into an irregular rhythm of rolls and crashes.

"The sea keeps count," Anya whispered. "The sea is a mathematician. The sea wants one of us."

Chapter 4

They woke early.

Morning light poured through the eastern windows.

The sun lay scarlet-and-gold on the horizon like a jewel on pale blue velvet.

The temperature had dropped sharply. It was Maine again. Chilly and windy.

Christina got out of bed shivering, and went to the window. It was low tide. The rich smell of the sea rose to greet her. Far out in the water the motors of lobster boats buzzed. She could not see as far as Burning Fog, and it was not one of the mornings in which the fog burned. Only bright, tossing waves quivered against the sky.

On a rock not quite large enough to be called an island, cormorants were spreading their wings to dry. These birds soaked up water when they dove for fish, and, eventually, as they paddled, sank so low in the water they were in danger of drowning. Then they had to mount a rock and hold up their wings for the wind to blow them dry. Christina had always thought it must be a very tiring way to live.

Anya rolled over and over until she had mummified herself in the sheets. "I hate getting up," she informed Christina. "Someday my life is going to begin mid-afternoon instead of dawn."

Christina just smiled. She loved mornings. The sun rose as early on Burning Fog Isle as any other place in the United States. In her bedroom back home, she liked to think she was the first American to see the sun coming over the horizon.

Anya sat up slowly, arching like a gymnast, hair draping her back. She yawned and stretched. Goose bumps rose on her thin, white arms. "Oh, no," she wailed. "It's cold out! Now the clothes we picked are no good. They were for hot weather."

The girls scrambled through their drawers, holding up sweaters, pants, and blouses, as if the correct choice would make or break the entire school year.

Christina settled for brand new jeans, a soft yellow shirt, and a cotton sweater with darker yellow cables. She tugged at the collar until she was satisfied with the way it poked up. So schoolgirl, she thought. She looked enviously at Anya, whose silver necklace and earrings glittered against the soft folds of her navy blue shirt.

Christina loved the way Anya's white throat showed where the blouse opened, and how the silver rope lay carelessly, and how Anya's cloud of black hair flowed over the clothing. Christina had never owned any jewelry to speak of. Now suddenly she wanted it — chains and ropes and bangles — a jewelry box that chimed when you opened the lid —

blouses with open necks instead of T-shirts and crew sweaters.

Anya tied a long, dark cranberry red belt around her waist and adjusted the tulip flare of her long skirt. She looked like a magazine ad. She was every adjective: romantic, tailored, seductive, and scholarly all at one time.

They went to breakfast, remembering to walk down the stairs. No guests appeared, although it was just after Labor Day weekend, and Christina thought if there were any hope of winter guests, there would surely be early September guests.

Christina was used to a huge breakfast. Her mother generally rose at four A.M. to serve the fishermen going out for the day. Today a single piece of dry whole wheat toast, a small bowl of cold cereal onto which half a banana had been sliced, and a tiny glass of orange juice were laid in front of her.

Christina got up and poked around in the refrigerator for jam to spread on her toast. She was leaning way down inside to inspect the back of the bottom shelf when something hard and cold jabbed her in the middle of her back. It felt like the tip of a gun, or a knitting needle. It dug between two of her vertebrae. Christina straightened up slowly.

Mrs. Shevvington removed her long, thick fingernail from Christina's spine. "Too much sugar is bad for you, Christina. Learn to eat your toast dry."

Mrs. Shevvington was wearing a royal blue suit with a lacy blouse. It covered her thick body as if she had zipped it off a store mannequin and zipped herself back in. She hardly seemed to be wearing the suit; it was just hanging there: It could as easily have been hanging on a closet door. Mrs. Shevvington's hand was still in midair, like a sea gull drifting on wind currents. The fingernail that had left a dent in her flesh was thick and hooked, like a hawk's toe.

Fingers, thought Christina.

She tried to remember last night, and Anya, and the voices Anya had heard. But the memories were slippery, like seaweed.

She had had no supper. Now she was supposed to have dry toast. Christina had a large appetite. "We have lots of time," she said, glancing at the clock. "I could make waffles. Who wants waffles?"

Mrs. Shevvington moved closer to the girl. Under the protection of her shirt and sweater, Christina shivered. If that fingernail had touched her bare skin, it would have slit her spinal cord.

Yarning, she thought, why am I yarning every minute now? I have to get a grip on myself! It's only a fingernail, she's only a seventh-grade teacher.

How could Christina have English with this woman? What could she ever write — what paragraph, what essay — that this woman would understand? What book would Mrs. Shevvington ever assign that Christina would want to read?

"Christina, I don't hear the others complaining about a perfectly nutritious breakfast."

Michael was crunching away at his cereal. He had dressed as carefully as the girls. He obviously wanted to look like Blake. He had untied the laces in his dock shoes, wound them in upright spirals, and gone sockless — this year's way to establish style.

Anya, who never ate anyway, was sipping from a thimble of orange juice. This was her kind of meal.

Benj was eating Anya's dry toast for her, having already wolfed down her cereal and banana.

"I'll cook the waffles myself," Christina said. "It wouldn't be a bother to anybody. I'll clean up, too. And I'm a very good cook. My mother taught me everything."

"She did not teach you manners," Mrs. Shevvington said. "It would be most unfortunate if, because of a bad attitude, you were not able to board here after all, and had to be moved *alone* to some other location." She smiled at Christina. None of the others could have seen that smile. Christina wished she had never seen the smile, either. It was the war smile. Just try to oppose me, Christina, it said.

Board alone. What did that mean? Without Anya and Michael and Benj? Then she really would have no friends!

Christina tried to eat the toast dry. It crumbled in her throat. She tried to enjoy the banana. It was too ripe and slimy.

Michael said to her, "Now don't let them get you crying. Those town kids like to pick on island kids."

"I never cry," said Christina, who was very close to it.

Anya gave her a queer, tight smile. "You might today," she said.

"They can be mean," Michael told her. "Everybody needs somebody to pick on."

"Nobody picks on me," Christina said.

"You mean nobody ever *has* picked on you, Chrissie," Benj told her. "You haven't experienced it yet. You're going to experience it today. All week. All September."

"Some of us," said Anya, "experience it all year, year after year."

People picked on Anya? How could anybody look at Anya and not feel a rush of pleasure in her beauty and her presence?

But there was one silver lining in this. Michael cared. For all his summer speeches about how if Christina tried to hold his hand he would flatten her, here he was, trying to give her courage.

"Now, you will need house keys," said Mrs. Shevvington. She handed each of them a shiny new duplicate. "The front door is to be kept locked at all times."

Christina held her key, feeling its unfiled edges, staring at the jagged profile. I'll get home first, she thought, and open that huge green door myself. I'll be the grown-up.

Mrs. Shevvington gave them instructions for cleaning up the kitchen. Then she made it clear that although Mr. Shevvington had a car (and had left much earlier) and although she too had a car (and was leaving now) the children were not going to be offered rides with either Shevvington. "You children have two choices. You may walk. It is only a quarter mile." She filled her lungs with air, making an exercise out of it, as if she were doing push-ups. "Good for you. Brisk. Or you may go down Breakneck Hill and catch the school bus at its last stop by the Mobil gas station." She waved good-bye as if she were a half mile from the children. "Have a satisfactory first day." She walked out of the house.

"*Satisfactory?*" exclaimed Christina. "That's the best wish she can give us? What happened to *wonderful, terrific, friend-filled,* or *rewarding?*"

The others did not pick up her lines. They neither joked nor contradicted. Was school so awful that Anya, Benj, and Michael already knew the best it could be was satisfactory?

Or were they on Mrs. Shevvington's side? Did they, too, think Christina had a bad attitude?

The girls got light canvas jackets because it did not look as if the day would warm up; the boys scorned protection from the elements and sauntered outdoors in shirtsleeves. Anya had a lovely briefcase with her initials on it, and pockets for pens, pencils, and a calculator. Her purse was a tiny dark red leather bag on a long thin spaghetti strap, which exactly matched her belt. Christina had only a five-subject spiral notebook with a yellow cover, and two pencils crammed into the spiral. The boys carried nothing. "Wait for me," Christina said. "I have to get my purse."

She raced upstairs, taking the steep steps two at a time. *This* was how stairs should be climbed! Her purse, so carefully bought with summer earnings, was not something she could leave behind. She had waited all these years to be old enough to have a purse at all.

But back downstairs, her precious purse felt clunky and dumb next to Anya's tiny bag. She was not used to holding it and it banged against her and took up space.

Outside Benj checked to be sure the door had locked behind him. He attached his house key to his Swiss army knife and jammed that into his pocket. Michael fastened his to his belt. Anya had a tiny zip pocket on her tiny purse into which she slipped her key. Christina's mother had made her a key ring, her name embroidered onto canvas in a leather oblong like a luggage tag. Christina and her mother had been so proud of the key ring. Now Christina thought, It's too big. And dumb. Nobody else bothers with anything like that.

She was suddenly horribly afraid.

Afraid of all those other children, all those rooms and corridors, all those times when she would have to walk alone, sit alone, eat alone. And be different, with her dumb fat key tag, and her dumb fat purse, and her strange tri-colored hair the other kids would say she dyed.

Wind lifted out of Candle Cove, billowing Anya's skirt and making a black storm cloud of her hair. Christina and the boys in their jeans and sweaters were as untouched by the wind as if it had steered around them. The first day comes only once, she told herself. No other day can be as bad as the first one.

So tomorrow will be fine. Stop being jittery. Don't yarn. Don't make it worse by exaggerating. Mrs. Shevvington is right; aim for a satisfactory day.

Christina bumped her fingertips along the wire fence that kept people from falling into Candle Cove.

Down in the mud flats, in almost exactly the same place as the day before, stood somebody in a brown wet suit. There was no water there to swim in. There was no boat to get into or out of. There was no bucket for clams. It was just a wet suit, gleaming.

It walked in the children's direction fluidly, as if being poured. Mud sucked on its feet. Christina could hear the sucking. She could see the mud, reaching up above the toes, grabbing the ankles. The wet suit came to a stop. It lifted its right hand, very slowly, very high, and beckoned.

"Listen to his fingers," whispered Anya. "It's not a wave. Not a hello. *Come here*, say the fingers. *Come down here and drown with me.*"

Out in the Atlantic, the waiting ocean chuckled and hissed.

The wet suit raised the other arm, as if to embrace them.

Christina was already suffocating in the embrace of her own fear and loneliness. She wanted to be hugged. The wet suit would hug her. She listened to the fingers, like Anya.

Come here, said the fingers. *Come here and drown with me.*

But her sneaker tip hit the fence and a button on her jacket caught on the wires.

I almost walked over the edge, thought Christina Romney, disengaging her button. Some guy down there waves, and I start believing Anya's yarns. She said the sea knew we were here. She said the sea kept count. She said the sea wants one of us.

Down in the mud the arms leaned toward them, longingly.

Christina wrenched her eyes off the wet suit.

Very slowly a car drove up Breakneck Hill. It was tiny and bright red, gleaming new, as if the driver were on a test drive from the showroom. It was shaped like a long, thin triangle, with the pointed end ready for take-off. The headlights were hidden under slanting hoods. Inside, the upholstery was even redder.

The driver stuck a casual sleeve out the window, followed by a casual turn of the head.

It was Blake.

How handsome he was! A catalog Maine model featured among the hunting equipment and camping accessories.

"Hi, Anya," said Blake. He did not smile. His heavy eyebrows lay neatly on his tanned face, and his deep set eyes matched them perfectly, as if they too had been ordered from the catalog. "Would you like to ride to school with me, Anya?" he said. He was nervous, as if she might say no.

He planned this, Christina thought, filled with romantic appreciation. He timed it. He probably test-drove the route so he'd arrive at just the right moment. Or maybe he's been sitting at the bottom of the hill, waiting to see the front door open, and Anya, whom he loves, emerge!

Anya smiled at Blake. Her whole face smiled — even her body seemed to smile. Shyly she touched her stormy hair, and the wind responded by covering her fingers as well as her face. From beneath the black mist of her own hair, Anya whispered, "I'd love to, Blake."

Blake's smile broke through his face like the sun through the fog, dazzling them. He bit his lip, a childlike expression that Anya returned with a wild, loving laugh. In this world of smart cars and fine clothes, only Anya could make Blake happy. Christina could tell by their lips, which were desperate with the need to laugh, kiss, and beg at the same time. Anya danced around the car to slip in beside Blake. He leaned toward her, as if to kiss her, and she held her face up, but in the end he did not, and Christina was disappointed. Instead Blake pushed the pedal to the floor and took off in a squeal of tires. From the back the car had no shape at all; its triangle was pointed away from them and it was nothing but a red cube.

Michael and Benj walked on. Michael's posture said, This is where I stop knowing you, Christina. Remember not to bother me.

They've abandoned me, she thought. I'll have to walk into the school alone. When I go up those steps, I won't have a single friend on the American continent.

Alone.

It was a word so horrible she seemed to hear it in the waves, repeating over and over, saying, *You're alone, Christina, alone, alone, alone.*

The school itself was plain; brick rooms squatting around a courtyard. But the front steps were pink granite from Burning Fog Isle — fifty feet wide, impressive as a state capitol. In fair weather, half the school sat on the steps to eat lunch. What if hundreds of teenagers, all with their best friends, leaned against each other, talked to each other, shared with each other — but left Christina alone? What if she, and only she, had to stand in the sun, shunned and unwanted?

Clutching her notebook and purse like a sword and lance, Christina looked back at the Cove.

It was empty. There was nobody in a wet suit.

There was nobody there at all but a little cormorant, drying its wings.

Chapter 5

Christina had math first. The teacher, Miss Schuyler, was a plain young woman with odd, old-fashioned braids. I like her, Christina thought. Oh, please, let her like me!

Miss Schuyler said how lovely it was to have new faces this year. "Let's welcome Brandi, who's moved here from Boston," Miss Schuyler said, pointing to a little dark girl cringing in the back. The class smiled. Everybody said, "Hi, Brandi. Glad to have you, Brandi." The little girl stopped cringing.

"And Kevin, who was here up through third grade, moved away, and is now back," Miss Schuyler went on, pointing to a tall, very thin boy in a sweatshirt so large it nearly touched his knees. The class welcomed Kevin.

Christina braced herself. Her purse, sitting on the desk, looked fat and stupid. Nobody else had spiral notebooks. Their paper was in three ring binders with impressive fold-out pockets and zips.

Nobody else wore brand new jeans. All their jeans were old.

"And our third new face is Christina, who lives on Burning Fog Isle, and is boarding on the mainland for the school year!"

There was no teasing.

Everybody looked as if this were the most interesting, romantic thing they had ever heard.

Miss Schuyler said it had always been her personal fantasy to live on an island, but she was not brave enough: It took courage to live on an island, she said, and she knew through the year they would find Christina a person of courage.

Nobody laughed at this. They looked awed.

Two girls asked Christina to be sure and sit with them at lunch.

Next Christina had science. Both the girls who had asked her for lunch — Vicki and Gretchen — were in science with her, and she sat between them. The science teacher said how well prepared island children always were; it put the rest of the class to shame.

Nobody teased Christina about that either; they looked respectful of Christina's superior knowledge.

Gym was what Christina feared most. Her knowledge of team games was almost zero. She discovered that nobody else knew how to hold a hockey stick, either.

She was as athletic as any of them.

It's going to be all right, Christina thought. I'm going to make it.

Changing classes was not as scary as she expected. Most seventh-graders stayed together, and the classrooms weren't spread very far apart. Choosing a desk wasn't awful; nobody saved seats for best friends; they just walked in and slid down. All desks were modern and slick, seats attached like one-room schoolhouse desks. Christina found it difficult to get in and out of them. Everybody else was graceful. Except the boys, who kicked things, stuck their feet out, wrapped their ankles around themselves, and honked like geese.

Christina was fascinated by the boys.

So many of them!

They were all like Michael, with immense feet and hands and noses. They were noisier than Michael, though, and had specialties Michael did not. The boys showed off their skills at hiccuping, burping, and jumping on each other's feet. This was what you were supposed to fall in love with? Where were the boys like Blake? She examined her classmates for potential Blakes and decided there were none. Seventh grade had a full complement of creeps, weirdos, future criminals, and nerds.

At lunch it turned out that Vicki and Gretch were fashionable. They were "in" — a phenomenon Christina had read about but never experienced, as the island had so few children. Other giggling seventh-graders angled for the chance to sit at the same table. Vicki and Gretch were given extra desserts. Vicki and Gretch's opinions were sought and their jokes laughed at.

The girls were much more attractive than the boys. They were neater, cleaner, and prettier.

Christina nevertheless could not take her eyes off the boys. How annoying that the boys sat at their own tables and the girls sat at others. Christina wanted to be next to the boys.

She was full of second-day-of-school resolutions. No purse, better notebook, memorize everybody's names, scruffy jeans.

"If you're not going to eat your Jell-O, can I have it?" Gretch asked. "I love it with whipped cream."

Christina handed Gretch her Jell-O. She wouldn't have eaten it anyway because she liked only dark-colored Jell-O (raspberry, strawberry) and never touched light-colored Jell-O (lime, lemon). It was a small price to pay for Gretch smiling at her, for being "in" like Vicki and Gretch, for sitting at what was obviously the best table.

The only thing wrong with lunch was that she did not pay for it.

Mrs. Shevvington had handed her a blue ticket to exchange for a hot lunch. Christina noticed that about a quarter of the students had these; the rest brought bag lunches, or paid money to buy a hot lunch.

"How come I have this blue ticket?" Christina asked Gretch.

"Because you're poor," Gretch said. "Island kids are always poor. The state is paying for your lunch."

For the first time Christina saw that Gretch, too, was dressed in catalog Maine. That while Christina's jeans were from a sale rack in a discount store, bought on a mainland shopping trip in July, Gretch's jeans had a brand name Christina recognized from full-page ads in *Seventeen* magazine. I might be able to afford the three-ring binder, thought Christina, but not the jeans.

She wanted jeans like Gretch's.

It was the first time in Christina's life that she had lusted after a brand name. She hated her own boring, unstylish jeans. They embarrassed her, they hung wrong, and they were too blue. She resented her parents for being poor and living where they didn't know anything about seventh-grade fashion.

Anya walked over to Christina's table.

An honor roll, drama club, soprano solo, tennis team, senior girl — pausing at lunch to chat with a seventh-grader? Even Christina, who knew nothing of the social life of schools, knew this was remarkable. Senior high kids ate on one side of the cafeteria and lowly junior high kids on the other. Nobody crossed the invisible lines, not with their feet, their speech, or their eyes.

Gretch and Vicki were awestruck. Their giggles were silenced. Their Jell-O spoons hung motionless. Anya had never looked so beautiful. The eyes of all the seniors and juniors followed her, and so, in person, did Blake. Now the younger girls almost swooned. Blake was perfect. Anya was perfect. Anya and Blake together were twice as perfect.

At first Christina thought. Anya had come over to make Christina look good and stop any teasing that might have begun. But Anya's eyes caught Christina's with a strange, dark desperation. Anya was not crossing the cafeteria lines to be sure Christina was surviving her first day, nor to borrow a dime for a phone call, nor to give her a message — but because Anya was not okay.

Christina did not know what to offer. She could not imagine what had gone wrong for Anya.

Anya held her arms out for comfort.

Blake caught up to Anya. Certainly Blake wasn't upset. Laughing, he took both of Anya's outstretched hands and twirled her away, like a dance partner. The seventh-grade girls sighed in delicious envy. "Do you see a lot of Blake?" breathed Gretch. "He's so wonderful! He's so handsome!"

"What's it like on that island of yours?" Vicki asked. Vicki was very tan, and wore a white cotton knit sweater, which made her look even tanner. Her light brown hair was absolutely straight, and it swung when she moved. She had a tourist look to her; she was the day tripper they scorned on the island.

"Oh, you know," Christine said, "just a rock and some sea gulls."

She flushed with shame. She loved Burning Fog. Why had she made it sound like a garbage dump?

"I *adore* sea gulls," said Gretch. "They're so *beautiful* and *pure*. I love how they tilt in the wind." Gretch had blonde hair, cut exactly like Vicki's, and they had a habit of tilting themselves toward each other, so their brown and yellow hair swung together and then swung apart.

"I don't think pure is the word," said Christina. "You should see them with baby ducks and baby terns. Why, one sea gull could goffle up a whole brood."

Gretch's blonde eyebrows lifted like punctuation marks. *"Goffle?"* she said, starting to laugh. She turned to Vicki, who giggled with her. They tilted hair. "Goffle. That's so cute. What other cute little words do you know, Christina?"

Christina said lamely, "I mean eat. Sea gulls eat anything." She would not tell them how her mother took the kitchen garbage, eggshells, crusts, and scrapings off plates to the top of the cliff, where sea gulls would swoop down like Roman gladiators.

Once they stood up from the table, junior high etiquette allowed the boys to join them. This turned the girls arch and silly. Christina did not know how to be arch and silly. One boy claimed to be able to spit tobacco farther than anybody, but as the cafeteria proctor was approaching, he could not substantiate this claim. One girl said out on Burning Fog Isle even the girls chewed tobacco. "I bet Christina can spit as far as you can," she said. "That's probably what she does when she's not canning fish."

Everybody laughed.

Another boy said he had been to Burning Fog Isle himself several times. Each summer his parents liked a day trip and a picnic on Burning Fog. Christina did not tell him what she thought of day trippers, but he was not so polite to her. He said he did not think much of islanders. He said they charged too much for soft drinks and yelled when you touched their silly dock.

It was probably Christina's mother who had sold him the soft drink. It was probably Frankie's dock.

Michael had told her to laugh it off. Christina could not find any laughs. But it was the other seventh-graders who laughed, closing in on Christina, talking louder and louder.

She had been afraid of being alone. Now she was afraid of being in the center.

"What's your house like?" said the boy. He had a funny, knowing smile. She felt wary, the way she would around lobster claws. "Is it one of those little shacks that always needs a coat of paint?" he said.

Vicki and Gretch giggled. "Jonah," they said, warningly — but coaxingly, so they could get credit for telling him to stop, but yet not stop him.

"It's a cottage," Christina said.

Jonah smiled triumphantly. "I know which cottage, too," he said to the rest of the seventh grade. "Christina's cottage has thirty-two rooms."

Gretch and Vicki looked impressed. They blended their hair together like a fence against strangers.

Jonah said, "And notice that, nevertheless, Christina is getting free lunch. Another welfare cheat. Welcome to our midst."

In English, Christina did indeed have Mrs. Shevvington.

The manners in her room were markedly different. There was no jostling or kidding. Even the boys behaved like human beings, without spitting, tripping their friends, or imitating tomcats in heat.

68

Mrs. Shevvington stood in front of the class, and the class sat in front of Mrs. Shevvington, and nothing else happened. Mrs. Shevvington gave a lecture while twenty-four children took notes.

When Christina picked up her pencil to take notes, her fingers smudged the page, and she left a sweaty palm print where the pencil couldn't write. Class seemed to last forever, and yet when the bell rang nobody jumped up. They waited until Mrs. Shevvington excused them. Then they walked quietly out of the classroom, just as Christina had to walk quietly down the stairs at the Schooner Inne.

In the hall Vicki and Gretch walked on either side of Christina as if the cafeteria scenes had never happened—and they were a trio of best girlfriends.

"What's it like living with the Shevvingtons?" said Vicki. "Mr. Shevvington is so handsome, don't you adore him? If he weren't a hundred years old, I would have a crush on him. But Mrs. Shevvington is so dull, isn't she? It's like being in first grade every year, absolutely nothing happens. Oh, well, at least she's sweet. Her first name is Candy. I think it fits perfectly, don't you?"

If they thought I was yarning about sea gulls, she thought, they'd never believe me about the Shevvingtons.

She walked down the hall, smelling school: a chalk-sweat-paper-floorwax-mimeograph smell she had never smelled before. As distinctive as low tide; the kind of smell you would never get wrong, you would remember all your life.

"Listen," said Gretch, smiling. "Don't be upset

about Jonah finding out you're a welfare cheat, Christina. He's really into honesty, that's all." Vicki and Gretch escorted Christina on down the long hall, telling her that the next class was art. "You'll hate art," Vicki said. "Everybody hates art. The art teacher stinks."

"I am not a welfare cheat," Christina said. "I'm into honesty, too. We don't own the cottage, we just — "

"And don't call it a cottage, either," said Jonah, coming up behind them. "Anybody who lives in a thirty-two room house lives in a palace. And then you're rude to the mainland tourists who end up paying for your free school lunch as well as buying your overpriced soda. It's disgusting."

Christina belted him in the mouth. When he staggered back, unprepared, she belted him a second time. This was so satisfying she was ready to do it a third time, when Miss Schuyler responded to the screams of Vicki and Gretch.

"That island girl hit him first!" yelled all the witnesses.

Miss Schuyler grabbed Christina by her sweater sleeve and Jonah by his pink oxford collar. "I cannot believe this," hissed the math teacher. "The very first day of school, and you are starting fist fights. We do not do this kind of thing here, Christina. Nor, Jonah Bergeron, do we fight little girls who are here for the very first day of their lives."

Jonah snorted. "Some little girl," he said.

Miss Schuyler hauled them down to the principal's office. They went through an outer office full of high counters and secretaries. Miss Schuyler knocked hard on a yellow door blackened around the handle with fingerprints, and pushed into Mr. Shevvington's office.

When Jonah finished his explanation there was silence in the room. Christina was aware of tall filing cabinets, piles of papers, books tumbling sideways, and an open window through which came the smell of the fish cannery. Mr. Shevvington seemed not to be a part of his office, any more than his wife had been a part of her clothing. He was simply handsome and silvery and sad. He fixed his eyes on Christina, and the eyes never blinked.

He'll call my parents, she thought. I've been away from home a day and a half, and look at me. In trouble with everybody.

Mr. Shevvington's voice was gentle, and yet rough, like a luxury car driving slowly over pebbles. "Christina," he said sadly, "I am so disappointed in you."

Christina's heart began to pound hideously, as if at thirteen she were going to have a heart attack. "I got mad at Jonah," she whispered. "I'm sorry." She felt as worthless as an empty soda can by the side of the road.

Mr. Shevvington sighed. Then he turned to Jonah. "Christina's father is caretaker of a millionaire's mansion. They don't have access to the house, but live in the servants' quarters because that's what they are, Jonah. Servants. Christina needs free lunch more than anybody else. I don't want you to gossip about her situation, but you might let people know that Christina is the kind of Maine native who knows poverty firsthand. So although yes, she's on welfare, no, she is not a welfare cheat."

Christina felt punched. "We have never been on welfare! My mother runs a restaurant."

"Her mother serves toast and coffee to lobstermen from a little shack near the harbor," said Mr. Shevvington to Jonah. "Now I want you two to be friends. That is your assignment for the fall, Jonah. You take Christina on as a friend and help her steer a safe passage among the rocks of junior high."

"Yes, sir," said Jonah. He was staring down at his shoes. Christina stared there, too. Yet another example of catalog Maine, only this time it was hunting boots, which most certainly had never been taken hunting.

I hate them! thought Christina. I hate them all. "I am not on welfare," she said.

"What do you think a free lunch is?" said Jonah.

Christina flung back her head to shout, *Then I'll never take free lunch again!* when she realized that her parents did not, in fact, have money to send for buying hot lunches, that Mrs. Shevvington was unlikely to buy her boxes of apple juice and Twinkies when the state would supply it free, and that she did not, at thirteen, earn any money herself.

Mr. Shevvington ordered her to apologize to Jonah.

"I'm sorry," muttered Christina without looking at him.

Jonah was excused to return to class, with a little

note from Mr. Shevvington to carry to his teacher. Mr. Shevvington's handwriting was delicate enough for wedding invitations. His muscular fingers did not look right making such thin, graceful shapes.

The principal dropped back down into his chair and smiled at Christina.

Christina had thought she would never smile again, but Mr. Shevvington's smile was so kind. Little by little Christina's face and mouth relaxed, and slowly she managed a smile of her own. The worst was over. Mr. Shevvington said that junior high could be something of a shock. Children age thirteen, he explained, were barbarians. He knew Christina was not, of course, but she was not used to the pressure of a whole grade around her. She would have to be calm, and pliant, and let them all have their way.

Christina did not see why they should always have their way. She didn't feel like being calm and pliant. She felt like belting Jonah again. But she did not say so. This is good practice, she told herself, and she made herself look pliant, like a flower stem in the wind.

"While you're here, Christina, why don't you fill out this form we will need to guide you through your school career."

Forms! she thought eagerly.

Christina loved to fill in blanks. Mostly she sent away for folders and leaflets about anything at all, just to get mail. This would be a *real* form.

Christina accepted the clipboard Mr. Shevvington gave her to write on and the pen he passed her to write with. With each item, she felt more like somebody too poor or too stupid to have brought her own. "My things are still on the floor in the hall where Miss Schuyler grabbed me," she said.

Mr. Shevvington nodded as if he did not believe her, but was willing to accept Christina's fibs to save her pride.

I won't cry, she told herself. I never cry. I won't now.

She took the pen purposefully. She could make her script just as beautiful as his. She'd show him.

The form was entitled *Getting to Know You*. Computer generated sixteenth notes floated in the margins, like a happy song. Christina filled in name, address, parents' occupations. Then she looked at the questions. Her brow wrinkled. They were very odd questions.

"How come I didn't get this in homeroom along with the medical forms?" she asked Mr. Shevvington.

"It's only for new students."

"But all the students in my grade are new," she protested, "starting junior high for the first time."

Mr. Shevvington wound a pencil around in his fingers like a baton twirler. "Christina, I hope this is not a harbinger of things to come. Do you have difficulty with authority? Are you going to be continually presenting problems and arguing? Mrs. Shevvington and I decided to overlook both last night and this morning, because we know how nervous you must be, an island child away from home for the first time — but I am beginning to have doubts about your ability to handle yourself."

Her hand grew sweaty around the pen. The metal chair poked her back like Mrs. Shevvington's fingernail. It's true, she thought. Nobody else argued. Nobody else got in a fistfight. Michael told me to laugh when they teased. I never even tried to laugh. I just socked Jonah.

Mr. Shevvington said gently, "Christina, I want you to think about counseling. We have a wonderful guidance department here. We have a social worker who understands troubled adolescents very well. I want you to consider working with her to sort out your emotional problems. Of course it will be your decision. We won't force you into anything."

Emotional problems? Christina thought. Me?

She had always been the granite of her family, the old strong stock of the island. It was Anya who was the endangered species, the fragile one.

Or was it?

"Now fill out the form," said Mr. Shevvington gently. His eyes were warm, soft: eyes to wrap a child in comfort.

"But these questions — " began Christina. She wet her lips.

"Will help us understand you," the principal said.

Christina lowered her eyes to the page. The letters were soothing; the alphabet never changed; the white rectangle of the pages never changed.

She tried to breathe evenly.

What are you afraid of? asked the first question. *Circle all that apply.*

Rats?
Darkness?
Being laughed at?
Pain?
Acid?
Failure?
Being alone?

Most of the time, Christina Romney thought, I am afraid of nothing.

Some of the time, I am afraid of everything.

But I am not telling anybody which I'm afraid of, or when.

"I won't fill this out, Mr. Shevvington."

"You must, Christina, dear."

"No."

The word sat alone, like an island in the sea.

There was a long silence. Christina did not look at his eyes. The eyes, like the beckoning hand of the wet suit, might force her into something.

The silence lasted and lasted. What would happen in art without her? Would Jonah be there even now, telling them all how poverty-stricken she was? How her parents were nothing but servants? It wasn't true. Her father was an excellent tennis player. Her mother was an excellent cook.

"Then you may go," Mr. Shevvington said. "But I want you to know that I am your friend. All I want is to help you. And Christina — "

She set the clipboard and pen on his desk and backed out of the office.

" — you desperately need help."

Chapter 6

After school Christina went to look for Anya, Michael, and Benj, but it was Jonah she found. Or actually, Jonah who found Christina.

"Get lost," said Christina. "I don't want any friends by marching orders from the principal."

Jonah said nervously. "I have to do what he says."

"Why? I won't rat on you. If he ever asks, I'll say you're very attentive, and helpful in every way. Now get lost."

Jonah stuck with her. "He's watching," whispered Jonah. "Let me walk with you as far as Breakneck Hill." The heavy hunting boots clumped along with her. Twice Jonah looked over his shoulder.

Twice Christina forced herself to look straight ahead.

Jonah was slightly shorter than Christina, but boys usually were at that age. All of him was thin: even his lips and his eyelids were thin. But it was not as thin as girls can be — anorexic. It was thin for the moment: Tomorrow, or next week, Jonah would grow six inches and gain seventy-five pounds. His hands were much too large for his seventh-grade body; his feet big as a clown's; his teeth too square. "You have funny hair," Jonah said. "Is it dyed?"

"No, it isn't dyed. And what kind of name is Jonah, anyway?" added Christina, getting in a dig of her own. "It sounds like a graveyard name to me."

Jonah stared at her.

Too late she remembered this was yet another island saying Anya had forbidden her to use.

Names fascinated Christina. So far in seventh grade she had met Kimberly, Jennie, Krystyn, Sable, Brandi, Vicki, and Gretch. But generations back, Christina's ancestors had names like Florence, Nellie, Phoebe, and HepsiBeth. They were in the graveyard on Burning Fog Isle, where their stones were routinely checked by graveyard buffs who wanted a rubbing of the angel on HepsiBeth's stone. Christina had always thought HepsiBeth sounded like a soft drink — Pepsi Cola, Coca Cola, HepsiBeth.

"We always give our cats graveyard names," said Christina to Jonah. "Off the old gravestones. One year the litter was Emmaline, Tristram, Jethro, Jemima, Dorcas, and Abiah. Jonah sounds like a good cat's name."

Jonah said, "You're weird, Christina."

"Good. Then you don't have to be friends with me. Forget your marching orders." Christina walked away from Jonah. Then she remembered something and turned around again. "There is one way you can help me. But you can't tell Mr. Shevvington about it."

Jonah did not look thrilled about something for which he got no credit.

"I want to see the house where Anya lived last year. It's in this neighborhood somewhere." If I get in even more trouble, she thought, the Shevvingtons will send me away. Probably there.

Her head ached with the day's events. She felt as if it would take all autumn to think through what had happened. And in only a little while she had to face the Shevvingtons again, and Anya and Michael and Benj. They would all know about the fistfight with Jonah.

Jonah took her down a narrow street, away from the cute little tourist-trade, sailor-trade shops. Past car repair places stinking of oil, and old sagging warehouses with weeds growing in the cracks of the buildings.

He pointed to a thick, squat house with seaweed-green asphalt siding. It was a house where poor people lived; where the smell of cabbage clung to the torn wallpaper and the ugly carpet curled up and collected spiders. Where there would be only one bathroom, and its tub would be pockmarked and its shower curtain moldy. There was no yard, no view of the sea, no color, and no wind.

Christina shuddered.

I, from my island of wild grass and roses, of leaping salt spray and seabirds floating in air currents — living *there*?

"Creepy, huh?" Jonah said. "Aren't you glad you live in Schooner Inne this year?"

Christina thought, Why did the Shevvingtons decide to take us? They don't have any other guests. I don't think they're going to have other guests. I think we'll live in the attic and they'll live on the second floor and nobody else will come. Ever. Anya says we're living with the Shevvingtons because they're so kind. Vicki and Gretch adore Mr. Shevvington. I don't think they're kind.

She remembered what the tourist on Frankie's boat had said. *Don't they look like ancient island princesses, marked out for sacrifice? Sent away for the sake of the islanders, to be given to the sea?*

"What's it like in the cupola?" Jonah said.

"I haven't been up there yet."

He was amazed. "A girl that slugs boys the first day of school hasn't explored the best part of the sea captain's house yet?" he said. "That's where the sea captain's wife stood when she dove to her death."

"Couldn't have," said Christina, who wanted never to agree with Jonah about anything. "It's all glassed in."

Jonah shrugged. "She didn't care if she got cut by a little glass, did she? She just jumped through it."

Christina was horrified. She had never thought of that.

Why had Mr. Shevvington smiled, saying, "I know," when Anya promised to do anything he asked?

Why had Anya said "The sea keeps count. The sea is a mathematician. The sea wants one of us"?

Jonah and Christina waited for the light to change at the bottom of Breakneck Hill. The waves crashed in Candle Cove. Six cars crossed the Singing Bridge, and the open metal floor of the bridge hummed loudly as the rubber tires spun over it. Christina had always loved the Singing Bridge.

"It sings when somebody drowns, you know," said Jonah.

"I've lived here all my life and I've never heard that," Christina said.

"Huh. You've lived on Burning Fog Isle all your life, not this town. I suppose town is pretty exciting for you, huh? Must be real quiet on that island once the tourists are gone."

"It's never quiet. The sea crashes, the gulls scream, the motors of the boats roar, chain saws cut wood, anchor chains rattle, shutters bang, the wind whistles — "

"Okay, okay, it's noisy on the island. I meant people."

"I do not," said Christina sharply, "consider tourists such as yourself to be *people*, Jonah."

She stalked up Breakneck Hill, not an easy thing to do. It was too steep for stalking. The glass of the cupola caught the sun and blinded her.

Neither of the Shevvingtons could be home from school yet. Christina would climb the cupola.

This had been the worst day of her entire life.

And she had no mother to greet her with something yummy, hot from the oven; no Dolly to share it with; no VCR to put her favorite movie in; no litter of kittens to play with on the kitchen floor.

Christina had never expected to be homesick, and certainly not the first day. Her sides hurt, as if she had cramps from running.

She unlocked the huge green door, shut it quietly behind her, and went inside.

No guests sat in the formal living room; no guests snacked in the formal dining room. The kitchen was dark and silent. The dingy den was empty.

Christina carried her books up to her room.

She got to the top of the stairs and the bedroom door was closed.

She distinctly remembered leaving it open that morning.

Mrs. Shevvington certainly hadn't gone in; she had left for school before they had.

Inside the room Christina could hear breathing.

She set down her book bag. Then she picked it up again to use its weight as a weapon.

The breath came in little huffs like a panting animal.

She swallowed. She cracked the door. No black wet nose of a dog or cat came through the crack. The breathing continued. Like somebody blowing out candles on a birthday cake. Like —

Oh, it's just the tide! thought Christina, utterly disgusted with herself.

She flung open the door, and the bedroom, of course, was completely empty. The huffing continued. Christina crossed the room to close the window, from which a sea wind must have blown the door shut.

"You be quiet, you cove, you," she muttered out the window.

She considered having a cry. Girls in books often curled up alone in the corners of their rooms and wept till they felt better. Christina had never felt bad enough about anything that she wanted to cry at all, let alone curl up for a weep. This was the kind of day that did it, then. If I'm going to do that, she thought, I'll need supplies. Kleenex. And a book in case I get bored.

"Christina, Christina!"

She jerked away from the window and ran to the stairs. Anya — Anya must be hurt — the wet suit — the tide —

"I'm so glad you're home," said Anya, running up the stairs. "Chrissie, I've had the worst day of my life. I have to tell you about it."

She hauled Christina back into the bedroom before Christina could tell her about the huffing, and flung them both on their beds. "Nobody has ever had a worse day," said Anya dramatically. She ran all ten fingers up into her hair and pretended to scalp herself.

The huffing stopped.

It's listening instead, thought Christina. Like me.

"First of all, Blake's parents say I'm nothing but a wharf rat and they want better for Blake."

A wharf rat. Girls who worked on the docks, knee

deep in fish heads and motor oil, and lost all their teeth before they were twenty-five. Girls who worked in the factories and had babies before they were sixteen and ate ten jelly doughnuts at a time because nobody cared whether they got fat and ugly.

"Anya, you could never be a wharf rat."

"That's what Blake says. But if we see each other, we have to sneak. Christina, I've never sneaked in my life. Blake's parents even told the Shevvingtons they don't want him to date me. They didn't actually order him not to, but they made it clear that he will upset them if he does."

Christina knew how it felt to be shunned. "Wait till you hear about *my* day," she said, settling in cross-legged on top of her mother's quilt.

"No. I'm not finished yet. Then I found out that the guidance department re-did my academic schedule. They put me in Public Speaking, Chrissie! Five days a week. Public Speaking. Do you know what that is? Each kid has to get up once a week and give an assigned talk. Out loud." Anya flung herself backward on the mattress and bounced. "When I filled out my form for Mr. Shevvington," she said, "I marked speaking in front of an audience as the thing I feared most. And here I am, in it. Mr. Shevvington says it's good for me. He says I have to learn to face my fears."

The huffing moved inside Christina's head like a warning signal. Christina said slowly, "What form?"

"The one we all had to fill out. The personality

one for guidance. Those questions were so awful. What did you put for that one?"

Christina's hands were cold. "I didn't fill that one out. I'm not afraid of anything." *Liar, liar, house on fire*, ran the nursery song in her head.

Anya popped up off the mattress. "You lucky thing. I might have known. Benj and Michael aren't afraid of anything either. They just laughed when Mr. Shevvington gave them the form."

"I thought the form was for new students."

"No, no, the *form* is new."

Christina was gasping again. I must have asthma, she thought. Great. One day away from the island and I need glasses and medication.

"Guess what my first speech has to be."

"What?"

" 'Describe your house.' "

"Oh, but Anya, that's an easy topic! You can tell all about the sea captain, and his bride, and the stairs, and the dark, dank, dingy den where we are forced to watch television."

Anya unexpectedly flung herself over the gap between the two beds and hugged Christina. "Oh, Chrissie, you lifesaver! I was thinking of my real house! My shack with the broken window panes and the chickens that live in the rusted-out station wagon and the privy for when the plumbing fails. I could never tell all these mainland kids about how I really live! Not when Blake's parents already think I'm a wharf rat!" She huffed a breath of relief. In Christina's ears the huff echoed and re-echoed,

Candle Cove in their bedroom. "Chrissie, you're always so sensible. Island granite, that's you."

"Absolutely," said Christina. "Nothing throws me."

Liar, liar, house on fire.

"But I saved the worst thing for last," said Anya. "First I have to look out the window. Make sure it's not still there." She pushed up the glass and leaned out.

Then she began screaming in horror. Her wails were high and thin like a siren in the distance.

Christina grabbed her, getting a handful of skirt.

Anya ripped free. "Chrissie, your house! It's on fire! Your parents are in it, they're burning up. Oh, my god, we have to save them, come on!"

Anya leaned farther and farther out the window, climbing over the sill, hanging over the cliff.

Christina hung on, fingers laced in Anya's blouse, trying to get a grip on her body. Like the sea captain's bride, Anya tried to go through the glass. "Let go, Chrissie, let go, it's calling me, they need me," Anya screamed.

Christina looked around Anya, trying to see the wet suit, or the cormorant, or the sea captain's bride.

Far out to sea, where they had been born, flames reached into the afternoon sky.

Anya was telling the truth.

My house! thought Christina. I lied, and it did set my house on fire!

Chapter 7

Anya was screaming, screaming, screaming.

Mr. Shevvington was racing up the stairs, Michael and Benj were racing up the stairs, even Mrs. Shevvington was running up the stairs.

Mr. Shevvington got there first.

"Christina!" he shouted. "Christina, stop it!"

Stop it? she thought. Stop trying to save Anya?

"Christina, what are you doing? Shoving Anya out the window?"

Mr. Shevvington jerked Christina by the shoulders, throwing her backward against the wall. Then he hooked his arms around Anya's frail body and pulled her into the room. He rocked her back and forth. "It's all right, Anya, you're safe now, don't be afraid, I've got you."

Michael and Benj burst into the room. Mrs. Shevvington clumped in moments later. Christina was dazed where her head had hit the door jamb. She lay on the floor trying not to cry out with pain.

"What happened?" cried the boys. "Christina, what happened?"

The burning fog. They, living on the island inside the fog, had never seen it. Christina had finally witnessed the apparition that so terrified generations of mainlanders — *Is it a house on fire? A ship in trouble? Are children burning? What shall we do?*

Anya, eyes closed, lashes black against her pale cheek, lay in the pillow of her own hair against Mr. Shevvington. A tiny red rim of Anya's blood decorated the white windowsill like a row of garnet beads.

Voice full of horror, Mr. Shevvington said, "Christina, were you trying to push Anya out the window?"

Michael stood over Christina. From this angle, he was enormous, with feet so large he could step on her, squash her like a bug. She did not recognize him — his folded arms, the underside of his chin, the bagging-out of his jeans at the knees. He was glaring at her.

Christina swallowed a sick dreadful taste in her mouth — a taste of metal, of seawater, of her own blood and bile. *Are they actually accusing me of trying to kill Anya?*

The huffing noise in the room was replaced by the quivering lungs of Michael, Benj, and Mr. Shevvington, by the strange whimpering of Anya.

"No, no, no," said Anya. "Christina would never hurt me — she — I — "

"What then?" said Mr. Shevvington. "Trust me. Tell me. I won't let her hurt you."

But Anya did not seem to remember the fire on Burning Fog Isle, the house she had needed to save, or the "worst thing of all" that she had not yet told Christina. She just mumbled and made no sense.

When Christina tried to tell, the boys said she was yarning, and Mrs. Shevvington said this was beginning to form a pattern, and Mr. Shevvington said he felt the girls should be separated.

"Separated?" said Anya faintly.

"There's another bedroom," said Mr. Shevvington. "We'll move Christina in there. This is not a good situation."

Above them the poster of the sea looked out the window. The fingers that rode the painted white froth beckoned, and the curl of the waves was like the curve of a smile.

It wanted her, thought Christina. The sea wanted Anya. If they separate us, who will keep Anya from the arms of the sea?

But what could she say out loud? Even Michael and Benj seemed to be wondering if Christina really had been pushing Anya! Not Michael, thought Christina, betrayed. Surely Michael knows me better than that!

Mr. Shevvington sat down on Christina's bed. He patted her mother's quilt. It was the flying geese square — tiny, equilateral triangles of calico that flew around and around. Christina made herself think of cloth, needle, and thread; her mother, patiently sewing for Christina, planning something beautiful for Christina. "Sit with me a moment, Christina," said the principal.

Christina did not.

I hit my head, she thought. I have a huge bump

on my head where he threw me against the wall. He *liked* throwing me. And nobody has asked if I am all right.

"You do not know yourself, Christina," Mr. Shevvington informed her, standing up. "I am very worried about you. This kind of emotional disturbance is sad and frightening to us all. We love you, Christina. Everybody in this room loves you. Talk to us about what's bothering you. Do you feel inadequate? Do the mainland children seem much more capable? Are you very, very jealous of Anya?"

Ah, boys. Michael and Benj did not like how the conversation was going. It promised to be full of emotion and blame and they did not want to get involved. They backed out, claiming homework, important re-runs on TV, snacks begging to be eaten.

Mrs. Shevvington smiled.

Anya began brushing her hair. She brushed it with such vigor Christina thought she would pull all her hair out. "I don't want to be by myself," said Anya, looking at Christina and the Shevvingtons only through the mirror.

"I'm only thinking of what's best for both of you," said Mr. Shevvington gently. "You're both denying that anything happened, but the fact is that we walked into a very frightening scene a few minutes ago. I am sure, Anya, that you were not screaming for nothing."

"I told you why she was screaming," said Christina. "She saw the fire on our island and — "

"Christina!" said Mrs. Shevvington. "These stories of yours border on the manic. Call it yarning, or call it criminal defense, I wish to hear no more of it."

"Criminal defense?" repeated Christina.

"Now, now," said the principal to his wife. "We didn't really see. We aren't really sure."

Mrs. Shevvington snorted. With a flick of her fingers she whipped Christina's mother's quilt off the bed and marched into the vacant bedroom beyond the boys' room. "No need to upack drawers," she said. "Michael, Benjamin!" she yelled. "Move Christina's entire bureau into this room."

The boys moved the furniture. Mrs. Shevvington supervised.

Mr. Shevvington began to talk about jealousy and how well he understood it.

Christina interrupted him. She would turn this terrible episode into a little package to be set aside — never opened again — perhaps donated to a church fair. "What's for supper, anyway?"

Michael said from the hall, "Good grief, Chrissie, we run up here thinking you two are being raped or mugged or thrown out the window and all you care about is what's for supper?"

"You know me," said Christina lightly.

But he did not know her. Michael, whom she had loved from birth, was a stranger to her; she was in trouble and he was not with her. Anya was a distant cloud. Benj was merely solid, moving furniture, showing nothing. *Christina was alone.*

It's what I feared most, she thought. I didn't fill

it in on the form but he knew anyway.

They walked down the stairs like a column of soldiers.

Supper was fish chowder, just the way Christina loved it; thick, with milk and butter and diced potatoes. A huge stack of puffy, fresh-from-the-oven baking-powder biscuits sat in a basket lined with a red cloth. Christina slathered hers with honey, and Anya ate hers plain, and the boys put on butter and maple syrup. Everybody had at least two bowls of chowder; Michael crushed crackers into his and Benj slurped his. Dessert was a wonderful cherry pastry from the bakery on the tourist street.

Food is the answer to everything, Christina thought. Especially if it's hot.

Her head no longer ached. Michael's stories about the soccer team he was trying out for were so funny. She planned to go to all his after-school games. She thought about the tape she had to dictate for Dolly. Good thing she had said nothing yet. She really would sound insane talking about posters and wet suits and cruel principals and forms asking if you were afraid.

She thought about her homework. She was eager to get started. She was sure girls like Gretch and Vicki would be perfect at homework; she could be no less.

Christina cleared the table, and Michael and Benj did the dishes. Anya opened her book bag. She looked into her physics lab notebook, with all its blank spaces for her to fill during the year. Anya had gotten an A average in chemistry the year before; no doubt she would do the same in physics. Christina took a little more dessert and nobody objected. Perhaps the Shevvingtons were going to relax the rules a little.

Michael and Benj just sighed. Homework was prison, and the bars had just shut, as they had known would happen, and there was nothing to do now but suffer, do time.

Michael opened to a chapter about comparisons between the Soviet Union and the United States. *"Government,"* he muttered. "Who cares about *government?"*

Benj began calculating on Anya's pocket calculator. "Fifty-eight school days," he informed them. "Then I'm sixteen. One and a half marking periods. That's all."

Anya said nothing. She filled in nothing.

Christina opened her book bag. For English they had to write a poem. It made her sick just to think about writing a poem. About having to read it out loud, while Vicki and Gretch and Jonah listened. Smirking. Talking about island girls on welfare.

Mr. Shevvington said, "Christina, you and I will have our talk now. It cannot be postponed any longer."

"What talk?" said Christina.

Mr. Shevvington took her by the shoulder and led her into the library.

His blue blue eyes kept trying to look into her ordinary dark eyes. She found other things to look at. She looked at the empty shelf for a while, and then the pattern in the rug, and next the three dull pencils lying at angles on the lamp table. There were dead bugs lying inside the globe of the ceiling light.

She thought, When did he get blue eyes? He didn't have blue eyes before!

"You're afraid to look at me, Christina Romney."

"I'm not afraid of anything," said Christina.

He said gently, "You didn't fill out that form precisely because you are afraid of *everything*."

The room grew thick and wait-full, like the bedroom upstairs, with the poster of the sea.

"Christina, talk to me about your fears. I'm here to help."

Christina said nothing.

He said, "You want to have no friends? Bad grades? Lonely afternoons?"

His voice softened. It grew thick and sucking like the mud flats. "Then you're doing just the right thing, Christina." The voice caught at her, dragging her down. "It's going to happen, Christina."

It was the dream sequence, being chased, feet stuck, and evil catching up. Christina said, "How can you call this a library when you don't have any books on the shelves?"

"When you try to change the subject like that," said the principal, "I know it is because you are filled with fear. You cannot admit yet that you are a very disturbed child. Christina, it's all right. I understand."

The evening passed.

Michael, Benj, and Anya did their homework at the kitchen table. Mrs. Shevvington prepared her class lessons at the kitchen table with them. Christina sat in the library, waging silent war with Mr. Shevvington.

"I have to do my homework now," she said to him, her final weapon. What principal could argue with that?

"No," said Mr. Shevvington. "I want you to go to bed early, get a solid night's rest, and be able to face the morning with a good heart. I am writing you an excuse to give every teacher."

In his delicate looping hand, he penned:

To whom it may concern:
Christina has suffered a severe emotional distur-
bance, and I have given her permission not to do
homework until she recovers from her distress.
Arnold Shevvington
Principal

The principal smiled. "Mrs. Shevvington will read this out loud to the class, Christina, so that they will understand why an exception is being made for you."

Christina sucked in her breath. She would rather die than have Gretch and Vicki and Jonah and the rest hear that letter! "I am not distressed," she said, "and I would like to do my homework."

"Now, now," said Mrs. Shevvington. She appeared as quickly, as silently, as before. There was something subhuman about the way she could appear anywhere — like an ant or a mouse, coming through the cracks unheard. "You heard Mr. Shevvington, Chrissie."

But how did *you* hear? thought Christina. Listening at the cracks, as well as arriving by them?

"I think," said Mrs. Shevvington, "the attitude I will take is that you are just very, very tired. You aren't used to the fast pace of mainland life and all those people around you, Chrissie. I think we will give you another chance."

Don't call me Chrissie, thought Christina. Only my very very very best friends may call me Chrissie. And then only sometimes.

"We're going to go on up to bed, now." Mrs. Shevvington took Christina's book bag as if taking custody of a child. She smiled, her teeth round and yellow like a row on a corncob. "With lots of good sleep, we'll behave ever so much better in the morning, won't we, Chrissie?"

Christina stumbled up the stairs.

Each tread caught her foot, and she banged her shins. There was a spider in the shower, and she could not find her favorite nightgown.

She could not imagine morning. Science — where the teacher had said how the island children were always so good! Math — history — what was she going to do?

Christina pulled the quilt over her head, and in the dark nest of her body and the sheets she tried to stay calm. The math was all review; she could do it in ten minutes during homeroom. The social studies she could read instead of having lunch. The science — well, she would just have to wing it. But English — Mrs. Shevvington had assigned them to write a short poem.

Christina hated writing.

Reading was fine; she could read anything and love it. But it did not work in the other direction for Christina.

How Christina loved paper! Fresh, new, first-day-of-school paper. Narrow lines or wide lines, spiral notebooks or three-ringed, arithmetic paper or construction. Blank paper was beautiful with its calm, clean look. But once she touched it messy thumbprints appeared, and violent black slashes where she had meant to cross a T. It wrinkled from the pressure of her clenched hand around the pen, and it tore at the wrinkles by the time she finished.

Blank paper — so nice when she bought it — such agony when she used it.

And writing her own poem?

I need a month just to think of a topic, thought Christina. She thought if she began crying she would never stop; she would be like the tide, and the salt water of her tears would cycle and recycle, endlessly ripping her back and forth.

Anya slipped into the new bedroom. Christina was so glad to see her. The girls hugged and did not let go. It was not like hugging at all, but like leaning. "What happened, anyway?" said Anya.

"I don't know," said Christina. They both knew they were talking about the window, and the burning fog, and the Shevvingtons.

"I couldn't do my homework," said Anya. "I couldn't understand any of it. The pages just sat there looking at me. Christina, I'm going to fail my senior year, I can feel it. And I can't give a speech.

I can't ever give a speech. I can't bear the thought of people staring at me and listening to me and analyzing my words and grading my talk. I'll lose my voice. I'll lose my mind!"

"Hush," said Christina. "You'll be fine."

"Listen to the sea. It sounds like a coffin being dragged over broken glass."

It does, thought Christina. Like the sea captain's bride. And of course there *was* broken glass. She jumped straight through the window.

Anya said, "Sleep in my room. I don't want to be alone in there."

You're not alone in there, thought Christina. The poster of the sea and the huffing are in there with you.

She shivered.

Surely Anya would not try to get out the window again. It had been the illusion of fire — she really had been trying to save the islanders — she had not been trying to jump like the sea captain's bride.

They went into the other bedroom. Anya undressed. She had a lovely body, as white as her face, as untouched by the sun as if Anya had been raised a mushroom. "So what should I do about Blake?" asked Anya.

Christina had forgotten Blake. She had forgotten that anybody but her might have problems. "I don't know."

"I have to see him. I'll die if I don't see him."

She said this with such certainty that Christina thought, Anya *will* die if she doesn't see him. We will all die. That is why we are here. To die. That is why there are no other guests. There must be no witnesses.

Anya put on a nightshirt — a huge man's shirt, with the tails reaching her knees. She was so thin within it, she seemed not to exist from the throat to the knees.

Christina said, "But what was the worst thing? The thing you were going to tell me before you saw the burning fog."

Anya said, "I don't remember. What could be worse than not being able to date Blake?"

Mrs. Shevvington came up to check. She made Christina go back to her room. Alone.

Christina lay in bed listening to the surf, waiting for everybody else to go to sleep. She had a flashlight. *Semper paratis.* Always prepared, that's me, just like the Coast Guard motto says, Christina thought. We island girls are prepared to survive.

Christina slid out of bed and stealthily opened the lid of her trunk, fishing among the sweaters and jeans until her fingers found the thin metal tube. She slid the narrow knob of the torch. The batteries were good. Christina tiptoed into Anya's room and got pencil and paper out of her book bag, since Mrs. Shevvington had confiscated Christina's. She took Anya's chemistry book for a writing surface and tiptoed back to her room. She nearly missed her footing at the top of the stairs and fell down them. In the dark green room Christina curled under the quilt and worked grimly on her poem. Version after version — stupid line after stupid line.

Finally she had something. She got a pen out of Anya's purse and made a final copy.

It was so messy she had to make a second final copy. I'm done, she thought, almost weeping from exhaustion and relief.

She re-read the poem by flashlight.

if I were a sea gull
I wouldn't have to stick around.
if people argued — I would fly off,
swerve, wheel, dip, scream.
a thousand wings of company if I have friends
two strong wings of my own
if I don't.

She liked it.

It was island strong.

Christina folded the good paper carefully and stuck it in her purse. She put Anya's belongings back exactly as she had found them. She didn't stuff the crushed versions in the wastebasket; Mrs. Shevvington might find them and use them for evidence. She stuck them back down in her trunk, under the Icelandic sweater. She slid the flashlight under her pillow. You never knew.

She collapsed in bed, comforting herself with the feel of the seams on her mother's quilt under her fingertips.

The huffing began again.

Christina's heart jolted.

"Fffff," the room said.

It's the tide, she told herself. I already went

through this once today, and it's the tide.

She lay in bed trembling.

"Ffffffff."

Her eyes burned from staring into the dark.

She identified the separate sounds of wind and waves and a distant motor — car, not boat. Her hands tightened around the flashlight, as if she might need it for a weapon, as well as to end the dark.

"Ffffff."

She got out of bed.

The huffing slithered around her nightgown and tumbled through her hair and penetrated her ears like a snake, crawling in, slithering in.

"*Ffffff.*"

It was not the tide. It was in the house.

In the hall a faint light came from the boys' room. Their door was open, their window shades were up. They slept deeply and breathed evenly. The open stairs yawned at Christina's feet and the delicate banisters around the balcony were thin as carved toothpicks.

"*Ffffff.*"

She turned on the flash. Some of the banisters stood straight in front of her, and others grew long and thin, and their shadows fluttered like moths. She swung the flash toward them, and they stood still while the doors to the boys' room and the bathroom vanished. She turned to light those places, and the shadows behind her moved forward and grew fat.

She could not move fast enough. The shadows ate her feet.

The sea captain's house looked down and up at her, exposed in her circle of light; the house all safe in its dark.

"*Fffff.*"

Christina walked into the jaws of the whispering sound.

It's not the Cove blowing out the candles, she thought, it's here, in this house, somebody having an eternal birthday, never getting the wish right, the candles lighting back up like evil magic tricks.

"*Fffff.*"

She climbed the open stairs into the cupola.

The stairs were very steep, and had only treads, not risers, so when she flashed the light at her feet, she could see through the stairs, down to the floors below. The shadow of herself was huge, like a flowing Arab robe. She climbed up and up, too many steps, far higher than the ceiling was high, like a cartoon creature climbing beyond the building into the sky.

In the moonlight the cupola glittered. She flicked the flashlight upwards and the glass turned black, reflecting her like a mirror.

She looked up, and left, and down, and right, flashing her torch, searching the shadows. The huffing was screaming at her now, "FFFFFFFF. *FFFFFFFFF. FFFFFFFFF!!!*"

The ghost of the sea captain's bride stood white, frozen by a winter sea, framed by glass, whispering, "*Ffffff. Fffffff. Ffffffff.*"

Chapter 8

Christina woke up slowly. Her muscles seemed to awaken before her mind, the waking up traveling down her limbs, out her arms to her hands, and finally arriving at her fingers, which hurt; they were cramped.

She opened her eyes.

She was in Anya's bedroom, lying on the bare mattress Mrs. Shevvington had stripped the night before. Anya was in her own bed, covers on the floor in a tangle. Wet salty air filled the room. The girls were holding hands between the beds.

Actually, it was Anya's hand holding Christina's. Her fingers were tight as death.

"Anya?" whispered Christina.

Anya woke up even more slowly than Christina. Her white face was smudged, as if by bruises or oil. The beautiful hair was lank and flat, the eyes dull.

"*Anya?*" whispered Christina again.

"I had the most terrible nightmare," said Anya. She began crying. She made no sound, nor did her eyes or chin quiver; tears spilled like brooks running into the sea. "Chrissie, you needed me. You were fighting the fingers of the dead."

Morning sun lay dazzling upon the sea, breaking through the window glass like a fist.

"What happened?" said Christina. Dimly she remembered the ghost.

"I don't know. The fingers had you, they were pulling you! I stopped them." Anya began shuddering. Her eyes did not seem to see past the iris. She was holding Christina's hand so hard Christina thought the bones might crack.

All memory returned. Christina was disgusted with herself. "That's not what happened, Anya. You were sleepwalking in your nightshirt. You scared me. You went right up the cupola stairs, and you were talking to the tide. You've got to get a grip on yourself." One by one she pried Anya's fingers loose. She tried to joke. "You've got a grip on me right now instead."

When Christina peeled her away, Anya's eyes stayed on her empty hand, and she held the hand up to her face to stare at it, the fingers who no longer had friends.

Christina got off the mattress and walked slowly toward the bedroom windows. There was seaweed on the glass. Forty feet above the cliff. Sixty feet above high tide. And seaweed had appeared on the window?

I won't look down, she told herself. I might see the wet suit. I won't look out, either. I might see the burning fog. I'll just look at the window pane.

And then Christina's fingers iced where Anya had clenched them.

The seaweed was on the *inside* of the window.

Christina lifted her index finger to touch the seaweed. The seaweed was still green and wet.

"Thousands of fishermen have lost their lives in that ocean," said Anya. "And children. And people on vacation. And sailors. And immigrants."

How could it be wet? thought Christina. High tide was hours ago. But even the highest tide of my life wasn't high enough to spray this window with seaweed.

In its time the ocean had yanked down oil rigs and lighthouses, thrown great ships to the bottom, tossed tiny dories onto rocky shoals. So it could hurl a wisp of seaweed in such a way that it landed on the inside of a window.

Anya was drawing dead children and sailors in the air with her hands. "And swallowed the salt water," she said dreamily, "and filled their lungs with ocean, and gagged their final convulsions." She sounded as if she had watched.

"And they're still here," she whispered, getting up, crossing to the window, and leaning way out to stare into the ocean.

"What do you mean, still there?" said Christina sharply. Haven't we said all this before? she thought. How often will we say this now?

Anya smiled madly. "Their shadows still swim. Fight the tide and fling seaweed. How do you think that green seaweed got stuck to the window way up here?"

Christina swallowed. "Uh — the high winds — extra high tides — "

"Don't be foolish. If a wave had touched the top of the house it would have swept away the shutters, it would have been a gale to tear off the town docks."

Christina looked away from the window. Looking at Anya was unbearable. She looked at the poster.

Quiet water. No whitecaps. No shadows beneath the raging sea. Just peaceful blue waves.

It was not the same poster the souvenir woman had thrust into her hands.

"The fingers of the dead put that seaweed there," said Anya. "Sea fingers."

How normal they all were at breakfast.

They had toast today, and bacon and fried eggs. Orange juice in tiny glasses with pineapples printed on them.

Michael talked of soccer practice, and Benj discussed his first project in woodworking.

Not the same poster. How could that be? What could be happening? What power of the sea had made Anya sleepwalk, singing to the tide in the tide's words?

Anya looked down at her plate fairly often, but seemed not to recognize anything on it. She held her fork but did not use it. Mrs. Shevvington said nothing about the rules of sound eating. Christina ate her own breakfast without talking. She stripped the fat off her bacon, which left her with a tiny strip of lean hardly big enough to chew. She ate the toast dry. Perhaps with her allowance she would buy her own jam. Strawberry, the only kind Christina liked. She would hide it between her knees and spread it on her toast while Mrs. Shevvington was pouring herself a second cup of coffee.

I do not believe in fingers of the sea, Christina decided. Anya and I both had nightmares, probably about school. I'm afraid of the seventh grade, and she's afraid of public speaking. It has to be the same poster, I just didn't focus. Today I will be granite again.

Mrs. Shevvington was wearing a cranberry red suit this morning. It was the exact same cut and material as yesterday's royal blue suit. Christina wondered if the woman had a whole rainbow of them — gold and purple and black suits, which would follow one after another, all with the same white blouse. "How are you feeling this morning?" said Mrs. Shevvington to Christina. She bared her corncob teeth.

"I'm very well, thank you," said Christina, peppering her egg.

"And you, Anya?" said Mrs. Shevvington. "How are you?"

Anya was clearly unwell. But Michael and Benj were already filling one of the two sinks with hot water and squirting dishwashing liquid under the flow of the tap. They did not notice that Anya neither heard nor answered the question.

"Any more trouble with the windows?" said Mrs. Shevvington, still smiling.

Trouble with the windows. Anya trying to step through them had been the trouble. Christina had forgotten all about that. Now she remembered Mr. Shevvington implying that she had pushed Anya. It's been one nightmare after another, Christina thought. Pretty soon I won't be able to keep track of them all.

Christina cleared the breakfast table, handing Michael the plates and glasses.

Anya simply stood there, looking disconnected from her own body. Her clothing did not match. She had on an ugly print blouse in faded grey and brown, with a yellow skirt and red shoes. "Did you look in the mirror?" said Christina.

"No," said Anya. "But I looked in the poster."

The fingers in the poster. Were they Anya's fingers of the sea? Had they come to collect?

Had they already collected Anya?

English class was very quiet.

Christina sat behind Vicki and Gretch, and Jonah sat behind her.

One by one, they were forced to walk to the front of the class and read aloud their poems.

Two of the boys could hardly get up there, they were so nervous. The first boy plowed into two student desks and the wastebasket on his way to the front, and whacked his elbow on the blackboard. There is no pain quite so awful as elbow pain; he moaned before starting his poem. "No sound effects, Robbie," said Mrs. Shevvington. "Merely the poem."

The boy had written about the beauty of his mother's smile when he got home every afternoon.

Christina was touched.

Her mother, too, had a welcome-home smile.

Mrs. Shevvington said, "How sweet, Robbie. Immature, however. I am afraid immaturity runs in the family."

Robbie flushed scarlet and tripped going back to his seat.

His mother's smile is ruined for him, thought Christina. Every day this year when he gets home from school and she flings open the door and smiles at him, he'll blush and get mad and avoid her.

She wondered what Mrs. Shevvington had meant about immaturity running in the family, and why she had said such a rude thing.

The second boy rhymed very carefully. To make sure the class followed the meter, he spoke in a singsong. His poem was about summer traffic.

Summer traffic, he recited.
Is very graphic.
Too many cars
Really jars.

He had eight verses like this. Christina loved it. She could see the poem illustrated with fat tourist automobiles and bumper-sticker size lettering.

"Wellllll," said Mrs. Shevvington, adding extra lllll's. She lifted her eyebrows, sharing a joke with the rest of the class. "You tried, Colin."

Christina's smile of enjoyment faded. Colin's head sank between his shoulders like a turtle's. He shuffled to his desk, trying to avoid everybody's eyes.

Vicki was next. Vicki's poem was stupid. It was about the meaning of death as seen in storm clouds. Mrs. Shevvington beamed at Vicki and gave her an A. "Now that," said Mrs. Shevvington, "is a meaty topic. A topic worthy of a poem."

Christina said clearly, "I think a mother's smile is a topic worthy of a hundred poems."

Mrs. Shevvington turned slowly and stared at her. Eyes of mud, skin of jellyfish.

Christina thought, I am granite. I do not flinch.

"Notice how the girl who did not do her homework feels free to make comments," said Mrs. Shevvington.

Christina's heart was hot with pleasure. "I did my homework," she said evenly. "Would you like me to read my poem now?"

The other children were staring at her, in awe, confusion, or amusement.

I have become different, thought Christina.

She had always been different. The one who was painted, the one photographed. But she had not wanted to be different in seventh grade. It was to be the year of being the same! The mainland year, the year of fitting in.

"Do read your masterpiece for us," said Mrs. Shevvington in silken tones.

Christina got up from her desk. Her feet seemed to have gotten heavier; she clumped to the front of the room; when she turned to face the class she saw a haze of unknown mouths and noses, queer staring eyes — strangers, strangers, strangers.

She swallowed.

She unfolded her wrinkled poem.

if I were a sea gull
I wouldn't have to stick around.
if people argued — I would fly off,
swerve, wheel, dip, scream.
a thousand wings of company if I have friends
two strong wings of my own
if I don't.

Jonah Bergeron clapped.

Robbie clapped with him.

The rest waited to see how Mrs. Shevvington reacted. The teacher said nothing about the poem. Instead she walked up to Christina, pushing against her, the cranberry red of her suit shouting as loud as a mouth.

"Why, Christina, you didn't do any homework last night. I myself forbade it. You wrote this poem last year, for some island school assignment. You're handing it in now, pretending you wrote it last night."

"I wrote it under the covers," said Christina, burning. "With my flashlight."

Mrs. Shevvington snorted. "I will give you a zero, Christina Romney. Cheating and lying may be acceptable on your island but they will not do here."

I could push her down Breakneck Hill, thought Christina, and applaud when she got killed.

Gretch and Vicki giggled. She knew they were giggling at her. At her poem. At her zero. At her shame.

After class three things happened.

Mrs. Shevvington said, "You will give me your flashlight at dinner, Christina."

"If you believe I have a flashlight," said Christina, "you believe I wrote that poem using it last night."

Mrs. Shevvington smiled. This time her teeth did not show. It was more a thinning-out of her lips: a challenge. "The flashlight," she said, "is to be given to me."

Why? thought Christina. To cripple me in the dark?

Who is this woman, that she wants to get me? Who am I to her?

"Christina?" said a soft voice.

Christina jumped as if ghost fingers were touching her spine. Then she flushed scarlet. "Hullo, Miss Schuyler," she mumbled.

"Are you all right, Christina?" said Miss Schuyler. Her fat braids lay like a thick honey pillow on the back of her neck. How cozy it must be, to live beneath that hair, thought Christina.

She thought of telling Miss Schuyler about what it was like to live with the Shevvingtons. But she could not do that. Teachers stuck together. Teachers had coffee together and meetings together, and if she told Miss Schuyler, Miss Schuyler would tell Mrs. Shevvington, and somehow Mrs. Shevvington would have more power. "I'm fine, thank you," said Christina, and she skirted around her math teacher and plowed on down the hall, alone.

Power, thought Christina dimly. What is power?

She thought of power plants, and electricity. She thought of nations and wars. Mrs. Shevvington has more power than I do, thought Christina. But what is the power for? Where are we going with it?

Robbie caught up to her, drawing her out of the hall traffic. "Christina? Is that your name?"

She was uncertain of them all now. "Uh-huh," she said cautiously.

How thin Robbie was. How powerless. "I don't want you to get in trouble with Mrs. Shevvington," said Robbie quickly, looking around to be sure nobody heard. "You're new here, Christina. You don't know. *Don't speak up again like that.*"

"But you're new, too," protested Christina. "We're all new. We just started junior high. How can you know Mrs. Shevvington any better than I do?"

Robbie's eyes were old and dark. He said, "I have an older sister." He said no more, giving the sister no name, no description; as if his older sister truly were nothing more than that — not a person, not a soul — just a thing. Christina shivered. Robbie swallowed. Whispering, he added, "She — she had Mrs. Shevvington last year for senior English."

"And?" said Christina.

Robbie shrugged. He walked away. "Just don't talk back," he said over his shoulder.

His sister, then — had she talked back?

But what had happened to his sister? Why did Christina feel that she had just received a gift from Robbie, a present he had been afraid to give her — news about the sister who had no name?

Next it was Blake who stopped Christina in the halls. Blake looked so handsome! Christina wondered if the painters and photographers who came to Burning Fog would want Blake to pose. He did not have an island look, though; she had never seen anybody so thoroughly mainland. "Christina, what happened to Anya?" said Blake. He ran his hands through his thick dark hair and it flopped across his part.

The fingers of the sea, thought Christina. They followed Anya all the way into the school. "I don't know, Blake. What's the matter?"

"She's being weird. She looks funny."

"She's worried about going out with you, and both of you getting into trouble."

"Yeah, I'm worried about that, too. But she was saying — " Blake broke off, embarrassed, because several lowly seventh-graders were listening. "She was saying the sea was gone," he said in a low voice. "She made it sound like the Atlantic Ocean had moved away."

The poster had changed. Could the ocean itself change? If the ocean could change, anything could; none of the laws of earth and life would be safe. If the world were about to collapse, Christina wanted to be on the island with her family, where she knew the rocks and the roses. "I'd better go see," she said. She pushed through the seventh-graders, running out of the building, down the wide steps, between the brick gates, heading for the Singing Bridge.

But it was not Blake running along with her — it was Jonah. Where had he come from? "Christina, you're crazy," he shouted, matching her steps perfectly, so their ankles locked like kids in a three-legged race. "Course the ocean's still there," he said. "If it had disappeared it would have been on the evening news."

"I can't rest easy till I taste it," she shouted to Jonah. "Run faster. We have to get back to class on time."

"Taste?" said Jonah.

"When you take a deep breath of low tide air," said Christina, "you taste it, too."

They reached the Singing Bridge. Cars hummed over it. The tide was high but the Cove was relatively quiet. Waves slapped in a friendly fashion against docked boats.

They stopped, panting.

Jonah said, "Um, Christina?"

The waves flecked a faint mist onto her face. "It's still here," said Christina. She sucked in lungs full of air, salting her mouth and throat.

"There's this dance," said Jonah.

Christina focused on him. She was granite and would not give in to yarns and fancies. A dance. "Oh, we're awful for dances on the island," she said.

Jonah looked relieved. "You're a terrible dancer, you mean? Good, because I've never danced at all. I've hardly even seen dancing except on videos, but

I feel as if I should know how. And this — "

"No, no," said Christina irritably. She grabbed his arm, turning him around, and they began jogging back to school. "*Awful for dances* means we love dances. We have lots of them on the island."

"Oh." Jonah considered this phrase. "Well, will you come with me?"

"Come with you where?"

"The dance."

"What dance?"

"Christina!" he yelled. "The seventh-grade dance! The Getting To Know You Dance! In two weeks."

There had been that form entitled Getting to Know You. There had been that order from Mr. Shevvington that Jonah was to be her friend. She said, "It's bad enough I have to get soup and sandwiches on a blue ticket, Jonah Bergeron. I'm not going to a dance on a blue ticket. Get lost."

Christina walked home with Anya and Blake.

The Jaye boys were not with them. Michael had started soccer practice, and Benj was looking for a job; he said life was too boring with nothing to do but school. He was hoping for a gas station. He liked engines.

Blake said, "Anya, please tell me what's wrong."

She still had her bruised look. Even though Blake clung to her hand, Anya seemed to be alone, lost inside her own body.

Blake pleaded with Anya. He said he loved her. He said he wasn't going to obey his parents; what did they know anyway? He said okay, if Anya wouldn't ride in his car, then he wouldn't either. He would abandon it in the parking lot and walk every step she walked. He just wanted to be with her. Something was wrong, please let him help.

Blake said, "Anya, tell me how you got that big bruise on your leg. And the cuts on your knee." Anya said nothing. Blake lifted the hem of Anya's skirt to show Christina the bruise.

Christina sucked in her breath. "Anya is sleep-walking," she said dubiously, although she did not want anybody to know. It sounded crazy; she was afraid a catalog Maine person like Blake would abandon Anya if she sounded insane. Blake would stick by Anya because he was in the mood to oppose his mother and father; but he wouldn't if everybody else said she was a nut case. Christina stared at the bruise. She could not remember either of them falling, and there had been no crashes among the huffing sounds.

"Listen," whispered Anya. "The sea. It sounds as if it's in chains."

"It's just the tide," said Blake. "It always sounds like that."

"Can't you hear?" Anya cried. "Chains scraping. Ankles caught. Children choking."

"It's the sand," protested Blake. "When the waves go back out, sand is dropped along the way."

Anya shuddered. "It sounds like dead armies marching."

Blake looked at her in despair.

"I will never sleep again," she told him. "You

didn't hear the sea last night. All the dead beneath the waves began breathing again."

Fffffffff, Christina remembered.

"It must have been the wind in the shutters," Blake said.

That night they did their homework at the kitchen table. Anya was writing an essay. "Write about young love," said Christina. "Write about Blake's car."

But Anya was writing about the tide in Candle Cove.

Every twelve hours (plus twenty minutes) the tide licks the barnacles, inching toward the village. Then a queer sickening whisper begins. Ffffff — puffing out a candle. And the entire ocean, laughing because it caught you by surprise, hurls itself into the Cove. You cannot get away. It has you. If you are in Candle Cove, wading, rowing a dinghy, digging for clams, you will die. Candle Cove is the Atlantic Ocean's toy. Like a birthday present, it opens itself every day, hoping, hoping, hoping, to catch you by surprise. And drown you. . . .

Mrs. Shevvington, like the English teacher she was, said, "Anya, two errors here. First, you refer to the sea as if it is a person. As if it thinks and plans. This is called personification. Attributing humanity to things or animals."

"I never said the sea had humanity," said Anya. "The sea is psychotic. The sea is a mass murderer."

"Your second error is pronouns," said Mrs. Shevvington. She was smiling. As if Anya had finally gotten the lesson right. "The reader cannot tell who the victim is."

"Me," said Anya. "The sea wants me."

Chapter 9

"Mother?" Christina said, clinging to the telephone. "Oh, Mother, I'm so glad to hear your voice."

There had been a phone line out to Burning Fog Isle all of Christina's life, but not during her parents' childhoods. They had had to use ship to shore radio. Christina blessed the telephone. She just hoped Mrs. Shevvington wouldn't come home and catch her in the forbidden living room before she had a chance to explain everything. "Mother, it's so awful here. I need you," cried Christina. "Please come."

There was a curious pause. It was not like her mother. For a moment Christina thought the connection had been broken, and she imagined the fingers of the sea, taking the underwater cable, tearing it asunder, laughing beneath the waves.

"Christina," said her mother in a queer voice, "the Shevvingtons have talked to us. They were on the telephone with us late last night. Honey, how could you behave like this? How could you forget your upbringing? Rude in school, lying about your homework, frightening Anya, refusing to eat the meals Mrs. Shevvington labors over? Christina, your father and I hardly know what to think."

The black-and-gold peacocks mocked Christina. "Mother, that's not what it's like." The telephone shook in her hand.

Her father got on the extension. She could see them, her mother in the kitchen, fragrant from baking; her father in the bedroom, sweaty from playing tennis. "Christina, when you left the island we were so proud of you, and now look. Cheating and yarning and refusing to obey authority! We don't know what's the matter with you, but luckily you're with people who are used to dealing with difficult adolescents. The Shevvingtons are going to handle it."

"*It!*" cried Christina. "You mean *me*? It isn't like that. The Shevvingtons are cruel people. I think they hate girls. I think they choose a new one each year, and this year it's Anya. The Shevvingtons made us fill out forms about what we're afraid of — acid, or rats! You have to — "

"You're making that up, Christina," her father said. "Christina, honey, no teacher, no principal, would ever hand a form like that to a child."

"No, no. It's true. And this house — I'm sure that the sea captain's bride — or maybe it's the poster, the poster of the sea — "

"Stop it!" shouted her father. "Christina, I won't have this! Mrs. Shevvington told us that you and Anya have some sort of sick game about that poster on your wall. Now you listen to me. When I was a kid, I had a hard time finding my place at the mainland school, too, and so did your mother, and so did everybody else, but we didn't resort to making up ridiculous stories and placing blame on other people, and pretending that the finest, most caring principal the school has ever had is cruel! We just worked harder, Christina. We obeyed the rules! And that's what we expect from you, too."

The phone crackled.

It's the sea listening in, thought Christina. The sea knows what's going on. The sea started it.

Mrs. Shevvington came into the room. She did not look powerful enough to control Christina's parents across the water. But she was. She took the phone, smiling her corncob smile. She told Christina's parents that visits would not be a good idea and phone calls would be worse. There should be no communication between Christina and her parents until Christina had learned to behave.

Christina willed her parents to refuse. Believe in me! she thought.

"Fine," said Mrs. Shevvington. "Arnold and I will keep in touch. The important thing is not to worry." Her smile stretched long and thin and yellow. "We are in complete control of Christina."

Dolly's first tape arrived.

Dolly was bored; it was no fun being the oldest in school; she had to help with the little kids, and this year the kids were really little: five-, six-, and seven-year-olds. Dolly missed Christina. Dolly was sure Christina was having a perfect year. Because that was the only reason Dolly could think of that

Christina wasn't sending tapes — she was too busy and too happy.

Christina had a blank tape. Benj had bought it for her. But what could she say to Dolly?

Dear Dolly, Remember my school daydream? Best friends, laughter, shared snacks, phone calls, compliments, a boyfriend?

I sit alone at lunch. Mrs. Shevvington punishes me for everything. Mr. Shevvington smiles and says I need mental counseling. As for your brothers, Benj won't listen to me; Michael never comes near me; word got around school that I'm weird, and he's afraid it's catching.

I sleep alone in a dark green room that talks to me at night. Mrs. Shevvington took my flashlight, and the light switch for the bedroom is on the far side of the room from my bed, and the light switch for the hall is all the way around the other side of the balcony. I just get under the covers in the dark and hope Anya doesn't jump out her window.

Anya said you can't tell anybody if it's hard; they just worry and they can't do anything anyway. I want everybody on Burning Fog Isle worried about me. But the Shevvingtons took care of that. Nobody's worried. Just mad.

Anya doesn't sleep much any more. She's afraid the seaweed on the window was a sign that the waves are going to come right into the room for her. Her grades are slipping. She breaks down in Public Speaking class and sobs. Mr. Shevvington comes in to give her moral support. She's always thanking him for being so good to her. He's not good to her! He's the one who put her in there to start with.

Mr. Shevvington wrote Anya's parents, Dolly.

> Dear Mr. and Mrs. Rothrock,
> Anya continues to work far below her capacity. Just what immaturity causes this, I do not seem to be able to find out. Instead of growing more mature, contributing more in class, acquiring and using skills, Anya moves steadily backward. . . .

I hate Mr. Shevvington, Dolly. You go to junior high to learn government, begin algebra, increase your vocabulary, start a foreign language. Me, I'm learning to hate.

I cornered Robbie. I asked about his sister. Robbie was afraid, but he told me in the end. Val was sweet and friendly once. Sang in the choir, won prizes in the art fair.

"Ordinary," Robbie told me. "But nice." He frowned; this was the real stumbling block. Val had been nice. . . . She became nothing. It wasn't that she stopped being nice. She stopped being anything.

Val slipped during her senior year; forgot to do homework, stopped washing her hair, avoided her friends, ate strange things, like Spaghetti-O's cold from a can. She adopted a single outfit — torn corduroy pants and an old shirt of her father's — and wore it daily for weeks. She was not on drugs, Dolly. She was not on booze.

She's locked up now. The Shevvingtons recom-

mended a really good adolescent mental hospital.

Jonah has fallen in love with me. I know. I wanted to have a boy fall in love with me. But I wanted to choose what boy. Jonah is overflowing with emotions that I do not share. I have to ask for instructions. "How do you feel now?" he asks. I say to him, "How should I feel?" He loves to hear me talk about the island, and whenever I finish my stories he laughs. I can't tell if he's laughing at me or with me. I want to be friends with the real kids! Like Vicki and Gretch. But they don't pay any attention to me. Except when they're laughing at me.

Oh, Dolly, it's so awful. The only good thing is you are safe on Burning Fog. I know you hate sixth. I hated it last year, too. But sixth grade is safe.

Sometimes when Anya wakes up at night, and slips into bed with me, her feet cold, her hands cold, and she says that the fingers of the dead are walking on her back —

We hang onto each other, Dolly, but I can't hold on forever. One of us is going to fall.

Well, of course she couldn't send a tape like that to Dolly.

So she sent nothing.

"I have to give a speech about the ocean," said Anya, twitching with nerves. They were up in Anya's bedroom, Anya staring into the poster of the sea, Blake and Christina staring into Anya. In the afternoon Blake was always at the Schooner Inne now. The Shevvingtons stayed late at the high school, Michael had soccer practice, and Benj had a job pumping gas at the Mobil station.

"Who says it has to be about the ocean?" demanded Christina. "Talk about the sky, or the grocery store, or Blake's catalog clothes."

Blake was sprawled on the floor of Anya's room. Christina was never afraid when Blake was there. She did not know what it was about Blake that kept away the fingers of the sea. Was it that he was a boy? That he was in love? That it was daylight?

"Mr. Shevvington says I have to overcome my fears. He says I have to tackle the scariest topics of all." Anya whispered to the poster. "He knows all my fears."

If I had those forms, thought Christina, if I showed them to my mother and father, then they would believe! Then they would realize that Mr. Shevvington is the one who is sick, not me.

She wondered where the forms were kept. Who else had read them? Who else had had to fill them out? What about Val's forms? What had Val been afraid of? How had Mr. Shevvington destroyed Val?

Anya ran her fingers through her hair and pulled it down over her face to hide herself. Blake sighed and pulled Anya off her bed and down on top of him, putting her hands and hair away from her face. "Anya, stop being so worried. It's only a high school class. The worst thing that can happen is that you'll forget your speech and have to sit down."

Anya burst into tears. She quivered when anybody raised a voice around her now. Mr. Shevvington never raised his voice, so she skipped a lot of

126

her classes and huddled near his desk. "Blake, don't yell at me. I can't date a person who yells at me."

"I'm not yelling at you!" yelled Blake.

"Anyway," said Anya, "Benj is not afraid of anything. If I have a job, I won't be afraid, either. So I'm quitting school, too. I found a wonderful job. Where the water is all locked up."

"What?" shouted Blake. "Quit school? Are you out of your mind? You *will* end up a wharf rat then."

Christina had thought romance would be fast red cars, billowing black hair, long drives down the coast, alone together, kissing, and in love. That's what Blake thinks, too, she realized, watching him watch Anya. But Anya — the most romantic-looking person in Maine — Anya doesn't even know.

Blake changed subjects. Perhaps he thought he could change Anya as easily. "I made you a present," said Blake pleadingly. "It's a calendar. Full of our dates. Nothing but our dates."

He had drawn the squares and the months himself. Each week was illustrated with cartoons cut from the newspaper — *Far Side, Funky Winkerbean, Peanuts, Cathy, Garfield* — cartoons about love and romance and boys and girls. Each Friday and Saturday listed a movie, a drive, or a dance that Blake would take Anya to.

"That's so romantic!" said Christina, hugging herself.

"A paper calendar?" muttered Anya. She never talked in a normal voice any more; she just whispered to herself or to the sea. "Silly little squares with numbers on them. The only true calendar is the tide. It speaks to you; it ordains the time."

"Anya," said Christina nervously, "when the tide speaks to you, don't answer."

Blake got up off the floor. Christina could feel his rage. No, no, Blake, don't leave her! Don't break up! You're all she has. I don't count. I'm just the seventh-grader in the other bedroom! She needs you!

But Blake was trembling; his muscles quivered strangely, and she could not tell if he wanted to hit something or hug somebody.

"I'm putting an end to this," said Blake. He slammed the window down, hard enough to break the glass. He yanked the paper shade so it snapped on the roller like a gunshot and jerked the thin cotton curtains closed.

"You can't get rid of the sea that easily," said Anya dreamily.

"Anya, I don't know what's happened to you. But it makes me nervous. And my parents — listen, the screwy way you talked in front of them this afternoon — Anya, it didn't help us any. *What is going on?*"

Anya turned very slowly, like a ballerina. She arched onto her toes and with a long, slow wave of her own, pointed to the poster of the sea. "Ask it," she said. "It knows."

How big he is, thought Christina. She was filled with admiration for him, for his body and muscles and anger.

Blake attacked.

For one horrible minute she thought she would witness a homicide after all, that Blake would kill Anya with his bare hands. His fingers were huge and curled, like the souvenir woman's, like Mrs. Shevvington's, like the waves on the poster of the sea.

Blake ripped the poster off the wall. Sliding his fingers under the paper, he tore it off in great strips and chunks. The sound filled the room, like the huffing of night, the sound of mutilating. He threw the strips of poster behind him. Bits of green ocean and blue wave fell in the four corners of the room.

Anya jumped onto her bed, getting off the floor, as if the bits of poster were rats about to bite her bare feet. "I didn't do it," she cried. "It wasn't me!"

"Who are you talking to, Anya?" shouted Blake, shredding the poster. "This thing was printed by the thousands in some factory in Boston. It's nothing. *Nothing*. See? I tore it up. It's gone."

Why didn't I think of that? wondered Christina. I could have torn it up myself. How clever Blake is.

The bedroom door was flung open, hitting the wall. The last strip of torn poster hung on the handle like a Christmas tree decoration.

"What is going on here?" Mrs. Shevvington said in a tight thin voice. "Anya, what are you doing, bringing young men up to your bedroom? Christina, why are you in this room? You have your own room, as I recall. Blake Lathem, I thought better of you. Since you have been associating with these island girls, your behavior has become worse and worse.

I plan to address your parents about this. They have been discussing the idea of boarding school with Mr. Shevvington, to remove you from Anya's influence, and I see that they were very probably right."

Anya cried out, draping herself over the bed like some old damp towel. Blake went white.

"Nothing has happened," said Christina. "Nothing was going to happen. We were just watching the tide." She hated how people yielded to Mrs. Shevvington. Why didn't they kick her in the shins? Why didn't Blake, who had enough rage in him to break windows, attack her?

"Oh, you were, were you?" Mrs. Shevvington smiled. It was a brighter, more challenging smile than any she had directed at Christina before.

War, thought Christina. We're at war now.

"Anya, Blake, go downstairs immediately. Christina, clean up the mess in this room."

They were gone, Mrs. Shevvington pushing Blake and Anya downstairs like a high wind shifting driftwood.

Christina was alone with the shreds of poster. From the bathroom she got the whisk broom and dustpan. She began sweeping up the bits of paper.

Fffffffffff, began the house.

She brushed.

Fffffffffff, said the house.

Fffffffffff, said the walls and the floor and the glass.

Christina tried to stand up but there was weight on her, as if she were standing under water.

If I can just get downstairs . . . she thought.

With the others. With Blake and Benj. I know it's just the tide. I know it funnels sounds up through the foundations and between the cracks and inside the cupola windows. I know it's just Candle Cove.

She dropped the whisk and dustpan in the hall. She grabbed the banister. She could not remember the way to the stairs. "I'm granite," she whispered, "it's Anya who is the tern." She felt herself tip, as if her granite was only a facade, and indoors, inside her rib cage, under her skin, she was as weak and scared as Anya.

She heard the ocean clapping with delight. It's the waves against the rocks, she told herself.

She smelled the sweat of the sea. It's just the salt spray, she told herself.

She fell, clinging to the rope, eyes squeezed shut against the salt water, praying for help.

"Christina," said Michael, laughing. "You look so funny hanging onto the banister like that. You know we're not supposed to run down these stairs. They're too steep." He helped her up. He said, "I've heard dumb rumors about you in seventh grade, Chrissie. You've got to shape up. What's the matter with you? Don't you want to fit in? You're giving island kids a bad name. You of all people!"

Chapter 10

In English class Mrs. Shevvington was doing adjectives. She would call upon a student, give him a noun — like "prairie" or "ocean liner" — and he would have to think up ten adjectives. Mrs. Shevvington had a stopwatch and they went fast, like a spelling bee. It was fun. Christina hoped she got a good word.

"Burning Fog Isle," said Mrs. Shevvington to Christina.

She made a face. That was no challenge. "Rockbound," she began, counting on her fingers, "salty, windy, isolated, pink, lonely, foggy, beloved, famous, and popular."

"Very nice, Christina," said Mrs. Shevvington. "Eleven seconds. Quickest of all so far. No hesitation. But why 'pink'?"

"The granite is pink. The pink flecks are called 'horses.' My grandmother was called a horse in the granite and so am I."

"A horse in the granite," repeated Mrs. Shevvington. "What does that mean?"

"Tough," said Christina. "Impossible to break."

She met Mrs. Shevvington's eyes, but there was nothing to meet. The woman was simply an English teacher working on adjectives. Today when I am strong enough to meet the enemy, thought Christina, there is not one.

"Do you have electricity out there on that island of yours?" said Gretch scornfully.

"Oh, we have all the amenities," Christina told her. "Hot water, telephone, television, microwave oven, the works." She ached for friendship. Who wanted telephones when you couldn't talk to your mother? What good were hot showers or the evening news when you needed love?

Mrs. Shevvington said that Burning Fog Isle had quite an interesting history. The class looked as if they found that hard to believe. "History," said Gretch, "is never interesting."

Mrs. Shevvington smiled. "Burning Fog has always been crime ridden."

The class laughed. Christina was enraged. How dare anybody say bad things about her island? "We are not crime ridden," she said furiously. "I don't think there's been so much as a wallet stolen in my whole life."

Mrs. Shevvington beckoned to the class, and everybody leaned forward, following the call of that powerful finger. "Before the Revolutionary War, the people on the island were simple fishermen or farmers," said Mrs. Shevvington with contempt. "Mostly they raised sheep," she added, as if sheep were invented to be laughed at.

The mainland kids giggled. They looked at Christina with pity.

"Before the Revolution, the islanders were very religious, very stern. After the Revolution, the only religion on the island was rum. Islanders were drunk all the time." Gretch and Vicki snickered. Mrs. Shevvington not only allowed this, but joined in. Mockingly, folding her arms across her chest, she faced Christina. "Burning Fog boys ceased to be sea captains," she went on, "and became pirates." The class laughed out loud. "This may sound quaint — an attractive little myth — but bad people populated Burning Fog. Vicious, amoral people. In fact . . . *murderers.*" Mrs. Shevvington savored the word. The children mirrored her, whispering the word to each other, letting it murmur like a distant motor. "Generation after generation the people of Burning Fog salvaged from ships they wrecked themselves."

"We did not!" cried Christina. "You're making that up."

Mrs. Shevvington raised her eyebrows. "No, Christina, I read it just last night in a book about the shoreline." She lifted the local Historical Society's privately printed book and proceeded to read aloud. The names of the supposed shipwreckers were Romney and Rothrock — her family and Anya's. "You, Christina," said Mrs. Shevvington, "come from a long line of murderers."

The fingers of the sea pressed into the small of Christina's back.

She remembered Anya stepping out the window toward Burning Fog.

She thought of Mr. Shevvington implying that she, Christina Romney, had been trying to push Anya out.

They are going to murder Anya, thought Christina. They are going to blame it on me. They are going to say that I come from a long line of murderers. That my great grandparents thought nothing of enticing ships onto shoals.

"Christina the Criminal," said Gretch, giggling. "I like that."

"Christina the Pirate's Daughter," suggested Vicki.

"No, that's too romantic," said Gretch.

The class laughed.

She went through the cafeteria line. She filled her tray. She passed in her blue ticket. She could feel them all watching her. She could feel them all waiting, getting ready to mock or laugh or sneer.

I will not break down, she thought.

She walked alone, threading through the filled tables. She did not attempt to say hello and she did not look to see if anybody would let her in. She knew that Gretch and Vicki controlled popularity and they had decided she could not have it after all. Christina walked steadily to one of the empty tables and pulled out a chair. It scraped a little on the floor, the sound her soul would have made if it could have cried out. The seventh grade smirked and turned its back.

It seemed that all the girls came in pairs and trios and quartets, and giggled together, shared candy bars, alternated arithmetic problems on homework. She wanted to sob, or throw herself at their feet, begging to be allowed to giggle with them.

Every time she reminded herself that she was granite, it seemed to be a little less true. They were chipping away at her.

Jonah sat down with her.

She hated him for it. No boy sat with girls. Not in seventh. It was better to be alone than have a boy take pity on her.

"I'm not here because of Mr. Shevvington's orders," said Jonah. "I really and truly want to go to the dance with you."

Christina made a foul noise.

Jonah said, "You're beautiful, Christina. You really are."

"Get lost, Jonah Bergeron."

"My middle name is also a graveyard name," said Jonah. "It's Gideon. Jonah Gideon Bergeron."

"So?"

"So don't you think you could go to a dance with Jonah Gideon?"

"What makes Jonah Gideon an improvement over Jonah?"

"He's more interesting," said Jonah. "More depth."

Christina snorted. Her mind was occupied with

other things. She wanted the flashlight. Her allowance was like nothing. One snack, one ticket, a single item at the pharmacy, and it was gone. If she needed a piece of posterboard for a school project, or Magic Markers, or more gym socks — there it went. "Jonah, would you loan me some money?"

"How much?"

"I don't know. I need a flashlight and batteries."

"What for?" said Jonah.

Christina studied him.

She saw nothing new. Jonah was incomprehensible. Why would he keep asking her to that dance when she was so mean to him? Was he a pipeline to Mr. Shevvington? If she said things to Jonah, would the Shevvingtons be told, line by line, betrayal by betrayal?

Jonah Gideon Bergeron, of graveyard names. Was that what it meant to be friends with Christina Romney? Graveyards?

Christina took a risk. "The Shevvingtons are trying to hurt Anya and me. I need a flashlight because we're isolated up there on the third floor in the dark and we're not safe." She stared at him, her eyes hot. Her own mother and father had not believed her. Her own mother and father had listened to half an argument and cut her off. Why would Jonah believe?

"I believe it," said Jonah slowly.

Christina's hair prickled, silver and gold.

Jonah wet his lips. He leaned toward her, his eyes darting like minnows in shallow water. "The Shevvingtons — there's something about them,

Christina. Nobody knows what it is. The parents think they're perfect, but — well, like, there was Robbie's older sister. And everyone thinks that Anya is next."

Christina felt herself grow lighter, as if she might float on fear. "Next what?" she breathed. "What is the end of it? Where are the Shevvingtons taking us?"

Jonah shook his head. "I don't know. Nobody knows. Robbie's sister just disappeared."

"You mean, like *murdered*?"

"No, no, she's there. Her body is there. She's just not — nobody knows, Christina. She doesn't have a personality anymore. It's like the Shevvingtons took it away, and now his sister is nothing. Vacant. Only the bones, but no soul."

Christina thought, What is a flashlight compared to the power of the Shevvingtons?

"Listen, Christina, tell somebody. You have to have help."

"Like who?" Christina was perilously close to crying, right here in the school cafeteria, with Gretch and Vicki watching. How they would love to tell Mrs. Shevvington that they had made her cry. "Did anybody help Robbie's sister? Has anybody offered to help Anya?"

"They don't see," said Jonah. "Only the kids see, and they don't do anything. They watch, though. They're like jungle animals. They watch the predator take the weak."

Christina felt Gretch and Vicki watching.

"But maybe a teacher . . ." Jonah's voice petered

out. He knew no teacher would take a side against the principal. They'd never believe anything awful about Mr. Shevvington. All grown-ups thought he was so wonderful, so kind — caring — careful — and that disgusting phrase all grown-ups adored, *such a good role model.*

"Miss Schuyler? In math? She's not too bad," said Jonah.

If my own parents don't believe me, thought Christina, if Michael and Benj don't believe me, why would Miss Schuyler?

And yet, and yet . . . only Miss Schuyler had ever asked if Christina was all right.

Jonah said, "I'll get you the flashlight." They were not Jonah's eyes looking out of his face anymore, but the eyes of somebody older and tireder. Had he aged, thinking about her danger?

After school she met Blake and Anya. She was their chaperone now, their stage manager.

Anya began whistling, face puckered up as if her lips were stuck in a Coke bottle. She whistled no melody, but a steady note, like the wind playing cello through the ropes of a high-masted ship.

"Stop it," said Christina.

Islanders never whistled. Whistling called up a wind. But you don't want a wind, it's Weather; nobody wants Weather.

"We're going for a walk," said Blake firmly.

That's what it is to be almost eighteen, thought Christina, full of awe. I can *say* I'm granite, but a person like Blake really *is* granite.

Blake took Anya's arm in his right arm, and Christina's in his left.

"Talk," said Blake. "I want to know. I know you're not crazy. Tell me what's wrong."

"I quit high school today," said Anya. "I'll show you where I'm working. You can visit me there if you like."

"Quit high school?" echoed Blake. "Mr. Shevvington let you? But Anya, you're first in the class! You're going on to medical school someday, remember? Remember your dreams?"

But Anya's dreams were no longer of school. Christina knew her dreams; dreams of the bottom of the sea. What kind of job? she thought. It will kill Anya's parents if she's really quit! She is the light of their lives.

And her own parents. What would they say? Would they blame Christina? And Michael and Benj, whom she hardly knew, and they were only three weeks into school — it was still September — still autumn. The longest month, she thought, in the history of the world.

Down Breakneck Hill they went together, feet sideways to keep from falling. By the bottom, gravity was making them run. Blake held the girls' arms to keep them with him.

Christina fell in love with Blake.

It happened in an instant, and she was no longer their escort, their advisor, their little sister. She loved him.

Oh, no, no, a thousand times no! thought Christina. He's Anya's! Anya loves him, he loves Anya and he's old, old, old. I'm only thirteen, and Blake is eighteen, it's impossible.

His arm linked in hers was heaven.

His scent was of men and wool jackets.

His shoulders were higher than hers. Wind blew Christina's tri-colored hair over his jacket. Ribbons of silver and gold danced over his shoulder and then blew gently onto his face. Blake smiled down at her. A ribbon of her own hair made a mustache over his lip.

Kiss me! thought Christina.

She tried to kill the prayer — for it was Anya he should kiss. Anya with whom he must have his romance.

But she looked at his lips anyway and dreamed.

She could have walked forever, hanging onto his arm, dreaming of him, pretending Anya was not on the other side.

"Here," said Anya happily. Her voice was warm and cuddly.

Blake let go of Christina's arm. "Anya, this is a laundromat."

Anya's bright smile was like gauze over her face, a bandage over her craziness. "See how safe the water is!" she told him. "It's trapped behind little glass doors. All the waves in here are under control." She spread her arms to embrace the laundromat.

Dreary people sat mindlessly staring at the clothing through the little glass doors of the washers and dryers. Lint lay on the floor and a few abandoned socks were pushed in a corner. A tired woman with seven baskets of laundry was struggling to fold sheets by herself.

Blake controlled himself. "Anya, you're an honor student. Like me. You're going to college. Like me. You're going to be a doctor."

"Folding," Anya nodded, hearing nothing he said. "It's clean and neat. You can keep track of things here."

Blake dragged them out of the laundromat. The humid, linty air stayed inside the building, along with the dirty linoleum and the broken change machine. It seemed to Christina he was crying, but that was impossible. People like Blake — men like Blake — did not cry in laundromats.

He's crying for Anya, she thought. He knows she's gone. She's already in the washing machines. The Shevvingtons, or the poster of the sea took her. Anya knew all summer they were coming for her. It was just a matter of time.

Christina did not know where they were going. Blake no longer held onto her; he needed both his arms for Anya. "Talk, Christina," he ordered her. "Anya can't."

Christina nodded. She flicked the switch on her cassette recorder. Benj had bought her blank tapes; it was time to use them. She would record it for Dolly at the same time. Then there would be two who knew. She began with the strange glassy weather the day they were given the poster of the sea. Anya said nothing, but nodded and nodded, as repetitively and as meaninglessly as the waves of the ocean. Christina finished with Michael catching her on the stairs.

Blake said, "The poster is just a poster. Maybe there is more than one. Maybe Michael or Benj thinks it's funny to put up new ones, or substitute different ones."

Christina knew they had not. Their lives were not interlocked with hers and Anya's; you could not tell that Michael and Benj occupied the same house. In some strange way, the Shevvingtons had housed them on the same floor, fed them at the same table, and yet they were not together.

"And the tide is just the tide," Blake said. "All this puffing of candles is famous. People visit this town just to hear that. That's why Schooner Inne will probably succeed — people who want to wake up in the middle of the night to the sound of Candle Cove. The house has the same foundation as the cove — the same rocks, Chrissie. You live in that building and you feel the same slap of the wave, the same cannon of sound. There's a pattern, but I can't see it. I'm going to, though, Christina."

A pattern, she thought. Like my mother's quilt: flying geese or feathered star pattern. This is an evil pattern. Not cloth, but paper and sound. But who? Only people make patterns? But who cuts this one, and why?

Anya said, "I feel the tide coming. I know because my fingers are on fire." She held out her hands. Long, slim, white fingers without polish, without rings. Christina took one of Anya's hands and rubbed it. "There," she said. "Does that put the fire out?"

Christina heard the hum of cars on the Singing Bridge. The more we talked of the sea, she thought, the closer we had to get to it.

Standing on the dock that summer people used for their yachts and power boats and cabin cruisers was the brown wet suit.

Beckoning.

"Blake," Christina breathed, tugging at his arm and pointing. "There it is. The brown wet suit."

Blake saw. He let go of Anya and began running. "I'll get him!" he screamed back at the girls. "Then we'll have answers!"

A storm had come up. It had not yet burst, but the air was full of electricity and salt wind. Black clouds against a pink-and-gold sunset swept in from the sea, fighting to see who got rain, who got thunder, who lightning.

The wet suit left the narrow gray painted dock. It ran lightly up and over the cliff opposite the Cove from Schooner Inne. It ran to one of the rickety ladders that led to the mud flats below. It began the descent into the cove.

Blake ran after it.

The wind came up, stronger than before, and the black clouds closed in. Christina shouted after Blake, but he didn't hear her.

"I could watch the waves forever," said Anya dreamily. "What I do is pick out one and follow it all the way in. Look, look!" she cried. "Look at the one I picked out. It's running away, breaking against the rocks, trying to get to safety."

Christina gasped.

The tide was coming in. The wet suit was going right into it. Blake was following right after him.

"Blake!" she screamed. "Blake!" She turned to Anya, pushing her onto a tourist bench flanked by yellow chrysanthemums. "Stay here, Anya."

"No," said Anya sadly, "the wave didn't make it. When my time comes to run, I will break against the stones, too."

"Anya!" screamed Christina. "Shut up. Be sensible. Just sit here!" She turned and ran after Blake, screaming his name, screaming for other people to help. But there were no other people. How could a town whose livelihood came from the sea, from these wharfs, from the tourists who usually sat there painting and photographing and absorbing local color — how could it be empty?

The storm gathered above Christina, so low in the sky she felt she could throw a basketball into it and break the clouds. It prickled with electricity. She could feel the lightning coming. "Blake! The tide is coming in! Don't go down the ladder!"

Christina did not know how she could have run so fast, over the outcroppings, over the crevices and cracks, to reach the top of the ladder.

But she was not fast enough.

Blake was halfway down. He turned to see, not Christina, but the water: a tidal wave, larger even than normal because of the storm. A great green blanket, eager to smother him, and carry him to the mattress below where he would sleep forever.

He seemed frozen on the ladder.

Instead of racing up to Christina and safety, he clung to the wood and stared at his death.

The tide slammed into Candle Cove like cannons going to war. It attacked the rocks and crashed against the crags. Its whitecaps reached like fingers to take Blake.

"Blake, Blake, Blake!" screamed Christina, reaching down. The water was so high it drenched her.

Blake looked up at her. The last thing she saw of Blake was his fear: the terrible knowledge of his fate written on his face as clear as print.

Chapter 11

"The poster," said Christina for the third time, "was torn into pieces. Blake ripped it off the wall. Now it's together again. That's why Anya dropped out of high school. That's why she's working in the laundromat."

Christina's father jammed his hands into his jeans pockets and stared out the window. Christina's mother began crying quietly.

Mr. Shevvington said, "Thirteen is a vulnerable age. There is often borderline behavior. I think we can be grateful that your daughter is not into drugs or alcohol. I think her personality can be saved." He paused. "I'm trying to think of a way to phrase this gently. But there is no gentle way. Island life is very isolating. Ingrown. Naive and unsophisticated. When a young emotional girl, full of hormones, full of dreams, finds herself facing reality for the first time, with classmates who are better prepared, more in touch with the times, better dressed, and so forth, it isn't surprising that there's a collapse."

Christina's mother had buried her face in the crook of her elbow. Christina's father had now turned his back completely. Mrs. Shevvington was smiling. Neither of the Romneys saw it. Mr. Shevvington's soothing, serene voice droned on and on. How much he was able to bring into it! Drugs, violence, "the times in which we live," "teenagers today," even the entire twentieth century.

Christina interrupted him, for which her parents scolded her. She said, "I have thought about it and thought about it. The only people who could have put up a new poster are the Shevvingtons. And they could have put a bit of seaweed on the inside of the window, and they could have told Anya story after story about the sea captain's wife stepping through the cupola and they could have — "

She stopped. She was frozen like a Stone Tag statute by the look on her parents' faces. "Do you seriously believe," said her father, through gritted teeth, "that a high school principal is going to do silly, childish things like switch posters in the middle of the night in order to frighten a vulnerable seventeen-year-old girl?"

Christina stared at him. That was exactly what she believed. She had said it over and over now. Why weren't they listening to her? She could make the facts no clearer.

"I feel so guilty!" Christina's mother burst out. "I thought we were doing so well by our daughter!"

"And you tried," said Mr. Shevvington sympathetically. "I believe that all parents do the best they can. Unfortunately, as in situations like this, the best is sometimes not enough."

Mrs. Shevvington had set the table in the Oriental dining room, amid the golden peacocks and the black gardens. She served a wonderful meal. She had a standing rib roast, with a delicious, smooth, dark brown gravy, and oven-gold potatoes. She had yellow squash, green beans, and brown bread and, even if you didn't like vegetables, the table was colorful and smelled delicious and looked thankful, like November, like harvest, like love.

The room gave off an aura of love, the way only a feast and a family can do, and only Christina knew it was false. Her parents thought it was kind and thoughful, full of effort and preparation.

"Mr. Romney," said the Shevvingtons gently. "Mrs. Romney." They sounded as if they were addressing an election crowd. "Although we do not wish to jump to conclusions, it looks as if Christina has always been very jealous of Anya. They were unable to share a room and had to be separated. Soon after that Christina even felt she had to take away Anya's boyfriend. Now it would be nice to think that Christina just flirted, but evidence is that Christina tempted Blake to show off. To save a life, supposedly. Some man in a wet suit that nobody else saw."

"Blake saw him," said Christina. She felt like a piece of wood. They could have nailed her to the front of a sailing vessel now and used her for a figurehead, and she would last through any weather. She felt varnished and she thought, That souvenir woman with the leathery skin. Anya said if she touched her she would turn to leather. I've turned.

"Blake," Mrs. Shevvington reminded them all, "was whisked away to boarding school the moment he could be taken out of the hospital. According to Blake's poor parents, the boy hardly knew what he was talking about."

"He knew," said Christina. She could not bear thinking of Blake and yet she could think of little else. He seemed to be beside her, talking to her, touching her. The Shevvingtons were right about one thing — she had had a crush on Blake. A crush that began as they ran down Breakneck Hill and lasted only that short, terrifying afternoon. Blake had been badly bruised, his shoulder dislocated when the summer person — some birder with binoculars — had jerked him to safety. Christina had not been allowed to see him. Anya had not been allowed to see him. When they telephoned the Lathems, Blake's parents hung up on them. "Don't harrass us," they said. They told the Shevvingtons (or at least the Shevvingtons said so) that those two island girls were such a terrible influence and so dangerous that they had to move their son immediately. And they did.

Move him where? Christina thought constantly. Where is he living? What school is he going to? Does he think about us? Is he worried about Anya? Does he remember he was chasing the brown wet suit?

Or does he truly, actually, think that I talked him into a suicidal run down the cove ladder?

Oh, how she yearned to see him! She thought of him so often and yet sometimes she could not quite remember his features; the more she thought of him the more his face eluded her.

Blake's scrape with death had been too much for Anya. The fingers of the sea had truly grabbed him. Christina was unable to convince Anya that the fingers of a real person — a birder walking by — had rescued him. That real people won! And so could Anya, if she got tough with her fears.

There was no toughness in her.

She had quit high school. She was working at the laundromat. Her parents had come to talk to the Shevvingtons. The Shevvingtons had very graciously agreed to keep Anya with them even though she was no longer going to public school and not rightly an island boarder. Perhaps she needs a year off, said the Shevvingtons sympathetically to Anya's horrified, heartsick parents. Every morning now when she left for the laundromat, in her ill-fitting jeans and unmatched blouse and sagging sweater they said to her, "This is good for you, this is right for you."

And Anya believed them.

Christina, remembering what Robbie had said, looked very hard into Anya's soul. She was not sure there was one left. Anya was empty, like an old Coke bottle in the recycling pile. The Shevvingtons were recycling her, all right. But into what?

Christina had made Robbie come to the laundromat to look at Anya. "Yes," Robbie had said, "that's just like my sister. Nothing left."

"Do your parents blame the Shevvingtons?" asked Christina.

"Of course not," Robbie had said bitterly. "They think the Shevvingtons are the ones who helped her last as long as she did. They think the Shevvingtons are kind and understanding."

All parents are alike then, thought Christina, looking at hers. They are actually grateful to the Shevvingtons! My own mother and father are probably going to end this dinner by thanking them!

Mr. Shevvington continued. "Christina knew better than anybody when the tide would come in; Christina is obsessed by that tide and by Candle Cove. She even pretends there is a tide right in her bedroom," said Mr. Shevvington sadly. "Brought us a piece of seaweed she claimed landed on that window sixty feet above the highwater mark." Mr. Shevvington paused. He had a wonderful sense of timing, Christina would grant him that. He said to her parents, "Christina knew Blake would reach that ladder just as the tide thundered in."

Nobody talked about that terrible sentence. It just lay there, implying terrible things.

Christina said to her parents, "*Listen* to me! Listen to *me!*"

But it never occurred to Christina's parents that the Shevvingtons might lie. The Shevvingtons were Authority, they were The Principal, and The Teacher, and The Innkeeper. They told The Truth.

They Knew Things, they had Experience, they were Understanding and Caring.

Her mother, weeping, said, "We have spent thirteen years listening to you, Christina. I guess we made a lot of poor choices. Now it's time to listen to the people in charge of you."

Her parents went back to the island. Without her. They cried, and they hugged her, and they promised to write and send her presents and they begged her to "shape up" and they said they loved her . . . but they left.

Christina thought, some people on islands *are* naive and innocent. Not me — but my own parents. There is evil in this house, and they didn't feel it. It took Anya, as it took Val, and now they're going to try to take me. Well, they won't. I am granite.

In English Mrs. Shevvington discussed a poem by Carl Sandburg. It was very short.

Christina did not consider it a poem. It was called "The Fog." She made a face at it.

"Christina?" said Mrs. Shevvington. "You have a thought to contribute?"

They waged war unceasingly now. The class knew it was war, and had divided into teams. Gretch and Vicki of course joined Mrs. Shevvington, bringing along with them every other girl in the class. The boys just loved a fight, any fight, and goaded Christina continually.

Christina thought she might not actually be the loneliest person on earth, but it certainly felt like it. She had had Dolly for a best friend all her life.

To have nobody, nobody at all — and yet rows of girls sitting inches away from her! — it was the worst thing on earth.

"Fog comes like wall to wall carpet, suffocating the view," said Christina, who had known more fog, more intimately, than any of them. She remembered vividly the day when she was five, out with her parents, suddenly caught at sea in a fog so thick they couldn't see each other, let alone navigate. Her parents began story-telling to keep their little girl calm; that was the day she learned about their courtship, how they saved money to buy their first couch, how her grandmother had given them the family's only wonderful antique, the Janetta clock.

But she said none of this. Anything she said would be used as a weapon against her.

"Time for our weekly extemporaneous essay, class. Put all books beneath the desks or on the floor. Take a fresh sheet of paper and a pencil." The class obeyed with the speed that always followed Mrs. Shevvington's requests, as if they were infantrymen saluting. Mrs. Shevvington got out her stopwatch. "Ready?" she said.

"Ready," they chorused, although none of them were. They hated spontaneous writing. Mrs. Shevvington had scheduled it every Friday until kids starting getting sick on Fridays just to miss it. Now she would spring the essay any time.

The topics were chosen to upset Christina; she could tell by the smirk on Mrs. Shevvington's face.

The fourth week in September — the morning after Blake — Mrs. Shevvington had said, smiling at Christina, "Two page essay. *How Will It Feel to Die?*"

The whole class looked at Christina — had not Mrs. Shevvington foretold what would happen? Had not their respected teacher told them how Christina was descended from murderers?

The following week, which was the first week in October — "One page essay. *Noises in the Night.*"

Now it was the second week in October. The children shivered, knowing the topic would be scary. Sometimes Christina thought they liked it — it was kind of like participating in a horror movie.

"What if," said Mrs. Shevvington, pausing suspensefully, "what if your parents . . . . decided . . . to abandon you?"

The class shuddered in delicious fear.

But what was Christina to write? Because her parents *had* abandoned her!

One parent of one child — only one — had come in to argue about the choice of writing topics. The parent left convinced that Mrs. Shevvington was a very *creative* teacher, with *meaningful* topics that made children *think* and *produce*. Now the parent went around town telling people what a *splendid* teacher Mrs. Shevvington was.

Sick, thought Christina. The Shevvingtons are sick. She looked at the blank piece of paper in front of her. What to write about? She had to pass in a paper or her failure to cooperate would be one more thing to tell her parents. She ignored Mrs. Shevvington's topic and titled her essay, "What is it like to live on an island?" It was important to write something that could be shared with the class, because Mrs. Shevvington always picked Christina's paper to read aloud.

She wrote, "Anything that happens on an island is important. A broken plank on the town dock, a large mail delivery to the Swansons, a litter of kittens at the Rothrocks, a new rope on the tire swing at the school. Everybody knows, and everybody cares."

The timer went off. Mrs. Shevvington picked up the papers with her sick, gloating smirk. Then she did an unusual thing: she read and corrected each paper on the spot. "Why, Brandi," she said, "I like this sentence. 'If my parents deserted me, I would collapse.' Now I want you to add two more sentences of description to that. How would you collapse? Describe your body and your mind in a state of collapse." She handed the paper back to Brandi. Her eyes were bright, hoping, perhaps that Brandi would collapse right then and there.

Brandi, however, had broken the point on her pencil and could think of nothing to add and the mood was not conveyed to her.

"Why, Christina," said Mrs. Shevvington, frowning over what Christina had written. "Having trouble?"

"Why, no," said Christina. "Whatever made you think that, Mrs. Shevvington?"

The rest of the class sat up in anticipation.

Not one child had ever told their parents about this war. Not one ever would. It was just something that happened in seventh grade — one person got picked on, and at least Christina could give back as much as she got. Besides, she was different anyway; she was from the island and probably expected to be picked on.

"A great big reader like you, Christina, ought to enjoy writing as well," said the teacher.

Christina thought this was ridiculous. Why should somebody who liked reading books also like writing papers? That was like saying somebody who liked watching basketball should also like playing it. What if you were three feet tall and crippled? Which was how Christina felt when she had to write something down.

The door to the classroom opened.

The class turned as one to look.

It was the eyes you saw first: eyes like drowned Peg's — blue husky dog eyes. Eyes like a doll's, rotating mindlessly in the sockets. It was the clothing you saw second — leathery, heavy stuff, like armor. And third — third — you saw the hands. Hands that were twin to Mrs. Shevvington's. Hands that curled and beckoned like a hawk's talons. Heavy with rings, shining stones that sparkled, the fingers laced across the chest, ten spikes looking for something to stake.

"Ah, yes, Miss Frisch," said Mrs. Shevvington, her s's hissing like snakes or sea water. "Christina? This is your mental health counselor. Misssssss Frisssssch."

They had brought the counselor right into the classroom.

Right in front of Vicki and Gretch and Robbie and Jonah.

"Christina?" said Mrs. Shevvington. Today she was wearing an emerald green suit. The green was a splat in front of the chalkboard. "I am so sorry you will be missing the rest of English class. Vicki will bring you your assignment. Vicki, she will be in the nurse's office."

"Oh, dear," said Vicki. "Are you sick, Christina?"

Christina sat locked to her chair. It was the souvenir creature, or her sister. I can't get up, she thought. I can't go anywhere with that.

The class was staring at her. Their eyes were wide, accusing holes, saying, *Are you sick? Crazy sick, demented sick, deranged sick?*

"Why, Christina," said Mrs. Shevvington. "I seem to recall you saying one day that you were a horse in the granite." She laughed. "Island children have such quaint sayings. Come, Christina. Be a horse in the granite for us."

She managed to slide out from under the desktop and straighten up.

No seventh-graders spoke.

They just watched.

And smiled.

Christina wet her lips. She tried to find her books on the floor beneath her seat, but they seemed too far away to reach. Her hands were too chilled to move and would not close around the edges of the texts.

Robbie got out of his seat to retrieve the books for her. The class giggled and became seventh-graders again, teasing cruelly in loud, high voices. "Robbie likes Christina, Robbie likes Christina, nanny nanny boo boo."

Robbie whispered, "Christina, that's the one they sent my sister to. *Be careful.*"

Chapter 12

Christina walked beside the thing. They moved past the other seventh-grade rooms and into the stairwell. Christina stayed on the landing, holding onto the heavy fire doors.

"Christina?" said Miss Frisch.

"I don't feel like talking," said Christina. She forced herself to look into the blue eyes.

"But we have so much ground to cover," said Miss Frisch. Anya had been right: Those were Peg's eyes. Husky dog eyes.

"Did you have the souvenir shop on Burning Fog?" asked Christina.

The creature's face changed expression. It seemed to be laughing. "Run a souvenir shop?" it repeated, amused. "On an island?"

"Are you the tourist who threw a hot dog to Peg, so Peg would go overboard and drown?" said Christina.

A body pressed up against her from behind. A flat hand in the center of the spine. It pushed lightly. Her heart screamed, her soul turned to ice; it was going to push her into the blue eyes, push her into the dead —

She turned to face it.

She would never let it get her from behind.

It was Mr. Shevvington.

But he did not speak to Christina. He was too busy smiling. "Did you get that taped, Miss Frisch?"

"Yes, of course."

"The parents will be most interested to hear those insane statements," said Mr. Shevvington. "Now Christina, let's all go downstairs together and talk for a while about your problems."

She was only thirteen. She was only five feet two inches tall. She weighed only ninety-four pounds. She was a little girl. Their shoulders were wide, their bodies tall, their strides long.

Mr. Shevvington's hand closed around her left wrist, and Miss Frisch's talons closed around her upper right arm, and they walked her down the stairs like a prisoner or a prize.

Christina thought, Somebody be with me! Please. Somebody. Mother, Daddy, Anya, Jonah, Blake, somebody!

But nobody came.

There was nobody to come.

Nobody believed in her.

Mr. Shevvington said, "You have destroyed your parents' love for you, Christina. Love is a fragile thing. You broke that love."

"They still love me," she said. "I know they do."

"Then why aren't they with you?" said Mr. Shevvington.

"Because you made them go!" she cried.

Mr. Shevvington frowned. "Christina, what parent would abandon a little girl just because somebody says so? Your parents have given you to us. Because you killed their love by being such a bad girl."

Down the stairs they went, through the doors, out into the hall near the cafeteria. The cafeteria was empty, chairs stacked on tables for the janitors to mop. The school was silent, as if every class had been dismissed or were taking final exams behind closed doors.

Mr. Shevvington was happy. Miss Frisch was smiling.

This is how they talked to Val. To Anya. And Val and Anya believed. Well, I don't believe. I will never believe. And I won't go into the nurse's office either, thought Christina. She said loudly. "What are you doing to try to get Anya back in school, Mr. Shevvington?"

"Unfortunately getting back into school is not easy," said Mr. Shevvington. "A girl nearly eighteen who leaves of her own free will. . . . We can't just re-enroll her."

"If Anya had the flu, she'd be out for a week and you'd let her back. If I can get her to — "

"You," said Mr. Shevvington, "are going nowhere near Anya. I've seen what happens when you and Anya are together, with your jealousy and your violence."

She lost control. "I am not violent!" shrieked Christina, hitting him with her book bag.

Miss Frisch dictated into her cassette, "The patient punctuated her statement that she is not violent by hitting the principal with all her strength."

Christina began laughing hysterically. Hysteria had never happened to her before, nor had she ever witnessed it. The laughs that bubbled out of her were creepy and frightening. She wanted to stop herself, to cut the laugh away, like the crusts off bread, but the laughter continued. Miss Frisch held her cassette right up to Christina's face, like an oxygen mask, and dictated over the sound of the crazy laughter. "The patient laughed at Anya's predicament."

Past the art room.

Past ninth-grade history.

Past the foreign language labs.

That must be where the fear forms are, thought Christina. In the nurse's office. They'll make me fill out one of those forms and then they'll know what I'm afraid of, and they'll attack, just the way they did with Val and with Anya.

I must not go into the nurse's office!

They passed the first set of auditorium doors and the row of pay phones in the lobby.

They passed Miss Schuyler's room. Christina's math teacher sat alone, correcting papers. She waved at Christina.

Mr. Shevvington coughed, politely putting a hand up to cover his mouth. The hand that had gripped Christina's arm. She was half free. She considered biting Miss Frisch to make her let go the other arm, but the thought of that creature's leathery skin against her tongue, inside the privacy of her mouth, was too terrible. She stomped on Miss Frisch's foot instead.

Miss Frisch cried out, wincing — and let go.

Christina ran into Miss Schuyler's room.

"Why, Christina," said Miss Schuyler. "You're here early. But never mind. I have it all ready. Good morning, Mr. Shevvington. Good morning, Miss Frisch. How nice of you to bring Christina for her tutoring." She smiled at them sweetly. "You need not stay. Christina and I will be fine."

Fine? Christina ached from fear. Her knees hurt, and her spine seemed fractured. It was hard to stand, impossible to walk. Miss Schuyler kicked a chair beneath her and she collapsed on it.

"Decimals," she said. "Quite simple, really, Christina. Begin on page forty-four of this workbook."

Miss Frisch said, "Christina is scheduled to have mental health counseling this period, Miss Schuyler."

Miss Schuyler laughed incredulously. "I could believe Christina would teach a class in mental health, but she certainly requires no personal assistance, Miss Frisch."

Christina held onto the workbook. Was there more than one war going on in this school? Was Miss Schuyler at war with Miss Frisch?

"Christina has been having a difficult time lately," said Mr. Shevvington, turning his serene, convincing gaze upon Miss Schuyler.

But nothing happened. Miss Schuyler was not convinced. She merely raised her eyebrows and touched her old-fashioned, honey-colored braids. Christina wondered how long the braids were. So thick that Miss Schuyler could be Rapunzel, and let them dangle out of a tower window. Miss Schuyler said, "Really, Arnold. I hope you have not been listening to rumor. That is the mark of a poor administrator." She turned away from him and said, "Christina, dear, page forty-four, please."

Christina could not even read the page numbers she was so nervous, but she flipped some pages and took the pencil Miss Schuyler handed her.

Mr. Shevvington and Miss Frisch left the room.

Christina said, "How did you know? Why did you save me?" Tears lay inside her eyes, and her chin and her knees were shivering, like separate leaves on a tree.

Miss Schuyler said, "You looked desperate, my dear. I thought I would give you a few moments to compose yourself. Now tell me what upset you, Christina."

Christina told everything. Not because she was sure of Miss Schuyler, but because it was time to tell. Time to let go and bring in an ally.

Time to surrender? thought Christina, half aware that Miss Schuyler could be another one. One of THEM. Am I falling into their hands? she thought. Is it a trick, like multiple posters?

But it was too late. She had told all.

There was not much time. Another math class would soon fill the room. No doubt Mr. Shevvington or Miss Frisch would be there waiting in the hall to catch her.

Miss Schuyler frowned. "Christina, that is quite a tale."

Christina felt herself turning to nothing, following in Val's and Anya's footsteps. It was a pitiful feeling. Not like a balloon being popped — sharply, with a pin, but oozing, air seeping out invisible leaks until there was nothing left of the balloon but an empty piece of color on the ground.

There would soon be nothing left of Anya. Anya would not even have color. She dressed in nothing but black and white now. Like a photograph of herself.

Miss Schuyler said, "I think I will get in touch with Blake first. A nice young boy. He's at Dexter Academy, as I recall. Now do not be afraid of the principal or that counselor. They have no supernatural powers, Christina. Nobody does. They have managed to upset you so much that you are imagining things. The wet suit is simply some out-of-season kook in a wet suit and the poster is merely a poster." Miss Schuyler frowned slightly, tapping her pretty cheek with her pencil. Christina had not previously thought Miss Schuyler a pretty woman. Perhaps the person who rescued you was always beautiful.

"However it is quite clear to a newcomer in the school, such as myself," said Miss Schuyler, "that there is some association between the Shevvingtons and Miss Frisch." Miss Schuyler pushed the pencil into the honey braids and left it there, like a miniature six-sided yellow sword. "Something unhealthy," said Miss Schuyler. Her pretty frown grew heavier, until it took over her entire face, aging her first one decade, and then another. "Possibly even, something cruel. But why?" She took Christina's face between her two hands, and held, it, as if Christina had more to tell.

"Val and Anya," said Christina, " were sweet and innocent. And — and they're doing one each year. Maybe they did girls in other towns. Maybe — Miss Schuyler, where did they come from, the Shevvingtons? What have they left behind? Are they teachers because — " Christina could hardly say it, because Miss Schuyler was a teacher, a wonderful teacher. "Are they teachers because every year there are new ones? New innocent girls they can rob of their souls?"

Because what fun would it be to destroy somebody nasty and mean? Christina thought. You would not enjoy destroying Gretch or Vicki. You would have the most fun ruining the nicest people.

Miss Schuyler took the workbook out of Christina's hands. Christina had not written a single number down, or even a single decimal.

"Christina," said the teacher dryly, "I am convinced that our principal is not a nice man. But I find it hard to believe he has an actual program he executes in town after town, destroying the souls of innocent victims."

I lost her, thought Christina. Grown-ups can only tolerate half the truth. I went too far, telling her all. Next time I tell anything, I must tell only little easy pieces of it. But then who will bother to help me?

Christina tried to stay granite. She tried to find the bright side. I have half an ally, she told herself. She half believes me.

Miss Schuyler seemed to look so far away she might have had a view all the way to Burning Fog Isle.

Christina thought, But Anya's parents and mine are quite literally at sea. How safe, how delightful for the Shevvingtons! They will take each of us from Burning Fog. They will take away our souls. "What can you do, Miss Schuyler?" said Christina, her hands knotted like the nets of lobster traps.

"I can do nothing. They have convinced the entire school system of their kindness, their understanding, their perfection. But I will watch them, Christina, and I will be your protector. So do not worry." Her eighth-grade class began coming in. Very gently Miss Schuyler added, "And don't magnify it either, Christina. It's not so dreadful as you're making it out to be. It's not nice. But it isn't deathly, either." She drew the pencil out of her hair, like a conductor closing off the chorus, and turned to her class.

Christina left numbly.

Out in the hall hundreds of teenagers knew exactly where they were going, and whether they had their homework done, and which book to carry. Christina knew nothing. Her head swirled. Her brain must look like her mother's marble cake — chocolate and white spiraled together as the wooden spoon drew through the batter. She felt loose and unconnected.

Out of the chaos emerged Mr. Shevvington. He connected to her wrist again. Firmly. "Come into my office."

"I don't feel well," she said. "I need to lie down." Miss Schuyler is wrong, she thought. It goes way beyond what she saw. *The Shevvingtons are evil.* And nobody knows but me.

Mr. Shevvington smiled. "That's fine," he said. "The nurse's office is just where we want to be."

Vicki and Gretch, arm in arm, stopped in the hall to watch them. "Why, Mr. Shevvington," they said, "is she still sick? Poor, poor Christina."

Mr. Shevvington said, "I think perhaps you girls have been hard on little Christina." He made her sound like a pitiful, stupid thing that people tried not to sit next to because of the smell. "Christina needs help, you know, and popular, pretty girls like you, Vicki, and you, Gretchen, could help her."

Vicki and Gretch tossed their hair like synchronized swimmers and preened in the hallway.

Remarkable, thought Christina. He can sound like Mr. Understanding, Mr. Deep-concern-for-troubled-girls, and yet he's made it infinitely worse. On purpose.

"A little bit of attention from girls who know how to behave properly," Mr. Shevvington continued, "would be the making of Christina."

Christina's loose, cake-batter brain became a loose, cake-batter stomach. It roiled and turned inside her like Candle Cove with the coming tide.

169

"We're pretty busy," said Vicki.

Gretch nodded.

Mr. Shevvington was very sympathetic. "Of course you are," he said. "You're the kind of girls who will be class leaders and team captains. I'm not suggesting that you adopt her as a cause and give up homework for her!" He laughed warmly. "Just a few minutes here and there."

Like taking a dog for a walk, thought Christina.

Vicki said, "Well, I suppose after school, maybe we — um — " Vicki tried to think of something she could fit Christina into.

Christina threw up.

It was wonderful. Disgusting, hot slime came up out of her stomach, burning her throat and mouth, and hurling itself on Gretch's designer jeans and Vicki's beautiful university logo sweatshirt. It dripped crudely down their chests and onto their pretty shoes.

Gretch screamed. Vicki clawed at herself. Christina said, "I need help. Please? Since you're so popular?"

Mr. Shevvington wrote out late passes for Vicki and Gretch. They went sobbing to the bathroom. Christina he hauled down to the nurse's office. What a weapon, thought Christina. She said to him, "I feel very unsettled. I may throw up again."

Miss Frisch was apparently not free this period. Mr. Shevvington told her to clean herself up and lie on the white cot in the corner behind the screen, and he would be back shortly. Christina drank from the water fountain until the horrible taste was out of her mouth, but she didn't have to clean her own clothing up; she had missed herself.

It's all in the timing, she thought, proud of herself.

And then she thought, *I'm in the nurse's office.* I am sure the fear files are here.

She looked around the room. White walls with posters on dental hygiene and sexually transmitted diseases. A large sink with jars of cotton wads, Q-tips, and tongue depressors. An arsenal of aspirin and some witch hazel.

Christina began flinging open doors. Behind the counter doors were rolls of paper towels, bandages, Kleenex. In the wall cabinets lay every size of Band-Aid known to man.

She whirled to go through the desks. Only one drawer was deep enough for file folders. It did not open immediately. Christina played with the pencil drawer until whatever catch attached to the file drawer loosened up, and she could ease it open.

She flipped through the tabs of the file folders. Statistics. Racial characteristics of the school system. Measles and inoculation data. No good.

She shut that drawer and went to the other desk. Reports on diseases, conditions, symptoms, and cures. Come on, come on, Christina thought, where are your student-by-student files?

She scanned the room.

There was a computer screen on the counter in the corner.

She turned it on, pawed through the little plastic

box of diskettes, and read the labels. They were individual files, all right, but the master disk was not among them. Christina turned to the nearest desk and began rifling through the shallower drawers.

There was a sharp explosive flash behind her. Miss Frisch had photographed Christina going through the desk drawers.

Chapter 13

All it takes is one rainstorm, thought Christina Romney. The lovely scarlet-and-gold autumn leaves are torn from the trees and the foliage season is gone: Bare branches and a dark horizon are all that's left.

She kicked her way through a pile of leaves, turning her socks gray with leaf dust, even though the leaves were gold. There was a chill in the air distinct from previous nights. It was winter-cold, not autumn-cold.

"Supposed to be a hurricane coming," said Michael joyfully. Michael loved fierce weather. Benj told him not to talk about it, not even to think about it.

Benj thinks the weather can hear us talk, thought Christina.

It was island thinking. Island superstition. A year ago Anya had thought no differently; now she had moved beyond superstition; she thought the house and the sea could hear her, too.

"Hurricane's down by Maryland and Delaware

now," said Michael, "but it might swing north."

"No," said Benj. "It's going inland. Stop your noise, Michael."

If I were home on the island, my mother would go on a winter hunt, thought Christina.

A winter hunt turns up matches for mittens, boots that fit, and the grocery bag that the long winter underwear was put in the year before.

Christina ached for her mother. She yearned for her father. But when they had come in on their own boat for an emergency meeting with the Shevvingtons — and with Miss Frisch — about Christina's thievery, when they had seen the Polaroid shot of Christina with her hand literally in the drawer where the petty cash was kept . . . they collapsed weeping. This time Mr. Shevvington did not have to recommend anything at all; they begged him. They said, "Please control her for us, please teach her better than we were able to, please take her!"

Christina marveled that it was so easy for the Shevvingtons.

Michael and Benj were going back to the island for the weekend, and they were going to try to talk Anya into accompanying them. They walked toward the laundromat.

"Bet we'll be stranded," said Michael hopefully. "High winds, gale force, can't come back to school for weeks."

Benj laughed. "Bad weather is always over by Monday morning, Michael. Don't worry, you won't even miss first period."

Michael was saddened. He said, "But maybe the

Shevvingtons' house will come down in the hurricane. I don't know how it's lasted so long on that cliff anyway. It's in a very vulnerable position."

"Don't say that," ordered Benj. "Christina has to stay there during the storm." Benj made a face. "Not that there will be a storm," he corrected himself.

She thought about Burning Fog Isle. She had experienced many severe storms, but none with a wind so strong that houses were thrown about like too small lobsters tossed overboard. Would her mother and father be all right?

She was finding it difficult to remember her parents' faces, or Dolly's laugh. She had made the mistake of saying that at breakfast and of course Mr. Shevvington heard and said, "Christina, this is serious personality disintegration. You have not cooperated with me on seeing a mental health counselor."

Michael and Benj went on eating cornflakes.

Mr. Shevvington put an arm around Christina as if they liked each other.

But he does like me, thought Christina suddenly. He likes what he can do to me.

They were at very close range. She could see now that he wore contact lenses. He *could* change the color of his eyes! So that was how his eyes darkened and grew bluer. How could she have been afraid of his eyes? They weren't even real.

"Boys," said Mr. Shevvington, "take this letter to Anya's poor parents. It isn't much in the way of comfort but at least they'll know we did our best by their poor daughter. We always thought she would become a wharf rat and now she has."

"You did not think that!" cried Christina. "You thought she would have an honor roll year, and be the star of the senior class, and — "

"Christina," said Mr. Shevvington, "stop yarning. Michael, Benj, have a good visit on the island. Say hello to your parents for us."

Miss Schuyler is on my side, Christina consoled herself. You can do anything if you have somebody on your side. She looked at her tormentors, who were both smiling, unpunctured by Christina's or Miss Schuyler's scorn.

Mrs. Shevvington's yellow teeth lay in her mouth like seeds waiting for winter birds to eat them. The teeth smiled, as if they too were thinking of eating.

Christina shuddered.

She stuck to the boys. The boys thought nothing of it.

The laundromat was stupifyingly hot and humid.

It was another whole world in there: linty and gasping and wet. Anya was even thinner, which hardly seemed possible, and even more beautiful, which was surely not possible.

She was wearing, because of the heat, a thin white cotton gauze dress with white lace around the throat. She had caught her black hair in a thin white ribbon and the bow lay against her cheek like a white rose. Her hair in the humidity of the laundromat had puffed like cumulus clouds.

176

"Jeepers, Anya," said Michael, "you look like a bride."

"I am," said Anya.

The boys stared at her.

At least this time they noticed something wrong, thought Christina grimly.

"Whose bride?" said Benj warily. "Blake's not around any more, they got rid of him."

"The sea," said Anya. "Nuns marry God. I will wed the sea." She folded a hot pink T-shirt, neatly turning the short sleeves in to the center and tucking the bottom up. She turned the shirt over, admired the flawless folding, and added it to a pile of somebody else's clean clothes.

Anya, who had been first in her class, future doctor, Blake's girl.

"Listen, Anya," said Benj, "come home for the weekend with us. It'll do you good to see your mom and dad. Frankie's boat leaves in half an hour. Everybody on the island is worried, Anya. Come on. Please?"

Anya shook her head. "I have work to do." She brought out a pen-and-ink drawing she was working on. At first it looked like waves from Japan or China, arching sea foam with hooks. But when you looked closely it was a hundred hands, a thousand fingers, all reaching for the same thing: Anya.

"I'll do the laundry for you," Christina offered. "I can't go home. My parents don't want me."

"They would if you'd behave," Benj told her. "Michael and I have about had it, Christina. I suppose you didn't really do anything wrong, but it looks wrong, and it makes the island look wrong, and it's time you stop and think before you do stupid, dumb things that hurt everybody else."

"What kind of friends are you?" she cried, stomping her foot. The sound was oddly drowned in the sogginess of the room. Anya added several more fingers to her curling waves. "Why don't you believe me? Why would you believe the Shevvingtons?"

"Mr. Shevvington is the principal," protested Benj. "He's not going to lie. Anyway, they caught you. They have the photograph."

"I wasn't taking money. I was looking for the files with those papers we had to fill out."

Benj shrugged.

Anya whistled mindlessly. Two notes, back and forth, back and forth. "Don't," said Benj. "You're whistling up a wind, and a wind right now means weather and we don't want weather. Hear?"

Anya gave no sign of hearing anything. She held up her own hands and studied them like a manicurist. "I can't figure out whose hands they are," she said.

Is there another town full of vacant, stunned girls, whose souls were sucked away? thought Christina. A town the Shevvingtons finished with and got tired of?

"Come with us, Anya. Okay?" Benj and Michael Jaye were uncomfortable. They didn't want to be in this ugly, damp place, with its mildewed walls and the madness that wafted off Anya like a breeze.

Christina wondered if the Shevvingtons were tired of Anya. If they had finished with her yet. If they don't have Anya to toy with, she thought, they'll need another girl. And the only one around . . . is me.

"We had boiled dinner last night," Anya said. She frowned. "Corned beef, cabbage, potatoes, and turnips. I hate boiled dinner. It makes me feel old and crippled and penniless."

The alternative to getting old is dying young, thought Christina. What have the Shevvingtons been saying to her?

"Mom's having a fish fry," said Michael. "We haven't had decent fish since we left the island. Come on, Anya. Chrissie'll fold your shirts."

But Anya just kept folding, smiling at the T-shirts as if she were tucking tissues in her trousseau.

Christina, Michael, and Benj sat on the dock, feet dangling toward the water. A stiff, biting wind blew in from the Atlantic but in the sun the boards were warmish. They felt splintery and familiar. Bird-lovers who visited Burning Fog Isle every autumn to witness migrations, binoculars and cameras hanging around their necks, waited with the children for Frankie's boat. Out on the rocks, seals sunned themselves and cormorants spread their wings to dry. They looked like dirty shirts hanging on the clothesline.

Christina thought of the island as heaven, a place of autumn colors and Thanksgiving coming. But she

179

was not there, and she could not go there, and sometimes she wondered if it even existed.

Autumn was Christina's favorite season. She loved fall: the carving of pumpkins, the early dark of afternoons, the cutting out of construction paper turkeys for Thanksgiving.

All these seemed a distant memory, something that grandmothers told their grandchildren about and nobody quite believed.

She made herself think of the letter Frankie would bring from her parents. The tape from Dolly.

If she knew Dolly, it would be a good tape, full of gossip and laughs.

"I just like to sit around aggravatin' people," Dolly liked to say. (That was what her grandmother liked to say, actually, and Dolly had just copied. But she was right. The trait had skipped a generation. They were both excellent at "aggravatin' " people.)

Dolly, as far as Christina knew, was ignorant of what had happened at Schooner Inne and school. Mr. and Mrs. Romney were silenced by shame and Michael and Benj by confused loyalties. As for the tape she had recorded when she was talking to Blake, it had vanished. Anya had been holding it, but by the time the ambulance came and Blake was taken away and the police had questioned Christina about the wet suit, Anya no longer had the cassette recorder in her hands and could not remember ever having it.

Frankie's boat nosed into the harbor. Rindge barked a greeting. Frankie tossed Christina a line, which she whipped around the cleat on the dock. Frankie unloaded the boat, saying good-bye to passengers who thought he was an exotic, exciting sea captain, posing for tourist photographs and helping nervous day trippers who were afraid they would fall between the boat and the dock.

Then he handed her something better than a letter: her mother's own baked beans.

Christina's mother put sliced onions, salt pork, brown sugar, and molasses into the beans, adding a little salt and dry mustard and a pinch of ginger. Her beans were wonderfully moist. Even people who didn't like beans loved Christina's mother's beans. Baked bean suppers had raised money for repairing the island fire engine and adding to the tiny school playground. Christina had loved that, but Anya used to yearn for a city, where they would raise money with art auctions and opening-night theater tickets.

And now Anya just wanted to fold other people's shirts.

Christina held the casserole in her two hands and warmed herself on her mother's love. She's not so mad at me after all, thought Christina. She baked me a dinner.

Benj was roughhousing with Rindge. Frankie was saying to a birder, "Course, it's exactly a century now since the last big one. So you can kinda feel it coming."

"Feel what coming?" said Christina.

Frankie shook his head. "Ocean gets tired of lying there, I reckon. Every fifty, every hundred years, she's got to kick up. Been fifty years since the hurricane that ripped down half the North Woods, tore the summer people's houses off the island. Figure we're due."

Christina shivered.

"Yep," said Frankie, looking out to sea at perfectly ordinary waves, "I think I see a swell. Beginnings of our own hurricane." Frankie sounded happy about this, as if, like Michael, he had been yearning for his very own hurricane. "Got to get back to the island and batten down," he said. "Got to close up shutters, tie down everything that moves, lay in a supply of bottled water and canned hash."

"That sounds like fun," said Michael. "Bottled water and canned hash. Gosh, Frankie, can I come live with you during the hurricane?"

"Yeah," said Benj, "at least lay in a supply of chocolate chip cookies, Frankie."

Frankie kicked the boys on board. He chewed on his pipe stem, looking Christina over from top to bottom. He knows, thought Christina, hot with shame. They know on the island; somebody talked; somebody said that Anya went crazy and Christina turned to crime. Do they all believe it? Do they all think I'm bad?

"You want to come, honey?" said Frankie. His eyes were full of affection. She wanted to kiss his weathered face a hundred times; somebody out there still loved her.

More than anything on earth she wanted to come with him. But she was not wanted. She shook her head, the barest movement, trying not to cry. "Say hi to my parents," she whispered.

Frankie grinned at her. "You're a tough kid, Chrissie. Now you lissena me. Don't let them get you down. I went to school on the mainland once, too. Hurricanes are easier." He rumpled her hair.

He was right; hurricanes had to be easier. But it was not school she was fighting. Why were all grown-ups so sure that if she only "adjusted to school," everything would be perfect? She could adjust for a hundred years and the Shevvingtons would still be evil. "I don't know if I'm that tough," said Christina.

He chewed on his pipe. "What you need is sumpin' to hang onto when the wind is bad. Take my baseball cap." He put his old red-and-white cap on her head with the bill backwards and yanked it down over her eyes. "Bye, kid."

She watched Frankie's boat until there was nothing left to watch, only a silver gleam on a satin sea.

The sea whispered to her, soft as a caress, lapping her ankles like a kitten. *I am your friend. Come to me. You'll be safe with me.*

"Never!" cried Christina Romney, straight into the wind. "And you can't make me, either! I am a horse in the granite! I am of the island and you will never win!"

The wind argued, flinging her words back into her mouth again. It tugged at Frankie's baseball cap until she had to hold it on with one hand. She pressed the baked bean casserole into her ribs and toted it on her hip.

The wind attacked.

Flags stood straight out, painted against the cruel sky, and people on sidewalks tilted their bodies to fight the force of the wind. Children laughed. Dead leaves went berserk.

Christina staggered up Breakneck Hill. The wind pulled her back down. Out at sea she could see the boats scudding at great speeds. Speeds that would be fun if you were Michael and not so much fun if you had a long way to go before you found a safe harbor.

Christina had no safe harbor.

The only place she could go was the Schooner Inne.

Mr. Shevvington closed the huge green front doors behind her. It took all his weight to push them shut against the wind. The wind screamed in anger, trying every crack in the house, finding some. The house whistled and shrieked like a demented orchestra. Candle Cove lashed its waves into the cliffs, which threw them back in a chorus of crashes.

She was locked in the sea captain's mansion, alone with crazy Anya, the Shevvingtons, and the poster of the sea.

Chapter 14

The house was completely silent.

Christina looked into Michael and Benj's room before she entered her own. How terrifying empty beds were. The neatness of the sheets and blankets was like the neatness of a mowed and trimmed graveyard.

Anya lay alone in her room, staring at the poster of the sea. The poster shimmered in the dusty dark of early evening, neon tremors of life struggling to be free. "Anya, at least turn on the lights," said Christina.

"You can't see the poster smile except in the dark," explained Anya.

Christina's hair lifted on her head. She could actually feel the colors of her own hair: brown, silver, and gold, trembling for Anya.

"I can't leave the room, either. The poster will come back off the wall again. I'll drown in a paper sea."

Christina backed into the hall, hands feeling the walls, stretching for the banisters of the balcony.

She's already drowned. She drowned inside her mind.

Behind her the house lay quiet, dark, and expectant.

Christina turned to face the house, and the house seemed to whirl behind her, laughing. She turned again, and again, spinning dizzily at the top of the stairs, trying to keep safe, as though something might attack her from behind.

She ran into her room, the house closing at her ankles, catching at her hair, and she dived, fully clothed, into her bed.

Under the covers, under her mother's quilt, she wept till she could weep no more, for Anya and for herself — unloved and alone. Out in Candle Cove the tide began to hum. *Fffffffff.*

The wind rose and cried out, and the house seemed to talk back, so they were screaming at each other, as if the house and the sea had different plans for the dark of night. *Tonight, Christina, tonight!* they both said.

There were nights when the dark seemed to be her friend, keeping her company through the night — Christina and The Dark — but now the dark was her enemy, keeping her prisoner.

She could feel the evil in the house gathering its forces. Alone she was weaker. She had been separated from her allies, from Michael and Benj and Jonah and Blake — like a gazelle cut from the herd by the lions who would destroy it.

She could not get warm. The bed was piled with

blankets and still the cold got under the covers with her and entered her bones.

Chrissie! Chrissie!

It was the tide calling.

It was the poster of the sea beckoning to her.

Christina whimpered under the covers. Then she remembered that she was granite, not a tern. That Mr. Shevvington did not have the eyes of a mad dog, but of a man who wore contact lenses.

Christina slid out of bed. She wrapped her mother's quilt around herself like a huge calico cape. Within the hood of the quilt she felt protected by her mother's love.

Christina stepped into the hall.

Christina's head and ears filled and pulsed with the huffing. It whirled around her like fans in summer. Humming like bees. *Chrissie, said the house, Chrissie, Chrissie.*

Her eyes and spine burned with fear. Anya was right. The house truly spoke. The sea kept count. It was demanding Christina herself.

A weapon, thought Christina. I need something to hit it with.

She would smother it in the quilt.

Christina walked forward, holding her quilt out like butterfly wings to wrap it in.

She walked into Anya's room. It was wet in there.

The sea is already in here! thought Christina, fear closing over her eyes like lashes. She heard the sea speak her name.

"Chrissie," moaned Anya, "Chrissie, something is wrong. Chrissie, I'm afraid of the poster."

The window was open. Anya was dampened by the rain coming in like cotton waiting to be ironed. The sea said nothing but its usual crash of wave and rock. It was Anya speaking her name.

Christina yanked the sash down, holding the quilt in her teeth so it would not slip off her shoulders.

Then she faced the poster of the sea. Its terrible fingers, its dim, drowning figures, stared back at her.

"I'm in charge here," she said to it. She kept her eyes fastened on the poster. She felt around in Anya's desk and came up with a handful of tacks. She swung the quilt off her shoulders and held it up as if to a charging bull. She rushed the poster.

Outside the wind screamed and the tide rose and Candle Cove fought a war with the rocks and the waves.

Christina covered the poster with the quilt. She tacked the quilt firmly right into the wall. The poster was gone. Calico squares and triangles and tiny firm stitches covered it.

"So there," said Christina.

Anya looked stunned.

"Come on, Anya, let's go downstairs. It isn't healthy up here." Christina dragged Anya out of the bedroom. They marched down to the kitchen, where Christina had her book bag. Anya sat in front of a TV she did not remember to turn on.

Christina tried to read.

From the school library Christina had checked

out a murder mystery Vicki and Gretch had been talking about. At the time she had thought she could read her way into the friendship. It seemed unlikely now. She held the book with her left hand and set the table with her right. Almost before there was a murder, she had figured out who the murderer was. How annoying to be able to add up the clues as easily as third-grade arithmetic.

Mrs. Shevvington had made eggplant lasagne.

"But — but my mother sent baked beans," Christina said.

"You should have refrigerated it," Mrs. Shevvington said. "I had to throw it out. It was no good."

All that love stirred into the molasses, to stick to her ribs like a hug on the island.

Thrown into the trash.

Christina began to cry.

"Everything you do is wrong," said Mrs. Shevvington. She put her hands on her hips, and her weight seemed to double. She rocked back and forth as if planning to topple onto Christina and crush her. "Take that silly baseball cap off."

I need padding, thought Christina. I should wear a soccer goalie's outfit around the house. She found Kleenex and blew her nose and mopped her eyes. Mrs. Shevvington caught the bill of the cap but Christina was ready for her. She whisked the cap behind her back, clutching it with white-knuckled fingers. It may be an anchor, Frankie, Christina thought, but what good is an anchor without a safe harbor?

There is nobody, she thought. I am a ship at sea

without a crew, without a harbor. Nobody loves me. Not Anya, who is hardly even in the room because she hardly even exists. Not Michael or Benj — they never paid enough attention to see anything. Jonah and Blake aren't here. My parents. . . Oh! my parents!

She knew she could never eat the eggplant. She wondered now if she could ever eat again. She felt cleaned out, like a scoured pot. There isn't much left of me right now either, thought Christina.

"Christina, honey," said Mr. Shevvington. He drew her close. He cared. His touch was loving, his embrace warm. Christina leaned on him, absorbing his kindness like a drug. Nothing else could evaporate loneliness. The texture of his jacket made her think of Blake and true love.

"Poor Chrissie," he murmured. "It's been a hard autumn, hasn't it? A girl has daydreams about junior high, and none of them come true, and it's hard to keep going, isn't it?"

Christina nodded, sniffling. The silky tie touched her cheek like a cool finger soothing a fever.

"Tell me all about it," said Mr. Shevvington. His hand closed over hers, warm and comforting.

How she wanted to blame her fears and failures on Mrs. Shevvington, or the seventh grade, or even Anya.

"What are you afraid of, Christina?" he said. "I'm here to help. I know you feel I've been against you, but it's not true, Chrissie. You have me on your team, honey."

His eyes welcomed her home, saying *you'll be safe now. Come to me.*

Very softly, he whispered, "Tell me your fears."

She had so many. They multiplied every day.

Being alone.

Having no friends.

The tide and the wet suit and the glass in the cupola.

The sea captain's bride and the honeymooners and the boy on the bike.

Anya going crazy, Blake gone forever.

How safe were his fatherly arms. His blue eyes were like robins' eggs in a nest, cozy in the tree.

"Tell me about Miss Schuyler," whispered Mr. Shevvington. He patted her hair, dividing the strands into their three colors, and braiding them as her father used to do. "Is Miss Schuyler really tutoring you in arithmetic?" His fingers folded around the baseball cap. His eyes were as soft as a baby blanket.

Perhaps he had looked into Anya's eyes like that, and Val's.

"I have this terrible fear of fractions," Christina told him. She put the baseball cap safely behind her back. "Miss Schuyler thinks she can conquer it. Also a fear of running out of popcorn. Nothing could be worse than going to a movie and they don't have any popcorn, you know?"

"This is not a joke, Christina," said Mr. Shevvington. His grip tightened. His fingers were half white, half tan. "I am trying to be kind, but I expect cooperation from you."

Christina said, "I know about the girls before Val."

The room turned utterly silent.

Mrs. Shevvington stood motionless at the stove. Mr. Shevvington's eyes lay like stones in his head. Beneath the veneer of his blue contact lenses she could see his real eyes. They were not blue. They were ice in winter, gray and cruel.

The Shevvingtons pivoted. Slowly. They faced her. Their eyes drilled into her skull.

"All about them," lied Christina. "All the ones before Val."

She thought of her ancestors who had drowned at sea, and she knew now how they felt: how they saw the power of the wave and the density of the water and knew that their end had come; that their ships were only pitiful bits of kindling in a great and powerful sea.

She had made a mistake. She had gone to sea in a storm. The Shevvingtons would destroy her now as easily as the Atlantic destroyed a sandcastle.

But they did not move toward her. They did not squash her between them. They did not discuss the girls before Val. Instead their horrible eyes met above her head, and their little mouths smiled secretly, and she knew that they had plans she knew nothing of.

Outside, the storm quickened and raged.

All Maine went behind doors and shutters, hunkering down; there was nobody to hear a scream for help, nobody who would be looking out any windows.

They sat down to eggplant. Her mother's casserole dish was on the sink. Scoured clean. Anya ate nothing. Christina ate only a roll. Nobody talked. A meal without conversation is an efficient thing. It was over in moments.

After supper Christina watched television. There was nothing on. This seemed unfair. On the island they hardly got TV at all, mostly watching rented movies on the VCR, and now when she needed electronic company and canned laughter, there was nothing on.

Anya drifted upstairs alone.

She'll be safe, thought Christina. I've locked the window and covered the poster. Sleep is what she needs anyhow.

She wrapped herself in an afghan. The Shevvingtons' eyes followed her every move.

She read her mystery, bored because she already knew the ending, and afraid because the pages were littered with bodies in car trunks, bodies in alleys. With every page turn, the Shevvingtons' eyes grew colder and the afghan protected her less.

But eventually they had to move. Mrs. Shevvington went to her room, Mr. Shevvington to the library.

She was momentarily alone. The rooms of black and gold creaked. Outside the wind lifted even more. She could hear metallic crashes as somebody's garbage can was tossed down Breakneck Hill.

Christina tiptoed from the TV room and into the hall, where she picked up the telephone. She dialed information and then she dialed the number they gave her. Less than one minute and Dexter Academy had connected her to Blake's room. "Blake?" she whispered.

"Hello?" said Blake.

Christina burst into tears.

"Anya?" said Blake. "Is that you?"

Christina shook her head.

"I love you," said Blake. "It'll be all right. I'll think of something. I haven't yet, but I will."

I love you.

"It's me. Christina. Blake, I'm alone with them."

"Chrissie, don't cry." His voice was rich with concern. "Tell me what's happening. How is Anya?"

"Leaning on the washers and dryers soaking up the lint."

"I don't understand why she gave up," said Blake. "Why didn't she keep fighting?"

"She thinks the enemy is her, not them." Christina could not bear to talk about Anya. She had to know whether Blake blamed her the way his parents did. "You don't think I tempted you to die, do you?" *You love me too, don't you, Blake?*

"Of course I don't. I was trying to see who was in the wet suit. I've lived here for years, I know better than to go down a ladder into Candle Cove, I was just being stupid. My parents refuse to believe they raised a stupid son so they're blaming it on you. Chrissie, I've thought and thought about it, and I think the man in the wet suit has a place to go. Under the cliff. Maybe even under Schooner Inne! Maybe that's why the sea talks so loud inside the house. Maybe there's actually a sea passage into the cellar!"

Christina found that almost more horrifying than Anya's belief that the wet suit *was* the sea. But I've never been in the cellar, she thought. I've never even thought about the cellar.

Was the cellar full of water now — full of storm and tide, crawling up the walls of Schooner Inne to drown her in bed?

Christina tried not to cry. She wanted more than anything just to keep listening to Blake's voice. His wonderful, rich, boy's voice. She told Blake about trying to find the fear files and getting caught like a cheap thief. "You don't think I'd steal money, do you?" she said anxiously.

"No, but you might do something else equally dumb. Leave it, Christina, just leave it. They're bigger than you are. More powerful. The Shevvingtons had one talk with my parents — *one!* — and wham! I'm two hundred miles west. I try to tell them it was important to go down the cliff after that man in the wet suit and they tell me not to make things up and how much I'll like boarding school."

She could see him, all lean and handsome and windblown. I love you, she thought. It's wrong and I'm going to stop tomorrow. She said, "We might get a hurricane."

Even as she spoke she heard something come off the house — a shutter or a storm door perhaps —

and rip agonizingly, and crash around in the alley.

"Take care of yourself, Chrissie," he said. There was a catch in his voice. She treasured it. "Listen," she began.

A thick, gnarled finger with chipped layers of red polish disconnected the phone.

"Christina," said Mrs. Shevvington softly, "I have told you not to use the telephone without permission. Who were you calling? We will find out when the bill comes, of course, so do not fib."

Christina did not fib. She did not speak at all.

"Bedtime," said Mrs. Shevvington.

Christina walked up alone, into the waiting dark.

The Shevvingtons stood below on their balcony, their arms folded like chains, and smiled at each other.

She would never sleep. The winds outside were trying to throw the house into Candle Cove. Perhaps the passage in the cellar was undermining the house so it would cave in from the bottom as well.

Every hundred years, thought Christina, turning Frankie's remarks over in her mind. I could read old newspapers, couldn't I? And find out about the boy on the bike and the honeymooners and the sea captain, and even the weather and the tides.

She tugged her hair into a ponytail and stuffed it up under the baseball cap. She had a lot of hair. It made a puffy pillow on top of her head.

On the very last page of the mystery book she found out who the murderer was. She had misunderstood every hint. She had never realized at all who the bad guy was. Christina had been completely tricked.

Had she misunderstood every clue in Schooner Inne as well?

She got out of bed and padded silently into Anya's room, making no noise to disturb her. Standing in the dormer, Christina looked out at Candle Cove. The waves did not curl in pretty frothy fingers. Tons of black and green water sloshed to the cliff tops and fell back. Wind cut canyons through the water. Even as she watched, a dinghy and a small motorboat filled with water and sank. A larger boat tore loose from its mooring and was dashed against its neighbor, hitting it like a sledge, until they both splintered.

The tall utility poles along the parking lot above the wharf threw a thick, mustard-yellow light over the chaos.

There was only one human being visible. Not a fisherman struggling to save his boat nor a house owner trying to fasten a shutter.

Anya.

White as a bride, clinging to the Singing Bridge.

So many clues! thought Christina. I missed every one. *Anya* was cut away from the safety of the rest of us — not me. *Anya* is the endangered species — not me!

Robbie had said that whenever somebody drowned, the bridge sang. Over the fierceness of the storm Christina could not tell if the bridge was singing. She could not call to Anya to stop her.

Tonight, the tide had whispered.

But it had been Anya whispering.

Anya announcing her plans.

Christina ran down the stairs. She had to get to Anya. Fast.

The front door, of course, was locked.

Christina clung to the big brass handle, unable to think at all. How had Anya gotten out? How was Christina to get out?

She raced back up the stairs and pounded on the Shevvingtons' bedroom door. (Did people like that sleep? Or just lie awake, gloating and planning?) "Open up!" she screamed. "We have to go save Anya. Unlock the front door. Get ropes. Call the fire department!"

The Shevvingtons did not open the door.

She shook it hard and kicked it. "I need you!" she screamed. "Help me get Anya."

"Christina, Anya is sound asleep. Go back to bed. This house has withstood a century and a half of storms, and it won't give way to this one."

Christina beat on the door with her fists. "Anya is on the Singing Bridge. She's going to step off into the Cove."

Mr. Shevvington ripped the bedroom door open. He wore a long, dark maroon robe, like Christmas kings. "Stop this!" he roared, louder even than the sea. "Go to bed."

"Look out the window!" cried Christina. She was sobbing now and it was hard to get a deep breath. What if Anya had already gone to the sea?

"We have had enough of your nonsense," said Mr. Shevvington.

She stared at him. "But Anya — "

"Is fine."

"Is going to drown!" she screamed, as if volume could convince, screaming so loudly she was raw in her throat just from those four words.

Mr. Shevvington folded his arms. He stood in the bedroom door staring down at Christina. It seemed to her that the corners of his mouth wanted to smile. Mrs. Shevvington, sitting up in the bed, did smile. Then she pushed the remote control button for her television.

Christina whirled and ran down the stairs to the kitchen. From her book bag she ripped her house key and flew back through the black-and-gold halls to the front door. She jabbed her key in the lock.

It did not fit.

"Your key fits only from the outside, Christina." How mocking was Mrs. Shevvington's voice. How sure of victory!

But victory would be Anya's plunge into Candle Cove. Anya, who thought the sea was keeping count . . . when all along it was the Shevvingtons.

Christina ran to the windows in the living room. Shuttered on the outside against the storm. She ran into the dining room. Shuttered and barred. The kitchen door was locked; the side door locked.

"Stop this!" she screamed. "Let me out! If you won't save Anya, let me!"

Behind their door, the Shevvingtons laughed.

She had thought that in the end they would be Good. That when push came to shove, they were grown-ups; they might be mean, but they would not stand by and let Anya walk off the cliff.

She had been wrong.

She did not live with people who knew the meaning of Good.

Trembling on the stairs, Christina tried to think. She cast her eyes up for some other kind of help. The glass in the cupola winked.

I can get out the top, thought Christina; they haven't closed the bottle entirely.

How long the ladder was. How many rungs there were. As if she were passing into another world, another time.

Christina pushed open the window through which Anya had talked to the sea. She slid out. There on the top of the house — so high it felt like the top of Maine — she stood, a tiny girl on a tiny ledge above the entire Atlantic Ocean.

The gale had gathered the sea and all its creatures and was hurling it mercilessly against the cliffs, reaching for the house. She stood on the roof like a twig in a blender.

I'm here, she thought, but how do I get down? Anya is still on the Singing Bridge, but she can't hear me over the storm!

"Blake!" whispered Christina. She did not have a real voice anymore. She spoke only with the ghost of her lungs. "Somebody — Mother — Daddy — Miss Schuyler — come get me, please!"

She yanked Frankie's baseball cap down hard on her forehead to keep it from blowing away.

Nobody will come get me, Christina thought.

And if anybody is going to get Anya, it has to be me.

Behind her, the window closed. A tiny sound, audible because it was not part of the storm, told Christina the truth. The Shevvingtons had latched the window.

Christina turned, terrified, and lost her balance, slipping backward toward the sea, her bare feet sliding on the cruel roof.

In the cove the waves clapped.

Chapter 15

There was a blur of stars and rain.

There was time to think of the outrage of it all: that she should tumble to her death like the sea captain's bride when she was the *good* one! The Shevvingtons, who deserved a watery grave, would live on.

There was time to think of the horror of her very own lungs filling with water instead of air. Would it hurt? Or would she merely cease to be?

She slanted between the sea and the sky, pummeled with rain, assaulted with noise. Her toes curled on the shingles, trying to hang on. Below her, the sea screamed and taunted. It tossed feathers of sea foam on her bare legs.

She screamed, throwing her hands out, tilting herself backward, trying to lie down, trying —

But there was nothing there.

Her feet reached into space, gravity yanked her body after them, and her hands held only air.

Christina landed immediately. Even her feet were surprised, and both her ankles turned in, having assumed, in a muscle and bone way, that they would never again hold up her body. She was standing on the sill formed by the odd little dormer of Anya's bedroom.

Her tears of terror blended with the rain, as if she were one with the clouds.

Below her the roof formed a very slanted passage away from the sea cliffs, toward the street. She crawled onto the shingles, trying not to think of the waiting arms of the waves below. The roof sloped more steeply than Breakneck Hill. There had to be a window she could get in. She caught the edge of a shutter and clung to it, trying to get away from the sea. It was the window of the Shevvingtons' bedroom. She could see their shadows.

She thought of the sea captain's bride. Had she tried to catch herself, too? She thought of Anya. Was this Anya's route — or had the Shevvingtons let her out, knowing Anya's state of mind?

Christina crawled forward, slithering closer and closer to the grim edge. The rain caught on the shingles and glittered like diamonds that would never be strung on necklaces. Don't slow down, she told herself. If you stop to think about what you're doing, you'll panic.

Below her was the nearly flat roof of the kitchen stoop. Christina inched down the wet shingles, clung for a moment to the gutters, dangled her feet as far as she could, and let go.

She could not even hear the thud of her own feet landing. The sound of the storm had drowned the sound of her crash.

Anya, wait for me! Christina thought. Her chest hurt from the desperate thudding of her own heart.

One more jump to go. Down into the back alley. But this last jump would be the worst; pavement was hard, unforgiving. The ocean might call, *Float in me*. The earth made no such promises. *Break your bones on me,* said the earth.

She jumped, landing knees first in a puddle full of sodden leaves. Her knees were skinned and bleeding. Her insides felt jarred loose. She stared up at Schooner Inne. She could not believe the height she had come down. She saw the Shevvingtons rushing from window to window, trying to figure out where Christina was now.

"I got down," she whispered. "I'm off the roof, Anya. I'm coming, just wait for me." Her knees buckled and left her in the puddle. She had to crawl. Like a whipped puppy she pulled herself forward, crying uselessly into the wind. "Anya, Anya, don't do anything!"

Every light in Schooner Inne went on.

It's not enough they won't help, Christina thought, they're going to come out and stop me! Oh, I hate them! How I hate them!

Christina hauled herself up, ran out the alley, and down the black steepness of Breakneck Hill.

How fast I'm going! she thought. I've never run so fast in my life.

It was like flying. She did not even seem to be using her feet. She was windblown, like a seabird in the air currents.

This is how the boy on his bike felt, she thought.

It was worth it to him. He was happy when he —

When he broke his neck.

Christina grabbed the fence, tearing her fingers on the thin, harsh metal. She slowed herself with her hands, braking with her palms.

Then she forced herself to walk. She counted her steps, making her feet land hard and flat. One hand was bleeding. She wrapped it in —

Oh, no, thought Christina. I'm wearing my nightshirt.

It was an XXXL barn-red T-shirt on which her mother had embroidered Christina's name in silver thread.

I look like a Christmas card. If they see me wearing a T-shirt and absolutely nothing else on a cold Maine October night, they'll lock me up. I'll be Val's roommate.

Singing Bridge was empty, no cars hummed over its metal treads.

She was too late. Anya had gone to the sea.

Sobbing, Christina rushed to the edge of the cliffs.

Candle Cove, too, looked like a Christmas card. Waves curled in shepherd's crooks, layers of white sea foam icing on green cakes. There, climbing down to the ledge where the honeymooners had picnicked, was Anya, clad all in white.

Anya glanced up and waved as sweetly as if they were at a school soccer game, cheering goals. "I heard you call," said Anya, happily, who could not have heard anything above the roar of the elements. "I heard you say to wait for you. I'm so glad we're going together, Christina." Anya's face was invisible, clouded by the black hair that frothed in the wind, glittering with diamonds of night mist.

Christina knelt by the terrible wet cliffs, and the shepherd's crooks of water tried to hook her body and drag her into the final fold. I have already climbed down a house! thought Christina. I can't face these rocks. I can't fight the sea again.

Anya took Christina's hand, light as air, and pulled her down. Over a sea-slippery ledge they went, and down to the next one, the waves crashing over their knees.

"No, Anya," Christina cried. "I figured something out. One evil attracts another. Each terrible thing makes space for another terrible thing. Terrible things and terrible people warm to each other. But we can defeat the Shevvingtons. I know we can, Anya. Stop going toward the sea, Anya."

Anya smiled. "We'll go together, Chrissie. They did that a lot in the olden days, you know."

"Did what?"

"Went back to the sea." Anya turned her face up to the storm.

"We didn't come from the sea," Christina pointed out. "We came from the island."

Anya shook her head. "We're not going that far." She pulled Christina with her.

The wind blew Frankie's cap off Christina's head and tossed it skywards. It spun in circles like a maddened scarlet bird and flew through the sky toward land. Christina screamed, and tried to reach it, but it was no use.

Anya nodded. "There is no magic stronger than the sea," she said to Christina. Anya had far more strength than Christina did. No matter how hard Christina pulled at her to go back up, Anya could pull harder to go down. This seemed odd to Christina, since it was Anya who was the tern.

If I were granite, thought Christina, I would be heavy enough to hold her.

She had nothing: no talisman, no quilt, no cap, no arguments.

And no strength.

She was sapped.

"Blake needs you," Christina told Anya. Even as she spoke, she thought, If only Blake could need *me*! Even as the water covered her thighs and the terrible steps they were taking were hidden beneath the waves, she saw his catalog Maine clothes and his windblown hair, and heard his warm voice, and wished that just once more, she could have his hand over hers. But Blake does need me, she thought. To save Anya.

Sea foam spun over them. Anya caught it in her hands, like lace to be measured for a wedding gown.

"Blake loves you!" Christina cried. "I don't have the quilt and I don't have the cap and I don't have the strength of granite, but I still have love. Come on, Anya, we're leaving the sea behind. It won't take us. Now or ever. It has all the dead it needs." She gripped Anya's hand with both of hers and lunged into the wind.

Anya fought.

The sea curled around Christina's bare feet. The

seaweed clinging to the rocks was brown slick. The barnacles tore her flesh.

"Anya, we have to go back up," shrieked Christina. "We'll die here! We don't want to die, we don't even want to catch cold!"

"Die?" said Anya, surprised.

"What did you think would happen under water?"

"I am of the sea."

"So am I, but mostly I'm of the island. Climb, Anya, climb!"

Christina looked back at Anya to smile at her, give her courage, but she saw only what Blake had seen: a wall of black water coming to get her. The sea was a mathematician. The sea kept count. They were the island princesses, marked out for sacrifice.

"Well, I'm not coming!" Christina Romney screamed. The wave hit her as hard as a boxer, filling her face and mouth with sea water. She spat it out. Gripping Anya, dragging her up, Christina stretched for the torn metal fence. She needed another hand; she could not hold onto Anya, and to the rocks, and to her own life, all at the same time.

The next wave knocked them back, down toward the honeymooner's ledge. Amidst the colors of darkness and storm she seemed to see a glitter of gold and silver, as if the ribbons from Dolly's package still danced on the waves.

My hair. Silver and gold.

Anya was right after all: the sea did follow me. It does want me.

Christina sobbed. Her fingers lost their tenuous

grip. Anya, who had never tried anyway, slid feet-first into the sea.

Christina tried to shout at Anya, but her mouth filled with salt water.

"It's no use," said Anya, saying good-bye to the world.

"It is so!" said Christina. "Now I'm mad. Now I've had enough. Get up, Anya Rothrock! Don't you fade into that water like some dumb honeymooner. Don't you slip down like some stupid kid on a bike. Get up, Anya Rothrock!"

Rage propelled Christina forward, up over the rocks, up over the fence, into the sodden street.

The only place in town that was open all night was the laundromat.

It was warm in there.

In a lifetime of swimming, diving, and boats, Christina had never been so wet. She was wet from her skin to her bone marrow. Her tri-colored hair ran like a river. She shuddered over and over, remembering the roofs and the rocks. Where did I get the strength to do that? she thought.

In the black glass of the laundromat door she saw her reflection: a small child. A seventh-grader. Nobody impressive.

Anya held out her hands to the warmth of the tumbling dryers and whispered, "Did we win, Chrissie? Did we defeat the sea?"

Where evil is, it multiplies, Christina thought. But goodness also multiplies.

"It wasn't the sea that was the enemy," said Christina. "The sea is just there, Anya. It never changes." Christina rummaged among the neat, still toasty-warm stacks of folded clothing Anya had left behind. She pulled on a pair of Anya's jeans, turning up the cuffs several times to shorten them.

The fogged-up door of the laundromat opened.

The Shevvingtons stood there. They were wearing yellow mackinaws. They dripped their own ocean of water onto the floor.

Anya was toweling her hair dry. She looked up vaguely. "Oh, hi there," said Anya, sounding sane, although rather forgetful. "Isn't it awful out?"

The Shevvingtons aren't actually murderers, Christina thought. They spill no blood, stop no hearts. Instead they cut away pride, they cut away purpose. So Val's body, or Anya's body, goes on — while the girl inside flickers and goes out.

Candle Cove.

I thought "candle" referred to the tide and the sea.

Perhaps it means the people who live by the edge: fragile flames struggling not to be blown out.

But I am not fragile. I was not blown out.

I saved Anya. Look at her, worrying about her hair like a normal person.

Christina had a tremendous sense of her power. Like granite she was: stone and rock. Her small body did not seem like something from the seventh grade. More like something cut from the quarries of the islands of Maine.

Christina drew herself up. She flaunted her

power before the Shevvingtons. They seemed to nod, almost to bow, their yellow mackinaws bending in the middle, as if they had become her puppets. Now she, Christina, would pull the strings.

"Is your car here?" said Christina to the Shevvingtons. She was almost laughing. The principal and the teacher were nothing. Tall, yes. In charge, no. "Pull it up in front," ordered Christina. "Take us home. When we get there fix us something hot to eat. Make hot chocolate for Anya."

She was obeyed.

They did not argue with her.

I have won, Christina Romney exulted. She tossed her silver-and-gold hair like banners of triumph, and she swaggered out of the laundromat, leading Anya by the hand.

She was only a seventh-grader. She knew nothing. She did not know that people do not surrender power so easily. She forgot the secret plans she had seen them make over her head during supper.

She did not see how docile Anya was. That toweling her hair dry was the most that Anya could achieve; that Anya took Christina's hand because Anya did not know where to go on her own. That Anya was alive . . . but emptied.

Christina thought she had won.

Chapter 16

It was a wonderful week in school.

There were no appointments with Miss Frisch. There was not a Miss Frisch at all as far as Christina saw.

In English class Mrs. Shevvington did not read Christina's paper out loud to sneer. The Friday essay was ordinary: Hallowe'en costumes they'd worn when they were little.

Vicki and Gretch were still popular and still ignored Christina, but another girl named Jennie, whom Christina had not noticed before, sat with her at lunch. Jennie was loads of fun — perky and silly. Soon they were joined by Kathleen, and then somehow Jonah and Robbie got the courage to sit there, too. They were the first in the seventh grade to have boys and girls at the same table. The rest were envious; even Gretch and Vicki were envious.

Jonah said he'd forgive Christina for refusing to go with him to the Getting To Know You Dance, as long as she promised to come to the Hallowe'en

Party at the Y with him. Christina allowed Jonah to hold her hand for just a moment. Hand-holding looked glorious when seniors did it, but it was pretty icky for seventh-graders.

Kathleen and Jennie giggled, ducking their heads and blushing and making incredibly dumb remarks.

Christina said she would dress up as an island princess for the Hallowe'en Party: what would Jonah be?

Jonah said since Christina thought he had a graveyard name, he was going to be his own tombstone.

Vicki and Gretch said loftily that seventh-graders were too old for that kind of silliness.

Three more kids, who felt being silly was much more fun than hanging around with Vicki and Gretch, moved over to Christina's table. Hers was now the most crowded. People offered her their desserts. They spoke wistfully of her hair, wishing theirs was three-colored, too. They even asked where she got her jeans.

I wouldn't be surprised if I can do anything, Christina thought. I will be able to get Anya back in high school. Blake will telephone me. Next time Michael and Benj go home for the weekend, I'll go, too. Mother and Daddy will love me again. I will get proof for Miss Schuyler and we'll get rid of the Shevvingtons for once and for all.

It was too bad that Miss Schuyler was sick all that glorious week and they had a substitute teacher for arithmetic. Christina wanted to tell Miss Schuyler everything.

Monday I'll tell her, thought Christina. She'll be proud of me.

Christina sauntered home from school.

The sky had cleaned itself up, swept itself clear.

There was something terrible, almost insane, the way there was never any trace of the weather in the sky.

Earth and sea carried debris. Broken tree limbs, downed wires, sunken ships.

But the sky was fresh and new, no ripples, no scars in its deep indigo blue.

The air was a symphony of rustles and shivers: distant wings of migrating flocks, softly slapping waves, the humming of the Singing Bridge.

Even the Shevvingtons realize, thought Christina, gloating, hot with pride, this time they tangled with somebody they cannot frighten. I can walk down roofs during gales. I can save people from drowning. What is a mere school principal to me?

She swaggered a little, although it was difficult on the slant of Breakneck Hill.

Mrs. Shevvington had gotten back to Schooner Inne before Christina.

Mr. Shevvington, strangely enough, was also home early.

Together they opened the great green doors, and, together, smiling, they welcomed Christina home. Because I'm in charge and they know it, thought Christina.

She walked in between them.

Behind her they closed the great green doors and turned the lock.

Christina merely shrugged and carried her book bag up to her room. She had bought her own snack today; it didn't matter whether the Shevvingtons thought there was too much sugar in it or not.

She ran up the stairs, just to show them they couldn't dictate anything to her, including the speed of using the stairs.

In her dark green room, her mother's quilt lay soft on her bed.

Ffffffffffff, said the house.

Christina stood very still in the hall. She turned very slowly. She walked around the balcony. The boys' room was the same as ever, Marilyn Monroe smiling down from the wall. But in Anya's room, the empty second bed was now made. Suitcases sat unopened on the floor by the second bed. Another chest of drawers had been set by the dormer window.

Her mother's quilt had been taken down.

The poster of the sea was exposed.

No, thought Christina.

The room stank of low tide, of clams and mussels and dead things. Christina reached for the wall but it slid away, like a fish under water. *Fffffff* said the walls and the floor and the glass. She tried to stand up, but there was weight on her, as if she were standing under water, with a million tons of green ocean pressing down.

It can't happen again! she thought. The poster

is only a poster. The sea is only water.

She licked her lips and they tasted of salt.

It's Candle Cove, it's the tide, she reminded herself. The house is just a house. I identified the evil, and it's the Shevvingtons.

She grabbed the banister.

She could not remember the way downstairs. She smelled the sweat of the sea. Clinging to the rail, she swam down the stairs.

"Christina," said Mrs. Shevvington. She was laughing. The laugh rattled, like dried peas in a half empty jar.

Christina turned the corner of the stair where the carpet began. She could see the Shevvingtons now. The surf inside her head ceased. Whose suitcases are those? she thought, confused. Not Anya's.

Mrs. Shevvington's little corn teeth matched her laugh. "We have a surprise for you, Christina," she giggled. The giggle was hideous and out of season, like Christmas tree bulbs in July.

Why did the room seem colder? What draft curled around Christina's heart?

Christina reached the hall. Mr. Shevvington stood on her right, Mrs. Shevvington on her left.

"You're lonely," said Mrs. Shevvington. "You need the companionship of another girl. One closer to your age than Anya, Christina."

"Of course, a principal has a certain amount of discretion," said Mr. Shevvington. "Rules of school attendance can be altered for special situations. The rule is, Christina, that a child goes to school on the island until seventh grade. But we petitioned to have that changed, Christina. Your parents are so happy, Christina; they feel you're going to be calmer now that you have a friend."

"I have plenty of friends," Christina said.

There was a patter of feet from the kitchen.

The Shevvingtons turned, laughing, to see who came.

It was Dolly.

Sweet.

Innocent.

Another Val. Another Anya.

How Dolly danced, red curls free from braids. Her body was elementary school size; a fragile collection of bones in bib overalls. "Isn't it wonderful?" she cried to Christina. "Can you believe my luck? I'm off-island, too!" She turned her pixie smile into the towering faces of the Shevvingtons. "I get to attend sixth grade here!" She took the Shevvingtons' hands and swung their heavy arms back and forth like a set from a square dance. "The Shevvingtons have been so wonderful to me, Chrissie," she said. "I'm going to love living here!" She hardly saw Christina. She beamed into their eyes. Mr. Shevvington's eyes were as blue as they had ever been, and, like the sky, they were swept clean of the past.

They were nothing, they were blanks.

On which to compose the storm that would take Dolly Jaye.

Christina's pride dwindled away like a ship vanishing over the horizon. She wet her lips. "I told Miss Schuyler," Christina began.

Mr. Shevvington's smile spread wider and wider, exposing more and more teeth, like a crocodile. "Your little math teacher? I'm afraid she found another job, Christina. Out west somewhere. Such a loss."

Mr. Shevvington put his arm around Christina. It might have been a hug or the beginning of a strangle. "You'll never be able to replace her, Christina. Will you?"

Ffffffff, said the house.

But only Christina seemed to hear.

"Now, Dolly, remember, this is a special privilege," said Mr. Shevvington. How caring he looked. How fatherly and kind. How blue his eyes were. "You must try very hard to prove that I am right to bring you among us a year early, Dolly."

"I won't let you down!" cried Dolly eagerly. "I'll do anything you say."

"I know," said the principal.

Don't miss Losing Christina 2: Snow,
the suspenseful second book in
Caroline B. Cooney's compelling trilogy.

Dolly had the right constitution for reading. She could curl up in the old chair and sit for hours, flicking pages.

Christina sometimes preferred to have movement and space. She wanted to kick and run and swing her arms. Books sometimes slowed her down; she had to be in the mood for a book. Dolly was always in the mood for a book.

Sometimes Dolly thought she was wrong to spend so much time choosing books. Especially after the principal said, "Too much reading, Dolly. I'm suspending your library privileges."

Dolly went to the town library instead.

Mr. Shevvington had her library card taken away.

Dolly had her friends in the sixth grade smuggle her books. But they had no book sense. They checked out junk like *Ronnie and the Little League Mystery*, or *The Story of the Boston Fish Market*.

"I always thought I would make an excellent invalid," said Dolly one night at supper. "I like bed. I like sheets and pillows. I'd lie there and read. All

I need is enough strength to turn pages."

"Perhaps you could have an accident," said the principal softly.

"I would be very brave," Dolly agreed.

The principal smiled.

SNOW

Chapter 1

Christina was alone in the cold mansion. January winds screamed off the Atlantic Ocean and tried to tug Schooner Inne off the cliffs and dash it onto the rocks far below. But Schooner Inne was very old, and the wind always lost the battle. Christina did not know why the Shevvingtons called it an "inne," because although there were eight beautiful guest rooms, there were never any guests. Just the five island children boarding on the mainland for the school year. And the children were stashed up on the cold, dark third floor, not in the sunny guest rooms. Criminals, thought Christina, have better housing than we do.

It was Saturday morning. Mr. and Mrs. Shevvington had taken Dolly shopping. They said Dolly needed new mittens. Christina knew it was true. But she felt so betrayed by Dolly, she wished Dolly's fingertips would freeze off instead. "You may not leave the house," Mrs. Shevvington had said to Christina. "Perhaps losing your weekend will teach you manners. What kind of example are you setting for Dolly? Accept your punishment as a thirteen-year-old should. If you leave the Inne, you will be confined to the house next weekend as well."

If Christina didn't have a Saturday and a Sunday to run and be free, to hold the sky and the wind — then she had nothing.

Dolly, hardly aware of Christina at all, let alone Christina's agony at being shut up in the house, had smiled lovingly at the Shevvingtons. How could Dolly adore them, with their eyes like mad dogs? wondered Christina. They were evil. But Dolly took their hands and skipped between them.

Schooner Inne was the highest building in the little Maine village. Christina could see all the way to Blueberry Hill, where children were sledding and skiing without her. Scarlet, gold, and green ski jackets dotted the snow like splotches of kindergarten paint spilled on white paper.

Anya came in. Christina had forgotten Anya was even alive, let alone at home. "Hi, Anya," said Christina dully. "How are you?"

"It's so cold in here, Chrissie."

Christina got her a sweater. Sometimes Anya even forgot how to dress. Then Christina took Anya into the kitchen, where it was warmer.

"Shall we watch TV?" said Christina hopelessly. Christina hated Saturday TV. "Shall we play a game? We could draw. Do you want me to get out the watercolors?"

Anya did not respond. She just stood there, thin and lost among the kitchen cabinets. All her romantic, fragile beauty was lost, as if she had put her own face somewhere and forgotten it.

After a while, Anya cleared the table of breakfast dishes. This winter Anya had ceased to be a teenager boarding for high school and had become a servant, good for laundry and dishes. She scraped every plate carefully, as if proud of this skill.

Christina could not bear seeing Anya and remembering what she had been. Anya used to love the telephone, giggling continually in her soft, happy chuckle to any of a dozen girlfriends or Blake. Anya used to read aloud from her English books. How well Anya could memorize! One night it would be a speech from *Hamlet*; Anya's slender body would take on a stern masculine pose while she flung her cloud of black hair like a cape. Another night her voice would deepen while in tragic tones she recited some grim poem about death in the trenches of World War I.

Christina stared out the window at the fallen snow. She loved snow. It softened the edges of the world and hid things.

"Do you remember Blake?" Anya said unexpectedly.

Do I remember Blake! Christina thought. I think I remember him better and more often than you. I'm glad you don't know the inside of my mind, where I pretend I'm on the dates you used to have with Blake, where I pretend he comes back to town . . . *and it's me he wants*.

It was wrong, this dream that had her heart. Christina remembered Blake standing on the rocks that bound the coast of Maine, framed against a blue sky and a black sea; that posture in which he looked like the owner, or even the conqueror, of any place he stood; those clothes, so casual, so expensive. "Yes," said Christina. "I remember Blake."

"Is he alive?" asked Anya.

"Yes. He's at boarding school." Where Blake's parents had sent him after the fall from the cliff, which they had blamed on "those island girls," meaning Anya and Christina. The school Mr. and Mrs. Shevvington had suggested.

"Why doesn't he write to me?"

"I guess because you don't write to him. I'll help you write a letter to him," Christina offered. If Anya is thinking about real things again, Christina thought, if she does a school-type thing like writing a letter, maybe part of her will be real again. Maybe she just needs to get cranked up, like an engine in cold weather.

The big house shuddered as the tide hurtled into Candle Cove, slamming against the rocks on which Schooner Inne was built. Living with the tide was like living with a battalion of insane drummers, who every twelve hours beat on the foundations of the sea captain's house.

Christina had come to believe that the sea captain's wife, who threw herself over the cliff a hundred years before, had done it because she couldn't stand the noise anymore.

"What shall I say to Blake?" Anya asked.

" 'Dear Blake,' " dictated Christina, and to her delight Anya laughed.

"I could have thought of that myself," Anya said. *Dear Blake*, Anya wrote, and her handwriting looked like the old Anya, the Anya who should be graduating first in her class, come June. Not the Anya who had dropped out of high school and taken a job folding laundry at the laundromat.

In the cellar, somebody giggled.

Christina raised her head and listened again.

They were alone in the house, she and Anya. Dolly had gone with the Shevvingtons. Dolly's older brothers, Michael and Benjamin, had left hours before: Michael to basketball practice and Benjamin to his job pumping gas.

The giggle came again, low and taunting.

You can't find me, it said.

Christina's eyes frosted, as if it had snowed in her brain. Nobody giggled, she told herself. The sea can make any noise. It can whisper, chuckle, clap hands. This time its noise is a giggle. That's all.

"Chrissie, I'm still cold," said Anya sadly, as if there were no cure for this.

The cellar giggled again. Christina looked at Anya, but Anya had heard nothing. Last fall, when Anya had been so afraid of the sea, the tide, and even the poster on her bedroom wall — when Blake had been pushed off the cliff into the oncoming tide and would have drowned except for the tourist who happened by — last fall Christina had thought the Shevvingtons must have a partner. Somebody who was able to do these terrible things for them. But she had found no evidence, unless you counted the

227

man in the wet suit she kept seeing everywhere, but who vanished whenever Christina tried to show him to people.

Christina pushed the thermostat up ten degrees, so Anya could toast along with her whole wheat bread. This was forbidden; it wasted fuel oil.

Who cares? Christina thought. The Shevvingtons get paid to have us here.

The furnace came on, rumbling. The house filled with deep shuddering noises from the sea, from the cellar. If there was still a giggle, it could not be heard over those growls and claps.

Maybe I'll go down and find out what's in the cellar, thought Christina Romney. It's probably just the tide and my imagination. That's what Michael and Benj would say. "You know what?" she said to Anya. "We've never explored the cellar. There are supposed to be passages from Candle Cove right up into this house. It's one of the legends, like the sea captain's bride falling to her death from the cupola. Let's see if we can find the passages." She located a flashlight on the shelf in the pantry and checked the batteries. Nice and strong. "You coming?" she said to Anya.

Anya stared at her in awe. "You're not afraid of anything, are you? I like being here with you." She smiled as trustingly as a kindergartner at Christina, who was thirteen to Anya's seventeen. "Listen to what I've written so far. *'Dear Blake. It's me, Anya. I miss you.'* How does that sound, Chrissie?"

It did not sound like a girl who had memorized Shakespeare.

Christina slid the bolt on the cellar door. She clung to her flashlight as if it were a grown-up. There is nothing down here, she told herself. "It's a great start, Anya." All fall her parents, her teachers and friends, and especially Michael and Benj had said to Christina, "Why do you blame the Shevvingtons for all the awful things that have happened? Why do you blame the Shevvingtons for Anya's mental collapse? The Shevvingtons are wonderful people trying their very hardest! You are making up all the connections you tell us about."

Anya said, "Shall I tell Blake we're having toast and tea, Christina?"

Christina turned the switch at the top of the splintery wooden stairs. The air was thick and dusty. "Yes, tell Blake that, Anya." She thought, We'll find out who's making what up. This giggle is the kind of thing the Shevvingtons would do to frighten one of us. The fall before, when Mr. Shevvington's eyes kept changing color, so that they were cold as gray steel one day and gaudy as bluebirds the next — why, it turned out to be as simple as two sets of contact lenses. And when the poster on the wall kept changing personality, so that Anya screamed whenever she looked at it — why, Mrs. Shevvington was just switching posters. Nobody would believe me. Grown-ups don't do things like that, everybody would tell me. Why, Mr. Shevvington is the best high school principal we've ever had, and Mrs. Shevvington is the most creative seventh-grade English teacher! *You're* the one making things up, Christina. That's what they would say.

I bet I'll find a tape with remote control down here, so they can turn on insane giggles and try to make us insane, too.

Down the stairs Christina went, flashing her light in the corners. She reached the bottom step and stared into the musty dark. A few old wooden saw-horses, a big wooden barrel, some discarded furniture, a broken table, old toolboxes, cans of paint. At some point in its long history the huge cellar had been divided into rooms. The doors of each room sagged on rusty hinges. One door had had a small glass pane in it once, but the glass was gone, and there was only a hole, as if a hand might inch through and touch Christina.

Don't think things like that, she ordered herself.

"There's a draft on my ankles, Chrissie," said Anya from the kitchen. Her voice was a thin, distant whine, like her life.

I'll follow the electric wires first, Christina thought. She looked up. A single lightbulb hung over the rickety treads. And no wires went anywhere; the only electricity stopped right at that bulb.

It could run on batteries, then, she thought.

Cautiously, Christina walked into the first room. Stone floor, stone walls, and cobwebs. She backed out and tried the next room. Stone floor, stone walls, and cobwebs.

The ocean in Candle Cove whiffled and whispered through the rocks.

She flashed her light in the corners. She flashed her light at the ceiling.

Up in the kitchen, Anya was muttering, "A draft. A draft. A draft." Christina heard Anya push back her chair and cross the room. Then slowly, as if not sure she knew how to do it, Anya shut the cellar door. The door closed with a thick wooden slap.

The light that had poured down from the kitchen vanished. The single bulb was weaker than Christina had realized. You could hardly even call it light; it was more like a fog.

From the depths of the cellar, Christina heard the flat, solid sound of a footstep.

Christina froze. It had not been her own foot. And Anya was too light.

Outdoors, muffled by the rock walls of the cellar, the Atlantic Ocean forced its way into Candle Cove. She swallowed. That's what it was, she told herself. Tide slapping rocks.

For a moment Christina wanted to flee back upstairs. But this was like a test, and Christina intended to pass. So she walked past the furnace, going deeper into the cellar.

She was tiptoeing. Why am I being quiet? she thought. Do I really think there's a creature down here I don't want to frighten? If there is anything down here, I definitely do want to frighten it.

Now the light from the single bulb was behind her. Her shadow was long, darkening her own path. With her flashlight, she split her own shadow in two. "Now one of you go in that room," she said to her two shadows, "and you there — you come with me." She giggled.

A deep, throaty voice giggled back.

Chapter 2

She did not scream.

The giggle sucked the air out of her lungs and kept it. Christina turned blue. Fighting her lungs, fighting the giggle, she tried to reach the steps. She stuck out her skinny little seventh-grade arms to defend herself.

The giggle thickened and grew deep until it became a groan. It was no tape. It was no trick. It lived; its inhuman noises reached for her like dead hands.

It was between her and kitchen door; the furnace, black and banging, hid it. She swung her flashlight, trying to catch the giggle in its beam. Her arm jerked with nerves and the light leaped around the cellar like fireworks, illuminating nothing. "Go away," Christina whispered.

Immediately: silence.

Christina and the giggle both ceased to breathe.

She circled, trying to keep her back safe, but not knowing where safety lay. She felt like a slow-motion ballerina. "Anya, open the door!" Christina whispered.

She passed the furnace, and nothing attacked.

She passed the sagging door of the empty room, and nothing touched her. "Anya!" she croaked.

The giggle began again, slithering off the stone walls like spiders.

Christina bolted up the cellar steps and grabbed the tiny handle. The handle spun, opening nothing. "Anya!" screamed Christina, pounding on the door with the flashlight. "Anya, you locked it! Open the door! Let me out! Anya!"

The foggy bulb above her head flickered.

"No!" screamed Christina. "Don't go out!"

It went out.

She turned, pressing her back against the kitchen door. "Please don't swim out of the dark," she prayed. "Please go away." She was whispering, as if she could not allow the rubbery giggle to hear her beg.

Christina touched her hair.

The strange hair that always protected her. The hair of three colors, with its streaks of silver and gold and chocolate brown. She felt that in the dark the charm of her extraordinary hair could not work; the rubbery giggle would not know that she was Christina of the Isle, with tri-colored hair.

She was afraid to aim her flashlight into the cellar.

What if she saw it? Its rubbery fingers ready to crush her against the kitchen door?

"Anya!" Christina kicked backward with her foot.

There was no sound in the cellar. No sound in the kitchen.

She could almost hear her own tears spilling down her thin cheeks. She was pressed so hard against the kitchen door, her own back ought to break through the solid wood like a tank.

But it didn't.

She was alone in the dark, in the cellar, with the giggle.

After a long, long time, she remembered her watch. It was digital and glowed in the dark. She stared at the tiny square numbers as they flickered away the seconds of time. Her skull filled with numbers and colons.

10:32:01.

10:32:02.

10:32:03.

At 11:17:45, Christina knew she was alone in the cellar. She did not know how she knew. But the giggle had gone. Evaporated like water? Or had it walked out another door? But there were no other doors.

She slumped against the kitchen door. She could cry no more; her face was so blotchy her eyes felt swollen shut. "Anya," she muttered once or twice, "please open the door."

How had this happened to her?

How had Christina, born on Burning Fog Isle, only daughter of the most wonderful parents in the world, ended sobbing and defeated in the cellar of a sea captain's house on the mainland?

Burning Fog Isle lay far out to sea. There were so few year-round residents that once the children finished the sixth grade, they were sent to board on the mainland for junior and senior high. (*Boarding*. It turned out to be a terrible word. Flat and hard and full of splinters.)

Christina had never been in a school with classrooms, a cafeteria, hallways, bells that rang, art, music, gym, and hundreds of kids. How thrilled she had been when at last, like Anya Rothrock, and Michael and Benjamin Jaye, she was old enough to get on Frankie's boat with her trunks and bags, and land at the town dock.

This was to be the year of being normal.

The year of being just like everybody else.

She had trembled with the joy of being ordinary.

It was Anya's senior year; Benjamin was a sophomore and Michael a ninth-grader. They would have friends; she would have friends; Michael would be on all the teams; Anya would gleam like a new moon; and Christina would be special and spoiled.

But Anya — lovely Anya, with her black hair like a storm cloud around her fragile, white face — had lost her grip on reality. Anya had been terrified of the sea, of the tides that rose every twelve hours and smashed against the cliffs below the mansion. Anya had been terrified of a poster of the sea that hung on her wall and seemed to change texture and color with Anya's sanity.

Slowly Christina had seen the truth. Perched on the cliff over the glittering sea, with its cupola and many roofs — Schooner Inne looked romantic on the outside. But inside . . . the Shevvingtons were destroying Anya on purpose and enjoying every minute of it.

No parent saw it. No matter what Christina explained to Michael and Benj — who were right there, who should have seen! — they just got irritated. "Stop telling yarns, Chrissie," they would say. And sometimes they even complained to the Shevvingtons, "Christina's yarning again." The Shevvingtons convinced Michael and Benj that Christina made up these things in order to attract attention.

The only teacher who realized what was happening, Christina's math teacher, was fired.

So Christina turned to Blake, Anya's boyfriend. Handsome, preppy Blake, who dressed in catalog Maine clothing, and whose watches cost more than a lobster boat. Anya and Blake had walked and danced and kissed, looking like a photograph in a slick magazine. They could have been modeling jeans or perfume or fast cars.

But even with Blake there, Anya collapsed. Her honor grades vanished like snow in the sun; her mind faltered; she quit high school. Blake struggled on; Blake never gave up.

But there was nothing the Shevvingtons did not plan for.

Somehow they arranged for the creature in the wet suit to entice Blake into chasing him. Their timing was perfect. As the twenty-foot tide rolled in like a living army, cannonading off the cruel cliffs,

Blake was to be dashed to pieces. But even the Shevvingtons could not plan for the lucky chance of a tourist strolling by. Blake was saved, though he was in the hospital for weeks. But he went straight from the hospital to the boarding school, and for Anya it was the final blow. She never saw Blake again; Mr. and Mrs. Lathem, his parents, refused even to give Anya Blake's address and phone number, because they held Anya responsible for everything that happened to Blake.

Oh, Blake had phoned once or twice. But he was swept up in another world now, and who knew what he believed about what the Shevvingtons and his parents had told him? And so they had lost Blake, their only ally.

But Christina, golden hair bright as summer apples, silver hair bright as stars, fought back. She was of the island: she was granite, like the rock she was born on, and nothing would stop Christina.

She had shown the Shevvingtons a thing or two! They finally saw she could keep Anya from falling off both the real cliff of the sea and the mental cliff of her mind.

There had been a week — a wonderful moon-bright week — in which Christina knew herself, age thirteen, to be stronger than the principal. The Shevvingtons had bowed down to Christina.

And then, laughing in the way of adults, who are always more powerful in the end, the Shevvingtons had brought forth Dolly, Michael and Benjamin Jaye's little sister. Christina's best friend on the island. Dolly was supposed to be in sixth grade, safe on the island for another whole year. But Mr. Shevvington used his power as principal, announcing that Dolly was "far too bright to be isolated on that remote little island with its pitiful excuse for a school." And Dolly's parents had agreed to let her go to the mainland early.

Had Michael and Benj protested? Had they said "No, no, the Shevvingtons are evil"?

Of course not.

Michael and Benjamin Jaye were oblivious to any of it.

Christmas vacation arrived. The five children went back to the island for two glorious weeks. And on those beautiful December days, filled with sweet song and crispy cookies, never had Burning Fog Isle seemed so remote from the mainland. It was a world of mothers and fathers, of being tucked in at night. It was a world of peace and laughter and people you had known all your life.

Her parents had said gently, "Chrissie, honey, you're exaggerating. You're getting such wonderful grades in school. Writing such fine papers. You seem to have so many friends to write us about, so many interesting activities. It is a terrible shame about Anya, but she's always been fragile, you know."

"The Shevvingtons," Christina said, in her last attempt to convince her parents, "took Anya's fragility and snapped her like little bones."

But they all sighed and said Chrissie was yarning. It was comforting to believe that Michael and

Benj saw nothing because there was nothing to see. Christina even made a New Year's resolution to stop yarning about the Shevvingtons.

They had gone back to Schooner Inne: Michael to basketball, Benj to slog on in school until he turned sixteen and could quit and be a lobsterman; Dolly to sixth grade; Anya to her laundromat; and Christina to her new resolution.

January classes began.

It seemed to Christina in those first days of January that the Shevvingtons hovered over Dolly like birds of prey, circling in the invisible air currents of the threatening sky, waiting for the time to strike. The Shevvingtons were drilling into Dolly's soul with diamond-tipped bits. Christina had no evidence. She hadn't even figured out yet how they were doing it.

She did not know that she had fallen asleep against the cellar door.

The door opened.

Christina fell backward into the kitchen.

The cold, harsh ceiling light blinded her. Blinking, she stared up to see Michael, Benjamin, Dolly, and Mr. and Mrs. Shevvington staring down at her. The Jayes wore jeans. The boys' huge feet were encased in huge, dirty high-top sneakers. Dolly wore tiny, brand-new white sneakers. Mrs. Shevvington's nylons gleamed like water. Mr. Shevvington's creased pant leg rested on his polished leather shoe.

"May I ask, Christina," Mrs. Shevvington said, "why you have chosen to spend your morning in the basement?"

"I was trapped down there," Christina said. She sat up. Now she was staring into their kneecaps. Awkwardly she turned herself over and struggled to her feet. Dolly was giggling. Michael and Benj were shaking their heads in tolerant amusement. "There was somebody down there!" she said. "Somebody — he kept giggling at me."

The boys rolled their eyes. "Chrissie," said Benj, "stop yarning. We've told you and told you. You'll never make friends when you spend all your time yarning."

"It's true," she said. She sounded like a bleating sheep. "Somebody lives in that basement! He's huge and rubbery, and he — "

"What have you been reading!" exclaimed Dolly, giving Christina a little punch in the side. "Chrissie, get a grip on yourself. You're falling apart like Anya."

Anya appeared. She had a tray in her hands. A teacup and a small plate with toast crusts lay on the tray.

"Anya, where were you?" Christina sobbed. "I called and called! You didn't rescue me."

The rest burst into laughter at the idea that Anya could rescue anybody. Anya, frightened by the guffaws, flushed and nearly dropped her tray. Benj rescued the teacup and set the tray down for her. "I was so cold down here," Anya whispered. "And you went away, Chrissie. I went up to my room.

It's safer up there, so high. Away from the waves. Things don't reach me there."

Mr. Shevvington lost his temper. "Christina, look what you've done. Anya was improving. Now you've terrified her again. She's lost all the ground she gained. Why do you do these rotten things, Christina? I think you purposely plan to destroy poor Anya's self-esteem." He turned to Anya. "Christina loves to exaggerate, Anya, dear. You must learn to ignore everything she says."

Dolly giggled softly.

Christina hardened her jaw to keep from showing hurt.

Mrs. Shevvington said, "Wipe that expression off your face, young lady. March back into that cellar."

Christina backed up against Michael and Benj. Save me! she thought. Don't make me go back down there ever again!

The boys pushed her to Mrs. Shevvington, who said, "I will escort you, Christina. We will examine every room. We will look in the dust beneath the furnace, and we will measure the spaces behind the unused sawhorses. Then you will march back up here and admit to everybody that this is yet another of your attempts to get attention."

Chapter 3

"Aw, Christina," said Jonah. He was laughing at her! Christina grew hot with hurt and anger. How could her best friend — a boy who was always saying he wanted to be *better* friends, be a real *boyfriend* — not believe her story? "You have the most active imagination in the state of Maine," he teased. "You see a fishing boat out at sea and you think it's an invading navy. One seal pops its head up in the harbor and you're sure that little brown thing means the harbor is mined with bombs."

Christina stalked away. How could she ever have found Jonah pleasant company? How could she ever have thought he would understand anything?

Jonah ran to catch up. "It was probably just Anya up in the kitchen, being crazy," Jonah offered. "Giggling to herself." Jonah was growing at such a great rate that his blue jeans, new in November, were too short for him in January. Even his hair grew more quickly, and it was bunched up in his collar. His huge feet thumped in the school hallway. He didn't have much control over them. He was always running into something. Beside Jonah Christina always felt graceful. It was a nice feeling, and sometimes she was quite grateful to Jonah for being clunky.

But not today.

"Don't be mad, Chrissie," Jonah said.

She wanted to sock him.

"It was dark down there, and you were scared. You're just being silly, is all."

Christina socked him.

Jonah knew her pretty well. He stepped out of range. Holding up his palms like a warrior's shields, he said, "The Shevvingtons are rotten, I agree with that much. But nobody is living in the cellar, Christina."

She stared at those hands. A man's hands on a boy. The feet and the hands were finished growing; the legs and arms were rushing to catch up.

Slowly, as if unsure that his arm would obey his brain's order, Jonah extended his arm and put it around her shoulder.

What comfort! The weight and the warmth were like a signed contract: *I'm your friend.*

On the island there had been few boys: Dolly's brothers, a couple of little kids in first and second grade, one or two older boys already lobstering for a living. Here in school there were hundreds.

Christina's mind filled and swirled with boys, like a plastic paperweight you shook in your hand to make it snow. In her paperweight were all the seventh-grade boys and of course Blake . . . but in her heart they vanished, as if covered by snow. There was only Jonah. Her eyes and ears filled up with him. She forgot school, its hum of talk, the beginning of classes.

"We'll be late for English," Jonah whispered, as if it were a secret. They took each other's hands, and his hand was very hot in hers. It was like holding a fever.

Mrs. Shevvington stood in front of the blackboard. She held a sheaf of corrected papers in her hand. In her class the seventh-graders, even the boys, were subdued. Nobody had a set of dueling pistols that shot heavy-duty rubber bands into the girls' rear ends. Nobody had forged love letters to pass around the room.

Yet again Mrs. Shevvington made them write an essay in class. Her voice cut like the wind at ten below zero. "A brief essay," she said to her silent thirteen-year-olds, "on January daydreams. One or two paragraphs. Good adjectives. Nothing dull. What you daydream about on the longest, darkest days of winter."

They wrote. The usual kids tried to get sent to the nurse, and Mrs. Shevvington as usual replied that they were welcome to throw up in the wastebasket if necessary, but she expected a finished essay first. The timer on her deck ticked mercilessly. Christina scribbled. She broke her pencil point, and Jonah silently handed her a new pencil. I love you, she thought, but he had looked back at his own paper before their eyes met.

"Time," said Mrs. Shevvington triumphantly. As always, Gretchen and Vicki collected the essays, their mean little faces smirking down on the pages, knowing trouble was out there for somebody — but not them. Never them. Mrs. Shevvington leafed slowly through the sheaf of essays. Nobody breathed. They were all praying not to be ordered to read theirs aloud. Mrs. Shevvington tapped the papers rhythmically against her palm, as if spanking herself.

"Christina?" said Mrs. Shevvington. "Read, please. We will all be so interested in what you have to say."

The class sagged in relief. Christina could handle anything. It was better for her to be Mrs. Shevvington's victim than any of them.

Gretch and Vicki stroked their silken hair in identical motions and leaned back in their chairs, the better to laugh at Christina.

Christina walked to the front of the class. She knew her essay was good, even funny. So why was she picked? What torment awaited her? Mrs. Shevvington handed her the paper. For once there was an expression on the teacher's flat face, but Christina could not fathom it. It was power, that much she knew. Whatever was going to happen, Mrs. Shevvington had planned it.

The panic from the cellar rose up in Christina. All things dark and slimy trembled in her brain. She tried to control her voice, but couldn't. It quivered. Even her chin shook. In her hand the essay trembled.

Gretch exploded in a silvery giggle.

Christina looked at Jonah for support. His smile

gave her courage. She began reading out loud. " 'My January Dream. By Christina Romney. I have cabin fever. The snow, the cold, the ice, and the early dark are like demons. I am going winter mad. The sweater I put on so eagerly when the first cold wind came up in September had the prettiest pattern. It was cozy on my shoulders. Now the same sweater is an instrument of torture. My January dream is of burning all my winter clothes. I have worn the same heavy sweaters and the same thick flannel shirts week after week after week. In my January dream I light a huge bonfire in the middle of a field of snow. We all throw our old boring winter clothes into the fire. Then we feel a thousand times better, and we can laugh all the way through February.' "

Christina finished. How clever the essay sounded. Surely the others felt the same way about their winter wardrobes. She half thought her classmates would applaud, and she got ready to smile back.

But instead, Vicki screamed with laughter. "Then you'd be naked all through February, Christina."

Gretchen said pityingly, "The rest of us have tons of clothes. Why, I've hardly even started to show off my sweater collection. I have thirty-four sweaters. How many do you have, Christina?"

Vicki said to Mrs. Shevvington, "Maybe we could get up a collection for Christina. So she'd have something decent to wear."

Mrs. Shevvington said that island girls had too much pride to accept charity, but it was very, very thoughtful of Vicki to think of such a thing. Fine people like Vicki, she told the class, were always putting others first.

Christina found her way to her seat. She could feel Jonah's pity. She hated pity. She didn't love him anymore, if that's what that minute of heat and touch had been.

Vicki touched Christina's sweater sleeve and said, "It really is ratty, Chrissie. Maybe you should just wash your wardrobe once this winter and that would make you feel better." Vicki and Gretch laughed together, like music boxes, all tinkly. Christina yearned to throw the silver laughter against the wall and smash it.

Mrs. Shevvington delivered a strange little lecture as she walked up and down the rows of desks. "January daydreams," she repeated. "Daydreams are dangerous things, children. You must be very sure you want what you daydream of." She was right in front of Christina's desk, and her heavy-lidded eyes in the oatmeal of her face stared at Christina. "Sometimes when things come true," said Mrs. Shevvington softly, her voice crawling into Christina's ears like mice in the night, "you are sorry."

Class, like all tortures, ended eventually.

The rest of school was a summer breeze compared to English. At lunch Christina looked for Jonah. Ahead of her in the hall she saw Mr. Shevvington. In his hand he held a large, swollen briefcase. Christina had never seen it before. It was old but cherished. The leather was supple, kept soft and shiny with polish.

He loves that briefcase, Christina thought.

She stood quietly among the teenagers going to and from the most important thirty minutes of the day — lunch. Mr. Shevvington entered his office. A few minutes later he came out again — without the briefcase.

Christina slipped into the girls' bathroom to avoid notice.

While she was there a thought crossed her mind.

She took a paper towel from the shiny box on the wall. She folded it several times. She waited while girls entered and left the stalls, brushed their hair, played with lip gloss. When she was alone Christina unlocked a window, opened it a quarter inch, and wedged the paper in the crack so that the window would not lock.

Chapter 4

After school Christina stood near the playing fields waiting for Dolly.

The wintry days were so short! Class was hardly over when the sky began getting dark. January closed in like a fat dictionary on a pressed flower. Christina felt squashed between the pages of January days.

She swung her ice skates in a circle.

The village fire department had ruled that nobody could skate on the pond this year. It never froze hard enough because of the brook flowing beneath it. Instead, the parking lot behind the old hardware store was flooded. The curbs held a few inches of water, which froze smooth and black, and there the children skated safely.

Christina was just an ordinary skater, but when she laced up her skates, she felt like an Olympic star, and in her head she heard nations applauding.

Dolly came running down the street from elementary school, her book bag, skates, and scarf flying behind her like separate people.

You could never mistake Dolly for anyone else. Her thick red hair was still in two braids, because she was only in sixth grade and had not started to care yet about hair. Her skinny little legs and long thin arms flung about her as if they were barely stapled to her body and might come off if you jerked too hard. Dolly never cared if any of her clothing matched. Today she wore a neon-pink ski jacket and killer-whale-blue pants with a screaming yellow scarf.

Dolly always had so much to say; she began talking long before she was close enough to be heard, so Christina came into the middle of Dolly's conversation. " . . . because of people watching. I fall down too much. I'd rather read about skating than actually skate. So we won't go to the parking lot ice. People would laugh at me. We'll go to the pond." She took Christina's hand. Dolly was a great hand-holder. She held hands with teachers and boys, crossing guards, and cafeteria aides.

"We can't skate on the pond," objected Christina. "There are rules now."

"I hate rules," Dolly said. Dolly believed the entire world should revolve around her, and it often did. Dolly had been born on Thanksgiving Day and her mother let them use Dolly for Baby Jesus in that year's Christmas pageant. She was only four weeks old and a ten-year-old Mary had dropped Dolly headfirst into the manager. There wasn't any brain damage, the doctor who had flown in told them. (Her older brothers always said there was plenty.) Dolly wanted to be Baby Jesus every year. She thought it was boring to have Jesus always either in diapers or dying on a cross, and they should have a nice six-year-old Jesus (Dolly) or a really decent nine-year-old Jesus (Dolly).

Nobody could pout quite as well as Dolly if things did not go her way.

But everything was going her way right now. While Christina felt farther away from Burning Fog Isle than Siberia, Dolly had not been homesick once. Christina could get so homesick she'd open a window and let the wind carry her tears back to the island, but Dolly simply adopted the Shevvingtons as parents. And no matter how many warnings Christina issued, Dolly never listened.

Dolly said, "You don't really want to skate, do you? Let's go home and be cozy and read." Dolly's life was stacked with books. Books to underline, to read under the covers, to read out loud to Christina.

Christina could not imagine wasting a daylight hour on the written word. "Please, Dolly? I love to skate." Christina wrapped her scarf around her throat. She loved the soft woolen caress under her chin. "Look at that field. Untouched snow!" cried Christina. "Let's make a chain of angels."

They lay down in the snow, swinging their legs and arms outward to make robes and wings, then stepping carefully across the fresh snow to make the next angel. Christina yearned for some of the toughest seventh-grade boys, so she could have a snowball fight. Christina believed in serious fights.

"I'm too thin for this," Dolly said. "I don't get enough blood to my extremities. I'll die of exposure and it'll be your fault."

"No," Christina said. "Playing in the snow makes you stronger. It's reading all those books that weakens you."

They made an angel chain all the way to the snow fence. "Come on," Christina said. "Let's go to the parking lot after all. They won't laugh at you. I'll hold your hand. We'll skate partners. Then you won't fall."

Dolly shook her head. Christina felt that Dolly was just not interested in her anymore. They were no longer friends, just two people with a history, who were now living in the same building. The Shevvingtons had eaten their way into Dolly's heart like witches through a gingerbread house. Dolly gave them her art projects and dedicated her social studies papers to them.

If the Shevvingtons keep eating at her, Christina thought, Dolly will have no heart left. She will be empty.

The winter shadows were long and blue. The sky drowned the snow in darkness. Emptiness was everywhere: her lungs, the fields, the wide sky. Today it begins again, Christina Romney thought. I can feel it coming. The Shevvingtons are ready to attack.

"Look at the pond," Dolly said, pointing. "It's waist deep in snow. The fire department is just too mean and lazy to clear it." Dolly pouted.

Christina took Dolly's hand again, relieved. Now

they'd have to skate on the parking lot. "You didn't want to skate anyway."

From the pond came a deep groan. Like a grizzly bear. A huge grinding roar like a chewing monster.

The girls stood still as statues in Stone Tag. Their bright jackets were targets in the white snow.

The groan came again. As deep as a cave.

Or a cellar.

"Something's under the ice," Dolly whispered. "It's going to get us!"

The third groan was stronger, as if the ice were attacking.

The girls turned and ran. Across the fields, past the trees. Dolly's braids flew in Christina's face like soft branches. Her yellow scarf flew off, and Christina caught it like an escaped canary. Through the deep snow they staggered. Over the snow fence, up to their chain of angels.

The wind — or something else — had been at work.

None of the angels had heads.

Chapter 5

Puffs of color against the white snow, they ran until they reached the school. But school was long over, and the door was locked.

It amused Christina in a grim way that she was seeking refuge in the building where the Shevvingtons reigned. All the parents admired Mr. Shevvington. When Mr. Shevvington spoke the parents would repeat what he said, as if quoting the President or the *New York Times*.

Dolly and Christina ran around the school, trying two more doors. Locked. "Let's go home," whimpered Dolly.

Home? Christina thought. She was snow-blind in the glare of the setting sun, and she kept seeing those horrible headless angels. There is no home for us, she thought. Home is on an island, far away. All we have are the Shevvingtons and the cellar, where a thing of rubber lives.

"Chrissie, I wanna go home," Dolly said, almost in baby talk.

But Christina had stopped running.

In front of her was an enormous passenger van, sparkling like jewelry. Gretchen's mother drove. Inside, laughing seventh-grade girls and boys were packed.

Christina forgot the pond, the angels, and the groans.

"They're all in your class," Dolly said. "Chrissie, are they going someplace? Why aren't you going, too?"

Gretchen, who practically ran the seventh grade, looked down on Christina. Vicki, beautiful in a black-and-silver ski jacket, smirked from another window.

"I wasn't invited," Christina said.

Was there a more terrible sentence in the world? Her heart ached. Even her joints ached, as if being left out had given her back pain.

All her friends were in the van. They were going to Pizza Power, where they would play video games and eat pizza wedges till they dropped. They saw Christina and waved. You weren't invited. Gretchen and Vicki smacked upright palms, like winners in a tournament. You weren't invited.

The fight went out of Christina. When Dolly still refused to skate at the parking lot, she shrugged. They walked back to Schooner Inne, through the village so loved by tourists, and across the Singing Bridge. From here they could see beyond the harbor and out into the ocean. Their beloved Burning Fog Isle was beyond the horizon.

The wind was so icy it must have come straight from the Arctic. Christina could smell snow in the sky.

Dolly said dreamily, "I have the best library books for tonight. I can hardly wait to start reading." Dolly had the right constitution for reading. When she was tired, she was very tired and would curl up in the old chair and sit for hours, flicking pages. "Sometimes I think it's wrong to spend so much time choosing books," Dolly confided, showing Christina the titles of her weekend choices. "It's probably like a drug. I'll get so addicted to the library shelves I'll cling, sobbing, to the library door when they try to close for the night."

Above them loomed the white bulk of Schooner Inne, its shutters dark and creaking. The front door opened, as if by remote control. Mr. or Mrs. Shevvington must have opened it, but nobody was visible. Only darkness, as if the house had no inhabitants who needed to see. Headless angels, perhaps.

Christina shivered.

But Dolly shouted joyfully, "Hi, Mrs. Shevvington! How are you? Did you have a nice day? Wait till I tell you about my day!" She ran ahead of Christina, swinging her precious books, throwing herself into an invisible embrace.

Wind knocked the doors shut again before Christina got there. She stood alone on the narrow top step, fumbling at the handle.

Tiny flecks of snow, hard as diamonds, whipped her cheeks.

* * *

They had a classic blizzard supper: pancakes, maple syrup, and sausages.

Dolly's two brothers ate like starved animals, pouring maple syrup over melting heaps of butter on top of pancake mountains. Michael, who was a ninth-grader, was on Junior Varsity; he talked about basketball practice, games past, and games to come. Benj, who was a sophomore, worked afternoons at a garage. He talked about transmissions, brake fluid, and fan belts.

Christina thought it remarkable that they cared about these things.

There had been a time when she had been in love with Michael, when she had never been off-island and had no comparison. Now she found Michael self-centered: aware of nothing but teammates and games.

Besides, she had other boys to think of now . . . Jonah, also in seventh grade . . . and Blake.

Blake had been gone for so long. It was difficult to remember Blake the person, but she could imagine him as a photograph: glossy and perfect, his clothes as rich as summer people, his smile as deep as the sea. She had touched his shoulder once, and he had touched hers. Daily Christina had had to remind herself, You're just a little kid. He hardly notices you. He's in love with Anya.

When Blake went away, Christina's memory built him stronger and more brilliant. She thought of him as a demigod, or a Greek hero, who, if only he would return, could save them all.

No other boy measured up to Blake. Benj and Michael were just two more Schooner Inne boarders who were noisier, messier, and hungrier than she was.

Mr. Shevvington sat at one end of the table. His suit today was herringbone gray with an elegant wine-red vest.

Mrs. Shevvington sat at the opposite end of the table. She was opposite her husband in all ways. Thick, graceless, and ugly, her fingers were stubs, like burned-up candles. Whenever she passed a plate, Christina was surprised that those short, fat fingers could even grip the edge.

Poor Anya floated around the table, not coming to rest, not touching the food set out for her. Nobody noticed Anya anymore. She was just a fixture, like a coffee pot or a blender. The lovely dark hair that had once drifted like a cloud around her ivory princess's face was lank and thin. The dark, mysterious eyes were dulled, as if nobody lived behind them anymore; the house of Anya lay empty.

Christina dusted her pancakes with confectioners' sugar instead of maple syrup. She spooned it out of the box and into a tiny sifter, shaking the sifter so that the sugar fell like snow on her food. She didn't like the edges of pancakes any more than she liked the crusts of sandwiches. She cut each bite into a triangle, leaving discarded pancake curves all over her plate.

"Christina," said Mrs. Shevvington, "you are too old to play with your food. Simply eat, please."

She had fought them over food issues before.

They always won. Once when Christina had diso-
beyed right up to midnight, they had telephoned
her parents on the island, and her parents had sided
with the Shevvingtons. ("Christina!" said her
mother furiously. "What is the matter with you?
Going to war over creamed potatoes! Grow up.")

Christina studied her pancake edges. Then she
squashed them down with the back of her fork and
crammed them all in her mouth at one time. It was
like eating wet pillows.

Dolly said, "The sixth grade is getting French
Exposure this week."

"What's that?" said her brothers. "Like getting
exposed to the sun?"

"We get Spanish Exposure, too," Dolly said. "To
see which language we want to take next year in
seventh grade, when we study a language for real.
I am sure that the French teacher swears when he
mutters under his breath. I am memorizing all his
swears. Wouldn't it be nice to swear in lots of lan-
guages?" Dolly's laugh was like finger cymbals: tiny
and tinkling.

Her brothers roared. Their laughter was like
lions in a cave. Benj and Michael demanded to be
taught the swears.

Outside, the snow came down thick as winter
blankets.

Dolly, who had hardly touched her supper, said,
"Ooooooh, that was good, Mrs. Shevvington." She
slipped out of her chair, slowly circled the big ugly
table with its legs as thick as thighs, and rested her
head on Mrs. Shevvington's shoulder. Mrs. Shev-

vington did not yell at her for not finishing her milk and eating only the middles of the pancakes.

Dolly drew her two braids around her mouth, like a Christmas wreath. "You know what?" she said through her hair. "Christina made me go skating. We went to the pond, and — "

"What!" cried Mr. Shevvington. He swung his distinguished face in Christina's direction. The eyes were blue today and as cold as the tips of Dolly's fingers. "Christina Romney! I am appalled. You took Dolly to that unsafe ice?"

His eyes today were bright blue, like a husky dog ready to bite. Mr. Shevvington's stare slowed her brain. Christina's tongue stumbled, trying to explain.

Dolly's brothers remembered there were things in life besides basketball and cars. "Christina!" Benjamin yelled at her. "You're the one who's older! You're supposed to take care of Dolly!" His big bony face, shadowed where he was starting a beard, was dark with anger.

"What's the matter with you, you jerk?" Michael said.

Christina waited for Dolly to admit that it had been *her* idea.

But Dolly said nothing. She snuggled closer to Mrs. Shevvington and Mrs. Shevvington rocked her like a baby.

Mr. Shevvington's eyes glittered at Christina like beach pebbles. "The pond, indeed! Do you want Dolly to fall through the ice and drown?" Mrs. Shevvington pointed her fat index finger at Christina.

The nail was bitten down into the quick, but she had polished it anyway, red as blood.

"Dolly, tell them what happened," Christina ordered.

Dolly said, "We made angels in the snow. The wind blew their heads away. Like executions. And then the ice on the pond screamed at us."

"Expansion," said her brother Benj. "When ice gets colder or warmer it expands and contracts. Makes terrible noises."

Mrs. Shevvington smiled, exposing her horrid little teeth, yellow as birdseed. She played with Dolly's thick braids. "Dolly, darling, what are you going to do tonight?"

They were finished with Christina. The Shevvingtons would pay no more attention to her that night.

Anya drifted, thin as paper, having said nothing, perhaps having thought nothing, certainly having eaten nothing.

I just became a tiny bit like Anya, Christina thought. Empty. Invisible. Why, Dolly can't be bothered to stick up for me. Even to Michael and Benj, I am nobody. That's how the Shevvingtons destroy. Look what they did to Val, Robbie's sister! Robbie doesn't even call her by name. Now it's happening to me. Even to my own mother and father, I'm just a person who ought to obey the Shevvingtons.

"Read," said Dolly with immense satisfaction. "I have two mysteries, two romances, and two science fiction."

Mr. Shevvington said, "You are reading too much, Dolly, my dear. A well-rounded young lady uses her body as well as her mind. You must become an athlete."

Dolly shuddered. "I'd rather read about sports. How about if I get out a really great book about ballet? Or horses?"

Her brothers lost interest. They attacked dessert.

"I may just have to suspend your library privileges," Mr. Shevvington teased.

"I'm going to read in bed," Dolly said, ignoring all suggestions of athletic activity. She hoisted her stack of books slowly, as if eating supper had exhausted her. "I've always thought I would make an excellent invalid," she told the Shevvingtons. "I like bed. I like sheets and pillows. I'd lie there and read. All I need is enough strength to turn the pages."

"Perhaps you could have an accident," said Mrs. Shevvington softly.

Christina's blood seemed to stop flowing. Would the Shevvingtons really go that far?

"I would be very brave," Dolly agreed.

Down the length of the kitchen table, the Shevvingtons smiled at each other.

Chapter 6

When Schooner Inne lay silent in the night, when the snow had stopped and the tide was out, Christina left her bedroom. She crept in the dark around the tilting balcony with its little forest of white railings. Down the bare, slippery stair she tiptoed, hand sliding on the old bent rail.

Hardly breathing, she paused on the second floor, where the pretty guest rooms and the Shevvingtons' beautiful master bedroom surrounded the lower balcony. There was no sound.

The mansion and its inhabitants slept.

The next set of stairs was carpeted: rich, soft, toe-tickling carpet.

At the bottom, Christina knelt and put on her boots and jacket. She checked her house keys, zipped them carefully into her side pocket, and slid out of Schooner Inne.

The night sky was so clear Christina felt she could taste the stars. If she opened her lips and stuck out her tongue, the stars would fall like snowflakes and taste like bitter lemons.

It was two o'clock in the morning. The village was silent. No cars stirred. No lights were on in houses. Nothing moved but a small thirteen-year-old girl named Christina Romney.

She walked one block and turned a corner. Her shadow leapt ahead, like a black giant. The only sound was the light crunch of her own boots in the snow.

Behind her the snow crunched.

Christina's heart crunched with it. She spun on the street, whirling to face the crunch. From the cellar? she thought numbly. No, no, it couldn't have heard me.

Headlights wheeled around the corner. The faint roof light of a police car twinkled.

Christina backed into the doorway of the nearest shop.

A police car was not reassuring when you were planning to break into a building.

But the police had not seen her. The men in the car looked straight ahead, cruising by in boredom. When they had vanished, Christina crept on in the dark toward her school.

In the night the school loomed like a monster with square edges: dark and wicked in the moon-tinted snow. She pulled off her ski cap, letting her tri-colored hair fall free. Nobody had hair like Christina. She counted on her silver and gold locks to protect her from the demons of the dark.

The winter wind bit through Christina's heavy coat. Who would have thought she would start the second semester with breaking and entering?

What if I get caught? Christina thought, flattening herself against an icy brick wall. In the blackness she could not see herself. Her shadow no longer existed: she was a non-person.

If I get caught, it will be exactly what the Shevvingtons want. But nobody else can stop the Shevvingtons. "Maybe you could have an accident," they had whispered down the table.

The Shevvingtons had a grip on the adult community like it was a dog on a leash. No parent, no grown-up, no teacher would save Dolly.

She knew the Shevvingtons well. Other people might rent a movie or read a library book for weekend entertainment, but the Shevvingtons loved to gloat. Somewhere, someplace lay a stack of papers and photographs of all their previous victims.

Last fall she had believed any incriminating papers would be in the Guidance Office. There had been no papers there, though, only computer disks, and she had gotten caught trying to find the right disk.

Then she had searched every inch of Schooner Inne. She had even looked and measured for secret compartments and hidden backs on cabinets and bookcases.

But there was nothing at Schooner Inne except the weird whistle of the wind off the Atlantic Ocean crying, *"Fffffffffffff!"* until Christina grew dizzy and sick trying not to hear it.

But now she knew about the briefcase. A container Mr. Shevvington stroked like a pet.

Christina could imagine Mr. Shevvington . . . the

office door locked . . . his secretary told to hold telephone calls . . . she could see his fine suit, his gleaming vest, the dashing little scarf he liked to wear . . . taking a beloved file from the deep, dark leather. How well she knew that private, gloating smile.

The power of adults! How they could humiliate a child in class. How easily they could manipulate and frighten. How they could control a child's future by vicious rumor or carefully planned coincidence.

Anya had been the hope and pride of Burning Fog Isle. And now, thanks to hard work on the Shevvingtons' part, Anya was a high school dropout who worked at the laundromat, folding other people's clothing . . . if she remembered how. And the Shevvingtons were so clever! They convinced everybody that it was Anya's fault. "Poor Anya has a week character," they said.

Before Anya, the victim had been Robbie's sister Val. Christina would always remember Robbie's warning, when school started last fall. "You're new here, Christina. You've been out on that island, protected from things. You don't know. Be careful of the Shevvingtons."

And Christina had said, "Why?"

"I had an older sister," he replied, giving the sister no name, no description, as if she were truly not a person, just a thing. Robbie's eyes were sad and dark.

But later Christina found out. Her name was Val. She was even worse than Anya. She'd been stuck in an institution. Was still there. "Why don't your parents do something about the Shevvingtons?" Christina had cried.

Robbie raised his eyebrows. "They are grateful to the Shevvingtons," he said quietly. "For trying so hard to help Val. For finding her a counselor, and when that didn't work, for helping them put Val away."

So among the files Mr. Shevvington would smile over would be Val's. He had truly triumphed with Val. There was nothing at all left of her.

Before Val, Christina had no knowledge. The Shevvingtons had not been in Maine before that.

I will find out, Christina thought. I will get the truth. I will stop the Shevvingtons before they can fill any folders full of Dolly or me.

A pink overhead light in the parking lot buzzed like a swarm of hornets. Christina gripped a wire trash basket and rolled it over the ice-pocked snow. She stood it up under the girls' bathroom window.

What if Mr. Shevvington had gone into the bathroom to check, once he'd spotted her coming out? What if he knew her errand? What if he had heard her sneaking out of Schooner Inne and gotten here ahead of her?

The rhythm of her breathing was frantic. Her lungs slammed against her ribs. She climbed on top of the garbage can. With cold fingers she felt the window sill.

Neither the janitors nor Mr. Shevvington had found her folded paper towel. She forced her fingers under the crack and opened the window.

Swinging one foot in, Christina rested her stomach on the sill and then lowered herself sideways inside the school. Her heart was pounding so hard her chest hurt. She took the flashlight out of her inside jacket pocket and turned it on.

The compartments and sinks of the girls' bathroom glittered cold and metallic. The dozen mirrors threw Christina's reflection back and forth. She crept out of the bathroom. The door shut silently and slowly behind her.

There were no windows in the halls.

The darkness was complete. As sick, as abnormal as the Shevvingtons.

The thin circle of light from her flash was pitiful. Her hand shook with fear, and the light shivered with her wrist.

Somebody in the blackness was breathing.

Christina froze like an icicle. She could not think.

The breathing was heavy and irregular and thick. It — it —

— it's me, she thought. I'm so scared I'm panting.

She leaned against the wall for a moment, remembering gym exercises. Three deep breaths, she told herself. She sucked air into her lungs, held it, heaved it out. Three times.

It actually worked. She was calmer. She moved her feet again. Left. Right. Left.

She was strong with purpose, as strong as the island granite from which she had come. They can't stop me, Christina thought proudly.

She forgot how many girls they had stopped before her. Girls who were older, stronger, smarter.

Chapter 7

Mr. Shevvington's office door was open.

This surprised Christina so much she was almost afraid to push it after she found the handle would turn. Could he be waiting inside?

No. If Christina had made any noise leaving Schooner Inne, it had been covered by the slapping of ocean waves. If poor Anya had heard Christina creeping, she'd think it was a ghost and tremble beneath her covers. Michael and Benj slept with their radio on and never heard anything but drums. Dolly slept as only a small child can sleep, thickly and completely.

Now Christina pressed against the outer office wall. With the tip of her toe, she pushed the principal's door, like a policeman afraid the bad guy inside would have a gun.

The door moved without sound and without resistance. But it did not stay open. She had to hold it. She was terrified it would close on her, trap her inside Mr. Shevvington's office, like a lobster in a trap: easy to crawl in, impossible to back out.

She used a huge telephone book to prop the door open.

She planned to touch nothing. Mr. Shevvington might even use fingerprints against her. Her mother's hand-knitted mittens would keep her fingers safe.

The briefcase sat by the desk, half in the cavity where his feet went. Where he could reach down, just as Christina had imagined, to stroke its leather skin and remember gladly what it held.

Christina lifted the briefcase. It was full. These have to be the papers I want! she thought.

She did not want to turn on lights to examine the papers. She did not want to be there another second longer than she had to. She would take the briefcase —

But where?

She could not hide it in her bedroom at Schooner Inne. It was too small, too barren, for hiding places. She could not hide it anywhere else in the Inne either. Mrs. Shevvington spent all her spare time polishing, keeping the Inne gleaming for the guests who never came. Perhaps Anya's laundromat — that hot, damp back room full of lint and lost socks?

Christina slipped out of the office, letting the door close. It made a little *snick*. She put the telephone book back exactly as it had been. She let herself out into the hall.

Far down the hall, an EXIT sign gleamed hot pink and dusty.

A man stood under the sign, his shoulders pink with EXIT light. He laughed, a low, insane giggle.

His dark rubbery body gleamed. She knew he was a man by his great size — and yet he was too smooth-edged to be a person. He was something else. Something not human.

Giggling, the thing moved fluidly toward her as if underwater . . . swimming Christina's way.

She felt underwater herself — eyes, brain, lungs, and legs clogged with terror.

The thing waved at Christina.

It swam down the hall, arms out to catch her.

There was nowhere to go but down the hall.

Christina fled toward the opposite EXIT sign. But it was blockaded by a diamond-crossed grill — one of the moveable walls strung out to block the halls at night, so the people who came to the basketball games in the gym could not just cruise throughout the school.

The rubbery, giggling thing had long legs — much longer than Christina's. Nor was the thing weighed down by a heavy briefcase.

It came so close Christina could even smell it. It smelled like low tide — like the ocean in summer.

Christina swerved into the gym.

It was black as velvet in there. She turned off her flashlight and scooted under the bleachers. She ran down into the middle of them and crouched, motionless.

Her lungs refused to stay motionless. They heaved, sucking in air as if they belonged to somebody else entirely. *Sssssshhhh*, she said to her lungs and *Hhhhhhhhh*, her lungs said back, screaming for oxygen.

The gym doors clanked open.

For a horrible moment the gleaming creature was framed in the faint pinkish light from the center hall.

Then the gym door closed.

It was in the gym with Christina.

Getting closer, coming toward her as if he could see in the dark. As if the whites of her eyes or the heaving of her lungs was a sign to him. The giggle was part groan, part insanity.

The scent of the sea was so strong it was like the tide coming in. Did he live underwater? Was he human? Did the Shevvingtons' evil extend to some other world Christina could not even imagine?

The thing approached the bleachers — not from the side, where he could slip in where she hid and grab her — but from the front, where he could push the bleachers together. Shove them against the wall.

Crush Christina.

She was hollowed out with fear. So this was how Anya felt — kneeling, helpless, caught — a victim. Without an exit, without hope.

The creature in the wet suit pushed the first row of bleachers under the second row. She was staring at his knees, and then his knees vanished because he shoved both those rows under the third row. He was making a wood-and-metal wall. He would shove on until there was no room for Christina. *Until there was no Christina.*

The bleachers protested. They clanked. Their joints fought back a little bit.

Christina, of the island, strong as granite, choked back sobs. She would not beg. She would not plead. She would not give in!

She had her proof in her hand, but there would be a different kind of proof in the morning.

The body of Christina Romney.

I want my mother! Christina thought. She clung to the mittens her mother had knit her. They gave her strength. There was love knit into that wool. Duck walking, Christina crept toward the side.

Now the thing pushed the three stacked bleachers under the fourth. He had to use his shoulder to force them, but all it cost him was a little grunt. Usually it took the whole basketball team to shut the bleachers.

He's so strong, she thought.

Christina emerged at her edge.

If he catches me . . . Christina thought.

She waited until he was throwing his shoulder against the stacked seats. Then she ran.

She fled the gym, flinging the door open. She skidded on the waxed linoleum and raced down the hall to the girls' room. Please let me get in here and close the door before he sees where I'm going! she prayed.

In the bathroom she was reflected in the mirrors: fear was painted on her face like a melted, deformed Barbie doll.

She climbed up onto the window sill but couldn't get a grip with her mittens on. She slipped back onto the floor.

Behind her the bathroom door opened and the

giggle pierced the room like knives.

Christina dived face first out the window, missing the trash can by inches, and falling instead onto a mattress of new-fallen snow.

The weather had changed as it did in Maine, instantly and without warning. She leaped to her feet and ran on. In the parking lot horrible buzzing lights illuminated her like a moth to be stabbed on a pin.

She ran across the playing fields toward the village.

Snow blew in her face and obscured her vision.

For three steps she ran on top of the snow. Then her foot broke through the crust. She floundered up to her knees. The wind whistled around her head and through the three colors of her hair as if she were a barn roof.

She could not hear the giggle, but that was because the snow had become a storm, and the Atlantic Ocean was pounding and the wind shrieking. She came to the Singing Bridge, whose open iron fretwork made the car tires hum when they passed over. The iron was solid with ice. With each splash of the extremely high tide, another slick layer was added.

To get to Schooner Inne she had to cross the Singing Bridge.

It will sweep me away, thought Christina Romney. The sea will take me down into Candle Cove and take me out with the tide. I will be frozen solid, like a maiden in an old poem: all ice. Even my heart and soul.

Exactly what the Shevvingtons want.
They planned this.
They knew.
They're inside even now.
Laughing.

Chapter 8

She clung to a steel cable.

The mittens her mother had knit her were double layered: black with white angora stars. The yarn froze to the steel, and the leaping seawater soaked the mittens, freezing them into hand-shaped curls.

I was wrong, thought Christina Romney, her hands frozen to the bridge. It was not Dolly they were after. It was me.

The air from the ocean was so full of salt and snow that she could actually see the wind.

Christina was lashed to the bridge by the very mittens her mother had knitted her. She pulled her hands out of the mittens, leaving them frozen to the steel. "You won't win!" she shouted to the wind. "I am Christina of granite. So there!"

She fought the wind like a wrestler until she got off the Singing Bridge. She turned her back on the wind and half crawled up Breakneck Hill Road. She reached the huge green double doors of Schooner Inne. She found her key in her pocket. Her frozen blue fingers forced it into the lock. She opened the door, slipped in, and shut it behind her. The wall-paper was flocked and formal, put up by the sea captain of so long ago. But the air in the house was chilled, infected by the Shevvingtons.

Christina's throbbing heart did not supply enough energy for the climb to her room. I am old, thought Christina. Perhaps my hair is gray now, instead of silver and gold and chocolate.

She touched her hair, but all she felt was melting snow. I don't have the briefcase. I dropped it somewhere.

She stared at her empty hands. How, oh how could she have done this? Gone through such torture, only to have lost the documents — the proof?

She began crying.

She hung up her coat. She took off her sneakers and set them to dry over the heating vent. She peeled off her soaking socks. The ice that clung to them melted in her hands. She looked up the whirling stairs and the white banisters that blurred like a forest. The first flight was not so bad. Thick plush carpet softened the way for her frozen toes.

The second flight, bare and slippery wood, was cruel and unwelcoming. This is home? Christina Romney thought. This is where I live?

At the top of the stairs, out of the dark behind the balcony came a waft of white. White that swirled like snow or ghosts. Christina was enveloped in white.

She tried to scream, but the white smothered her.

"It's me, Anya," whispered the white. "Where

have you been, Chrissie? The Shevvingtons came up and checked your bed, and when they saw you weren't in it, they laughed and went back to their room. Where have you been? Are you all right?"

Anya's swirling lacy nightgown, like a bride's trousseau, folded around Christina. "You're freezing," Anya whispered. "Come, I'll get in bed with you. Body heat will help." They tiptoed to Christina's room. It was tiny and dark, with bare floors and cracked plaster. Christina had added flower pictures and her mother's vivid quilt and a little white rug, but the room stayed dark. There were times when Christina and The Dark were like best friends, huddled together under the covers. But tonight The Dark was laughing, ready to bring out its real friends, creatures of the shadows and the sea.

Anya peeled away Christina's soaking jeans and hung them to dry. The wind came through the electrical outlets in prong-shaped drafts. "I turned on the electric blanket after the Shevvingtons left," Anya whispered, "so the mattress would get hot for you."

Usually Christina hated the electric blanket. She wanted the layers of wool to weight her down. Now the hot blanket was hope and safety.

"There," said Anya, rubbing Christina's feet, "you're all right now." Under the covers, they wrapped their arms around each other until Christina stopped shivering.

"Anya?" said Christina.

"Mmmmm?"

"Are you back?"

"What do you mean, Chrissie? I've never been away. I've lived here for a long, long time."

"But — you waited up for me." Be sane again, Anya, pleaded Christina silently, like prayers. Be my friend, I need a friend, I need you on my side. And you're older than me. Oh, Anya, I want somebody older than me! When I was a little girl on the island, I always wanted to be the oldest. I wanted to be in charge and decide everything and run the show.

I was wrong, Anya. It's awful being the oldest.

Anya, be the oldest! Come back! I need you, Anya.

"I hardly ever sleep," Anya said. "I just lie there and listen to the sea. The sea keeps count, you know. It wants one of us. I don't mind if it's me. But I don't want it to be you."

She still isn't back, Christina thought. I can't tell her about tonight. I still don't have an ally. It isn't the sea who is the enemy.

Christina wanted to weep for Anya or for herself. But she was too tired. She slept.

Anya lay awake, her black hair draping the pillows. She dreamed no dreams; she thought no thoughts. She was empty.

In the morning, at breakfast, Christina clung to Anya. She thought that Mr. Shevvington was watching her more than usual and that Mrs. Shevvington bent closer than usual, but perhaps she was wrong. Mr. Shevvington's soul was hidden by his elegant clothing, and he stayed smooth and gleaming, no matter how dirty his deeds. Mrs. Shevvington's soul was hidden by a body so thick and solid it had no feminine curves whatsoever. Her little black eyes were holes in her flat face, and when she smiled her little yellow teeth lay in rows like corn on the cob.

They did not look as if they belonged together. Grown-ups were always startled when they first met Mr. Shevvington's wife, with her complexion like oatmeal. What does he see in her? they would whisper afterwards, for he was inspiring and she was a pudding.

Dolly sat, thin as a rag doll, in her chair next to Mrs. Shevvington. "I washed the windows in my bedroom again," she said, her voice high and trembly.

Salt spray from the whipping waves below the cliffs constantly turned the windows opaque. Christina loved the feathery scrawls of frost, but Dolly whimpered. "They close me up," she said fretfully to Christina. "They stitch me inside my room. They turn my room into the inside of a sleeping bag."

"Don't say that out loud," Christina whispered. "You must not let the Shevvingtons hear you say that."

But Dolly thought Christina was just being hard. She turned to Mr. Shevvington and told him, because he cared when a person was afraid of something. "Poor Dolly," he said. "You're afraid you might suffocate, aren't you?" He smiled.

Then he walked them to the front door, checking that everybody had a book bag and gym shoes.

"And there's another thing," said Dolly, although Christina was signaling her not to talk about it. "I don't like the balcony or the way the bathroom door opens onto the stairs. I don't even like the stairs. Please, may I have a bedroom on the second floor instead? Nobody ever stays in the guest rooms. Please, may I have a guest room? So I don't have to go all the way up to the third floor? I'm afraid I'll fall. At night I can't even go to the bathroom because I'm afraid I might trip over the railing." Dolly shivered with her fear of heights.

"You must learn to cope with your fears," said Mr. Shevvington.

"Why?" said Christina. "Why not just change bedrooms?"

Mr. Shevvington said that Christina did not want anybody but herself to be strong. That Christina approved of Dolly being weak and afraid. "That way you will always have a meek little follower," Mr. Shevvington said.

Christina would have stayed to argue, but Michael and Benj were running down the steps, heading for school. Today of all days, Christina did not want to be alone with a Shevvington. She dragged Dolly after the boys. At the bottom of Breakneck Hill, Dolly turned left for the elementary school. Christina walked in the boys' footsteps through the snow. How would she get through the school days now, knowing what lurked in those halls by night?

Michael and Benj threw snowballs at everything that moved.

Would she see a mound of snow the size of a briefcase?

Or had the giggling creature found it and put it back under the knee cavity of the principal's desk?

In English the essay topic had been "cozy spots." Christina had written about the thickets of blackberry canes on Burning Fog Isle, where she and Michael and Dolly and Benj used to play War. But Mrs. Shevvington chose fat, ugly Katy to read aloud.

" 'I like sitting under the hair dryer at the beauty parlor,' " Katy read. " 'It's a noisy, wheezing, hot-air world. I can't hear anybody's conversations. I read high-fashion magazines and think about being beautiful.' "

Gretch laughed viciously. "At least you can *think* about being beautiful, Katy," she said.

Katy withered and flushed.

Mrs. Shevvington smiled and said nothing. She passed out sets of vocabulary cards. Gretch took advantage of the movement in the room to whisper to Christina, "I'm having a slumber party this Saturday night. You could come this time. I wouldn't mind."

It took all Christina's control not to beat Gretchen black and blue with the vocabulary cards. "I'm afraid I'll be busy," she heard herself say. "I'm having a slumber party of my own."

She could not imagine what had made her say such a thing. The Shevvingtons would never let her have a friend spend the night.

And besides, did she really want the seventh grade to know how the island children lived?

The beautiful parlor downstairs with its black and gold Oriental furniture, furnished by the sea captain from his voyages to China, for his bride. They weren't allowed in there; they might soil something.

The magnificent dining room — nobody could approach that gleaming table; island children might rest their shoes on it.

The adorable guest rooms, with the frilly canopies on the four-poster beds. No, island children were confined to the kitchen, the ugly little back room with the black-and-white television, and their barren rooms on the third floor.

And did she want anybody to see Anya? Seventh-graders were cruel. They would poke fun at Anya, and Anya might be hurt.

Besides, nobody could have fun when Mr. or Mrs. Shevvington was around. It would be the worst slumber party in the history of junior high. Girls would telephone their mothers and ask to be brought home, they would hate it so much.

But all day long, Christina found herself inviting people to the slumber party she could not have.

Jenny was delighted to come. Joanne couldn't wait. Susan and Rebecca and Emily all wanted to come.

Christina found herself madly inviting everybody

she had ever met — everybody whose name she remembered — just so that Gretchen couldn't have them at her party.

What price am I going to pay for this? Christina thought.

Part of her was sick and wanted to run away to California.

The other part of her kept asking more and more girls to come to the party.

Chapter 9

I wish I were beautiful, Christina thought. She twined the silver locks with the gold, and then the gold with the brown. I'm interesting, she thought. I'm unusual. But I'm not beautiful.

She borrowed Anya's hot rollers to set her hair. She thought of poor, fat, ugly Katy, whose favorite cozy nook was the hair dryer at the beautician's.

Suddenly, critically, Anya said, "You have too much hair on each roller. Here. I'll do it for you."

It always surprised Christina when the old Anya surfaced, as if bits and pieces of her were floating around and latched occasionally onto things like hot rollers. Last night she was partly aware, Christina thought. She stayed up for me, warmed my feet. And now tonight she's partly here.

Perhaps the Shevvingtons had misjudged. They thought Anya was completely destroyed, but perhaps she was healing.

The Shevvingtons must not know, Christina thought. They must not see Anya coming back. Or they would go after her again. This time, like Val, they would get her put away.

When Anya gently took Christina's hair off the curlers, gone was the tangle that usually capped her head. Elegant, smooth waves fell past her shoulders and gleamed in the lamplight. She felt older and romantic: she was a woman now, not a mere seventh-grader.

"Me, too!" Dolly cried.

If Dolly sees changes in Anya, thought Christina, she will tell the Shevvingtons.

"Anya, fix my hair," Dolly ordered. Dolly unbraided her hair. The braid pattern stayed in the hair, as if she had been run over by tank treads.

"Leave it like that," suggested Christina.

Dolly looked annoyed. "Make me look older than Christina, Anya," Dolly said.

Anya fussed with Dolly's hair. She arranged it in long, soft loops, like a girl at the turn of the century, and fastened it with hidden bobby pins and one large glittering barrette.

Dolly's prettier than I am, Christina thought. I am granite, like the island. I am strong and tough. But I am not pretty.

For a strange, painful moment she yearned for prettiness more than anything on Earth. It hurt inside, crying out, Let me be pretty, too!

The telephone rang. Mrs. Shevvington answered downstairs, calling up, "It's for you, Christina. Do not stay too long on the phone unless it's homework. The telephone is not a toy. Do not abuse your telephone privileges."

Christina walked sedately down the three flights, because if she ran Mrs. Shevvington would punish her by not letting her take the phone call. "Hello?" she said cautiously. Mrs. Shevvington stood right next to her.

"Hi," said Jonah. He sounded breathless and eager, like somebody going Christmas shopping.

"Hi, Jonah." Her hair was as silver as stars, as golden as summer apples. She felt pretty.

Jonah said, "I had a nice time this afternoon."

She and Jonah had gone skating on the parking lot ice. They had raced, flinging insults and snowballs at each other. It had been loads of fun, but it had not been romantic. A phone call, though, that was romantic.

Mrs. Shevvington's little black eyes were hardly a foot away. "Page ninety-eight," Christina said. "First twenty examples."

Jonah said, "Chrissie. Is this code or is she listening?"

"Both," Chrissie said.

Jonah said, "Let me know what they say about having the slumber party, Chrissie. See if they'll let you have boys come, too. Now that would be fun."

He was flirting with her. She touched her hair, reminding herself she was an elegant woman with gleaming tresses. But Mrs. Shevvington laughed and walked away and Christina turned back into a pumpkin: seventh grade, dumb and young. "See you tomorrow," she said, which was not even conversation, let alone flirting.

It occurred to Christina that there might not be a price to pay for setting up a slumber party. At dinner when she asked for permission, the Shevvingtons would simply say, "Absolutely not. Twenty screaming, animal-like, seventh-grade girls in our perfect inn? Never."

Then at school, Christina would just say, "They wouldn't let me. You'll have to go to Gretch's after all. Too bad."

This began to sound rather nice. It would be the first time this year that Christina had not only gotten herself into trouble, but also out of it.

But to Christina's amazement, the Shevvingtons said, "What a grand idea! Why, Christina, that will be lovely. We'll have such fun! We'll play all kinds of games. We'll make popcorn balls and pull taffy. We'll play hide-and-seek all through the house. We'll draw lots to see which girls get which guest room. You must tell them to bring their very best robes and slippers. We'll have a midnight fashion show and drink hot chocolate before we retire to our suites, like English ladies."

Christina stared at them. They appeared to be serious.

Michael and Benj made faces, groaned, and clutched their throats. Junior-high girls, they announced, were the lowest creatures on earth. They would sleep at friends' houses, so they wouldn't see or help or clean up after this slumber party.

"Who is coming, Christina?" said Mr. Shevvington, his smile still resting on his face, as if he had borrowed it at the library and forgotten to return it.

She rattled off as many names as she could remember, hoping she was not off by more than five or ten

They made her invite Vicki and Gretchen.

"It's not nice to leave people out," Mr. Shevvington reproved Christina. "If you are going to invite all the others, you really must invite Vicki and Gretchen. Or you will cause hurt feelings." He turned to Mrs. Shevvington. "It's an uphill battle teaching Christina manners, isn't it?"

Mrs. Shevvington nodded sadly.

Michael and Benj did not listen; they had never been interested in good manners. Only sports, food, and cars.

Dolly frowned. "Christina," she said reproachfully. "And you said the Shevvingtons never did anything nice. They're being wonderful to you. Plus, you set up the party before you even asked permission. Chrissie, you owe them an apology."

Christina had planned to warn Dolly yet again: They'd like you to have an accident, Dolly. Then think how they could control you! Every minute and every muscle of you. So be careful. Be careful on stairs, and at the top of Breakneck Hill Road!

But now she was shaking with fury.

"What kinds of games will we play?" Dolly asked, bouncing around.

Christina nearly said, "*You* won't play any of them. I didn't invite *you*. You're only in *sixth*." But she didn't.

Mr. Shevvington stroked the silk scarf he had tied around his throat. He looked like a fashion ad from a Sunday paper. He smiled across the room at no one Christina could see. He said very softly, "A nice game for little girls is Murder. We'll all hide, and I'll choose the victim."

The next day after school Christina stood in the sun waiting for Jonah.

But it was Dolly who found her. Running up, braids swinging — and no books in her arms. Without books, she looked unattached, as if her tiny body might come loose from the earth and blow away in the wind. Christina could hardly remember seeing Dolly without something to read.

Dolly's pixie face puckered with tears. "Mr. Shevvington talked to the elementary school principal about my reading. They agreed that I am too sedentary."

"Too what?"

"I sit too much. They say I have to take dancing lessons. Every single day after school. At Miss Violet's." Dolly's legs and arms flapped like pages of a book. It was hard to imagine her learning graceful patterns for her feet. "I don't want to take dancing. I just want to read, Chrissie. Can't you talk them out of it for me, Chrissie?"

Christina had two fine daydreams. In the first, she ordered the Shevvingtons to let Dolly read books and be sedentary forever and they knelt and obeyed her. In the second, Christina was the dancer — clad in shimmering silver, leaping across the stage to wild applause.

"Walk with me to Miss Violet's?" begged Dolly.

They walked together, Dolly swinging Christina's hand. "Chrissie, what will I do?" Dolly cried. "I'll fall down. I won't be able to learn the steps. I won't get the rhythm right, I'll go in the wrong direction. Everybody will laugh at me."

Miss Violet's School of Dance was a pretty brick building with outside stairs that swooped: the sort of stairs a famous dancer would stand at the top of to receive photographers and journalists who wanted to interview her.

You could fall dancing, Christina thought. Is that what they want Dolly to do? "The Shevvingtons are making you take dancing on purpose," she said. "That's what the Shevvingtons are like."

Mr. Shevvington unfolded like a huge paper doll from a parked car next to Miss Violet's. "Christina," he said sadly. "Still fighting that sick and twisted jealousy, aren't you? We are doing this to help Dolly overcome her fear of failure, to build her frail body and fragile confidence. This is our gift to Dolly. And you, poor girl, are eaten up with jealousy." He patted Christina's shoulder. She wanted to bite him.

Dolly clasped both her hands in front of her, like a child in the nativity scene seeing an angel. "Oh, Mr. Shevvington!" she cried. "*You* paid for the lessons! You are so wonderful! I love you so much!" She turned to Christina. "You don't have to come in with me, Chrissie. Mr. Shevvington's here. I'll be fine now. You go skate in the parking lot. 'Bye."

Jonah and the boys had taken over the parking lot ice. They were speed skating: bent low, thrusting forward, circling as hard and fast as they could. All the little kids had been pushed away and were sitting sadly on the benches over by the tennis courts. All the girls who wanted to practice figure eights or spins had been knocked down enough times that they had given up and left. Christina laced on her skates and skated hard and fast. She pretended her skate blades were slicing Mr. Shevvington.

"Jonah," she said, skating even with him, "do you think I am sick and twisted?"

Jonah grinned. "Sure. That's why I like you. I'm drawn to sick and twisted people."

Jonah's legs were long. It didn't matter how determined Christina was; Jonah could cover more ground. Her muscles cried out for rest, but she disciplined herself, pretending it was the Olympics, her country's honor at stake.

What's really at stake, thought Christina, is being a friend to Dolly. How can I be Dolly's friend when she listens to Mr. Shevvington, not me?

Jonah pulled ahead. Two tenth-grade boys spun by Christina as easily as birds on the wing. Jonah called back over his shoulder, "Hey, Christina, you wanna come over to my house? Have something hot to drink? My toes are freezing off."

"Hot date!" shouted the tenth-graders. "What an invitation — his toes are freezing off! You gonna warm 'em up, Christina?" One of them swiped at Christina, knocking off her cap. Her hair spilled out, blowing in the relentless winter wind.

A true friend, Christina thought, is a person who

helps even when the friendship isn't close anymore. "You're jealous, aren't you?" she said. How nice to call somebody *else* jealous.

The wind separated the strands of her hair: silver and gold, chocolate laced. The tenth-grader grinned and slowed down. They skated in step: her right leg swirling across the ice in tempo with his, then left legs together and right again. When his hand reached toward her hair, Christina knew he was not going to yank it, the way seventh-grade boys would. "I love your hair," said the boy softly. "Silver and gold and brown. It's — "

Jonah skated between them.

The huge clumpy feet he tripped over in class were graceful in long, black, men's skates.

Jonah said firmly, "Leave it alone."

Jonah's mother acted as if Christina came every afternoon. They made hot chocolate in a big, friendly, messy kitchen, with Jonah's little sister swinging her legs from the counter and Jonah's little brother yelling because it was his turn to sort the laundry. They played Monopoly on the table, and Mrs. Bergeron hardly noticed when chocolate got spilled on a Community Chest. There were dripping winter boots and newspapers sliding off their stacks; school books tumbling into the unsorted laundry; and between Monopoly turns they all investigated the freezer for things to microwave.

It was like her own home, cluttered with love and talk.

Christina bit into a sugar cookie, and suddenly

she was so homesick she wanted to weep. She could actually taste home: a taste of crunchy sweetness, of cookies still hot from the oven.

Jonah walked Christina home because it had grown dark. She felt the way she might after Thanksgiving dinner: stuffed. But with friendship, instead of turkey. Jonah's mother had said to come back anytime.

Can I come back to live? she wanted to beg. Can I stay with you? I'll sleep in the hall, I'll sleep standing up — oh, please let me live here instead of at Schooner Inne! But of course she didn't. She said, "Thank you, I will."

And when Jonah said good-bye on the steps of the Schooner Inne, and she went inside all alone, it was truly a temperature change. The chill of loneliness lowered Christina's resistance. All her fears lived here, and none of her allies.

In the gloomy front hall, where the slender white railings twirled up and up toward the black cupola, she remembered her slumber party and the game of murder. In the dark, she thought, there will be an accident.

After all, little girls get silly. Would it be surprising if one toppled off the balcony onto her spine? The Shevvingtons would be absolved of all blame. People would feel sorry for them and bring casseroles and potted plants.

Chapter 10

Mrs. Shevvington rented a charming, antique maid's costume for Anya. It was a long, black cotton dress with a starched lacy white apron and cap. "That's sick," cried Christina. "You should make her wear school clothes and go back to school. Not dress her like a maid!"

"She's happy, Christina," said Michael irritably.

"I think she looks pretty neat," Benjamin added. This was amazing. Benj never expressed the slightest interest in girls or their looks.

Christina tried to explain her point to the Jayes. Benjamin, Michael, and Dolly Jaye frowned at Christina, an impenetrable family unit.

Mr. Shevvington said sadly, "Can't you rejoice when poor Anya has a moment of pleasure? Must you always keep happiness for yourself?" He put an arm around the trio of Jayes and the other arm over Anya's black shoulder.

Christina, the outsider, flushed.

Benj and Michael teased their little sister, told her to have fun, and dashed out before the guests arrived. The girls came in a clump, giggling and pushing. Including Gretchen and Vicki; Katy, who never got invited anywhere; and Dolly, who wasn't in seventh grade at all.

The first game Mrs. Shevvington organized was Pin the Tail On The Donkey.

"Mrs. Shevvington," protested Gretch, laughing. "Nobody's played that since they were little. That's a baby game."

"Ah," said Mrs. Shevvington, "but we need to be in a certain order, and however well you do in *this* game is the order in which you will enter the second game."

Christina was not surprised when Gretch won, Dolly came in second, and Vicki third. She was not surprised when Mrs. Shevvington lined up the girls in order of winning, so that fat Katy was marked the loser, last in line, while Dolly stood up front, between Gretch and Vicki.

"Everybody pair up now!" ordered Mrs. Shevvington. "Next game is in pairs!"

"I get to play with Gretchen!" cried Dolly joyfully. She beamed at Gretchen, who said to her, "I love your red hair, Dolly. And your name! It's so sweet. You are sort of a dolly." Gretchen and Dolly held hands and talked about dancing class.

Christina stood with Katy. We're the losers, she thought.

She gave Mrs. Shevvington the dirtiest look she could. Mrs. Shevvington said loudly, "Why, Christina! As hostess I expect you to make sure *every* guest has a good time. Are you complaining about your partner?"

Poor Katy bit her lips and stumbled. Her plain face turned splotchy red and her eyes welled up with unshed tears.

Dinner was wonderful: huge platters of lasagna, soft hot rolls with sweet butter, and salad for greenery. "Nobody is actually required to eat any salad, of course," said Mr. Shevvington, smiling down at the girls, "because this is a fun time, and we want even vegetable haters to have fun all night long." The girls applauded Mr. Shevvington, who bowed and escorted each girl into the formal dining room. During dinner Mr. Shevvington told wonderful scary stories about the sea captain who built the house and his bride, who flung herself to a horrible death from the cupola of this very house, exactly one hundred years before. "Tonight, when it's dark," he whispered, "I'll tell you what happened to the sea captain after his wife vanished in the terrible tides of Candle Cove."

Gretch and Vicki screamed with delight. "Horror stories!" shouted Vicki. "I love them."

"You are one," muttered Katy.

Christina laughed for the first time that night. Katy had potential.

After supper they popped popcorn and made caramel popcorn balls. They sang crazy songs — the sort with twenty verses you learn in summer camp. Mrs. Shevvington had them play Charades of brand names. Gretch did Wrangler jeans; Vicki got Coca-

Cola; Dolly got Burger King. Mrs. Shevvington explained that Christina would go last, because the guests always came ahead of the hostess. Then, when it was finally Christina's turn and she was aching to act, Mrs. Shevvington said everybody was bored now, and they would do something else.

Mr. Shevvington looked across the popcorn at his wife. Mrs. Shevvington looked back. Their smiles seemed to fit in midair like a key and a lock. Their eyes slid around the room and landed on Dolly. Dolly was sitting between Gretch and Vicki. Vicki was feeding Dolly a popcorn ball, Vicki holding it, Dolly nibbling. Gretch talked about Dolly as if she really *were* a doll. "Isn't she adorable?" giggled Gretch.

"She's so sweet," agreed Vicki, stroking Dolly's braids as though she had just purchased Dolly in a department store.

Dolly preened.

"We're going to play," said Mr. Shevvington softly. *"Murder."*

The girls all screamed joyfully.

"Now you must listen to the rules very carefully. Especially the first one. This is a big house and a scary one. You must not go into the cellar. Is that absolutely clear? Everybody repeat the promise. 'I will not go into the cellar.' "

They all promised.

There is something down there, Christina thought. They don't mind if I am trapped by the thing. They don't mind if it comes and goes from the school and the cellar. But they mind if people like Gretch and Vicki find out.

"Next rule," said Mrs. Shevvington. Her eyes never left Dolly. She was smiling, her little corn teeth lying between her thin lips. "You will all hide in pairs." She was breathing heavily, excited about things to come.

Christina thought how the stairs narrowed on the third floor and the balcony tilted. "If we hide in pairs," Christina shouted, "I want to be Dolly's partner."

"No way," said Gretch, irked. "She belongs to me."

"I'm with Gretchen," Dolly agreed. "You stay with Katy, Christina."

Katy hung her head. "You don't have to stay with me, Christina," she murmured. "You can find somebody else."

Mrs. Shevvington looked at Christina. Every girl at the party could read that expression. Really, Christina — can't you be nice to that poor, ugly, little fat girl for one evening?

They've won a round, Christina thought. They're making me look like the bad guy when *they're* the bad guys. "They'll never find *us*, Katy," said Christina. "I know all the best spots in the house. Stick with me! We'll get that Murderer." She lifted her chin, staring into Mr. Shevvington's eyes, blue tonight. But Mr. Shevvington looked youthful and innocent, as if all he had in mind was a silly game in a silly house with silly girls.

But Mrs. Shevvington's lips curled, like an animal preparing to eat raw meat. It's her, Christina thought. She's the dangerous one.

Mr. Shevvington explained the complex rules of Murder. They had to keep on the move, avoid being killed, and yet find out who the killer was. They had to stay with their partners. They could not get in large groups.

Mr. Shevvington put a cassette into the stereo and flipped the switch, which played the music in every room. The slithering strings of violins trembled in the air like old ghosts.

Mrs. Shevvington turned out the lights.

The guests scattered through the house, banging their shins on furniture. The stairs creaked as they dashed up and down. Crazy giggles ricocheted like bullets.

In the dark, Christina could watch nobody. Katy held so tight to her hand Christina thought her bones might break.

Wherever it would happen, it would happen up high in the mansion. So Christina dragged Katy up the first flight of stairs and then up the second. "I don't wanna be up here," Katy wailed. "It's too scary up here."

"Sssssshhh," Christina said.

"Let's hide under the dining-room table, Chrissie," Katy whispered.

"Shut up," Christina hissed.

The house began to fill with screams as heavy hands and cold fingers unexpectedly touched a player in the dark.

Then the girls began screaming just for the fun of it. Somebody turned the eerie violins up higher.

Anya began screaming for real: the ghastly high scream Christina remembered so well. Once, screaming like that, Anya had tried to step out the third-floor window, seeing fire where there was only fog.

Anya screamed like an animal. Christina imagined Anya frozen with fear in the dark. Was Anya to be the victim, not Dolly? Had the Shevvingtons seen Anya's improvement after all? Was playing with Dolly just intended to confuse Christina?

"Chrissie! Chrissie! Chrissie, where are you?" screamed Anya.

Once Anya's fears had pulled her to the edge of the cliffs. Now — during the slumber party — was something pushing her instead?

"I'm coming, Anya!" She abandoned Katy, racing in the blackness down the stairs. "Stand still, Anya, so I can find you. It's all right, it's just a game; don't be afraid."

"Christina, shut up!" Gretch yelled from some other location. "You're ruining the game. Let her scream. It's wonderful. She has the best scream of all."

Christina felt her way into the kitchen, to the source of the screams. "I'm here, Anya." Christina edged forward. A white splotch appeared in the dark. Anya was only inches away. Christina reached for the lace trim on the apron.

Too late, Christina heard the giggle.

She caught desperately at the wall, at chairs, at

anything — but there was nothing to hold.

The giggle turned into a groan.

The white vanished. The dark turned into a black hole.

And it was Christina who fell. Down the cellar stairs. Hitting the steps, hitting the rail, hitting the stone floor.

Down into the waiting giggle.

Chapter 11

Morning sun glittered on new-fallen snow.

The snow had blown into wonderful drifts, like whorls on top of a lemon meringue pie.

Christina's knees hurt. She stumbled to school.

Jonah came running to meet her. "What happened, Christina?" he asked. "I know Mondays are pretty bad — but limping?"

Gretch and Vicki bounded up. "We had the best slumber party ever!" cried Gretch. "They live in the most wonderful house. You should just see all the treasures. Mr. and Mrs. Shevvington are so terrific to those island children. We should all be so lucky. We had the best food and the best fun. I got to sleep in a bed with its own little stepstool because the mattress was so high: me and Dolly and Vicki. It was perfect."

"I was asking about Christina's limp," Jonah said, turning his back on Gretch.

Gretch and Vicki threw back their heads and howled with laughter. "When we played Murder, Mr. Shevvington said the only rule was, 'Don't go near the cellar.' So who goes into the cellar? Christina!"

Jonah knew Christina's cellar stories. He knew she would never have gone into the cellar again in her life. Jonah put a brotherly arm around her and said, "Chrissie, are you all right?"

It was comfort, not romance, but Vicki and Gretch were furious with jealousy. "She just skinned her knees," said Vicki, brushing it off. "Anyhow it was her own fault. She opened the bolt on the cellar door herself."

"I did not!" cried Christina. "The door was wide open when I got there! I was trying to save Anya."

"Save Anya?" they repeated. Vicki and Gretch fell on each other, laughing. "Christina, it was a game. Nobody needed saving. We were all having a good time screaming. Anya's elevator doesn't go all the way to the top anyhow, you know. Her mind melted last year. Only the world's best shrink could save her now."

Christina was trembling. "Somebody opened the cellar door on purpose, Jonah."

"Oh, right," Vicki said. "You're always trying to blame somebody, Christina Romney. You tell people you have this terrible life, but it's all lies. The Shevvingtons are fabulous. And no matter how rotten you are to your guests, like poor Katy, and no matter how demanding you are and how you try to force Dolly into stuff — the Shevvingtons forgive you and try to help you. Now you're even trying to blame somebody else because you went and opened

the cellar door, which you're not allowed to do."
They flounced away.

Jonah asked, "Did you fall, Chrissie? Or were you pushed?"

He believes me, Christina thought.

At the party not even Anya had believed her!

She had felt the thing's fingers on her skin. They were cold, and they stank of the sea. It was like being stroked by a fish.

But the crash of her body on the stairs had saved her. The noise brought Katy, Jennie, Amanda, and Linda running. The slimy fingers retreated to the shadows in the back of the cellar. Christina lay in a crumpled pile at the bottom of the rickety stairs.

Every guest at the party gathered in the door to tell her what an idiot she was, falling down the steps in her own house.

"Jonah," Christina whispered now. "It was there. It's real. It lives. It touched me." Everything granite in Christina disintegrated. She put her arms around Jonah, hung her troubles around his neck, and wept.

But they were too young, and it was too soon. Jonah was appalled. His friends would see; it was too intimate; they were in public; what was she doing? He forgot the cellar and the giggle and the Shevvingtons and pulled back, trying to disassociate himself from all that affection and need. "I — um — I'll see you in — uh — class," he said desperately. "And — I'm busy this afternoon — I — I hope your knees are okay." And he fled.

Christina snapped an icicle off the row that lined the school and threw it like a tiny javelin into a drift of snow. When she turned around, Jonah, Vicki, and Gretchen had disappeared. Christina stood alone.

It was seventeen below. The cold chewed her fingers. By the time the last warning bell rang and she forced herself into the building, her fingers were stiff and blue.

In homeroom they had to fill out forms for state-wide testing, which would take place later in the month. When she tried to write, the letters came out looking like Egyptian hieroglyphics. My mind feels like that, thought Christina. Meaningless curves and twitches.

The day passed in a similar fashion, twitching and curving.

Who was the next victim of the Shevvingtons? Did they want Dolly or Anya or Christina? Who was the thing? What did *he* want?

"The essay," said Mrs. Shevvington in English class, "is to write a contemporary parallel of a fairy tale. I will assign the fairy tale. Jonah, for example, will have *The Little Red Hen*. In this story, of course, no farm animal will help the little red hen raise the wheat or grind the flour, but when the loaves are baked, they all want to eat it. The moral, of course, is that if you want to enjoy the results you must put in the work first."

Mrs. Shevvington circled the room. She stopped at Katy's desk and smiled at Katy. Christina knew that smile. She tried to think how to stand between fat, ugly Katy and that smile, but no solution came to her. "I'm hoping to make each story match the student," Mrs. Shevvington said to the class. "That way it will be more fun."

Fun for whom? wondered Christina.

Katy must have had the same thought. She gathered herself, ready for the blows.

"You, Katy," said Mrs. Shevvington, the smile growing like a blister on her skin, "will do the story of the ugly duckling."

Katy went so white the pimples stood out on her face like a rash.

Gretchen and Vicki giggled.

Mrs. Shevvington turned to Christina.

Die, you hateful woman, Christina thought, willing Mrs. Shevvington to have a heart attack.

Mrs. Shevvington simply smiled wider. "Christina, you will update the story of the boy who cried wolf." Her little teeth lay between her thin lips like pellets from an air gun. "Of course in the new version, it will be the *girl* who cried wolf."

The class had expected something that would make Christina cry. This was nothing. They were disappointed.

But Christina understood. The message was very clear.

You may scream for help all you want, Christina, my dear. Nobody will believe you. And then, when you really need help, when the screams are loud and real — no one will come, Christina of the Isle. You are alone.

Chapter 12

It used to be that the ending of school was a clock thing: the big hand on twelve and the little hand on three. But now the close of school was a physical relief of body and soul. I'm out. It's over for a while.

"Everybody's coming over to my house," said Jonah. "Want to come, Chrissie?"

Benjamin bounded by, headed for his garage job. Suddenly it struck Christina that Benj was still in high school, though he had always planned to quit at sixteen.

How clever the Shevvingtons were. Benjamin and Michael Jaye were the balance. If anybody noticed that right after Anya fell apart, Dolly developed strange fears and Christina behaved oddly — why, Mr. Shevvington could point out how successfully he had kept this fine young lobsterman in school.

"Yes, I'm coming," said Christina.

Across the school yard Dolly flew, her new jeans so long that the rolled cuffs made pale blue saucers around her skinny ankles. "Chrissie?" she called.

Her voice was as thin as a snow flurry.

Traitor, thought Christina. Her eyes stung with hot tears that Dolly should have joined up with Gretchen and Vicki and the Shevvingtons.

"Chrissie, don't be mad."

Christina turned her back on Dolly to go with Jonah.

"Chrissie, I need you," Dolly said.

They were Christina Romney's words. Her love of helping people was as strong as her love of life itself.

"Chrissie, dancing class is so scary. I'm in the advanced class, but I'm not as good as the advanced girls. I have to dance alone, and they laugh at me. I've begged the Shevvingtons, but they won't let me drop out. They say it's good for me to face some competition for a change. They say on the island we didn't know anything about the real world." Her pixie face was turned up into Christina's, waiting for Christina to solve her problem.

A very heavy hand landed on Christina's shoulder. Mrs. Shevvington had materialized. Her candle-stub fingers pressed painfully between the bones of Christina's shoulder, and then attached themselves to Dolly's head. "You must try your very best," said Mrs. Shevvington to Dolly.

Dolly's tiny diamond-shaped faced was skewed by grief. "My best," said Dolly, "isn't good enough."

The Shevvingtons do not destroy by any evil of our times, thought Christina. Not by drugs, not by alcohol. But by an evil as ancient as time: cutting

away strength, beauty, confidence, friendship —
until there is nothing left, just a shell.

"Dolly, that's wonderful!" cried Mrs. Shevvington. "I'm so proud of you! If you get nothing else
out of dancing class, you've learned a very important lesson. Sometimes your best just isn't enough,
and you have to accept being ordinary. You island
girls oft times have difficulty admitting your ordi-
nariness. You are so sure you are special."

Dolly's red hair seemed duller, her fair skin wan-
ner, her bright eyes dimmer.

Mrs. Shevvington smiled. "You run along to your
class now, Dolly."

Dolly obeyed instantly, like a slave, like —
like Anya.

In Jonah's yard the snow was thigh high. Jonah
brought out snow shovels and brooms. The children
shoveled paths. He had drawn a maze on paper and
was shouting directions, but nobody listened, shoveling joyfully at their own routes. The paths interlocked and dead-ended. White walls of shoveled
snow grew higher and higher, until only the fluffy
pompons on their ski caps showed above the passage
walls.

Above their heads, the sun set in a sky the color
of frostbite. Pink channels appeared in the heavens
as if dead children frolicked there in a maze of pearl.

Jonah's mother leaned out the back door. "Getting late, kids!" she called. "All you who have to be
home before dark, set out now!"

Christina hoped Jonah would offer to walk her

home, but he was too busy finishing the maze. When she called good-bye, he hardly glanced up.

Don't cry, Christina told herself. You had a great afternoon. Shoveling snow with your friends. Maybe I want too much. Maybe I have to learn to enjoy less instead of craving more.

She did not want to go back to Schooner Inne.

From Jonah's she went the long way, staring at front doors, wishing she could board with anybody but the Shevvingtons. She passed a phone booth and thought of telephoning her mother and saying, Mommy come get me. Come understand. She passed the laundromat, where Anya presumably stood in the hot, humid air, emptying detergent into washers. She went to the harbor, where the few boats in the water were crusted with ice.

High above her on the opposite cliff loomed Schooner Inne, cold and white as ice. A wisp of smoke drifted up from behind the roof of Schooner Inne. Christina could not remember the Shevvingtons lighting a fire before. Christina wanted to warm her blue fingers at that fire and stare into the flames, a comfort as old as mankind.

She ran up Breakneck Hill.

Mr. Shevvington opened the door for her. He did not speak. His face was hard and cold as the winter sky. Gripping her shoulders, he yanked Christina through the long hall with its flocked emerald paper and the staircase rising like a wedding cake. Michael and Benj were standing there; she stumbled past, her feet catching on their big winter boots, and they did nothing. They might have been framed photographs on the wall. Dolly was on the second step, making a mustache of her braids, staring at Christina.

Mr. Shevvington pushed her ahead of him, into the kitchen. For a moment she thought he was going to lock her in the cellar, and she came close to screaming. But he opened the back door. He's throwing me out, thought Christina, numb with confusion.

Mr. Shevvington held Christina in front of him as if preparing her for a firing squad. She felt smaller than Dolly: little-girl weak.

"Look at that!" said Mr. Shevvington through gritted teeth.

Spirals of fire shot like gold silk into the air.

A bonfire in the snow.

"You put your entire wardrobe on that fire!" said Mr. Shevvington. "All your clothes, Christina. You set fire to them."

"She warned us," said Mrs. Shevvington. "We have to admit that. She even wrote an essay and insisted on reading it aloud to the class, detailing how she would dispose of all her possessions in a fire."

"I didn't, either," cried Christina. "You made me read that out loud. You know I didn't really mean it. It was your assignment."

"It was your January daydream," said Mrs. Shevvington. She jabbed a poker into the fire. In the ashes Christina recognized her snowflake sweater. It *is* my clothing, she thought. "I would never do that. I was at Jonah's all afternoon," she said desperately.

"On the contrary, Christina. You left Jonah's house an hour ago. I telephoned his mother. You sneaked into Schooner Inne, got your wardrobe, found matches and a can of oil from the cellar you so love to explore, and set this fire. Then you ran away to the harbor so you could return later and pretend to be innocent."

Mr. Shevvington shoveled snow to smother the fire. It hissed.

The loss of her clothing became real. She had nothing to wear. The presents of Christmas, only a month ago: gone. Burned. Her mother's hand-knit sweaters. The memories of their shopping together in the distant city for school clothes.

Mr. Shevvington took Christina's shoulder, roughly hauling her back into the kitchen.

What will my mother say? Christina thought. Tears spilled from her eyes, hit her cold hands, and spattered on the floor.

She looked at Michael, whom she had loved the first twelve years of her life and wanted to marry, so they could live happily ever after on the island. Michael avoided her eyes.

She looked at Benj, who had been the older brother for them all: organized the games, been the referee, the baby-sitter, or sandwich maker. Benj stared at the ceiling.

She looked at Dolly, and Dolly looked steadily back. "Chrissie," she said. "Mrs. Shevvington explained to me how jealous you are because I have new clothes and you don't. Because I have dancing lessons and you don't. Because I'm happy here and you aren't. If I had known you were going to start setting fires to get attention, Chrissie, I — "

"I did not!" cried Christina. "How could you think that, Dolly? You know I would never do a thing like that."

Dolly frowned. "But Christina," she said patiently, "the Shevvingtons said so." Dolly, Michael, and Benjamin Jaye nodded in unison. *The Shevvingtons said so.*

"That doesn't mean it's true," Christina whispered.

Dolly, Michael, and Benj looked at her reproachfully. The room echoed with their thoughts. *The Shevvingtons said so.*

Christina sat down before she fell over. "Where's Anya?" she said. Her mouth felt thick, as if the dentist had just given her a shot before filling a cavity.

"She's resting," said Mrs. Shevvington sharply. "You are not to disturb her. Naturally, she is very frightened by this. You know how fragile Anya is, Christina. No matter how selfish you are, no matter how determined to spoil things and terrify others, I truly thought you had enough concern for Anya to protect her. Clearly I was wrong. You will do anything for attention."

Mr. and Mrs. Shevvington telephoned Christina's parents.

They gave their version of the fire first.

How clever they were. "Of course you tried so hard," said Mrs. Shevvington sympathetically. "It's terribly difficult to deal with an adolescent. How could you have known you were spoiling Christina so badly in your effort to give her a good life?"

Christina wanted to rip the telephone out of their hands, but she restrained herself. It would not help.

"Christina in her terrible jealousy," said Mrs. Shevvington in the gentlest voice in the world, "was forced to extremes to get attention. Her mental and emotional state is very unfortunate. I'm so sad about it, Mrs. Romney. We want you to know that Mr. Shevvington and I will help you in every way. When families are hit by tragedies like this, they must be brave."

Christina touched her hair. Sometimes she could actually feel its colors — the silver and gold like ribbons of honor spun through the brown. Tonight she could feel nothing. She was running out of courage.

"Christina needs serious professional help," said Mr. Shevvington when it was his turn. How soft his voice was. Velvet.

This is how they finished Val off, thought Christina. They got her parents to put her in a mental institution. *Would my parents abandon me like that?*

Mrs. Shevvington handed Christina the telephone. The little black holes in the middle of her eyes looked like the black hole of the cellar.

"I'd like to speak to my parents privately, please," said Christina. She was reaching bottom.

315

If she did, the Shevvingtons would win. She imagined them going into her bedroom, emptying her bureau drawers, taking blouses off hangers, keeping Michael and Benj and Dolly away from windows. Setting that fire.

I know the truth, she thought, but that doesn't matter. The truth by itself is nothing. You have to be able to convince other people or it doesn't count. Christina took a deep breath. "Mommy?" she said. "Daddy? It isn't true. They're making it up."

Her mother was sobbing. The sobs continued all through Christina's talking. Her father was breathing deeply, as if he were in a tennis match. "Are they making it up, Chrissie?" said her father sadly. "There was a fire, wasn't there? And your clothing on it?"

"Daddy, I didn't put it there! The Shevvingtons did! It's part of a plot they have."

"Oh, dear God," said her mother, who never swore, who would only say that as a prayer. "Mr. Shevvington is right. That is true paranoia. Believing you are surrounded by evil plots! Chrissie, darling. Mommy loves you, do you believe that?"

"Yes, I believe it!" cried Christina. "I always believe you! It's your turn to believe me. That essay was an assignment. But it gave them a clue about how to get me. I know Mr. Shevvington is the high-school principal, but he's the one who is insane. Just because you're a teacher doesn't mean you're a good person. Don't you remember what happened to Anya? It's part of their plan. I'm next, you see!"

She turned to her audience at the Inne, to see

316

the effect of her speech on them. Benj and Michael looked incredibly sad. Benj — strong, tough Benj — had tears in his eyes.

It has worked, thought Christina. They think I'm crazy. This is how it worked with Val. I never knew how they pulled it off, but when you are the authority, it's easy.

Mrs. Shevvington's silver tongue had done its evil work.

To every protest Christina made, her parents replied, *But the Shevvingtons said so.* "Mommy," said Christina over and over again, "Mommy, believe me." But her mother did not.

Chapter 13

Several years before Michael and Benj had been fascinated by torture. They loved reading about the gruesome things man had done to man. Michael's favorite torture was Assyrian: the warriors slowly slit their prisoners' skin away. Benj's favorite was from Merrie Olde Englande, where they would chain the prisoner to a rock by the sea and let the tide rise up to drown him inch by inch.

As the whole seventh grade shunned her (that creepy girl from that creepy island, setting fire to her own clothes) she wondered which was more horrible. Physical torture or psychological?

There was only one day of school before her parents' arrival on the mainland. It lasted as long as the thirteen years of her life.

Only Jonah stuck by her — and for that, nobody would associate with him either. "What really happened?" Gretch asked viciously in the cafeteria.

"The Shevvingtons did it," Christina said. The teacher on cafeteria duty was shocked; Christina could already hear the report on her insanity.

"They're grown-ups," Gretchen said. "They wouldn't set fire to your clothes. It's sick."

Christina imagined her parents' visit. They'd take her shopping (with money they could not spare) for a new, plain, serviceable wardrobe. Three pairs of Brand X jeans, socks that came six in a plastic package. Even the clothes would be a punishment. "The Shevvingtons are sick," said Christina.

But of course nobody accepted this. They all loved the Shevvingtons.

Only Katy, whom Mrs. Shevvington routinely whipped, and Robbie, who had lost his sister Val, believed. But Katy and Robbie were Nobody. To be believed, you had to have the support of the Somebodies.

"Maybe Anya did it," said Katy, trying to find an acceptable "out" for Christina.

The children and teacher considered this and were willing to believe it.

If I let them blame Anya, thought Christina, I will be safe. I will have friends again. Nobody will get me "professional help" like Val.

How she wanted to blame Anya. Why not use Anya for that? What good was Anya anyway? She could hardly even keep a job folding clothes.

But if I let them blame Anya, thought Christina, I will be even more evil than the Shevvingtons. She straightened, knowing she would never have a friend again. Maybe not even Jonah. "It was the Shevvingtons," she said. "Anya would never do that."

They stepped back from her. Gretchen chewed

on a ribbon of her thin hair. "If it wasn't Anya," said Gretch, smiling, "then . . . it was you."

In the middle of science came a summons for Christina to go to the office to see Mr. Shevvington. The class snickered. "Here it comes," they said. "He'll lock you up, Chrissie. You'll have shrinks from here to Texas."

Cheeks scarlet, heart ice, Christina stood up and walked alone to the principal's office. The metal lockers on each side of the hall were like prison doors, opening and slamming, row on row. What was it like for Val? Was Val scared all the time? Did Val whimper and beg? Did Val even know?

Mr. Shevvington was wearing a charcoal suit with gray pinstripes, a vest, and a crimson tie. He looked like a diplomat on his way to catch a plane somewhere important. The secretaries at their desks and two mothers waiting in the office looked at him with adoration.

"Christina, dear," he said. "We need to have a little chat about counseling." He sounded so caring. The secretaries and the mothers smiled, happy that he loved the strange, sick little island girl.

Christina said nothing. The mothers were Vicki's and Gretchen's mothers. He had brought her down here on purpose to display her to them!

Mr. Shevvington hugged her. She wanted to throw up. But if she showed how she felt, it would be a mark against her, not him. So she pretended to be comfortable. "I want to be sure you aren't upset or anxious, Chrissie, honey."

They beamed at his understanding support of a little girl.

"Chrissie, sweetie," said Mr. Shevvington, ruffling her hair.

"Don't call me Chrissie," she said hotly. She flattened her hair back down the way it belonged. She took three steps away and glared at him. "I am not anxious. I do not intend to have counseling."

The mothers looked at her reprovingly. The secretaries exchanged resigned shrugs.

Mr. Shevvington coaxed, "I bought a new rock tape I know you'll enjoy."

"No, thank you," Christina said. "I have to get back to class." She lifted her chin and exited. She was so filled with fury she paused right outside the office, leaning against the wall, wanting to go back and slug him.

The conversation continued, and she heard it perfectly.

"Ungrateful little thing, isn't she, Mr. Shevvington?" said Vicki's mother. "It's so generous of you to take care of these island children. We all have the greatest respect for you and Mrs. Shevvington, putting up with their shenanigans. I know Michael Jaye is an asset to the basketball team, but the *rest* of them! Frightening little monsters!"

"That Anya practically threw her boyfriend off the cliff last fall. Why, Blake's parents had to ship him off to boarding school to keep him safe," said Gretch's mother. "And this Christina child! You should hear the stories my daughter brings home about Christina."

"That hair's weird, don't you think?" said a secretary. "Those three colors, like a painted flag? She's stained. *Marked*."

Christina could hardly breathe from shame and rage.

She remembered the September morning when she and Anya, Michael, and Benj had stood among the tourists on Frankie's boat, headed for the mainland and the first day of school. The tourists had whispered about Christina's three-colored hair and Anya's chalk-white countenance. *"They look like ancient island princesses. Marked out for sacrifice. Sent away for the sake of the islanders, to be given to the sea."*

Had it been a prophecy? Was it coming true?

But Mr. Shevvington laughed. "Now, ladies. Christina is a difficult child, but she chooses to be. It is not a result of her unattractive hair."

Christina almost put her fist through the cement block wall. I have beautiful hair!

"You must love teaching," one mother said to Mr. Shevvington.

"Yes, indeed. I think of each class as a zoo." He laughed. "Twenty-six to a cage."

We are animals to the Shevvingtons, thought Christina.

The mothers matched chuckle with chuckle.

"Mrs. Shevvington and I are very fond of the island children, for all their flaws," said Mr. Shevvington. "We're taking them all skiing over the next three-day weekend. You know how isolated those island children are. Not one of them has ever been on skis. Isn't that amazing? In Maine? We're trying to broaden their horizons a little bit."

"Mr. Shevvington, how generous of you! Downhill skiing? Lift passes, ski rentals, ski lodges, and everything?"

"Of course," said Mr. Shevvington.

Christina could actually *hear* his smile. It had a stretched, false sound.

"Little Dolly Jaye has a fear of heights," Mr. Shevvington said lovingly. "I thought we would cure her of it in the most delightful way. We've bought her a darling little ski outfit. I can hardly wait to see Dolly going down the slopes at full speed, all her fears behind her."

And what accident, Christina thought, do you want her to have in front of you?

She might never have a friend again, but she still had a mother and father. Her parents' visit was wonderful. They made no mention of the fire, the weeping phone calls, or the expense of new clothes.

Refusing the Shevvingtons' offer of a guest room at Schooner Inne, Mr. and Mrs. Romney drove to Boston to a huge city hotel. Christina sat squashed in the front seat between her parents, her father's hand on her knee, her mother's kisses on her cheek.

They went to the Children's Museum and the Science Museum; they all played the strange games and tests at the Computer Museum. They hiked the historic walks and talked of Paul Revere and John Hancock.

At night they sat in an enormous lounge, where

the pianist played long, slow, soothing pieces, and a waiter in black tails brought trays of steaming hot snacks.

Her mother and father told the island gossip — who was mad at whom, who was late paying the oil bill, whose kids were shaping up to be good at basketball. After supper they went to a late movie she had yearned to see but the Shevvingtons had said was too "mature" for her.

"It wasn't very mature," said Christina afterward. "Just violent."

When they went shopping, instead of the plain sweater Christina had expected, they found two lovely shaker knits: one peach, one so green and foresty that Christina knew Dolly would want to borrow it. Her father found a sweatsuit of bright yellow with orange parrots floating among lime green leaves. It made her feel safe as summer and lemonade.

Her father gave her more spending money than she had ever had at one time, all in new, crisp one-dollar bills, so she felt like an executive, with a real wad of money. "I like that word, *wad*," she told her father. They measured the bills across, and it was really nice and thick and waddy.

Christina knew she was safe. It was time to tell the truth. "We have to sort out what's been happening at Schooner Inne," said Christina. She thought, They will rescue me somehow. And Dolly and Anya. I won't need the proof in the briefcase, just my own mother and father. I should have known that all along.

"Chrissie," said her parents. "No matter what happens, we will stand by you."

Ice touched Christina's heart. "What happened was something Mr. and Mrs. Shevvington did," she said.

They looked at her sadly. "Christina, at some point a person must take responsibility for her own actions. You cannot blame the Shevvingtons for Anya's mental collapse. You cannot blame the Shevvingtons that Dolly is afraid of heights or doing poorly in dancing class. And sweetie, you cannot blame the Shevvingtons for your own uncontrollable rages."

Christina could not believe this! All their cuddling and shopping meant nothing! They were on the Shevvington's side! They too, like Michael and Benj and Dolly, thought if the Shevvingtons said so, then it was so. "If somebody accused *you* of bad things," she cried, "I would know they were lying, no matter how much proof there was."

Her parents talked gently of counseling, of telephoning every single night to keep in touch, no matter what the cost of the calls out to sea. Their talk was like the sea itself, lapping away at the shore.

Her father wiped away her tears with the flat of his big, thick thumbs, and her mother rocked her. "Try to stay calm, darling. See if you can last until vacation. If it's still bad, I'll rent an apartment in the village, and we'll live together."

Christina wanted to scream *Yes, yes, yes, do that!*

But her mother and father would be separated.

He on the island, she on shore. She would have to close down the tiny restaurant that supported them through the winter. They would have to admit to the islanders, as Anya's parents had before them, that her daughter could not survive on the mainland. They had splurged on this lovely weekend as a way of saying, We love you. They would also pay a second rent to say, We love you.

But it was Christina's task to say, No, I'm fine, don't worry about it, it'll all work out. So she said it. "No, I'm fine now," she told her parents. She hated her words. They sounded like an admission that she had burned her clothes. But some of the lines on her father's face smoothed away, and her mother's cheeks seemed pinker. So Christina did not say to them, the Shevvingtons are going to take us to a ski resort! They are going to get Dolly there! Instead she said softly, "Don't worry about it."

Now more than ever, what the Shevvingtons had planned must be stopped. For her own sake . . . for Dolly . . . for Anya . . . for her mother and father.

Chapter 14

In English, an amazing thing happened. Mrs. Shevvington picked on Gretchen. This had never happened before.

The essay was to be about the most precious possession in your household — perhaps a baby photograph or an old dish of a grandmother's, a cherished wedding present. Mrs. Shevvington had Gretchen read aloud.

"The most precious thing in my house," read Gretchen proudly, "is my private telephone line." She knew she was the only person in the seventh grade with her own phone book listing. "I have three different phones I can plug into the jack. My favorite is an Elvis phone. It — "

"I beg your pardon," said Mrs. Shevvington, sparse eyebrows raised contemptuously. "Are you saying that *the sound of your own voice* is your most precious possession?"

The class laughed at Gretchen. She was not used to it. She stumbled. "No — I — um — it's the phone I like."

"Oh. I see," said Mrs. Shevvington in that cruel, silken voice. "So that all your admirers can reach you?"

Gretchen turned beet red. She looked ill.

"Nobody else listed herself as the most precious object," said Mrs. Shevvington. "I'm fascinated, Gretchen. I don't know which is more interesting. That you consider yourself an object, or that you consider the sound of your voice so magnificent."

Gretchen's essay pages shivered in the air. The meaner boys — the boys Gretchen herself had trained to do this — began flapping their arms to match her shaking hand.

"Try to be less self-centered, Gretchen," said Mrs. Shevvington. Mrs. Shevvington sat calmly, her thick body like a piece of the desk, her oatmeal face solid. "Think of another subject."

The mean people leaned back and smirked. Gretchen was as exposed as if she had been stripped of clothing.

"Well?" said Mrs. Shevvington.

Gretchen was now white as kindergarten paste.

"I can't think of anything," mumbled Gretchen. "My head is empty."

Empty, thought Christina. Mrs. Shevvington had emptied her. Just for today, of course. Nothing permanent, like Val.

A minute passed. The big old school clock made a slight tick as the minute hand twitched and moved on. Gretchen stood hot and stupid in front of the class. Even Vicki did nothing. Gretchen had not a friend in the world.

Christina knew how that felt. "If I had an Elvis phone," said Christina, "I would list it first, too, Mrs. Shevvington. I don't think it's fair of you to decide what is important to other people."

She had truly caught Mrs. Shevvington by surprise. "I do not think I was addressing you, Christina Romney," said Mrs. Shevvington.

"No, I don't think you were either, Mrs. Shevvington. But I would like to hear about the other two telephones. Could you read the rest of your essay, please, Gretchen?"

Gretchen looked at Christina suspiciously to see if it was a trap.

The clock clicked again, with a little quiver of the long black hand.

The passing bell rang. But neither Gretch nor anybody else fled. It was Mrs. Shevvington's class. The hallways filled with shouting and noise.

Mrs. Shevvington said at last, "Class dismissed."

I had the last word, thought Christina, her grin of delight tucked safely inside her face.

Jonah was the first to stand. He walked straight to Christina's desk. He looked down at Christina with a curiously gentle expression. He touched her hair with his fingers spread, as if resting one finger on each color hair. "You know, Chrissie," he said, a grin crossing his face, "I'm kind of attracted to you."

"Kind of!" teased the other boys.

Jonah's grin filled his face, along with his new braces, and all of him seemed to shine and laugh.

Mrs. Shevvington became nothing — merely a toad behind a desk. The entire room belonged to Jonah, and all the faces of all the seventh graders were upon him and upon Christina.

"I'm sorry I've been such a creep since that fire thing," said Jonah, loud enough for everybody to hear. "Come on, let's get out of here."

In May Christina would be fourteen. It seemed very significant. Thirteen was too young to be in love. Thirteen was playing games, imitating high school kids.

But fourteen: fourteen would be just right.

Behind Christina's house on the island grew apples. They were called Northern Spy. She loved that name.

I am the Northern Spy, thought Christina.

One advantage to old houses was that each door had a big old keyhole. Mr. Shevvington was in his study, which had a traditional mice-talking-to-Cinderella-shaped keyhole.

Christina, the Northern Spy, put her eye to the hole.

"Come in, Christina," said Mr. Shevvington. He was laughing at her. "What did you want, my dear?" he said. He waved her toward the high wooden seat in front of the desk. It was the kind of seat you could not get comfortable in. The back cut into your back, the bottom made ridges in your bottom. She remained standing.

On his desk was a stack of ordinary manila file folders. The top one was open. Stapled to the right side were papers, and to the left cover, a photograph of Dolly.

Mr. Shevvington closed Dolly's file. Then he counted the stack. Ten files: not new — wrinkled, much used.

Not future victims, thought Christina. *Past* victims. The file beneath Dolly's is Anya's, and behind that Val's. I knew there were papers! I knew it!

"How is your counseling coming along?" said Mr. Shevvington. Slowly, lovingly, he closed the briefcase. "Are you making progress?"

He knew perfectly well Christina had not said a syllable to the counselor he had picked out. And never would. "I am making a great deal of progress," said Christina. "I know the truth."

Mr. Shevvington smiled, unworried. He patted the briefcase in a friendly way, like a dog. The files were his pets. He fed them with his horrible appetites.

Neither Dolly nor Christina had homework. They played with Dolly's Barbie and Ken. Dolly had everything, from the swimsuits to the miniature hair dryer to the wedding gown. But she looked as if she would rather be reading about Barbie and Ken than dressing them. "Why aren't you reading?" said Christina. It was fun to play with Barbie and Ken. They always did what you told them to. And they always smiled and were happy to get new clothes.

"Mr. Shevvington took away my library privileges."

Christina laughed. "No, really," she said. "Why aren't you reading?"

"Mr. Shevvington says I'm not living in the real world," explained Dolly. "He says when you live entirely through characters in books it's a sign of dementia. He says I'll do demented things like — well — like — " Dolly had the grace to blush; obviously Mr. Shevvington had said she might burn clothes like Christina or go crazy like Anya. "Anyway, I'm not supposed to read every single minute."

Dolly looped her braids around her throat, chewed the tips for a while, and put high heels on Barbie. "I slipped going down Breakneck Hill, Chrissie. And yesterday I fell on the stairs. Every time I see a slant, I feel as if I'm falling. I was telling Anya and she said she always feels that way. She's felt that way since she moved here."

Christina held tighter to Ken and Barbie.

No! I'm not ready! I'm trying to survive without people to sit with at lunch. I'm trying to get through each day knowing my parents think I'm half crazy. I can't save Dolly now. I haven't saved myself. How can you be somebody else's savior when you can't be your own?

"Sometimes I think it's named for me, Chrissie."

"What is?" Christina decided to set up the barbecue for Ken to broil steaks.

"Breakneck Hill. I think I'm the one who's going to break her neck."

"No, you're not. It was named a hundred years ago for some little boy who rode his bike down it."

Christina stood Ken by the barbecue. If I don't think about what Dolly's saying, it won't be true, thought Christina.

Dolly folded her Barbie so that Barbie reclined in the bubble bath, her white toes poking up out of the tub. "Mrs. Shevvington told me that sometimes things repeat themselves when it's exactly a hundred years."

A tiny gold-and-red foil fire glinted in Ken's barbecue.

Christina thought of falls and fires. *Was it just one step from burning a person's clothes to burning that person?*

"Dolly, don't worry. You won't fall. I promise. I'll be there for you."

Dolly beamed. "And will you do another little favor for me, too, Chrissie?" A voice half whine, half love. "Would you get books for me out of your school library? I have a list. I can't get them from the elementary school library."

"Why not? Are they sex manuals?"

"Of course not. They're just stories. I can't get through the week without some good books to read."

"You mean you've read every single good book in the elementary school library?"

An odd, sly look came over Dolly's face. "Yes," she said. "That's it."

So the following day, Christina checked out five books from Dolly's list and brought them home. It was near supper. Everybody was there. Mr. and

Mrs. Shevvington, Michael, and Benj. You could not count Anya anymore. She seemed to occupy no space. Hardly more than air.

"Here are your books, Dolly," Christina said. "Hope these are good enough. The librarian had to substitute one."

Everybody stared at Christina.

"Christina," said Mr. Shevvington, "I don't know how much farther this can go. You know perfectly well we are trying to wean Dolly from her obsession with fictional characters. You know we are struggling to get her to dance and have friends over to play, instead of curling up with escape stories. And here you are, undermining our decisions, boldly and blatantly marching in here with the forbidden objects."

Christina said, "Since when do high school principals and English teachers forbid a kid to read books?"

Michael whirled on Christina. "Since they have gotten concerned for her *health*, Christina. You think we want Dolly to be some nut case like you or Anya?"

But I'm the good guy! Christina thought.

"She was always spoiled," Michael said. "The Shevvingtons are good for her. If you'd ever follow their rules, they'd be good for you, too."

What did Michael see, upstairs at night? Did he see happy, funny Dolly? Did he not notice that Dolly was afraid of more and more things every day? Did he not think that when his little sister was even afraid of frost on the windows there was something radically wrong? "She's your sister!" cried Christina. "Put her first."

Michael said very quietly, "Do you ever put me first? How many of my games have you come to since the season started, Chrissie? You and I used to be really good friends. Do you even know whether I'm a starter or whether I warm the bench? Do you know how many points I'm averaging each game? Do you know who we're playing next Friday? Have you ever brought my own sister to see me play?"

Christina flinched. While I was busy trying to be a savior, she thought, Michael stepped out of my mind like a stranger out of a bus.

"On the cupola of Schooner Inne," said Mr. Shevvington, the Perfect Principal, "is a weathervane. A copper fish. Frozen in place. No matter how the wind blows, he points the same way." Mr. Shevvington looked sadly at Christina. "No matter how the wind blows, Christina, you point only at Mrs. Shevvington and me. It's time to melt, Christina."

Michael and Benjamin and Dolly Jaye nodded.

Anya floated, unhearing.

Dolly slipped into a chair. She was small enough that her feet did not touch the floor, and she swung them a little, like a toddler.

There was ice in Christina's heart, put there by the betrayals of her parents and friends. If she melted that ice, people would be her friends again. But if she ceased to fight the Shevvingtons, nobody would fight them. They would win forever and ever, whether they wanted to humiliate Katy in English or push Dolly off the balcony.

"We're trying to help Dolly grow up," explained Benj.

Christina abandoned melting. "Why does growing up in this household always mean you can't do the things you like to do?" said Christina. "Dolly likes to read, so why can't she read?"

"I suppose the corollary to that," said Mrs. Shevvington, "is you like to burn your clothing, so why can't you burn your clothing?"

Christina hurled all five of the library books straight at Mrs. Shevvington. None of them missed.

Chapter 15

And so Christina lost her Saturday privileges again. While the others went out, she was forced to stay inside. It snowed all day: a light, friendly snow, the kind you turned your face up into and held out your tongue to collect a flake from the sky.

Mr. Shevvington went to the school, where he said he would be all day. He took his briefcase, waving it at Christina as he got into his car.

Mrs. Shevvington went to get groceries. Dolly went with her. Dolly said she loved doing errands.

How strange, thought Christina. Why doesn't Dolly go out with her friends in the sixth grade?

Dolly has no friends.

She had not asked a single sixth-grade girl over to the Inne. Nor telephoned one. Nor talked about one. She was alone every day when she met Christina after school.

Am I Dolly's only friend? thought Christina.

It was frightening. Christina's dream of coming to the mainland had been to have rafts of friends —

crowds — rooms full. At times she did. At this time she did not. But Dolly had never even used the word "friend."

Christina sat alone in the house. Even Anya was gone, working at the laundromat.

Outside the tide fumbled in Candle Cove, whispering *Fffffff, Ffffffff, Ffffff*. It sounded like a giant blowing out candles on a birthday cake. In a moment the whispering would turn slushy, as the rising water crawled forward, gathered momentum, and then began slamming against the rocks like trapped thunder.

No sun glinted through the mansion's windows. The color of the air was gray. The white banisters of the stairwell curled above her, like twirling cake candles. Christina climbed the stairs. She did not want to be near the cellar door.

Fffffffffff, said the cove.

At the second floor she paused.

The door to the last guest room — number eight — was open.

It seemed to Christina that she heard someone laughing.

Ffffffff, said the cove.

Christina slid into room number eight, back against the wall, in case the giggle or the tide began to rise up in the house as well.

She had never noticed before that Room 8 had a definite personality. The pencil-thin posters of the high antique bed lent a fragile air to a room decorated in lace. The colors of the room were pale, the color of ghosts. And the surprise of the room was a thick black rug with silver and gray streaks, like a storm cloud on the floor.

The colors of Anya.

Ten file folders, thought Christina Romney. Mr. Shevvington counted out ten file folders and tucked them into his briefcase.

The last two aren't yet closed — me and Dolly. Because we aren't destroyed yet. That means eight folders of girls they *have* destroyed.

Eight guest rooms.

Val, Robbie's older sister, must be the folder beneath Anya. Folder Seven. Room Seven. Slowly, as one opening a casket at a funeral home, Christina entered the room with 7 on the door.

She had been in these rooms several times. They were all different, but never before had she noticed *how* different.

Here the carpet was blue as the sea in summer, and the walls a rich violet, like sunset. The curtains were deeper blue, like night at sea. The room was small, but the dark colors did not close it in: they opened it, like a flower in a crystal vase.

It was a rich, sensuous room.

Val, sister of Robbie, on your narrow cot in your hospital room. Is this you? Are you a girl of violet and blue?

The room was as clean as a sanctuary. Waiting for its guest. But Val would never visit this room. She was trapped in another.

Christina backed out of Val's room and crossed to Number 6. She peeked in from the hall, as if Number 6 would resent being trespassed upon.

Number 6 liked yellow. Number 6 was sunshine and gold, glinting like sunrise on glass. Number 6 would love dancing and music and laughter.

Christina did not want to see Number 1, or the personalities of Numbers 2, or 3, or 4, or 5.

But she thought about Number 6 all day.

Where are you, Number 6? From what high school did they take you? Into what laundromat or what institution did they put you?

Several days later, over supper, Michael talked relentlessly about basketball. The team was sixteen and nine, and if they won tonight's game, they would go into the regional play-offs. He said almost shyly to Christina, "It was nice to see you at practice this afternoon."

"You were terrific," she said to him. "Especially at suicide."

Michael grinned. "I love suicide."

"You *what*?" said Dolly.

"Suicide," explained Christina, "is when the coach makes the boys run full speed into the wall, slam into it, pivot around, race back across the gym, slam into that wall, pivot, race back across the gym, slam into — "

"I get the point," said Dolly. "And this is what my brother is good at? Why don't they give it a peaceful name, like, say, Double Wall Approach?"

"Because it's not peaceful," said Benjamin. "It's supposed to turn the team into warriors. Make them want to stomp the other team." Benjamin was teasing his younger brother.

"What is it you guys yell when you huddle on the edge of the court just before the game begins?" Dolly wanted to know.

Michael grinned again. "Sometimes we yell *'Defense!'* and sometimes we yell *'Team work!'* but last week we yelled *'Crunch 'em!,'* and we scored so high that we're always gonna yell *'Crunch 'em!'* from now on."

Dolly said, "I hope skiing is more civilized."

The Shevvingtons smiled.

Michael said, "I phoned Mom and Dad and got permission. But there's one little problem. I don't want to go. We're having an extra practice that weekend and I'd rather do that. So if you don't mind, Mrs. Shevvington, and thanks a lot for offering. I'll spend the weekend with George instead."

No! thought Christina. I need you. You haven't noticed anything wrong with Dolly or the Shevvingtons yet, but I need your body and your muscles and your presence over the ski weekend!

"Fine idea," said Mr. Shevvington. "George's family are fine people. I approve heartily of your dedication to the team spirit, Michael."

Michael did not notice the falseness in this silly sentence; it was the kind of remark he expected from a principal. "Gotta run. You coming to the game, Chrissie?"

"Yes," said Christina. "Dolly and I both are."

"Oh, no," said Dolly. "I have homework." Her brother stood very still. Christina had been stabbed like that many times this year. She had not known Michael was getting stabbed. "I bought tickets,

Dolly," said Christina. "You can do your homework at halftime. We need to see Michael play."

"Don't worry about it," said Michael. He was into his coat and out the door in moments.

Anya said, "I'll go to the game with you, Chrissie. May I use Dolly's ticket?"

They were so startled that Anya was still a living, speaking presence that nobody spoke. "That's great, Anya," Christina managed. "I'd love that. Finish your supper. We have to leave pretty soon."

They had plenty of time actually, but to get Anya ready to appear in public might take half an evening.

Dolly asked Mrs. Shevvington if they could do her homework together. "It's more fun that way," she said, smiling up at Mrs. Shevvington.

Benjamin said, "Listen. If Michael's not going skiing, I don't want to. At the gas station they'll pay me overtime. How about I stay at George's, too? They have lots of room."

Benj's expression did not change like his brother's or sister's. There was no excitement, pleading, or enthusiasm. It was stolid. A fisherman's face. He waited patiently for the Shevvingtons' decision.

It came as no surprise to Christina that Mr. Shevvington felt this was a Fine Idea. Dedication to a Personal Goal. It was What Growing Up Was All About. Benj grunted and left the table.

So it would be Dolly, Anya, and Christina going skiing. *Anya can't even comb her hair, and Dolly wants to be crunched.*

She would probably begin giggling with hysteria when they reached the ski resort, get locked up like

Val or Number 6, leaving the Shevvingtons free to manipulate Dolly's fear of heights on the Killer Slopes.

There was, Christina remembered, a ski trail called Suicide.

Perhaps they would start Dolly out on that one.

Anya came running down the stairs. "Are we going?" she said anxiously to Christina. Christina could remember when Anya wore a dark navy blue coat set off by a crimson scarf and soft, supple gloves with a purse that matched. Now Anya had gotten into an old ski jacket whose down was leaking out the seams. She'd rammed a ragged ski cap over her hair without checking in the mirror. One ear showed, the other didn't.

Christina wanted to shake her by the shoulders. *Why can't you pull yourself together? Why do you have to keep rowing with one oar?*

But she loved Anya. "Here," she said quietly. "Let me button your coat for you." Anya had started with the first button, but the second hole. Christina fixed her and walked her to the front door.

Anya took her hand when they reached the sidewalk. "Slippery," she confided.

You don't know how slippery, thought Christina.

The two girls hiked.

If Blake were here, he'd drive us in his beautiful red sports car, thought Christina. She wondered if Anya had finished that letter to Blake and put a stamp on it and dropped it off at the post office. It seemed far more than Anya was capable of. Anyway, she hadn't asked Blake for help. Only told him they were having tea and toast.

By now Blake surely had a new girlfriend to match himself: beautiful and well dressed and sleek. Why would he bother again with Anya?

Anya said, "Chrissie, I can't wait to go skiing."

Christina was amazed. Anya was being brought on the ski trip rather like a suitcase or a bathrobe. Nobody expected her to ski. "That's great, Anya," said Christina. "Do you know how to ski?"

"No," said Anya. She laughed — a real laugh — her old laugh. "But Blake does."

Christina repeated, "Blake?"

Anya's joyous laugh rang like church bells. "Blake answered my letter," she said. "His boarding school is only a few miles away from the ski resort we're going to. He's meeting me!"

Christina gasped. Blake — an ally! Right there! Blake had known more about the Shevvingtons than anybody, and Blake had believed. "Anya, you didn't tell the Shevvingtons about this, did you? They don't know, do they?"

"Tell the Shevvingtons?" said Anya. "What — do you think I'm crazy?"

They both laughed. Gales of sane girlish laughter.

At last, at last — they knew something the Shevvingtons didn't.

Chapter 16

"Don't tell Dolly," whispered Christina.

Anya nodded. "I won't. Dolly loves the Shevvingtons."

"But how did you get a letter back from Blake? The Shevvingtons get all the mail first."

"I put the laundromat as my return address," said Anya. Her huge, dark eyes flickered in her chalk-white face, like a poster child from a country filled with starvation. "I don't have any clothes to wear, Chrissie. I've never been skiing."

"Neither have I. The Shevvingtons bought Dolly a beautiful emerald-green ski suit. She looks like a Christmas tree ornament."

"I know. I saw. You and I will have to come up with something. I have to look perfect for Blake."

Christina thought this was the most romantic thing ever to happen. True love was going to rescue Anya.

We'll whip the Shevvingtons! she thought. Blake and Anya and I.

Now Christina could hardly wait for the three-day weekend.

The joy of revenge bubbled in Christina like soda pop. When she and Anya entered the high school, she was all but dancing. They handed their cardboard tickets to the kid at the gym door and got their hands stamped with the school initials. Biting their lips to contain their wild laughter, they took two steps — and Mr. Shevvington blocked the way.

She had forgotten that the principal attended home games.

"Anya," he said. His voice was soft. He wet his lips. "You look so lively. Has something happened?"

Anya put up quivering hands to protect herself from the piercing shaft of his eyes. They were blue tonight, blank as insanity.

Mr. Shevvington took Anya's wrists and lowered her hands. "Tell me, Anya," he coaxed.

She would tell. Christina knew it. Then the Shevvingtons would know, could protect themselves, and what was worse, would laugh at Christina for deluding herself that she could beat them.

"I decided to kick butt, Mr. Shevvington," Christina said crudely. "I'm gonna shape her up. I put lots of makeup on her. She's gonna scream for the team or else."

Legs flaring left, pompons rustling right, the cheerleaders were shouting, *"Michael, Michael, he's our man, if he can't do it, no one can!"*

"Christina, Christina, she's our man," said Christina to the principal. "If she can't do it, no one can."

Mr. Shevvington laughed. "Getting her cheeks

rosy with rouge, Christina, is hardly putting her back together again."

Anya said fretfully, "It's noisy in here, Crissie. I wanna go home."

"I'll be with you," said Christina. "Don't whimper."

Anya dipped further into baby talk. "I'na go home," she mumbled.

Mr. Shevvington smiled and turned away to greet a basketball parent.

"Oh, Arthur," said the parent adoringly. "You're not only here for every game, you don't miss the Junior Varsity either. It gives the boys such a boost that their principal always supports them. With your schedule I just don't know how you do it."

Christina yanked Anya by her coat collar. On the bleachers the kids were kicking the boards with their heels. "Air ball, air ball, air ball!" screamed the kids hopefully.

At games the kids bunched by grade, and within that bunch by cliques. Christina had never been to a game before and did not know where to sit. Anya no longer had a grade or a clique. There's Jennie, Christina thought with relief, and behind her is Robbie.

Christina hauled Anya over coats, between couples, and up four rows. Anya continued whimpering and resisting. Christina could not tell if Anya was acting for Mr. Shevvington's sake or if she had slipped back into her old self. She could hardly ask. ("Are you sane or not right now, Anya?") Christina found a space big enough for two and shoved Anya down. She sat — and found Gretchen and Vicki on her right.

"What're you doing here?" said Gretch.

"We came to see Michael."

"It's about time," said Vicki.

They watched the game. Two minutes by the time clock, eight minutes in real life.

Gretch said critically, "Anya looks pretty decent. She must be getting someplace with her psychiatrist."

Anya's cheeks stained red. Christina considered snapping off Gretchen's fingers, when she realized it was the first time in months that Anya had been sufficiently aware to be hurt. Christina squeezed Anya's hand for comfort, and Anya squeezed back. She's in there! thought Christina, and her joy soared to the gym ceiling.

"So are you going skiing on the three-day weekend?" said Gretchen to Christina. "We always go. We have our own condo, of course. And season passes, so we don't have to wait in line the way you'll have to. What kind of boots do you have? Mine're new this year, of course."

Christina had nothing.

Gretch said, "You've never seen my new ski outfit either, Christina. It's the height of fashion. I'm a very good skier, of course. Which slope will you be on? The bunny slope?" She giggled. "Last weekend when we were skiing, two kids broke their legs right there on the bunny slope. We laughed so hard."

You are pond scum, thought Christina. Sewer sludge.

Vicki leaned over. "I suppose you'll have blue jeans on. The first time you fall you'll be soaked."

"That'll be in sixty seconds," said Gretch.

Vicki and Gretch laughed and laughed.

Anya flushed.

Christina had seen the outfit Gretchen had ordered. She had shown it to the whole seventh grade. Gleaming synthetic skiwear that clung to the body like colored water. The kind of clothing perfect people wore.

Christina thought, Blake will be a fine skier. He's that kind of person. He won't want an Anya who falls over and is clumsy and wearing wet jeans. He'll want somebody beautiful and graceful and brilliant.

What if Anya did not measure up? What if Blake abandoned them?

Christina shut it out of her mind. She watched Michael play. He was very good. Not enough height, but he made up for it in speed.

I don't have enough height, either, thought Christina. But I am going to make up for it in cleverness. So there.

The next morning the Shevvingtons said they were signing Dolly up for Beginner Ski Class. "You'll have such fun, Dolly, darling," they said. "It's children your age, with a very understanding, gentle instructor. Before you know it, you'll be a pro!"

Christina could not help herself. "A class?" she said eagerly. "I don't know how to ski either. May I take the class, too? I don't mind being in with little kids."

Mrs. Shevvington raised her caterpillar eyebrows above her bran-muffin face. "Really, Christina," she said. "I hardly think your recent behavior warrants such a reward." She turned back to Dolly. "And guess what else I got for you," she said.

Again Christina could not help herself. She looked to Anya for comfort. Anya rolled her eyes and pantomimed.

What if the Shevvingtons saw? What if the Shevvingtons found out that Anya was healing? What might Mr. Shevvington do to get her soul back?

Dolly said, "I don't care. I don't want to ski. I don't want to go downhill anywhere, ever."

Christina studied her breakfast cereal to keep herself from looking in Anya's direction. She must never look at Anya again. It would betray them both.

"You won't break any bones," said Mr. Shevvington. "You're so light and graceful, Dolly, you'll land like a baby bird."

"I won't! I'll land on my face. I can feel it. I dream about it. The ice will rip my face and tear my hair. Please don't make me! Give the class to Chrissie. She wants it. I'll just sit in the ski lodge and read a book by the fire. Please don't make me go!" Dolly put her hands over her face, not to weep behind her fingers, but to save herself from landing face first.

"Dolly, see the lovely gloves I bought you?" said Mrs. Shevvington. "And you won't fall. You'll have poles to keep you up. All those dancing lessons will stand you in good stead now."

Dolly took the gloves.

Christina had never seen such gloves. A green so dark and shimmering it was like the sea underwater, fabric so supple it was like skin — yet thick and waterproof.

The mittens her mother knitted seemed made for a heavy, ugly farm wife.

I want gloves like that, thought Christina.

She wanted to take them from Dolly's hands and put them on her own hands, and —

Jealousy was alive in her, snatching her good thoughts to make them bad. The Shevvingtons were smiling. The gloves aren't for Dolly, Christina thought. They're for me. To bring out the worst in me. To make me abandon Dolly.

At lunch in the cafeteria she told Jonah everything. He listened with his whole body. His sandwich hung untouched in his hand; he ate her words instead. "It's looking good," said Jonah. "Blake's a great guy. With him there they can't do much."

"They did before. They convinced Blake's parents to ship him off to boarding school, and Blake couldn't fight back. All of a sudden he was gone."

"They can't manage that in a weekend," Jonah pointed out. "Blake will protect Anya just fine." Jonah frowned slightly. He took a huge bite out of his sandwich. Through layers of ham and cheese, he said, "Blake always liked you. And you always liked him."

"I think he's terrific. That's why I feel so good about this weekend."

Jonah took a more savage bite. "He's old," he said contemptuously. "He's got to be eighteen."

Jonah was jealous. Christina, ignoring several hundred witnesses, leaned across the cafeteria table and kissed Jonah on the mouth.

He couldn't kiss back — he was eating. His eyes flew open with amazement, and he struggled with his ham and cheese. By the time he finished chewing, half the seventh grade had begun a football cheer — *"First in ten, do it again!"*

They gathered around Christina and Jonah, saying, "Well? Going to return the favor, Jonah? Come on. Let's see your technique."

Jonah threw his lunch bag at them but paper bags are poor weapons, and nothing happened, so he threw his orange.

Kenny threw back an apple. Jonah threw his half-empty chocolate milk. Ellen hurled her pudding, and within moments they were having the food fight of the year. People were taking advantage of this wonderful moment to even scores with people they had detested. Hot lunch people, who had spaghetti, emptied spaghetti down each other's sweaters. Christina found a plate, its tomato sauce untouched in a puddle on the white pasta, and considered Gretchen's white cashmere sweater.

"Who started this?" shouted the cafeteria proctor, racing among the tables.

"Christina did," said Gretchen.

Christina stood very still, the spaghetti plate balanced on her palm as if she were a waitress serving dinners.

The proctor said grimly. "Well, Miss Romney, Mr. Shevvington will not be surprised to have you brought to his office yet again."

Christina set down the spaghetti.

She had unknowingly played right into Mr. Shevvington's hands.

He would take away the ski weekend.

Dolly and Anya would go without her.

Chapter 17

"Mr. Shevvington is not in the office at the moment," said the secretary, barely glancing up. It was what secretaries did best at this school — ignore the students. "He's showing the school board members the leaking roof in the west wing. You'll have to wait."

Christina sat quietly on a bench in the outer office. One secretary typed, one filed, one talked on the phone, and one scrolled down a computer screen. The clerk who was typing finished. "I'm going to take this down to the science department," she said. The one filing said, "I'm going on break now," and waltzed out. The clerk on the phone argued with her caller, glaring into the receiver. The computer operator moaned, pressing her hands over her eyes. "Oh, no, I did this wrong; I have to do it over."

Christina glided without sound across the office. She turned the handle to Mr. Shevvington's office, opened the door, and crept in.

The briefcase, bulging, sat under Mr. Shevvington's desk.

I have it! she exulted. I knew eventually I would win. Good *does* triumph over evil.

She wrapped her fingers around the handle. She walked past the clerk with computer problems and the clerk with telephone problems. Neither paid any attention. She walked out of the office.

She had taken two steps toward her locker when Mr. Shevvington appeared way down the hall, coming toward her. He was with a man and woman: the school board members.

Christina walked the other way. She did not run. Running made people realize there was something wrong. She knew she was recognized. Only Christina had the hair of three colors. And no student, even the most geeky nerds, carried a briefcase. But Mr. Shevvington had his image to keep up. He was not going to shout, "Stop thief!' in front of school board members. Besides, she might show them the contents.

Christina walked quickly the opposite way. It was a high school wing; the junior high students were not normally in the same halls as high school kids. The school had many wings radiating outward for the junior and senior high, with gymnasiums, auditorium, music rooms, and art department in the middle.

"Please excuse me," said Mr. Shevvington in a leisurely voice. "I have a discipline problem to attend to. I will telephone you after I have the figures on what it will cost to repair the roof."

Christina reached the end of her corridor. She could turn left or right. And once out of Mr. Shevvington's sight, she could run.

Any exit, she thought. Leave school. Run through town. Go to the harbor. I'll hide the briefcase on somebody's boat. If Frankie is there I'll talk him into taking me back to the island right now.

Her mind raced over hiding places, escape routes, dark corners.

"Always a pleasure to deal with you, Arthur," boomed the school board member.

She wanted to look back and see if they were shaking hands or if he was already headed her way. She made herself keep going. She turned right. Shifting the heavy briefcase to her other hand, Christina began to run.

A high school teacher lecturing in his doorway stepped backward into the hall and frowned. She smiled back. "You have a pass?" he demanded.

Christina hoisted the briefcase instead of a pass. "Mr. Shevvington asked me to bring him his briefcase," she said, slowing her pace. The teacher nodded, watching her as she walked on. Now she could not run anymore. Heart pounding like a sprinter's, she kept her steps slow. The corridor was horribly long. She was two thirds of the way down, approaching the next crossing of corridors, when Mr. Shevvington turned the corner behind her. "Christina," he called after her.

She continued walking.

"Christina," he said again.

She reached the next turning. Each hall had an

EXIT sign at the far end. But where did they come out? The hall had no windows for her to figure it out. What if she came out in the teachers' parking lot, where walls enclosed the cars, and she had to run around the entire building? What if she came out the rear and had to cross the open playing fields like a rabbit in front of a shotgun?

Passing bells rang.

High school students spurted out of their classrooms. Screaming, shoving, laughing, shouting, they filled the hall like a volcano erupting. She turned right.

Boys who stood a foot higher than Christina, girls whose sweaters swirled like choir robes, academic types with books stacked like chimney bricks, surrounded her. She hugged the briefcase to her and slipped through, dodging and curving.

Taking advantage of a swarm of enormous football-shouldered boys, Christina ducked into a stairwell and ran up the stairs.

Mr. Shevvington's voice rang in the shaft below. "Did you boys see a little seventh-grade girl? Strange multi-colored hair?"

"The little island girl," said one agreeably. "Anya's little friend." This speaker must have pointed, because Mr. Shevvington said, "Thanks," and his feet pounded on the stairs like pistons.

She flung open the door and emerged on the second floor.

Terrible place to be. If only she could dump the briefcase somewhere.

How barren the school seemed, now that she

needed a hiding place. Hallways of gleaming tile and no furniture. Doors opening into classrooms filled by waiting teachers. Every closet locked by janitors, every office staffed.

"Christina! Christina Romney!" Mr. Shevvington was shouting now. It was too late to be subtle. He was afraid. The briefcase mattered. She had to win!

But now she was in the junior high wing, where everybody knew her name. Where some teacher was sure to grab her and hold her prisoner. In seconds passing period would be over. The halls would be empty. She would be exposed.

"Christina!"

She was panicking. The hand gripping the briefcase cramped and ached. Seventh-grade faces caught hers, staring, surprised, confused. Christina rushed on. Mr. Shevvington strode after her.

She reached the other stairwell and yanked open the door. Down she ran. Behind her the bells rang; passing period was over; when she got to the bottom and came out again in front of the office where she had begun, she would be the only child in sight. Carrying the only briefcase in sight.

The tears began. How she hated Mr. Shevvington for having the power to make her cry! How she hated herself for being only thirteen and weak!

Halfway down the stairs she ran straight into Gretchen.

How could it be that Christina had prayed for assistance — and it was Gretchen who appeared! She whispered, "Gretchen, please help me. Take this briefcase. Hide it in your locker. Don't tell anybody. It's a matter of life and death."

Gretchen stared at her. Christina thrust the briefcase into her hands. "Run, Gretchen! Please!"

"But Christina, this is Mr. Shevvington's. I recognize it. He carries it everywhere he goes. What are you doing with it?"

"I stole it. It has papers I have to have."

Gretchen gasped.

They both heard the heavy pounding of feet. Mr. Shevvington running. She might not accomplish anything else, but she had made him desperate.

Gretchen took the briefcase and fled.

Mr. Shevvington yanked open the stairwell door. Christina watched his shadow. He looked up to see if she had tried to get out on the roof. He looked down to see if she had returned to the first floor. Christina caught the door behind Gretchen and let it close without a sound.

Mr. Shevvington raced down the stairs.

"You scared me, Mr. Shevvington," she said calmly. "Chasing me like that."

He stopped two steps above her, trying to see the briefcase. Alone in the stairwell they faced each other. How tall he was, with those two extra steps for height!

He put his hands forward, as if to shake her until her spine snapped. Christina jumped away, ripped open the door, and came out in front of the two school board members, still talking. She pretended her shoelace was undone, and knelt to tie it up again.

"Why, Arthur," said one pleasantly, "that was

quick. You're always so efficient. We had another thought about how to solve the roof problem. Do you have a minute?"

Christina double knotted it. She untied and tied the other shoe.

"Of course," said Mr. Shevvington smoothly. "Come into my office."

Christina was alone in the hall. Unsteadily she got to her feet. Where was Gretchen's locker? She tottered toward the junior high lockers.

She heaved an enormous sigh of relief, and the extra oxygen calmed her. I'll take the briefcase. I'll skip the rest of school. I'll —

Gretchen popped out of the girls' bathroom. "You're safe, Christina," she said. "I owe you for being nice to me in class. So I will never tell anybody you stole Mr. Shevvington's briefcase. I snuck into his office and put it under his desk. Those dumb secretaries didn't even look up. I even locked the door after me. Mr. Shevvington can't accuse you of taking it now. It looks like it was there all along."

Christina stood very still.

"Are you all right?" whispered Gretchen nervously.

He was in his office right now with the school board. When he sat down, his polished shoes would hit the briefcase. He would have the last laugh.

He will always have the last laugh, thought Christina.

I am no longer sure that good triumphs over evil.

I am afraid that evil will win.

Chapter 18

After school the children all gathered around Christina. "What was your punishment?" they said. "What did he do to you?" The food fight was ancient history. She had almost forgotten it.

My punishment, she thought, is knowing that he has won and will always win. Knowing that someday an empty room in an empty inn will be decorated with my personality. "Nothing. Just gave me a hard time."

Jonah marvelled. "You must have a silver tongue, Chrissie," he said.

Mr. Shevvington had thought she put the briefcase under his desk herself, from fear of him. He couldn't figure out how she had done it, but he had excused the food fight because the briefcase was such a joke.

"Everybody come to my house," Jonah called. "I turned on the outside water faucet and sprayed the snow maze with the hose. It iced up. We can slide on it!"

Half the seventh grade wanted to go to Jonah's.

Christina said she was coming but she had to wait for Dolly. The children ran on.

Dolly appeared almost immediately. Christina extended her hand, but Dolly didn't take it. "I've outgrown holding hands," said Dolly. "Mrs. Shevvington says I must learn to stand alone."

Christina knew that none of them could stand alone against the Shevvingtons. "How awful!" said Christina. "Dolly, sometimes you need to hold hands."

Dolly was blue from cold. She looked, in the island phrase, peak-ed. Christina told her about Jonah's ice maze and how they would all slip and slide together. Dolly was not enthusiastic.

Jonah's mother gave everybody old holey socks to slip over their shoes. About twenty seventh-graders — kids Christina most and least liked: Robbie, Katy, Gretch — slithered through the ice mazes on socky feet. They collided at intersections, made trains of themselves, and pushed each other into dead ends.

Dolly refused to go into the maze. "I might get lost," she said seriously.

The seventh-graders howled with laughter. "It's just my backyard," said Jonah nicely. "And the maze isn't very deep, Dolly. If you stand up straight, it's waist high. Nothing can happen to you."

"It looks like Breakneck Hill Road," said Dolly. "All ice and downhill."

The seventh-graders ignored Dolly and chased

each other, slipping, sliding, and shrieking in the maze.

Kenny had a long stadium scarf, knitted in purple-and-white squares. Everybody hung onto it, and Kenny dragged them after him.

Dolly went inside to have hot chocolate with Jonah's mother. Mrs. Bergeron said, "Christina, honey? I wonder if you'd come in, too, for a moment. I have something to show you."

Christina was suspicious of adults with something to show her. She went in uneasily, keeping her back to the wall.

Outside, Jonah led an ice war.

Mrs. Bergeron poured a mug of hot chocolate for Dolly and dropped five tiny marshmallows into it. Dolly stirred happily, watching them melt.

Mrs. Bergeron put a large white cardboard box on the table. Tissue poked out of the sides. "Ooooh, clothes," said Dolly. "I love clothes. Did you buy something new, Mrs. Bergeron?"

"Yes, but this is the old one. I wore it only once, and it just wasn't me. It made me feel sallow and fat." She took off the lid. Color as bright as lemons sang from the box.

Mrs. Bergeron unfolded a ski jacket so beautiful, so sunny-yellow and snowy-white that the little girls blinked. She held it up against Christina. "It's a tiny bit large," she admitted. "But that doesn't matter when you're skiing." She unfolded the ski pants. "A tiny bit long," she said. "But when you ski, you need that extra room for flexibility."

Christina trembled.

Mrs. Bergeron said, "Let's just slip it on. Make sure it's right for you, Christina. I will feel so much better if this ski suit gets some use."

Christina put it on. She said nothing. Her heart was too full for speech.

Dolly whispered, "Ooooh, Chrissie. Your hair glitters. It's like you're wearing new-fallen snow."

Mrs. Bergeron led her upstairs to a full-length mirror, and Christina stared at herself, a daffodil in the snow.

"I look perfect in mine, too," said Dolly. "Mine's emerald green. It's just right for my hair, too. My hair is red," she added, as if Mrs. Bergeron could not see.

Mrs. Bergeron said, "Everything is easier to handle when you're dressed just right and your hair is perfect."

Christina wanted to hug Mrs. Bergeron and to be hugged: have her anxiety hugged away as this ski suit would take away the grief of having to wear old blue jeans. But she was too weary with fears to raise her arms.

Mrs. Bergeron hugged her anyway.

Mothers — the most wonderful people in the world. Christina pretended Mrs. Bergeron was her own mother. She sank into the hug. Jonah's mother said, "When you reach the ski resort, why, you'll slip into this and be the most beautiful girl on the slopes." Folding the lemony snow puffs of jacket and pants, she tucked them into a dark brown shopping bag. It was hidden in there, a secret victory for Christina.

"Thank you," Christina whispered.

Mrs. Bergeron said, "Nonsense. Now you two go out there and get some fresh air. You need a little color in your cheeks."

Outside the snowball battles had reached war proportions. Teams were spread across the yards with snipers in trees, while officers built caches of snowballs to supply their soldiers with.

Christina ran to find Jonah. "You told your mother I didn't have a ski suit," she said.

"Are you mad?"

"No! It's so beautiful!"

Jonah looked at her with that new intense heat that had shocked her before. But neither could act on it. They were pelted with snowballs as the opposite team caught them unaware.

The sun sank in the sky: ripples of pink and purple flung like ribbons into the snow-threatening distance. The children were incredibly beautiful against the snow. Scarlet, blue, green, and gold were their jackets and scarves. Like a medieval pageant, they trooped on a white world.

And Christina, when it was time to go home, held in a brown paper bag her second secret: clothes that would give her the strength to ski.

Chapter 19

The girls shared a bedroom. It had one bunk bed and one double bed on each side of an enormous diamond-shaped window that looked right out on the ski slopes. The bare wood floor was slippery and smelled of wax. On the bathroom door was a mirror panel, in front of which Dolly preened. She was a pixie. Anya had French-braided the gleaming red hair in a single tight row from her forehead back to the nape of her neck: Dolly's lovely little head, slender neck, and tiny wrists were all that showed beneath the emerald green wrapper of ski suit. Dolly turned left and turned right, looked back over her shoulder and dipped.

"You're perfect," said Mrs. Shevvington, entering the room.

Dolly looked up shyly, as eager for Mrs. Shevvington's compliments as Christina would have been for Blake's. Dolly said, "I'm still afraid of falling." She shivered, looking fragile as glass.

Mrs. Shevvington was already shaped like a refrigerator. In her padded ski suit she looked like a wicked, beardless Santa Claus. Next to her, Dolly was a miniature person, a pet, like a miniature poodle. Mrs. Shevvington patted Dolly like a dog, too.

Christina was undressed, but she had not taken the yellow ski suit out of its brown paper bag. The jeans she had peeled off lay in a messy inside-out pile on the floor. Anya had nothing to change into. The pitiful old ski jacket with its stains and tears hung loosely on her narrow shoulders.

Mrs. Shevvington's eyes passed over Christina and Anya, and she was satisfied with what she saw. To Dolly she said, "Of course you'll fall. Beginners always fall. But it's just tipping over, and slithering on the snow for a few feet. The bunny slope is made for falling. And before you know it, you'll be sailing down Gentle Deer, which is the advanced-beginner trail and then Running Deer, which is intermediate."

Into Christina's ear, Anya breathed, "What if he doesn't come?" Her beauty was like a thread — anything could cut it through. He will, promised Christina soundlessly.

Dolly took Mrs. Shevvington's hand. "Are you sure I won't fall very hard?"

"Even if you do, look how padded you are. A baby doesn't get hurt when it sits down because of its diapers. And you won't either."

Dolly beamed up at Mrs. Shevvington. "You always know what to say."

"We decided," Mrs. Shevvington added, "that it would be best to sign you all up for a beginner class. After all, we don't want any broken bones in the first five minutes, do we?" She smiled, her little corn teeth the only color in her oatmeal face, as if she had scheduled the broken bones for later on. "So Anya, Christina, hurry and get ready. We'll meet you at the bunny slope in a few moments."

They had to cover their tracks, of course. Adoring school parents must be able to compliment the Shevvingtons no matter what happened to Dolly.

Dolly said to Christina, "And you didn't trust the Shevvingtons to make this a perfect weekend." She hugged Mrs. Shevvington. "You knew I needed beginner company to fall with, didn't you?" she said lovingly. "Thank you for being nice to Christina even when she's difficult." Dolly and Mrs. Shevvington left the room without a backward glance.

Christina took her turn in front of the mirror. Slowly she slid her legs into the puffy, satiny folds of the ski pants. She fastened the suspenders and adjusted the high waist. Holding her turtleneck sleeves with her fingertips so they wouldn't get caught in the jacket, she put on the daffodil-yellow top. Slowly she zipped it up, watching her reflection. She ran her ten fingers into her hair and fluffed it around the collar. I'm pretty, she thought. She wondered if Blake would tell her so, if he would grin when he saw her and yell, "Hey Chrissie, I've missed you!" If he would say, "Gosh, you look pretty; yellow is your color."

Anya whispered, "Chrissie! Look out the window!"

Outdoors, the snow fell thickly and steadily in a harsh wind.

It was like seeing through a lace curtain. People were blurred and snow laden.

Like the Shevvingtons, most people on the slopes wore dark fashion colors: magenta, jade, or navy. When I am out there, Christina thought, I will blend with the weather and the mountains and the sky — lemon yellow with white. I will be beautiful. Different. Memorable.

Anya was pointing. Her thin, ringless finger was trembling.

Christina looked harder and saw Blake.

Blake! No cap, even in this cruel wind, just a scarlet headband that lifted his dark hair and protected his ears, and a high-necked scarlet jacket that snuggled under his chin. Across the ski suit was a silver metallic slash from chest to knee. He seemed taller to Christina, and he was certainly broader. He wore his ski boots and held his skis, which he was resting in the snow as he examined every person coming out the lodge doors. After a while he turned to look in other directions. The snow glittered white and furious, and he slid sunglasses onto the bridge of his nose.

He held the snow as an actor holds the stage. It was his.

People paused when they saw him, admired him for a moment, and gave him space: he was too impressive to shoulder out of the way.

Blake, I love you! Christina sent her message by heart. Then, guiltily, she turned to look at Anya, who loved him, too.

Anya's hair had worked loose. Its dark tendrils

curled around the ragged old hood. Her thin ivory face was as translucent as the sky at dawn. "He came," she breathed. Tears filled her eyes, and she rested both palms on the icy window, staring down at Blake. The wind attacked Blake and lifted his hair but he did not move, surveying the skiers, looking for Anya.

Anya looked down at herself. At the ugly maroon jacket, the wrong length for her, not quite warm enough, the rips she had not mended. Her cheeks stained red. She took a painful little breath, lifted her chin, and said, "I love him. Love doesn't need perfect clothes."

She kissed Christina. "Cancel me out of the beginner class," she whispered. "Blake will teach me."

Christina held her daydreams for another second: a wonderful instant of Blake's love, Blake's touch, Blake's company. Then she said, "Quick. Switch clothes with me. You have to look perfect for Blake."

"No," said Anya. "Mrs. Bergeron gave them to you. So Gretch- and Vicki-types wouldn't laugh at you."

"I know how to laugh back," said Christina. She was unzipped, she was unbuttoned, she was peeling it away. She was trying not to cry.

Anya bit her lips, staring not at Christina but at the lemony fluff piling by Christina's feet. Then with desperate speed she ripped off her ugly old things and yanked on the yellow. They had been too big for Christina; they were slightly too snug for Anya: but it made her slim and fragile instead of the padded pillow so many skiers resembled. Christina teased Anya's hair into tiny black curls beneath the daffodil trim.

Anya whispered, "Thank you, Chrissie," and hugged her, and ran out of the room. Christina, slowly putting back on her own jeans and her regular old winter jacket and scarves, stood by the diamond window, watching Blake.

All her life she would remember Anya coming down the steps of the lodge — how Blake half knew her and half didn't. How he suddenly flung back his head, and laughed, and tore off his sunglasses. How he strode forward, folded back the yellow hood and, with his bare hands in that terrible cold, held her face up to his. Tilted her head back, kissed her cold lips, and spoke to her and kissed her again.

Christina was a silly little seventh-grader, alone in a snow-cold world.

Blake loved Anya. Always had, always would.

The bunny slope was hardly even a bump. There was no chair lift to the top, but a rope, like a clothesline on a pulley. The class had all ages in it: nervous middle-aged women and fearless toddlers. Nobody else was wearing jeans. Dolly frowned. "I thought you said you had gotten good clothes somewhere," she said. "Were you yarning again, Chrissie? You have to stop that. It's a very bad habit."

Mr. and Mrs. Shevvington said, "Now, Dolly. Be generous. Forgive Christina her lies."

I'm the one who's generous! thought Christina, yearning for credit.

But she could not tell them; they still didn't know about Blake, and they certainly would not recognize Anya in her lemon yellow. The more time Anya had with Blake before the Shevvingtons knew, the more her strength would return.

The wind went through the denim fabric as if her legs were bare.

Skiing turned out to be like riding a bicycle: once you had it, you had it. The first time down Christina was fine; the second time she fell twice; the third time she fell once; the fourth time she was fine again. "This is fun!" she said to Dolly, and to her astonishment Dolly's little cheeks were red with joy, and Dolly nodded. "I love it!" she cried against the wind. "I think I'm going to be good at it!"

The wind lifted Christina's hair like banners of silver and gold. The instructor cried, "What beautiful hair! I've never seen hair like that. Is it real?"

Christina and Dolly laughed together.

The snow and the slopes had turned them back into friends: it was like the island: it pulled them together, it made them one.

The Shevvingtons had vanished. They were dressed in dark blue. The moment they skied away and got in line somewhere they became invisible. I will never know where they are, thought Christina Romney, and felt a chill that was not wind factor.

In only two hours they graduated. "Great work, girls," said the instructor approvingly. "Now right over there are Gentle Deer and Running Deer. Use the ski lift. I'll watch you the first time, and then you're on your own because I'll be starting another class. Don't try Running Deer yet. It's a little tricky for the first day."

"Gentle Deer," repeated Dolly. "Doesn't it sound like an Indian mother, rocking her papoose?" The two girls got in line for their first chair lift. The brutal wind had kept many people indoors. Only a dozen skiers were in front of them: several adults wearing navy. Nobody looked thick enough to be Mrs. Shevvington, nor lean and elegant enough to be Mr. Shevvington.

The ski lift had a metal seat no wider and no more substantial than a backyard swing's. The back was a wide metal bar, and in front a thin metal bar snapped in place. The wind rocked the chairs back and forth. Each time the lift stopped for the next passenger, the skiers higher up jerked. Their legs dangled above the open snow. They went higher and higher in the sky, until far up Gentle Deer they vanished in the swirling snow, eaten by the mountain.

"I can't," whimpered Dolly. "I'll fall, Chrissie. I don't want to do this, Chrissie, don't make me, Chrissie, let's go inside and get warm at the fire, Chrissie — "

An attendant plopped them backward onto the thin metal seat, swung the bar closed, and they were snatched up the mountain, two by two.

Christina was terrified. She had not known how high it would be. How flimsy. Gripping the bar in her mittens she choked back a sob of fear. When Dolly twisted around, the chair swung hideously. They both screamed. Behind them two kids about five years old called, "What are you so worried about? This is nothing. Don't make a big deal over it." Shamed, Christina and Dolly grit their teeth and prayed, teetering over the tops of the pointed firs. Every few yards the horrible little container jerked again, picking up more skiers.

At the top came the next terror — how to get off. They desperately studied the people ahead but couldn't quite see how it was done. An attendant thrust open the bar and Christina lurched out, tumbling ingloriously and falling on her bottom. Dolly vaulted off, landing perfectly and then tipping over slowly. "We're alive," whispered Dolly, lying on her side, giggling like a maniac. The five-year-olds rolled their eyes and took off immediately, sailing on the snow as easily as island children sailed on the sea.

Bodies leaning left and leaning right, poles angled for balance, scarves flying out, skiers hurtled down the hill. Quite a few skied in pairs: an expert father held hands with his beginner child. Nobody fell.

Behind them towering evergreens blocked the sky. Every branch of every tree held its armload of snow, dumping one now and again with a smothering *plop*. The shadows of the great trees were black and blue, like bruises. The wind screamed. The ski lift clattered. Christina took a deep breath to steady herself, and the wind tore the air out of her lungs, leaving her gasping. The patch on her thigh, where she had fallen on the bunny slope had soaked through and was now ice.

"You go first," said Dolly.

Gentle Deer seemed miles long. Bumps and dips made the skiers fly into the air. By the time they reached the bottom the skiers were as tiny and indistinguishable as little colored Legos. "I can't," said Christina. Her lips were chapped, and her hands ached.

"Sure you can," said the attendant, and he gave first Dolly and then Christina a push.

Dolly screamed, knees bent not for style but folding up to stay alive. Christina knew the meaning of "heart in mouth." Her whole insides lurched. The world seemed to slam into her face, speeding toward her as she rushed through it, but she hit nothing. She passed Dolly, she hurtled forward, thinking, How do I stop? I'll go through the building; I'll have a face full of logs.

She and Dolly were caught by their instructor. "Great work! You two are naturals. Not a twitch of nerves. Well, enjoy your day! Keep in touch."

Gentle Deer was boring. Christina knew its rises and falls and was accustomed to the speed. She wanted to try Running Deer. She had become good in a short time, and she knew why: she had forced her mind and body to it because otherwise her mind would have been wrapped around Blake.

Blake and Anya had vanished. Christina's heart ached. Her jeans were so cold! How she wished she could be Anya! Or at least be wearing the yellow suit.

Hours had passed. The shadows of the pines and

firs at the top of Gentle Deer stretched halfway down the mountain, and the snow no longer seemed white but blue.

Dolly said, "I'm cold, Chrissie. I'm going in."

"Don't you want to try Running Deer?"

"My feet are killing me," said Dolly. "My ankles are killing me, my back is killing me, my hands are killing me."

"That's pretty bad," said Blake, who was suddenly there, smiling down at them both.

But Dolly did not know Blake, because he had left for boarding school before Dolly arrived from Burning Fog Isle. She thought he was just a cheerful stranger, and she smiled without interest. She was too chilled for a real smile — the corners of her blue lips merely twitched. Taking off her skis, Dolly trudged toward the lodge.

Christina was inches away from him. She had not grown over the winter, but he had. And he was as handsome as she remembered. His cheeks were windburned, and around his eyes were white patches where his sunglasses protected him. "I'm glad to see you," she said formally.

Blake grinned at her.

Christina felt as weak as Dolly. She wanted to fold against him like a baby blanket and be snuggled. "Where's Anya?" she said.

"Same as Dolly. Wiped out. What's the matter with you island girls? No inner strength?" He was laughing.

Christina's inner strength had deserted her the

moment Blake appeared. And when he gave her a hug, she wanted to spend the rest of her life with him.

"You don't want to go in yet, do you?" he said anxiously. "Ski with me, okay?"

"You're too good for me," said Christina. "I haven't even tried Running Deer."

"I'll ski it with you. You can do it fine. I've been watching you. You have a real knack for this. I think skiing is going to be your sport." He took her hand; or rather, his thick glove took her mitten. They seesawed across the snow toward the ski lift. "There was an English assignment; we had to describe something unusual. I wrote about your hair."

Christina trembled. Blake said, "Anya told me the ski suit is yours. Tomorrow you wear it. She doesn't really like skiing. It was sweet of you to give it to her, but I have to say that it hurts my feelings. You two thought I wouldn't like her anymore if she wore old clothes. Clothes don't have anything to do with it. Jeans aren't warm enough, Chrissie."

She fell even deeper in love, that Blake cared whether she was warm enough. She said, "If clothes don't have anything to do with it, why do you care who wears what?"

He laughed. "Clothes have nothing to do with love, but a lot to do with skiing."

They rode on the ski lift together. Where Dolly had taken up no more space than a straw, Blake filled most of the seat. His bulk was comforting.

"I'm not scared now," said Christina. He grinned at her and ruffled the hair that stuck out from under her raggedy cap.

For that ride, there was no age difference, she was not thirteen going on fourteen, and he was not eighteen. They were a handsome boy and a beautiful girl; there was no world but snow and speed and each other.

Jonah had a crush on her, tenth-grade skaters were tempted by her hair, and Blake . . . Blake wanted somebody. And Anya had left; had she run away? Had she drifted into her lost soul so he couldn't reach her?

"Let's ski partners," said Blake.

"How?"

"Like dancers. You stand at my side and I hold your left hand with my left hand, like this." He held their hands in front and his right hand circled her back. "And I hold your right hand at your waist, like this."

Perhaps that's all there is to love, thought Christina. You both have to need it at the same time.

Blake wants to be in love.

Anya is not here.

I could have him.

Chapter 20

She and Blake glided on and on, his hand steadying her waist, while her heart lost its balance. Over the cry of the wind and the pounding of her pulse, Christina heard a giggle.

An enormous man skied past at tremendous speed, his poles digging into the snow, his body low over his knees. His eyes were hidden by bulging goggles; the skin of his face was protected by a cap with holes, only his lips protruding from lumpy knitting. From the thick lips came a sound Christina knew only too well.

Christina lost her balance, but Blake caught her effortlessly and steered her like a little truck.

The creature of the wet suit and the crunching bleacher — *here*?

On Running Deer?

I am safe, thought Christina. But where is Dolly? Where is Anya? They went inside — but to what?

Blake glided to an easy stop and swung Christina around, their skis in a row, so they were looking up the mountains. "Don't you think skiing is the prettiest sport on Earth?" said Blake. He was smiling at the view, not at Christina. "Mountains under snow. Evergreens against sky." He pointed at the slopes, now nearly bare of people. The day's skiers had left an enormous crisscross of slithery tracks, blue with shadow. Three chair lifts rocked in the wind, carrying almost nobody as the dark of evening settled in: the easy one at Gentle Deer, the medium one at Cardinal, and the incredibly high one — its cables silver thread in a blackening sky — that took advanced skiers to Suicide.

"Come on," said Blake. "Let's go down Cardinal."

"Blake," she protested, "I've only been skiing one day."

"Coward."

"I am not!"

"Yes, you are, Christina of the Isle. I'm going to ski with you, and you can do it. Unless you're a scaredy-cat. Come on. Cardinal. With me."

Laughing, he skied away from her. He looked over his shoulder once to make sure she was following. His long, experienced legs slid swiftly over the hard, rutted snow toward the lift for Cardinal. She was so much shorter and hardly knew how to make the skis walk. Slithering around, struggling, she tried to follow him. "Blake!" she called. "Drag me! Come on, be nice!"

The red suit with the silver blaze came to a halt. Giggling, Christina gripped the loose bottom of the jacket, and Blake skied forward, towing her. She had to concentrate just as hard, though, or the fronts of her skis would tangle with the backs of his. Studying the ground and the backs of his boots, she hung on.

They were in luck.

Only one pair ahead of them at the lift.

But then, it was getting dark. The snow fell even harder, like flecks of sand dashed off the beach in a hurricane. She protected her face with her elbow. I wonder how cold I am, thought Christina. I wonder if I have frostbite from wearing wet jeans.

She dropped into the seat next to Blake and leaned on him. He did not tell her to move over. Perhaps he doesn't miss Anya at all, thought Christina, and at the same time her soul was glad, her guilt washed over her as cold as the wind. She had the strange thought that Blake did not smell right. The preppy leather and aftershave smell were not there. She frowned slightly, tilting her head up toward him. The snow flung itself in her face.

How high they were! No other skiers sat on the chairs around them.

Beyond him, she watched the other two chair lifts jerk toward their mountain tops. Both were on her left. But Cardinal was on the middle. She recognized the bunny slope, Gentle Deer, and Running Deer, way, way over there beyond Cardinal. "Blake!" she breathed. "Blake, we're on Suicide! Why did you do that?"

He said nothing.

She looked up.

It was not Blake.

It was the creature of her nightmares: the wet suit, the smell of the sea crushing her behind bleachers. *It was him.*

Christina screamed.

There was no place to go. Nothing protected her: no safety belts, no enclosures. The lift on Suicide jerked. Christina seemed closer to airplanes than Earth.

The thing began giggling, laughing and laughing and laughing and laughing. Christina screamed to match. "Don't touch me! Don't touch me!"

She looked down. This mountain was not Gentle Deer. It was fierce with weapons — rocks and trees, gullies and chasms. It was not called Suicide for nothing. Below her a cliff yawned, its rock face so sheer that no snow could collect on it.

She clawed at his face mask, trying to rip away the goggles, peel off the lumpy knitting, see who this was.

But it shoved her.

And at the same time, it released the metal bar.

Christina rolled off the narrow seat.

Her screams ran like a streamer into the sky. She went out frontwards, saw the snow coming toward her, heard his giggle, heard the chair lift snap forward, having dumped her, all unknowing. From the ground a chorus of screams from every skier sang.

My folder, thought Christina. It is closed forever now.

Chapter 21

Orange.

Everything was orange.

"It's okay, honey," orange people kept saying.

What did she own, who did she know who was bright neon-orange?

"You're all right. It's a miracle." Even their heads were orange.

"We're just going to strap you onto this sled, honey. Don't be scared; we're right with you."

There seemed to be a vast crowd of people. Legs everywhere, bright-colored legs, not just orange, but all colors: blue, green, yellow, red —

Red, thought Christina. The red suit I thought was Blake. It pushed me off the ski lift.

She tried to raise her head, but orange hands pressed her back down onto the sled. "Lie still, honey. You fell into soft snow. You didn't break bones; you didn't suffocate. That was a one in a million fall — we're guessing just bruises, but you lie still until a doctor looks at you."

They were a rescue crew. Over their ski clothes

they wore plastic orange smocks like firemen or highway workers, so they would be visible in any weather. And the colored legs: it was a gathering crowd of skiers at eye level. They were making a great deal of noise. "Why is everybody shouting?" whispered Christina. She was no longer on the mountain. They had moved her off the treacherous ski slope to the cleared area in front of the lodge and were waiting for the ambulance.

"They're pretty glad you're okay," said a rescue worker. "A lot of people saw you fall out of that chair lift. I guess it's everybody's nightmare."

"I didn't fall," said Christina. "I was pushed."

But the rescue worker just knelt beside her and patted her. "You're still shaken up, sweetie," said the woman in a motherly voice. "Nobody pushed you. The metal bar came undone somehow."

"The man in the red suit," protested Christina.

"There was somebody in the lift ahead of you," agreed the rescue people, "but that skier may not even have seen what was happening. At any rate, whoever it was apparently reached the top and skied on down Suicide. We're hoping he'll get in touch with us and let us know what he saw, if anything."

The Shevvingtons were pushing through the crowd to reach Christina.

Blake got there first. "I thought you were right behind me!" he said. "I looked around and no Christina!" He felt her, up and down her ski clothes, as if expecting to find and set any broken bones himself. His face was white as snow. "She was with me!" Blake said to the rescue squad. "I was going to take her down Cardinal, partners. And then she vanished."

"Got on the wrong ski lift," said one man. "We've got signs everywhere. I don't know what else we can do to make it clear that Suicide is very advanced. Imagine a beginner getting on that lift! Didn't you read any of those signs, honey?" he said, angry with Christina.

"I didn't look up," whispered Christina.

"Great," said the rescue worker. "We have a dozen signs, and the kid doesn't bother to read."

"Blake, listen to me. It was that man. The wetsuit man. He's here. In a snow suit. Red. Like yours. I thought he was you."

"I guess she did hit her head," said the woman rescue worker. "Listen to her babble. Let's get her down the mountain right away. Is the ambulance here yet? Is the doctor here?"

Mrs. Shevvington arrived and flung herself down in the snow next to the sled stretcher. "Chrissie, darling," she cried. "Thank goodness you are all right!" She gazed pleadingly up at the orange people. "It's my fault," she cried. "I didn't watch her closely enough. I had no idea she would try anything like that!"

The rescue squad was absolutely shocked. "You mean you think she may have done it on purpose?" one whispered.

"No!" screamed Christina. "Don't listen to her!"

"She is under psychiatric care right now," said Mrs. Shevvington. "I think the name of the ski trail must have stimulated her."

"It did not!" screamed Christina.

Mr. Shevvington stood over her, too. His ski suit looked black in the starlight. He had taken off his cap and goggles to show his distinguished hair. The crowd quieted a little, just as impressed with Mr. Shevvington as all adults always were. What did he have, that in moments he could make them admire him and believe his words? "We were so lucky," he breathed.

The crowd echoed, "You were so lucky!"

Christina felt like biting his ankles. The straps on the stretcher were not fastened down yet, and she jumped up, ready to beat on the Shevvingtons. Blake caught her. "Don't," he whispered. "You're playing into their hands! You have to act sane."

I'm going to kick them until I have kicked them all the way to the cliff, and then I'll kick them over! thought Christina.

Blake held her even tighter. "They want an excuse to lock you up," he breathed in her ear. "Don't give it to them! All these witnesses! Chrissie! Get a grip on yourself. Smile. Be a sweetie."

Once more, thought Christina, they've won. I refuse to believe it. I refuse to believe that I could be shoved off a ski lift, and all these people saw it, and still they think *I'm* the demented one!

Blake hissed, "I love you, Christina. Now save yourself! Do you hear me?"

Christina turned to the rescue squad workers. "I

cannot thank you enough," she said courteously, her clear voice ringing like an island bell in the mountain air. "I can't imagine how I could have been so dumb, getting on the wrong ski lift. I guess I just didn't shut the metal bar all the way closed when I got on. Please forgive me for causing such a stir. I'm perfectly all right. I don't need a doctor or an ambulance."

The squad looked uncertain. Christina was clearly able to stand and walk, but what was this woman implying about Christina's mental state?

But Christina was saved by Dolly, who hurtled through the crowd, her tiny emerald body like a bullet shot from a gun. "Chrissie, Chrissie!" shrieked Dolly. "Are you all right? I saw it from window! But I didn't know it was you up there!"

Dolly flung herself on Christina, and the little girls hugged. The crowd murmured, "Aw, isn't that sweet."

Blake said, "Let's go inside the lodge and get warm now. Chrissie's jeans are soaked through."

"Yes, she needs to get warm," agreed the crowd, as a single person.

Blake half carried, half led Christina up the lodge steps. The Shevvingtons tagged along. Blake was so handsome and debonair; Dolly was so adorable and vividly red and green; Christina was so appealing with her strange hair in the moonlight — nobody saw the Shevvingtons again.

But the price! thought Christina. This was my chance to corner them with the truth!

As if reading her mind, Blake said grimly, "This

was their chance to corner you, Chrissie. You nearly bought it. If you hadn't been paralyzed for life breaking your spine, they'd have locked you up with Val for attempting suicide. On Suicide Trail. It's pretty cute, when you think about it."

Christina remembered Blake's earlier words. *"I love you."*

The heat of his body had been merely warmth when she was cold; the support of his arms had been merely crutches when she was weak.

But now it was love. Christina was dizzy, sick, thrilled with love.

"Don't faint," said Blake, alarmed, half teasing. "Come on, girl of island granite. Be strong."

Dolly did not like tagging after Christina and Blake. She did not like all this attention for Christina when she, Dolly, was there. Dolly held out her arms to Mr. Shevvington. "Carry me!" she demanded in a high, piteous voice, like a kitten. "I'm so trembly after what happened to Chrissie."

Mr. Shevvington scooped her right up. He was tall, and Dolly was very visible snuggling against his shoulder. "Don't worry, little darling," cooed Mr. Shevvington. "You're safe with me."

The crowd sighed with pleasure. "Such a pretty picture," said everybody, tilting their heads like mother birds to watch Dolly being cuddled. Several people took photographs. Blake and Christina went ahead. Slowly the Shevvingtons followed them into the ski lodge.

Inside, a vast fire crackled in the towering two-story stone fireplace. Logs as big as Christina's room at the Inne smouldered in the stone cavity. "Heat," whispered Christina. "I could step right inside the flames to get warm, I'm so cold."

"Sssssssshhhh," said Blake urgently. "You want the Shevvingtons to quote you on that?"

"No, but I want to get warm."

"Where's Anya?" said Blake, getting irritable now. "She'll take you up to your room. You need to sit in a hot tub and get some warmth into your bones. And if Anya doesn't help, you'll have to ask Mrs. Shevvington."

A staircase, huge and solid, circled layer on layer above the stones. It was nothing like the tippy fragile forest of white banisters at Schooner Inne. It was made of great planks of oak, sturdy as trees.

Down the stairs came Anya.

She had dressed for dinner: a narrow white wool skirt beneath a delicate, lacy top with a row of tiny ribbons around the throat. Her hair was spun black and her lips were soft and pink. She was as beautiful as a princess, as fragile as glass.

Blake's grip on Christina loosened. His eyes were for Anya and Anya only. Vivid in scarlet pants and jacket, his dark hair windbrushed, his cheeks windburned, Blake crossed the wide room to Anya, and she descended the stair to Blake. Complete in themselves, Blake and Anya touched fingers. Reaching over the banister, Blake guided Anya down the last few steps, and when she reached the bottom and there were no railings between them he took her in his arms and kissed her. Then, synchronized as a single person, they moved across the room to Christina.

I never had you, she thought, grieving. You were always Anya's.

She turned her head away to keep anyone from seeing the pain it caused her. Grow up, she told herself. You wanted Blake to be the rescuer, and he was. You wanted Blake to be a hero, and he is. So stop pretending he can be your boyfriend as well. You're a little girl. Anya is a beautiful woman.

"Blake!" said the Shevvingtons, shocked, setting Dolly down so fast she nearly hit the floor. "What are you doing here, Blake? Why aren't you at boarding school? What is going on, young man?" They tried to be the fierce principal and the harsh teacher, but the ski lodge diluted their power with Blake. He bowed to them mockingly. "What a surprise to meet again," he said. His eyes were exactly the same as theirs: hard, fighting eyes. If they entered a ring — Blake vs. Shevvington — Blake would win.

For Anya he would fight any battle.

Christina ached with cold and exhaustion. But at least the Shevvingtons were beaten. Christina had survived; Anya had Blake.

The rest of the weekend, thought Christina, trying to summon up energy and gladness, we will ski and laugh and party and stay up late. There would be no more accidents — the Shevvingtons can't risk it.

We'll have food sent up to the room, she decided,

having always wanted to order from room service. Perhaps we'll order in the middle of the night. If there's dancing, I'm sure Blake will save one dance for me.

Mrs. Shevvington's little black-hole eyes landed on Christina. Mrs. Shevvington knew when she was beaten. Christina knew that the Shevvingtons would change plans immediately. She did not have the strength to fight back this time. But Blake is here, she thought. Blake will fight for me. So it's all right.

Mrs. Shevvington straightened. "Arthur, dear," she said loudly to her husband, "after this dreadful brush with death, I'm too shaken to stay longer. I simply cannot finish out the ski weekend. My nerves," said Mrs. Shevvington, who had none, "are frayed. Girls, you must pack immediately. Go to your rooms. As soon as Christina is warm and in dry clothing, we'll drive straight home. Tonight."

But now I want the weekend, thought Christina. She did not have enough energy to argue a single syllable. She could hardly stand up without Blake.

Dolly said, "That's very wise, Mrs. Shevvington. Chrissie can hardly stand up. She can sleep in the car."

"I'd rather sleep in the room," Christina mumbled.

Mr. Shevvington picked Christina up this time. Blake was too absorbed by Anya to notice. Dolly frowned with faint jealousy. Christina was too tired to argue.

Anya wilted against Blake. "Home?" she whispered. "Oh, please, no! I just saw him again. Not yet!"

Just as she manages to blossom again, thought Christina, they cut her back.

"Come, Anya," said Mrs. Shevvington. "Come, Christina. Do not dillydally."

"Anya is staying for the weekend," said Blake. "I'll drive her home."

"She most certainly is not staying. I do not give permission," said Mrs. Shevvington.

"Permission," said Blake, "is not yours to give. I am eighteen. I can vote and die for my country. And therefore, I can decide when to drive Anya back to Schooner Inne."

A chill that was not from snow or mountains settled all over Christina's heart. If I go home without Blake or Anya, she thought, if I go back to Schooner Inne and only Dolly is between me and the Shevvingtons . . . that means there is nothing between me and the Shevvingtons.

Mrs. Shevvington stomped her foot, like Dolly having a pout. "Well, I'm not paying for that room," she said spitefully. "Just where do you expect Anya to sleep?"

"I'll get her a room," Blake said.

My folder is not yet closed, thought Christina, whose eyes had closed of their own accord. And I am so close to the truth now that the Shevvingtons cannot wait much longer to be rid of me.

Blake. I need you. You have to come, too. Anya has to come, too.

But she had not spoken aloud. She was thinking it in her sleep. She had fallen asleep right on Mr. Shevvington's shoulder. She knew it and did not know it, wanted to move but slept on.

So they were back early. She slept through the drive back to Schooner Inne, slept through being put to bed upstairs, slept till way into the next day, when Dolly woke her up. "I've had breakfast!" said Dolly impatiently. "Let's go over to Jonah's. They're playing in the ice maze. We have to tell them everything. And I have photographs. One of the people in the ski crowd had a Polaroid, and he gave me photographs. We'll show them to everybody."

"Of me falling?" cried Christina, waking up immediately, thinking, Proof, proof! This is it! A photograph of the man in the red suit — proof that I was pushed, that I was not alone in that chair lift! I'm there, I have it, I won after all, I —

"No, no," said Dolly. "Nobody had a camera out then. Photographs of us rescuing you. See this pretty one of me in Mr. Shevvington's arms? And here's a really nice one of me snuggling down next to your cheek to be sure you're all right."

Christina stared at the cracked plaster on her ceiling. Do I laugh or sob? she thought.

"What do you want for breakfast, Chrissie?" said Dolly. "I'm willing to fix you something."

"I think I'll just chew on my pillow for a while," said Christina.

* * *

Everybody was startled to have Christina and Dolly join them. "But you were going away for a three-day weekend," protested Jonah.

"Did you wear the yellow suit?" cried Mrs. Bergeron. "Did you have a wonderful time? Are you a natural at skiing? I bet you are."

Dolly said importantly, "Christina fell off the ski lift."

"No!" they all screamed. "She didn't! How terrifying! Are you all right, Chrissie? What happened?"

Dolly gave her version of the fall.

Christina did not offer hers. She could just imagine what people would say. *Pull yourself together, Christina; stop telling stories; behave in a socially acceptable manner; do what the Shevvingtons say.*

Jonah said impatiently, "Dolly, shut up. I want to hear what Christina says. You weren't part of it at all."

"I was so!" said Dolly, pulling her lips together in anger. "Look at the photographs of me."

"Nobody cares about photographs of you," said Jonah irritably, brushing her aside. "Christina," he said, "that is so scary." He pulled her away from the rest, so they were standing in a corner of the house that made a sun trap, out of the wind. "Chrissie," he whispered, "was there something more to this than — well — you know — the Shevvingtons? They wouldn't really go that far, would they?"

The rest were screaming, yelling, pushing, and sliding in the ice mazes.

I could be skiing now, Christina thought. With Blake. Going fast, skimming over the top of the world with his hand on my waist. Wearing the lemon-yellow suit. The sun could be over Running Deer instead of this boring old backyard.

She wanted to share with Blake, not Jonah! She wanted Blake to care, not Jonah! Jonah was just another seventh-grader. Blake was man, handsome and strong and —

and Anya's.

Christina sighed. She said, "I don't know. Let's play."

When it was time to go home, she could not find Dolly.

She shrugged. Dolly never stayed unless she was the center of attention. Dolly had doubtless gone on home herself.

Chapter 22

But Dolly was not at Schooner Inne.

The sun set. The sky went black. The snow began. And Dolly did not come home. There were no little sixth-grade friends to phone to see if she was at their house . . . Dolly had no friends.

Michael, Benjamin, and Christina put on coats and boots and went to look for Dolly. They searched between Jonah's house and Schooner Inne. The snow came down thick and heavy. Hedges turned into white snakes, parked cars became white monsters. Michael brushed snow off fire hydrants and garbage cans, as if he thought his little sister had frozen upright at the side of the road.

"When we get home," said Michael loudly, "we'll find her with Mrs. Shevvington in the kitchen."

Or has Dolly already been in the kitchen with Mrs. Shevvington? thought Christina. Is she missing because the Shevvingtons decided she would be?

"Or she was home all along," said Benjamin. "Hidden in some corner reading a book."

They liked that idea. The island children ran back

to Schooner Inne. They searched Dolly's and Anya's room. They went into the closets and up into the cupola. They looked in Christina's room and under the piles of extra blankets. They went through each guest room, and then the formal rooms downstairs.

Dolly was not in Schooner Inne.

The boys and Christina stood silently in the kitchen, staring at the Shevvingtons.

Even I, thought Christina — and I know how evil they are — even I am waiting for them to be the grown-ups and fix things.

Mrs. Shevvington did not make supper. Mr. Shevvington walked between the back and front doors, opening them, looking around for Dolly. Snow whipped into miniature drifts inside each door.

"Maybe we should call our parents and let them know," said Benj.

Mr. Shevvington said there was no point worrying them yet.

The snow came down. The temperature dropped. The wind howled.

Christina had thought Dolly was pouting because nobody had cared about her photographs and everybody put Christina first. But Dolly could only pout in front of people: Dolly needed an audience for everything she did. Where could Dolly be — by choice — without a companion or a crowd?

At nine o'clock Michael said, "Maybe we should call the police."

Mr. Shevvington hesitated. So Michael picked up the phone and called them himself.

They came, asked their questions, and looked through the house themselves, from cupola to cellar. No Dolly. They looked in the Shevvingtons' cars, in case she had fallen asleep in one of them. Then they said most likely Dolly had finished her hot chocolate at Jonah's, felt sleepy, and crept into some corner right there and fallen asleep. Off drove the police to search Jonah's house. It was such a logical, cozy explanation that for a whole half hour Christina felt good: surely Dolly was safe at Jonah's.

But she was not.

The police came back to Schooner Inne. They wanted a good photograph of Dolly.

Outside the snow fell harder. Is she cold? thought Christina. Is she scared? Is she lonely? Is she hungry?

It's my fault, thought Christina. I should have let her keep the spotlight. I know she can't live without it.

Her words rang in her head. Can't live, can't live, can't live.

"Had Dolly been having trouble at school?" asked the police. "Would she have run away?"

But how could Dolly run away? In a village with no bus, train, or taxi? The only place Dolly would go for refuge was Burning Fog Isle, and no boats were on the water in this weather.

"Like many island children," said Mr. Shevvington sadly, "Dolly had a hard time in school. She was an unhappy little girl." He managed to imply that it had been immoral of the Jayes to bring up their sons and daughter on Burning Fog Isle. He managed to imply that he and his wife, however, had been doing all they could to cure Dolly of her island upbringing.

"Dolly was not liked," added Mr. Shevvington. "Her locker was defaced. Her notebooks torn. The sneakers she left in her gym locker were shredded. A child shunned like that, I'm afraid, might reach for a grim and final solution."

"You're making that up," said Christina sharply. "That never happened. If those things had happened, Dolly would have told me."

"She didn't tell us much," said Michael, fighting tears. "She mostly confided in Mrs. Shevvington. Mrs. Shevvington was really her best friend," he told the police.

Mrs. Shevvington smiled pityingly. "It's a sad thing when a little girl's best friend is a strange grown-up, officer. But it is not unusual for unhappy children to seek out the most stable adult. I think you know the recent history of Anya and Christina. What examples to have set for you! Stability is not an island product." Mrs. Shevvington shook her oatmeal face back and forth. "Poor little Dolly. Perhaps in the morning . . . you should . . . drag the pond. Christina made her go there. Poor little Dolly was always drawn back."

"She was not!" cried Christina. "It wasn't like that."

They will redecorate that guest room, thought Christina. The one that was black and cream, lace and gauze, the one that was Anya. They will make it a room of Dolly. Emerald green and full of books.

Mrs. Shevvington began to cry noisily. Her crying was as ugly and solid as her face. Mr. Shevvington put an arm around her to comfort her.

The police officer said quickly, "Nobody blames you. You did your best. Anything could have happened. Going to a friend's house without calling you. Falling through thin ice."

Nobody would blame the Shevvingtons.

Why, the Shevvingtons would act as horrified as anybody. They would weep in front of people, saying it was their fault. People would gather around to reassure them. "It wasn't your fault," they would tell Mr. and Mrs. Shevvington, adding in a whisper, "Those island girls . . . so unstable . . . so strange. In the end, Dolly was no different."

If Christina told the police that Evil stood before them, fixing coffee, they would say Christina had gone winter mad. If Christina said, "Guess what almost happened to me skiing," the police would say to the Shevvingtons, "You people really have all the loonies living here, don't you?"

"Also," said Mrs. Shevvington, "the island children, especially Dolly, are fascinated by the fact that exactly one hundred years ago, the wife of the sea captain who built this house flung herself to her death by leaping off the cupola onto the rocks. Dolly asked for the details. I thought it was historical interest, and I encouraged it." Here Mrs. Shevvington wept a little. "But perhaps Dolly was planning to do the same. Oh dear, oh dear, oh dear," sobbed Mrs. Shevvington.

"My sister wouldn't do that," said Benjamin. He

was as stolid and unemotional as ever. "My sister is afraid of heights," he said. "She was afraid of that ski weekend because she'd have to go downhill face first." Then he said, "I'm going back out to look for my sister again."

"But where?" cried Mrs. Shevvington. "Where haven't you looked already?"

Benjamin shrugged. "I can't do *nothing*." He turned to the police. "She'd go to the island if she were going anywhere. Let's check every boat in the harbor. She might have sneaked aboard a fishing vessel."

The police thought that was logical. They said Michael and Benj could come with them for the hunt. "Me, too!" cried Christina.

"You're too little," said Michael. "And she's our sister."

Christina was alone in the mansion with the Shevvingtons.

They smiled at her.

Her skin crawled. She could feel the three colors of her hair separating and shivering. She smiled back.

Mr. Shevvington said, "I will telephone the Jayes now."

"Now when you know they can't come," said Christina. "You know they'll have to wait for dawn. Nobody can take a boat to the mainland at night during a snowstorm. So you know they'll sit awake all night, weeping and terrified."

Mr. Shevvington smiled.

Mrs. Shevvington smiled.

She could not sit in the room with them. Their smiles were too horrible, full of holes and yellow teeth and knowledge.

Christina went up the curling stairs to her cold little room.

She turned on the electric blanket and wrapped it around herself, mummy style. The Shevvingtons can't hurt me tonight, she thought. It's not reasonable, not when the whole police force will be back shortly. So I must stay calm and think. Either Dolly is hiding from the Shevvingtons . . . *or the Shevvingtons are hiding Dolly.*

Could they hide Dolly at Schooner Inne?

Christina had often wondered if the giggle who lived in the cellar came up for meals; if when she was asleep on the third floor, the giggle crept up to sit in the chair where Christina sat for supper; to drink from the glass Christina liked; to eat the leftovers Christina had wrapped in aluminum foil and put in the refrigerator.

Now she knew the giggle could ski.

But did she know where he was? Ski resort? School gym? Or back here? With Dolly?

Chapter 23

At two in the morning the policemen brought Michael and Benjamin back with the order to get some rest. They had found no trace of Dolly.

The boys went upstairs. The Shevvingtons followed. The Shevvingtons entered their room on the second floor. Michael and Benj continued up to the third. Christina rushed out to hear the news.

"She's got to be all right!" said Benjamin desperately. "What could have happened to her? She's so cautious."

Michael said, "Remember Anya this fall? How over and over she said the sea wanted one of us?"

How could they forget Anya, in her white gown, hidden by the cloud of her own hair, like an ancient prophetess, murmuring, "The sea wants one of us"?

"I'm calling Anya," said Benj thickly, turning, pounding back down the stairs. Michael and Christina thudded after him. He dialed the ski resort, and over the phone lines, across the miles, they heard the terror of being wakened by a phone call in the middle of the night. "Dolly's missing?" cried

Anya, her voice breaking and cracking like old ice. "Not Dolly! We're coming, Blake and I; we'll drive as fast as we can."

"There's no point," said Benj. "I just wanted to know if you had Dolly, or if she had come to you or talked to you." He hung up almost with violence, frustrated by another dead end.

They trudged back up the stairs. The endless circling stairs, like an endless circling nightmare. "Benj," said Christina, "do you think that the Shevvingtons — "

"Chrissie!" snapped Benjamin, "you're as crazy as Anya these days. Dolly's just — I don't know — lost or something." His voice broke. Benjamin, too, was lost.

The Shevvingtons will have captured us all, thought Christina.

She shut the door to her room. Michael and Benj's shut, and down below, the Shevvingtons' door closed with a *snap*.

Christina looked out the window into the village. In spite of the heavy snow, she could see far more lights than the night she had walked alone to break into the high school. Rotating red-and-blue lights on police cars looking for Dolly Jaye.

She isn't out there, thought Christina.

Christina was wearing her sweatpants with the jungle parrots. Over it she added an old hooded sweatshirt. She put on two pairs of socks instead of shoes. She checked the batteries of her flashlights. She put one flashlight in the kangaroo pocket of the sweatshirt and held the other in her hand — combination weapon and light.

For two hours she sat on her bed watching the lights go on and off in the town. Mostly they went off.

It was four in the morning.

If people were going to sleep at all, they would be asleep now.

Down the stairs crept Christina in her stocking feet. Nothing creaked to give her away. She reached the bottom and looked up. No moonlight filtered through the ice-caked cupola windows. The banisters rose like bones in the darkness. Nobody's bedroom door opened. Nobody had seen or heard her.

Through the hall, into the kitchen. She turned on no lights. In the dark she found the bolt on the cellar door. She worked it slowly, controlling the sound of her own breathing until finally, silently, she could open the cellar door. At the top of the stairs, she stood listening.

Silence.

She listened harder and separated the murmur of the furnace and the tick of the water heater.

She listened harder and found the thump of her own heart.

Then she turned on the two flashes, pointed them ahead of her, and tiptoed down into the cellar.

Nothing had changed.

There were old sawhorses and paint cans. Rusting tools and cardboard boxes on shelves.

Into the first room Christina went. She felt the outer stone walls for rocks that moved or drafts that came through cracks. She pushed hard on the inner walls. But there were no hidden rooms where a creature could lie in secret. All the inner walls were moldy paperboard.

Into the second room.

Nothing.

By now the damp in the floor had soaked through both her socks. Her feet were cold and beginning to hurt. This is nothing, Christina told herself. Think how Dolly's feet must feel, wherever she is.

Into the third room.

It contained some cardboard boxes sitting on shelves and a large trunk half hidden by old rusting tools.

The trunk was large.

Large enough to contain —

Christina tapped on the trunk with the flashlight.

It sounded thick and full.

It was not locked.

She opened it easily.

Ruby red and emerald green — like Dolly's hair, Dolly's ski suit — glittered in the shaft of her flashlight. Christina cried out, covering her mouth to stop the noise.

The trunk was full of old, discarded Christmas tree decorations — tarnished bulbs and faded tinsel.

She stuck her hand down through it.

Nothing else was there.

She closed the trunk.

She went into the fourth and final room.

The door creaked behind her.

She whirled, flashing her lights.

Nothing moved.

Her hair prickled.

She crossed the room.

From the room with the trunk came the giggle.

"I knew you were here!" breathed Christina Romney. "I knew when you saw it was me, you would come out."

Her hair of silver and gold gleamed in the half dark.

She left the fourth room. She held flashlights in each hand, like a gunman in a western going for the final shoot-out.

But nobody stood in the door of the room with the trunk.

She stepped toward it. Her breathing seemed louder than blizzards, her heart slamming against her ribs louder than waves against the rocks.

Nothing giggled.

Nothing moved.

She took another step. With her icy foot, she kicked the door open.

Nothing stood behind the door.

Nothing at all stood in the room.

"Dolly!" whispered Christina. "Are you there?"

Around her ankles she felt cold air.

Somewhere a door had opened, or a window. Cold off the sea was sifting through the cellar.

But there were no doors here, nor any windows.

Christina walked into the room with the trunk.

She moved her two lights around the room, and the shadows of the sawhorses and the paint cans and the trunk leaped and dissolved and leaped up again.

The cold air was almost a wind.

Cold as ghosts, thought Christina.

The sea captain's wife. Had she come back? Did she consist of cold air?

But Christina did not believe in ghosts. No ghost had tried to crush her in the bleachers.

Now the wind was stronger. It lifted her hair like fingers going for her throat.

Christina walked into the shadows, leaving shadows behind her, making shadows before her.

She could smell the mud flats.

It was the scent of Maine: the scent of low tide, the essence of the sea.

She faced into the scent and followed it, as if it were the smell of chocolate chip cookies at the bakery.

The wall was not the same shape it had been. It had an angle she had not felt when she was in this room before. It now had, in fact, an opening. A passage out to the cliffs.

Legend was correct.

The sea captain had had a reason for building his home on this terrible spot, alone and wind-tormented: private access to Candle Cove. What had he smuggled in or out this grim little rock-bound passage?

It was narrow. The stones on each side were hung with ice.

No wonder the rising tide sounded like advancing cannons when the waves slapped the opening of this passage. But where could the passage come out, except on the exposed ledges and shelves of the cliffs? Nobody could dock a boat there; it was rock, with the most dangerous tides in Maine twice a day.

She could not see the end of the passage.

It was dark out and still snowing.

But wherever the giggle was, and wherever he had Dolly, that, surely, was the end of the passage.

I'll go wake Michael and Benj, she thought. I won't mention the Shevvingtons or the giggle; if I do, they won't listen. I'll say I found a secret room in the cellar. The three of us together will find out what's at the end of the passage.

Christina was filled with the image: herself, Michael, and Benj, standing in a hole in the cliff, Dolly reaching her fragile arms up for rescue. Dolly would tell her brothers about the Shevvingtons, and Christina would be free of the lies they had wrapped around her, from burning clothes to tempting Dolly onto thin ice.

Christina turned to go back out, but her cold-as-lead feet betrayed her. She lost her balance, staggered slightly, and slid into the passage.

She caught herself by taking two steps forward . . . and then she knew the truth. The floor was slanted toward the Cove so the water would run back out. Slick with ice, it was as smooth as the maze in Jonah's backyard. Christina slid and fell. She could not get up. The walls and floor of the passage were solid ice.

Christina slid toward the black unknown. She dug her feet into the floor, but it was glass ice. She dropped first one flashlight and then the other, but freeing her fingers did not give her anything to grip. She braced her feet against one wall, but her weight carried her relentlessly toward the cliff. Inch by inch, she gathered momentum.

This is what happened to Dolly, Christina thought. She didn't jump to her death, like the sea captain's wife. She just slid on through.

I will vanish, too.

My parents will live with the same terror and unending worry that Dolly's will have to. Sympathetic townspeople will deliver casseroles to the Shevvingtons to bolster their spirits in this sad hour. Nobody will ever know. The briefcase will acquire more folders, more photographs, more treasures for the Shevvingtons to look at by night.

Christina fought the ice.

With every kick she slid faster.

Now she could feel the snow on her face.

Now she could almost taste the low tide.

There was a gray ghostliness ahead of her.

It's the end, she thought. Of the tunnel.

And of me.

Chapter 24

She was gathering speed; Christina was her own toboggan now. She shot into the air. She tried to arch, so that her feet, and not her spine, would hit the rocks. But there was no time. She landed with a jolt she felt from the base of her spine to the top of her skull.

She was sitting on a ledge, only a few feet above the mud flats.

With Dolly.

"Chrissie, you scared me," whispered Dolly.

"What are you doing here?" gasped Christina.

"The Shevvingtons' son put me here. Chrissie, when the tide comes in, we'll be swept off the rocks."

"The Shevvingtons' son?" repeated Christina.

"He lives in the cellar, Chrissie. Isn't that terrifying? He's been here all along! He's a crazy person, and he used to be in an institution, but they let him out because the psychiatrists didn't think he was dangerous anymore, and poor Mrs. Shevvington, who loves him — she's such a wonderful person, Chrissie; she just loves anybody, no matter what they do — anyway, she brought him back home. But he only likes dark, hidden places, so he lives in the cellar."

The snow gleamed faintly, as if they were in a ghost cove, near ghost water. Christina shuddered. "But where did he keep you?" she said. The Shevvingtons' son! Now there was a ghastly thought: another generation of them.

"In the passage. We sat there with his hand over my mouth while he giggled to himself," said Dolly. "We heard the police searching. He has a secret door, and they didn't find it. It's thin slabs of rock cemented onto a regular door, Chrissie. Just like in the very best books. The kind I love to read." Dolly shivered. "But I want to read about things, not have them happen."

How were she and Dolly going to get out of here? They could not climb up the cliffs: that would take ropes and picks. They could not get back into the passage; it was iced and anyway, the giggle was in there somewhere. *The Shevvingtons' son!* She knew now that he really would have crushed her up in the bleachers. And that Blake really would have died last autumn if it were not for the tourist who had accidentally happened along. And that she had really been meant to fall onto rocky crags, not soft snow beneath the ski lift.

The Shevvingtons emptied bodies.

Their son tried to kill them.

"How did he get you?" said Christina.

"I came into the kitchen, and he dragged me into the cellar. The Shevvingtons were home, but they didn't hear me screaming. Poor Mrs. Shevvington. This will hurt her so much! She loves her son, and it isn't her fault he's a bad person. I don't blame her for keeping him at home."

"Dolly!" cried Christina. "Can't you see that the Shevvingtons arranged this for you? They heard you screaming and enjoyed it!"

"Don't be ugly," said Dolly.

A giggle interrupted her.

Above them in the rock opening was the Shevvingtons' son, freed from an institution because he was no longer dangerous. "It's him," cried Dolly. She clutched Christina like a monkey, fingers wrapping around her.

High in the sea captain's mansion a window was thrust open, and a light went on. Mr. Shevvington's head emerged. "Mr. Shevvington!" cried Dolly. "Come and save us! We're down here!"

The wet suit began giggling.

Christina knew why he was laughing: the Shevvingtons would save nobody.

"We have to cross the Cove," said Christina, jerking Dolly to her feet. "There are people in those boats over there. If we can get to them, we'll be safe."

"Nobody can cross the Cove!" screamed Dolly, trying to jerk free of Christina. "The tide will come in and sweep us away. And besides, it's all mud flat and salt ice and salt pools we won't see in the night, and we'll fall in and drown!"

The wet suit giggled again and began lowering his dark, rubbery legs, coming down to their ledge.

The Shevvingtons' window closed, the light went off. They were going back to bed. By dawn, when police and parents arrived, there would be a new tide and no trace of two little girls from the Isle.

The wet suit's slippery foot found the first stony step down.

"Run!" Christina ordered, and she leaped off the ledge, dragging Dolly across the treacherous, dark, unknowable Cove. Dolly fought her. The mud sucked on her. Nothing but thin cotton socks were between her skin and whatever lurked in the mud. "Dolly, pick up your feet. Run! Tide's coming!"

At last Dolly obeyed Christina.

She's weak, thought Christina suddenly. I always thought Dolly was strong, like me. We were best friends all our lives, and I thought we were the same. We weren't. Dolly can follow but never lead. She followed Mrs. Shevvington, because Mrs. Shevvington is stronger. Perhaps the most dangerous thing on Earth is the person who always follows. What if you follow the wrong person? The wrong idea?

A whiffling sound filled the air. Like somebody blowing out candles on a birthday cake.

It was the tide.

They would be battered against the cliff walls like small fish; they would be carried out to sea under the water, their hair swirling red and gold beneath the waves.

The tide inched in like pancake batter.

Now and then a tourist died when he kept clamming, not believing a tide could become a twenty-eight foot wall. Picnickers got swept off pretty ledges, where they sat with their potato chips.

"The mud is eating my sneakers," sobbed Dolly.

The water gurgled like a milkshake and came toward them. Christina ran faster, but the mud refused to let her speed up. The water came up her legs, lapping her knees. She could no longer run, only wade.

From the cliff came the happy giggle of the wet suit. Christina looked over her shoulder. He was standing in the passage, waving at them.

The tide began its roar of triumph. The water had seen them and was bounding forward.

Dolly was dead weight, nothing but tears and fear. Dragging her, Christina burst out of the water into a sludge of mud and ice.

The tide screamed in rage and desire.

They were near the boats. If they could pull themselves on board, they would be safe from the tide, for a boat would simply rise with it.

Her ear heard a new sound. A motor. An engine.

Feverish with need, Christina looked up. Were the police here? Had a car pulled into the harbor parking lot?

She had been wrong that the Shevvingtons had gone back to bed.

After all the times she had outwitted them, they would not leave this to chance.

Mr. Shevvington got out of his van.

Chapter 25

But the hands that pulled Christina up were not Mr. Shevvington's.

They were a policeman's. In the wonderful warmth of those big arms, Christina knew she was safe.

"How did you know?" she whispered.

The scream of sirens filled the air. Whirling red-and-blue lights rocketed on police cars.

"It's entirely my fault," cried Mr. Shevvington. "My son is not well, but I thought he could function like a civilized human being. I was wrong. Oh, this is terrible. I am fully, wholly responsible for whatever has happened." Mr. Shevvington told the police that he had never dreamed his son had a way to come and go from Schooner Inne. He had never dreamed that his son would steal poor Dolly.

"He must have been the one who set fire to your clothing, Christina," cried Mr. Shevvington, hitting his head like one who has just found a solution to a terrible problem. "And to think we blamed you! Oh, Chrissie, will you ever forgive me?"

Christina had no intention of forgiving anybody anything. In fact she hoped Michael and Benj were remembering various tortures of yesteryear to inflict upon the Shevvington family.

Up at the top of Breakneck Hill, Mrs. Shevvington coaxed her son to go quietly with the policemen. Giggling, gibbering, in his wet suit, the man climbed into the back of a police car and drove away forever.

It was too cold to stay on the docks. The police rushed the girls into their cars, drove quickly up Breakneck Hill Road and carried them into the Inne, although Christina said it was the last place she wanted to be. "There, now," said the policeman comfortingly. "We took the bad guy away. It's warm in the Inne. And your island friend Anya just got there."

Anya! thought Christina. It will be all right. Anya and Blake are there; I'll have allies, people who understand, safety in numbers.

And sure enough, Blake, whose arms were wrapped around Anya to comfort her, spread his arms wider to hold Christina, too, so he was rocking two girls back and forth. One was granite, one fragile as a tern in a storm, but tonight it was difficult to tell which was which. "I've got you, Anya," murmured Blake. "Everything's all right, Dolly's all right." And to Christina he said, "You're so tough, kid. I love how you're so tough. You can handle anything, but I'm taking Anya to live with my aunt in Portsmouth. She's had enough of this crazy town. She needs a city and a fresh start."

Benjamin and Michael flew down the stairs to

hold their little sister. This lasted about a minute, when brotherly love ran out because the neighbors brought over doughnuts and coffee. Interest in food always ran higher than interest in sisters.

Mouth full of jelly doughnut, Benj, whom Christina had counted on to figure out the truth, said, "Dolly's okay. All's well that ends well. I admire you guys for taking your son back. I'm just sorry that your son never got well."

Christina could not believe it. She wanted to kick him.

"And I'm sorry we didn't believe your stories, Chrissie," said Michael. "All those times I told you to stop yarning — the giggle and the cellar and the clothes — it was all true. This person did it all."

"He didn't do it!" cried Christina. "You still don't understand! Listen to me. For once, listen to me! The Shevvingtons gave him his orders. They planned this. They trained him."

She had lost her audience. They went back to doughnuts.

"I'm going to call all the parents," said the policeman, "to let them know you're safe and everything's fine."

Mrs. Shevvington had managed to turn her oatmeal face into a fairly good replica of a human being, with an expression of grief and shame. "We'll have workmen come and seal up that cliff passage," said Mrs. Shevvington. She shuddered noticeably. "It's so dreadful. I had no idea at all!"

"You were feeding him," said Christina. "You had to have had some idea."

Mrs. Shevvington looked reprovingly at Christina. "We had a little apartment near the harbor for him. We gave him an allowance, Christina. How were we to know he had found a means of sneaking in? We would never have kept innocent children in a house where such things were going on! Really! I am an English teacher. My husband is a high school principal. Children and their dear little lives are our greatest and first concern."

The grown-ups in the room and the three Jaye children all nodded. Even Anya and Blake nodded.

So this is what a scapegoat is, Christina thought. You find somebody to blame it on, and everybody is happy. Even the victims are happy. "I don't believe this," Christina said.

Mr. Shevvington, elegant and citified, looked both strong and hurt, dignified and crushed. "Mrs. Shevvington and I are so proud of you, Christina. And of course, we owe you our apologies."

Christina snorted.

"When I talk to Mommy and Daddy on the phone," said Dolly, "I'm going to ask if I can finish sixth grade on the island. I think I'm too young for the mainland."

Her brothers said she was being brave and sensible. The Shevvingtons said, Oh, how they would miss her!

And, oh, how empty your file will be! thought Christina.

Christina could no longer stand being around any of these people. She went upstairs to take a shower, where gradually she turned the water from lukewarm to boiling. She washed her hair twice till it squeaked and, when she got out, towelled it dry. The gold and silver hair dried more quickly than the chocolate brown, and the gleaming ringlets curled in layers.

Christina went back downstairs. Temper, she said to herself. I must not lose my temper.

Dolly, Michael, and Benj had finished telling their parents everything.

Now the policemen were on the phone to Christina's mother and father. ". . . and your daughter is a heroine. Such presence of mind, such courage. She knew the only hope was to cross the Cove, and she managed it. I bet they'll want to interview her on television. Probably re-enact the whole thing for the cameras."

By now the downstairs was filled with noisy, happy people. It looked, for the first time, the way an inn should: a place where guests came to celebrate. All smiled lovingly at the Shevvingtons. Anya and Blake sat on a sofa, Anya asleep against his shoulder, Blake calm and proud to be the one supporting her. "It takes courage, also, Arthur," said one neighbor, "to admit poor judgment. The town will stand behind you, Arthur. You did what you thought was best."

Christina ate a jelly doughnut in two bites, took the phone from the policeman and shouted, "I saved Dolly, Daddy!"

"We're so proud of you, Chrissie," said her father in a choked voice. "Your mother and I are coming over in the morning. Actually it's nearly dawn now.

We'll see you very soon. Honey, forgive us for our doubts. There really was an explanation for all the things that happened. And now I want you to thank the Shevvingtons for us."

"To do what?" repeated Christina.

"Thank them. When they realized who must have committed the terrible crime of taking Dolly, they telephoned the police right away and admitted the circumstances. What responsible behavior. I think he is the best principal we've ever had."

Far from being tarnished by this, the Shevvingtons would win gold medals!

Mrs. Shevvington was smiling.

Never would Christina Romney thank Mrs. Shevvington for anything.

"Dolly, darling," said Mrs. Shevvington, "let me tuck you into bed. You have had a long and terrible twelve hours."

"First I have to thank my best friend," said Dolly. Almost shyly she approached Christina. The room went silent, watching them. "I'm sorry, Chrissie," she said humbly.

"It doesn't matter," said Christina. Christina kissed Dolly.

It did matter. She did not know if they could be friends again or not.

The Shevvingtons had gotten away with everything.

But I'm alive. Dolly has not been hurt in an accident. Anya is sane . . . well, maybe she's getting there. Blake is back.

I fought a good war.

But I didn't win.

The enemy is still on the battlefield. Still teaching. Still running a school. Still living at Schooner Inne.

Christina had not, after all, brought Val back, nor located Number Six of laughter and gold. Nor produced the files of past Shevvington victories.

Dolly smiled trustingly at Mrs. Shevvington, trustingly took her hand, trustingly followed her up the stairs that swirled like mad white fences.

The Shevvingtons would start again.

It would never end.

FIRE

Prologue

At five-thirty in the morning, the rising sun touched the coast of Maine, passed through a window high in Schooner Inne, and rested on a pillow. Strange hair lay on the pillow: silver and gold laced with chocolate brown.

The hair seemed to burn in the sunlight, its three colors melting as if on fire.

In the doorway of the bedroom, someone smiled at the sleeping girl. The smile exposed stubby yellow teeth in a face as flat as paper. Above the smile, eyes glowed like phosphorescent mold. Fingers, whose bitten nails were painted blood-red, lit a match. The match rasped across the striking surface like a knife being sharpened. The yellow smile curled across a complexion like pie dough, and the visitor slid away, down creaking stairs, behind thick green doors.

Chapter 1

Christina Romney woke with a jolt so intense she wondered if thirteen-year-olds ever had heart attacks. She pressed her two hands over her heart to stop it from beating so hard. What woke me? she thought. Christina preferred to take an hour to wake up, slowly sifting away the sleep.

Outside on the ocean, lobster boats roared. One was playing a radio station Christina particularly liked. She hummed along.

She ran her fingers through her hair, taming it. Sometimes she could feel the separate colors, as if the silver and gold and brown grew from different parts of her soul.

She hopped out of bed, dressing quickly. Even in May it was cold in the third-floor bedroom of the old sea captain's house perched on an ocean cliff. Christina needed a long-sleeved shirt, a cotton sweater, and a hooded sweatshirt. One by one, as the day warmed, she would peel them off.

She decided to go down to the wharf and talk to

the lobstermen. She knew most of them. Christina was not from the mainland; she was boarding at Schooner Inne for the school year; her home was Burning Fog Isle, far out at sea.

Eighteen days until summer vacation! Christina exulted. I can last for eighteen days of anything. Even seventh grade. Then I get to go *home*.

She was much, much older than she had been the September before. She wondered if the islanders would see how changed she was. Probably not. She had learned that people saw only your outside. Christina was the only seventh-grader who had not gotten any taller. Perhaps fear was damaging to your height.

She tugged her sweatshirt down over her small flat chest and turned to leave the little attic bedroom.

A long, thin, pale candle was burning by the door. It was stuck in an empty coffee can, leaning sideways, hot wax dripping right onto the floor. The flame leaned toward Christina.

Her heart jolted again and thrashed in her chest like an animal trying to escape. Only a few nights before, she had been sleepwalking. Or so the Shevvingtons claimed. She had ignored them. Christina was solid as granite; she would never do anything as fanciful as sleepwalk.

She bent to look at the candle, and its golden flame leaned toward her, as if to kiss her lips. As if she and the tiny fire were old, intimate friends.

She had a vision of herself staring blankly, creeping silently down all the curving stairs of the mansion, like a blind butterfly, breaking her wings against the walls until she reached the kitchen. Finding a tin can. Finding a candle. Dropping it into the can like a blueberry into a pail and lighting it. Drifting up to the attic again like a ghost, leaving a trail of wax.

Schooner Inne, its timbers centuries old, would burn as easily as crushed newspaper. She would never have brought a burning candle up here.

The candle winked at her. It knew the truth.

She blew it out, but the candle re-lit itself.

She could not wrench her eyes away from the flame. It was shaped like a weeping tear. She knelt beside it, her hair falling forward, like tinder ready to catch fire itself. Holding her hair up in a ponytail, she blew the flame out forcefully. The candle sagged down into the coffee can.

Christina picked it up. Making no noise, she tiptoed out of her room, around the tilting balcony, and down the bare wooden stairs. On the second floor Mr. and Mrs. Shevvington slept. It would not do to awaken *them* so early in the morning. The Shevvingtons with their eyes like mad dogs? They would froth at the mouth and bite Christina if they did not get eight hours of sleep.

Two other island children were finishing out the school year boarding at the Inne: Michael and Benjamin Jaye, who were older, both in high school. Michael and Benj slept through anything. You would have to drop cement blocks on their feet to waken them at dawn. No worry that they would get up and ask what she was doing, playing with fire.

She did worry about the stairs. Twisting, open, lined with a forest of fragile white banisters, they creaked with age. On the second-floor balcony, carpet began: thick, rich carpet that soaked up sound and warmed bare feet.

She crept past the Shevvingtons' bedroom. They had a lovely suite. The island children were kept in attic rooms with only a coat of paint to brighten them up.

Criminals have better housing than we do, thought Christina.

Behind their door, she heard the Shevvingtons talking. Mrs. Shevvington was her English teacher and Mr. Shevvington the high school principal. Christina flattened herself against the wall. If she had awakened them, school would not be worth living through. She listened to their voices, furry like leopards. They were talking of something else entirely.

". . . sell the Inne," said Mrs. Shevvington. Her voice was thick and sucking, like the mudflats at low tide. "We should get an excellent price for it. From city people who think it would be fun to run a bed and breakfast."

Christina nearly laughed. Mr. and Mrs. Shevvington did many things with those eight pretty bedrooms, but not once had they had a living guest.

No. These guest rooms held only the shells of the past.

". . . list it with a realtor today," said Mr. Shevvington. "I've been accepted as principal in that Chicago high school."

Christina pictured him: elegant and lean. Probably even his pajamas were tailored and impressive. All the parents adored Mr. Shevvington. They quoted him as if he were *The New York Times*. Even after all the terrible things that had happened that year, the parents still were on the Shevvingtons' side. "They tried their best," the grown-ups said sympathetically, bringing casseroles instead of drumming the Shevvingtons out of town.

Even Christina's mother and father said, "They were only trying to help their son, Chrissie. Have some compassion." For the Shevvingtons' grown son had been found living in Schooner Inne's cellar, giggling to himself, coming and going at low tide through the opening in the rock cliff.

People were already forgetting about Anya and Dolly.

Anya . . . Christina had always wanted to be and look just like Anya. Anya was very fair, and never tanned. Like a princess in a fairy tale, Anya remained chalk-white, with a frame of black hair so thick and heavy its weight curled her slender neck forward like a swan's. Anya had been the academic star of Burning Fog, the one everybody expected would go out into the world and bring fame to her family. Her boyfriend was a preppy townie named Blake, who dressed in what the children called Catalog Maine: rugby shirt, boat shoes without socks, loose trousers made of imported cotton. But then the Shevvingtons chose Anya, and bit by bit, turned Anya's senior year — which should have been a sort of heaven — into insanity, taking away her grades, her looks, and finally, Blake.

Next they chose Dolly, the youngest of the island children boarding at Schooner Inne. Dolly was elementary school size: a fragile collection of slender bones in big overalls, her red braids nearly as wide as her shoulders. They turned Dolly from a laughing, flying sixth-grader into a trembling, nervous creature sure that life would suffocate her; and sure enough, Dolly nearly had fatal accidents . . . three times.

How close the Shevvingtons had come to their goal — two island children destroyed in one school year. But Dolly was back on the island with her parents for the rest of the school year, and Anya had left for the city to stay with understanding relatives of Blake's.

So people were able to set the horror aside. They had a handy person to blame things on: the crazy son. Now that he was locked up it would be tacky and tasteless to mention the "problem" again.

"The Shevvingtons," everybody informed Christina, "have suffered enough."

As if Christina had not suffered! As if Anya and Dolly had not suffered!

". . . beautifully cleaned up," said Mrs. Shevvington. "I'll light fires in all the fireplaces when buyers come to look. It will seem so homey and cozy with embers glowing."

Homey! Cozy! The Shevvingtons? Hah!

And then Christina truly listened . . . the words sank into her sleepy, crack-of-dawn brain. *The Shevvingtons were leaving town!* Putting Schooner Inne on the market!

She was free! She was safe!

Christina skimmed down the last flight of stairs, light as a tern. She slid barefoot out the front door and sat on the granite steps to put on her shoes. She stuck the can and candle behind the stone planter in which windbeaten geraniums struggled for life. The sun curled on her lap like a honey-colored dog, licking her with yellow warmth.

Christina began laughing. Life was good. She was soon to be fourteen; seventh grade was nearly over; the Shevvingtons were leaving town. What more could a girl ask for?

Mr. and Mrs. Shevvington also dressed early. Then, smiling softly, they walked into each guest room. They stroked the bright blue colors in one room and gloated over the soft yellows in another. Downstairs they paced through the beautiful parlors still decorated as the sea captain had fixed them for his bride so many years before.

Nearly every room had a fireplace. These were not big sturdy brick fireplaces where colonial women cooked stew. They were small and elegant, surrounded by imported tiles and mantels of sea-green marble.

In the front parlor, the Shevvingtons crumpled newspaper, stacked kindling, and rested slender logs on the andirons. Mr. Shevvington struck a match. It was a wooden kitchen match. The big old house was drafty. The flame quivered, thin as a thread, and then fattened up, solid gold.

"I heard Christina go out," he remarked. His fingers were long and thin, like fireplace pokers.

"Christina," said Mrs. Shevvington dreamily, "would make a good wharf rat, don't you think?" She smiled, her little teeth like yellow corn, dried on the cob.

Mr. Shevvington laughed. His laugh crept through cracks like January winds. "Yes," he said. "A wharf rat. A girl who works on the docks, knee-deep in fish heads and motor oil, and loses all her teeth before she's twenty-five."

"A girl who sits alone eating jelly doughnuts, getting fat and repulsive, and nobody cares," added Mrs. Shevvington.

"A wharf rat," they said together.

Fire licked the wood, stretching into the chimney, reaching for oxygen. Silver and gold flames consumed the brown logs. "The three colors," said Mr. Shevvington, "of Christina's hair." His eyes were soft and warm, like a baby blanket.

Mrs. Shevvington's yellowish eyes were like poached eggs in an oatmeal face. "We do have," she said, "eighteen more days."

"How nice," said Mr. Shevvington.

Chapter 2

Late that afternoon, the other seventh-graders on the beach began to think of supper instead of hacking around. They called their mothers from the public phone and got rides home. Christina watched enviously as mothers beeped their horns, calling, "Hi, honey, have a good time?"

I have a mother like that, she thought. But my mother's on the island.

She looked out to sea. Burning Fog Isle was lost in the thick fog that had started rolling in. Sometimes a trick of atmosphere occurred: The sun shone behind the fog, blazing like flames. Many times in the last three hundred years, mainlanders had rushed to save ships at sea or houses on the Isle from fire. But there never was a real fire; it was just the fog, catching the sun in its soft gray prism.

Christina loved the fog. It hugged her and kept her secrets. It belonged to the sea and went back to the sea; and you could neither hold it nor summon it.

The wind fingered her hair, until it was a mass of gold-and-silver ribbons. She walked alone up Breakneck Hill. The quick-moving fog walked with her, wrapping her like a wet scarf. Unlocking the heavy green door, she let herself into the gloom of the front hall of Schooner Inne. The only light came from the cupola three stories up. The paper on the wall was flocked and formal; nobody would ever crayon on those walls, or even lean against them. She passed the parlor where nobody ever sat, for the chairs were stiff and sharp, and the sofas rigid and unwelcoming.

In the fireplace was a silent fire.

Christina blinked, backed up, and looked in the door again.

Fire glittered. But it made no crackle, gave off no scent, produced no smoke. Christina moved toward the fire like an iron filing slithering toward a magnet. She stretched out her fingers for warmth but felt none.

A fire without heat.

Hair falling forward, blending with the flames, Christina bent to touch the cold fire.

An odd catlike smell filled the room.

Mrs. Shevvington's voice purred. She said, "Christina, darling, what is this fascination you have with fire?"

Christina jumped. There was something subhuman about the way Mrs. Shevvington could appear anywhere, like an ant or a mouse coming through the cracks unheard.

Behind Mrs. Shevvington stood the brothers, Michael and Benj. Michael was growing so fast you could hardly keep track of him; he was fifteen now, and getting muscular, his favorite cotton sweater shoved up past the elbow. He had cut his hair even shorter, as if the taller he got, the less hair he needed. Benj was just solid; Benj had always seemed like a grown-up. He had skipped childhood entirely. His face rarely divided into smiles or frowns. Christina always wanted Benj to shout and laugh. But Benj was just there.

Mrs. Shevvington said, "I've not forgotten that dreadful episode during the winter, Christina, when you set fire to your clothes."

Christina sucked in her breath. She hated looking at Mrs. Shevvington. Sideways, the woman had no profile.

In his heavy voice, dragging like a net on the bottom of the sea, Benj said, "Mrs. Shevvington, we all know it was your son who set that fire."

Christina nearly fell over. Benjamin was defending her?

Mrs. Shevvington's eyes grew dark and threatening, like a thunderstorm. But Benj was too solid for her. She went snarling back into the kitchen. "Benj," said Christina delightedly, "you stuck up for me."

"You saved my sister Dolly's life, didn't you," he said, without a question mark at the end, as if Benj did not have questions, only facts.

"Yes, I did," she said. For it was a fact. She had

thought everyone had forgotten the terrible night in which she dragged Dolly across the mudflats, desperately trying to reach the opposite shore, while the tide hurtled forward to claim their bodies, and take them out to sea forever. While the Shevvingtons' insane son stood on the ledge, ready to throw them back into the sea if they tried to go back into Schooner Inne. Sometimes at night she woke to the sound of his laughter, shrieking over the waves, and she was never quite sure if it was a nightmare — or his return by dark.

It was nice to have done a good deed, and even nicer to get credit for that moment of courage that kept Dolly alive. Christina bounced toward old Benj, feeling warm toward him, warm toward the world. "Benjamin, Ice Cream Delight opened for the season. After supper do you want to go there and get a sundae with me?"

Benjamin stared at her incredulously. You would have thought he had never in his life gone for ice cream. He was too amazed even to answer her and went on in to supper.

Christina paused to check the silent fire. It was crinkled Mylar paper. Yellow, orange, and scarlet paper cut into flame shapes, crushed down over black Mylar that gleamed like coals. Fire of foil. How well done it was. And how like the Shevvingtons, she thought, to think that a fake fire will be cozy and homey enough for all those prospective Inne buyers.

She laughed to herself. She was always giving

the Shevvingtons credit for supernatural abilities. And there always turned out to be dull explanations. Like the changing poster of the sea that had driven Anya crazy, its evil, curling waves beckoning her over the edge one day, and the next day its painted ocean flat and wall-poster blue. Eventually they found out that Mrs. Shevvington just switched two posters back and forth.

Christina went into the kitchen with the others. They never ate in the dining room, always in the kitchen, on a hideously ugly table, its top chipped, its legs as fat as thighs. Benj was setting the table.

He's sixteen and they already call him Old Benj, thought Christina. He'll quit high school and be a lobsterman like his father and grandfather before him, and he won't say another syllable unless he's forced to. I wonder how he'll ask a girl to marry him? Perhaps she'll ask him. Then all he'll have to do is nod.

Christina plopped down in her chair.

"Christina," said Mr. Shevvington, "sit gracefully. Do not just let go and fall into the chair."

Christina tried to decide whether this was worth a fight or not. There were any number of arguments about sitting techniques.

But Benj said, "I think she is graceful." Benjamin passed the creamed potatoes Christina's way.

Christina hated sauces. There was something sinister about them, whether they were milk-white, hollandaise-yellow, spinach-green, or tomato-red. They hid the true food. You could not be sure what those little chopped things were, down at the bottom of the sauce. It hadn't been so bad when Dolly and Anya still lived there. Anya could always be counted on to surface from her foggy world to identify lumps for Christina. "That's an onion. That's a mushroom." (Dolly never ate anyway, her skinny little arms and legs barely stapled to her body. So it hadn't mattered to Dolly.)

How Christina missed Anya! Anya was as beautiful as sea foam, her thick dark hair a cloud around her translucent skin. But Anya had had no strength. Not like me, thought Christina with satisfaction. I'm like the Isle: I'm granite. Behind the safe cover of her tilted milk glass, Christina sneered at the Shevvingtons. It felt pretty good.

"Guess what," said Benjamin Jaye.

Christina choked on her milk. "Since when have you ever told us anything at all," she asked him, "let alone said to guess at it?"

Benjamin grinned at her.

Even the Shevvingtons blinked at the sight of Benj grinning.

"Is that a grin?" Christina teased.

Benjamin grinned even wider.

"You know how!" she cried. "Benj! You're so cute when you grin."

Now he blushed.

His younger brother said, "This is disgusting. Stop it, Benj. Just tell them."

Benj said, "The marching band is going to Disney World next fall. All we have to do is raise the money for forty-four of us to make the trip, and we get to be the Disney World band for the day! *Me*."

"Oh, Benjamin!" Christina screamed. "Florida? You'll fly down? In those wonderful band uniforms! All scarlet and gold braid, and white shoes. All those years of playing the trumpet are finally paying off. That's so great!"

Benjamin, who had possibly the world's largest appetite, was too excited to eat. Christina had never come across a boy who could not eat. Benj kept filling his fork and then setting it back down on the plate, untouched. "We'll take a bus down to Orlando," he said. "Flying's too expensive. But a really nice bus, with a bathroom and a snack bar. We'll stay five days."

"Five days at Disney World," breathed Christina. "That is so wonderful, Benj. You'll have the best time. How much money do we have to raise? I'll help. You'll need tons. Millions. We'll have car washes and bake sales and hike-a-thons."

Mr. Shevvington said, "At this point, the school has not yet given permission."

Benj dropped his fork, his face speaking instead of his tongue. *You might refuse to let us go to Disney World?*

Christina glared at Mr. Shevvington. "You won't even be here next year," she said hotly, forgetting she had learned this by eavesdropping. "You're getting a job in another state. So there."

"It won't matter if they have permission or not,"

said Mrs. Shevvington. "They can't raise that kind of money. A scrubby little Maine village like this? Hah!" she sniffed. "Don't set your heart on it, Benjamin, because it will not come about."

"Anyway," said Michael, his mouth all pouty, "why should everybody raise all that money for just you guys? Forty-four of you get to go to Disney World, but we don't. I don't play an instrument. So why should I help?"

Christina was outraged. "Because he's your brother," she said. "You're mean, Michael. You've been getting all the glory all year with your games and your trophies. Now you don't want your own brother to have any?"

Michael said, "He doesn't work as hard as we did. Band is just a dumb class, like art or cooking. Athletic teams have to practice every day after school. And Saturdays. What do they have to do for Band? Just show up, is all."

The brothers glared at each other.

Mrs. Shevvington said, "You're right, Michael. Benjamin rarely practices. And of course, he doesn't make that much of a contribution to the band anyway. After all these years, he's only third trumpet."

Benj, on whose face emotion so rarely showed, flinched. He stared down into his creamed potatoes so he would not have to see his brother's jealous eyes and the Shevvingtons' cruel mouths.

Christina thought, So that's what they'll do these last eighteen days. Try to hurt everybody in sight.

443

Look how quickly they stabbed old Benj. First time he's ever been filled with joy, and they punctured him right away.

Benjamin tried to take a sip from his glass, failed, and put it back on the table. The glass shook.

"You don't feel well," observed Mrs. Shevvington, a tiny smile slitting her face.

Benj shrugged.

"Seconds please," said Michael, pointing toward the serving bowls.

"Eat what Benj left on his plate," suggested Christina, "since you're the one who spoiled his appetite."

"Christina!" said Mrs. Shevvington. "Your manners are deteriorating every day. I am appalled at you. Go to your room."

"No," said Christina. "Benj and I are going for ice cream." She stood up, heart pounding. Disobeying the Shevvingtons was scary. She did not look at their eyes. His would be glittering like a seagull's, as it swept down to peck open a tern's egg. Hers would be little stones, as if there were not a person inside; just gravel.

"Your fourteenth birthday is only a few weeks away," said Mr. Shevvington, "and you are behaving like a spoiled toddler."

Benj said, "I forgot about your birthday, Chrissie. That's neat. It's hard to believe you'll be fourteen."

That was so much speech coming from Benj she

felt they should write it down and save it for his grandchildren to read.

"We should do something special," added Benj. "Since your mom and dad can't give you a party until you get back to the island for summer." He touched his jeans pocket where his wallet made a rectangular bulge. Benj worked at the gas station and saved every cent toward the new motor he wanted for his boat. It had not occurred to Christina that he would pay for the ice cream. She had expected to use her allowance.

If he paid, it would be like a date.

She hid her giggle at the mere idea of Benjamin having a date.

"I'm coming for ice cream, too," said Michael, jealous over even a tiny thing his brother might have and he wouldn't. "We'll try to think of something for Christina's birthday."

Mrs. Shevvington's smile was horrid, her little yellow teeth lined up like broken candy. She purred, "Perhaps *we* can think of something to do with Christina."

Chapter 3

Christina, in the middle, was by far the smallest. Her tri-colored hair flew in the wind like flags.

Michael was on her right. He talked loudly of sports and teams. She had never noticed before that Michael was something of a spoiled brat. Look at him, she thought. He can't bear it that Benj would even have an ice-cream cone that he doesn't have, let alone Disney World. And he certainly isn't going to let anybody talk about my birthday.

Mrs. Shevvington's words battered her head. *Perhaps we can think of something to do with Christina.* It did not sound like parties and confetti; it sounded like doom and destruction. She kept thinking of that creepy candle in the coffee can.

Benjamin was on her left. She came up to his shoulder. And what a shoulder it was. Curving muscle burst out from below the T-shirt, threatening to split the cotton. Benj, who never talked, talked steadily — right through his brother's babble, as if they were unaware of each other. He talked of Epcot and Space Mountain and his marching band uniform.

Behind them came the Shevvingtons, who had decided that they, too, needed a first ice cream of the season.

The five of us look like a family, Christina thought. People who don't know us would think What an interesting set of parents, what beautiful children.

That was enough to make her lose her appetite for ice cream. The idea of being Christina Shevvington instead of Christina Romney! "Yuck," she said out loud.

"You don't like the band uniforms?" said Benj.

"You don't think I'm the best ball player?" said Michael.

They were on the sidewalk, going down the treacherous rim of Breakneck Hill. Below them the tide slithered into Candle Cove like a muddy pancake, and then, hitting the rocks, spewed violently, like a pancake being whipped in a blender. The highest tides in Maine occurred in this very cove. Every few years, the tide picked an ignorant summer person off the rocks, or caught him in the mudflats, and sometimes the body was found and sometimes it wasn't.

Christina shivered, although the evening was hot. What will the Shevvingtons do with me? she thought. Will I be found? Here she was with two strapping boys who liked her — and neither one would believe it if she said the Shevvingtons were plotting against her. They were too busy thinking of baseball and Florida. She wrenched her mind off cliffs and drowning, fires and candles. "It's such a terrible decision what kind of ice cream to get, don't you think?" she babbled. "I love vanilla. I love chocolate. But each year they kick off the season with a new flavor, and it would be criminal not to taste it."

"Criminal, Chrissie?" Benjamin considered her word carefully. "It's not that severe."

"She's exaggerating, Benj," explained Michael, making his brother sound stupid. "That's what Christina does best anyhow. Stretch a story to fit."

The Shevvingtons laughed. "That's true, Michael. Christina tells more yarns than anybody in Maine."

Christina knotted her fist. She felt like appeasing the appetite of the tide with Shevvington bodies.

"There's a solution to your ice-cream problem, Chrissie," explained Michael in a condescending voice. "It's pretty high-tech. That's why you never thought of it. Just get a three-scoop cone." He laughed at her.

Christina's fist came straight up to Michael's nose, but he had grown up with her, and he was ready for it. He caught both her wrists, disarming her as easily as he would a toddler. He laughed. "No point in struggling, Chrissie," he said. "I'm a hundred times stronger."

His fingers closed around her wrists like locks.

She scrabbled at him, trying to get free. Nothing happened.

"Michael, you are so strong," said Mrs. Shevvington, full of admiration. "Why, you could toss Christina over the cliff as easily as an empty lunch bag." The wind tore her chuckle out of her mouth and tossed it into the sea.

Empty. It was the Shevvingtons' word. That was what they did to their victims. They emptied them. Emptied their bodies, and put their souls to rest forever in the silent guest rooms of Schooner Inne.

Christina struggled. She felt like a little animal, a kitten dragged to the vet — to be held down for shots — to be put to sleep forever.

Michael will be their instrument, she thought. That's how they'll do it to me. Mrs. Shevvington isn't going to let these eighteen days go unused.

Benjamin had his brother in a wrestling lock. "Let go," Benj said, for whom two words would always be enough. Michael's fingers went limp. Christina was free.

"My goodness but you're prickly, Benjamin," said Mrs. Shevvington. "Can't you take a joke?"

Benjamin glared at Mrs. Shevvington. If her eyes were pebbles, his were boulders. Suddenly Christina felt herself sister to Benj. They were carved of the same granite, from the same quarry, from the same island in the sea. "Come on, Benj," she said, grabbing his hand, "let's get there first."

* * *

In the morning, Benjamin did not stride off to school by himself but waited for Christina. She was astounded. Last summer the brothers had informed her in no uncertain terms that friendship must be left back on Burning Fog Isle; she must not expect them to associate with a lowly seventh-grader. She of course had tagged after them anyway, until they growled, "Christina, buzz off."

Today, the sun came up like a trumpet announcing *summer! Summer! Summer!*

And Benjamin Jaye held the heavy green door open for Christina, and shortened his big strides to match hers. The wind tugged her tri-colored hair, separating it. This was a good sign. (Christina never read horoscopes. She listened to her hair.) "You really want me to help with the fund-raising, don't you, Benj? I promise I will. You don't have to walk with me. Anyway, I'm meeting Jonah at the gate."

Benj said nothing, but she had not expected him to. They walked on. Such a glorious day! She was wearing a pretty cotton dress, with a tulip-flared skirt in watered pastels. She even had a new purse, nubby cotton, all fat and sagging and full of her own things. She loved purses. They were sacred. People might say how pretty your purse was, but they never went into your purse. You could have secrets in it if you wanted. "You know what I was thinking last night?" said Christina. She hoped for a syllable, but Benj raised both eyebrows instead. "At least it's a two-eyebrow morning," she teased him.

He laughed.

"I was thinking that for Disney World, we'll need grown-up money, not kid money," explained Christina. "We need to do things that attract tourists. They're the ones with the money. Now listen up. Clam chowder is the town specialty."

"Lobster is," Benj corrected her.

"Lobster, too, but listen. I need clams."

They were at the gate, and there was Jonah. Jonah was sort of Christina's boyfriend. Nobody in seventh grade actually had a boyfriend, but Jonah was a boy, and he liked her a lot, and sometimes they said they were "going together."

"Clams?" said Jonah. He poked Benj in the chest. "Well, you got one, Chrissie." He laughed hysterically.

Benjamin took Jonah's extended finger and began to snap it off. "Benj!" said Christina, getting between them. What could have made Jonah — a scrawny thirteen-year-old — start something with Benj, who could have modeled for a gym-equipment ad?

"I don't like clam or lobster jokes," said Benj. "Just because I keep silent when there's nothing to say, Jonah, doesn't mean I'm a crustacean."

Christina looked at the pair of them. How obvious the age difference was! Jonah was actually slightly taller than Benj, having grown like a stilt all winter. But he was skinny, with a lopsided, loping bounce. Benj's arms were twice as thick. His tan had never faded because he worked year round at the sea and at the gas station. He already had a lobsterman's squint, from the sun glaring off the water. It did not seem that two and a half years separated the boys; it seemed like ten.

"Anyway," Benj prompted her. He ignored Jonah, as sixteen-year-olds always ignored seventh-grade boys.

"Anyway, I think we could get all the restaurants in town to donate a vat of their own special recipe of clam chowder. We could set it up at the wharf. Decorate each dock like a particular restaurant. And people could buy a ticket and taste twenty kinds of chowder."

"Yuck," said Jonah. "I hate clam chowder."

"Nobody cares about you," said Christina. "It's tourists we're interested in. We need money so Benj can go to Disney World."

Jonah rolled his eyes. "Christina," he said, just as Michael had, "that's the high school. Who cares? It's their problem whether they can raise the money. Do you know how much time and effort it would take to do that chowder thing? Let them raise their own money. Besides, you couldn't do that till July or August when tourists are really here, and you'll be out on that island of yours." He made Burning Fog Isle sound like a garbage dump.

Her island of wild grass and roses, of salt spray and seabirds floating? Christina lowered her head as if to batter Jonah to his senses. Nobody got away with saying bad things about Burning Fog when Christina Romney was alive to stop them. Jonah dashed off with a bunch of boys who were climbing up on the school roof to retrieve the mittens, tennis balls, and book reports thrown there during the year. "I'll get you later!" yelled Christina. Jonah, safe on the roof, lay down on the shingles and shrugged.

Benjamin took a breath as if to ask Christina something. The wind suddenly ripped in from the sea, and a whiff of low tide filled their noses. Christina's cotton dress whirled up. She caught the hem, and from her windblown pocket fell a book of matches.

"What's this?" said Benjamin, frowning. "Christina, you're not experimenting with smoking cigarettes, are you?"

"Of course not. Don't be dumb. Those aren't my matches. They must have been on the pavement."

Benjamin gave her a strange look. "Chowder's a good idea," he mumbled, and walked away.

What was that all about? thought Christina.

"Christina," came a whisper.

She looked around, seeing nobody. There were dozens of kids outside because the bell hadn't rung yet. Why would anybody whisper?

"*Christina!*" it hissed.

She shivered. It sounded like the tide calling her name. That was what Anya thought, Christina remembered, when she was going mad. *The sea is a mathematician*, Anya had cried; *the sea keeps count, the sea wants one of us.*

Anya had been entranced by the tides. *Listen,*

she would whisper, her long fingers holding Christina like a net holding fish under water. *The tide is saying, "Come! Come here and drown with me!"*

A cloud covered the sun.

The trumpet-gold day turned to shadows.

Christina shivered uncontrollably.

A damp cold finger touched her neck, and she screamed, leaping backward.

It was only Robbie. Ordinary old Robbie Armstrong from English class. "Robbie, you scared me," she accused him, panting for breath. "I dropped my purse." Why am I so jumpy? she thought. A minute ago I was happy.

Her scream had drawn attention. A strange, silent, serious attention. Eyes stared at Christina — and at the ground around her.

On the pavement, where children of another generation had painted hopscotch lines, lay a dozen books of matches. Her cloth purse was not as fat as it had been: all those matchbooks had spurted out when the purse hit the ground.

The principal had been standing on the school steps, waiting for the warning bell to summon the children to class. Now Mr. Shevvington walked down the wide granite slabs, his polished black shoes clapping like hands against the rock. He was very tall. Christina had to look way up into his face. The sun was behind him, flooding her eyes, so she had to duck her head. Mr. Shevvington pointed to the match pile. "Christina," he said into the listening silence. "What have you been setting fire to?"

Chapter 4

Twenty people heard.

They each told their friends.

By lunch, the entire school had heard. *Mr. Shevvington says Christina Romney's been setting fire to things. You should have seen all the matches she had. But you know what those island girls are like. Remember when Anya tried to push Blake over the cliff into the tide? Oh, they tried to blame it all on the Shevvingtons' son, but still . . . when things like this happen . . . you wonder.*

In the cafeteria Vicki and Gretch smirked. They told the story of the match pile again, making it bigger, more convincing, and scarier.

"What were all your matches for?" Jonah asked her.

"They weren't mine. Mrs. Shevvington must have stuffed them in my purse."

"I told you," said Jonah, in the voice people always use with that sentence. A nyah-nyah voice.

"I told you something was going to happen, but did you listen to me? No. You ran off with Old Benj."

Several kids giggled, as if Old Benj were a well-known joke among them.

"Honestly, Chrissie," Jonah went on. "You want to be a wharf rat? Married at sixteen, have ten kids, make fishnets all winter, and get gray hair?"

"I will not be a wharf rat," said Christina fiercely. "And neither will Benj." Her fists doubled up under the cafeteria table. Don't get into a fight, she told herself. You don't have to defend Benjamin Jaye. He can defend himself.

"Then why are you hanging around him, all lovey-dovey like that?" demanded Jonah.

"Lovey-dovey?" cried Christina. "Jonah, get a grip on yourself. He's like my brother."

Jonah snorted. "*You* get a grip on *your*self," he said. "He's going to quit school, he won't be back for junior year. He'll ask you to marry him, and you will."

"I'm fourteen!" shouted Christina, rounding off a few weeks.

"So? Big deal. He's sixteen. What's two years? My father is eleven years older than my mother." Jonah folded his arms across his chest as if he had just won an important argument.

Mrs. Shevvington walked into the cafeteria. She never did that. She did not have a free period when the seventh grade had lunch. She looked around the cafeteria, her eyes roving inside her one-dimensional face, like movable eyes in an oil painting.

Her eyes seemed to cut Christina out of the crowd like a sheep dog isolating one of his flock.

The cafeteria was filled with sunlight and the laughter of others. Other people split Oreo cookies, one taking the filling and one the chocolate side. Other people handed around Doritos and brownies. Other people discussed with Jonah whether or not in the state of Maine you could get married as young as Chrissie and Benj were. But for Christina, participation ceased. Something is here, something has come, she thought. But what?

Slow as low tide, Mrs. Shevvington drifted over to Christina. She touched Christina's cheek. Her finger pad was mushy as a jellyfish dying on the rocks. "Christina," said Mrs. Shevvington. Lovingly, for the benefit of her audience. To other people the Shevvingtons always seemed to be the good ones. "Mr. Shevvington is quite worried about you, dear. Do you want to discuss something with me?"

I want to throw you off Breakneck Hill, thought Christina.

But for once she was wise enough to stay silent.

"Mr. Shevvington thinks you are smoking cigarettes. He thinks that's why you carry a purse full of matches. But I am afraid it's more serious than that, isn't it, Christina?" Mrs. Shevvington nodded her head, like a guillotine in slow motion. "Because you don't need a dozen books of matches for one cigarette, do you, Christina?"

Across the cafeteria Vicki hissed, "Chrissie's done something terrible! I bet she's gone mad, the way island girls do!"

Christina was usually alert during English class, but today she was anesthetized by what had happened to her. She could not seem to hear what was going on. Every time she looked up she snagged on Mrs. Shevvington's eyes. Christina could not feel herself inside her dress; she was the dress; she was nothing but a piece of cotton. She could not feel her hair: The three colors had withered away. There was nothing now to protect her.

All I have to do is hang on, Christina told herself. They have only seventeen days now, and what can they do in such a short time? If I stay calm, and don't play into their hands, I'll be all right.

"We will want to have a class party, of course," said Mrs. Shevvington, "to celebrate the end of school."

Everybody wanted a party. Even people who had had a terrible school year wanted a party.

"We'll have it at my aunt's summer house," Vicki commanded. Vicki was wealthy, and never lost an opportunity to say so. Her aunt owned a house right on the ocean, one of the few with actual sand rather than rocks and cliffs. The beach was only a few yards wide, but you could spread a towel on it. Maybe two or three towels. Above the beach was a wide meadow, and there they could play volleyball, softball, and Frisbee.

"How generous of you, Vicki, dear," said Mrs. Shevvington. She was sticky, like the back of a stamp. She caught children to her: first their eyes, later their souls. The smile searched the room like a fisherman trolling. The children ducked their heads, staring into the corners of the room, or down into their laps. They all had their own ways of avoiding the smile.

It was Robbie that the smile caught today. It changed his posture, made his breathing ragged. His thin, little boy's chest plopped nervously up and down.

"Robbie," said Mrs. Shevvington, in her cruel, teasing voice, "I will put you in charge of organizing the class party."

"*I* want to be in charge!" cried Vicki. "It's on my aunt's beach."

"I think Robbie has hidden qualities of leadership," said Mrs. Shevvington. Her lips were thin as pencil lead. She drew a smile with her pencil lips and laughed. "Well-hidden qualities, of course."

Robbie flinched.

"But we want to encourage Robbie, don't we, class?" said Mrs. Shevvington. "We want to bring out his best, don't we?" Her sticky eyes absorbed their snickering laughter. "Come to the front of the class, Robbie."

They all knew Robbie hated standing up alone; he couldn't talk once their faces stared at him; his cheek would twitch. It would not bring out his best. It would destroy him.

Destroy, Christina thought.

For a terrible, selfish moment she was glad that the smile had caught Robbie and not her.

"Oh, Mrs. Shevvington," Vicki pouted. "He can't do anything right. It'll all be spoiled."

"That's been true in the past," Mrs. Shevvington agreed. "But every student of mine should have many chances." Her eyes ceased to blink. They narrowed; they pierced Robbie like Indian arrowheads. Slowly Robbie got out of his chair. Mrs. Shevvington's eyes hauled him past Vicki, past Gretch, up to the front of the class. Two dozen pairs of eyes watched him now. "Don't shuffle, Robbie," said Mrs. Shevvington. "You look like a second-grader who needs to be excused."

Robbie flushed an ugly mottled purple.

The class tilted toward Christina, waiting for her to stand up for Robbie, the way she always did. Christina avoided their eyes. How many times have I gotten involved? she thought. Complained to my parents, told other kids' parents, let the guidance office know what she's like. Don't you see how Mrs. Shevvington undermines us, and lays traps for us, and lets us bleed in front of everybody? I say to them. But the grown-ups always say, Christina, why must you always exaggerate? Why must you tell so many yarns? Mrs. Shevvington is trying to build your self-esteem; she's a fine teacher; you just have a bad attitude.

Christina ignored Robbie. She pretended to study her English book. There on the inside cover were penciled doodles. Candles, flames, and the tips of matches. A shiver took possession of Christina's spine and slithered over her tanned skin. She could not remember drawing those. She usually doodled tic-tac-toes.

Fire, she thought. The candle. Did I — ? No, I couldn't have. I don't do things like that.

Mrs. Shevvington's little black eyes abandoned Robbie; they focused on Christina; a smile like fungus on a rotted log grew out of Mrs. Shevvington's thin lips. Christina traced the fire doodles with her finger.

Robbie's cheek jerked. He wet his lips.

"Robbie's older sister was also weak," said Mrs. Shevvington, her eyes centering on Christina. "It's in the family genes. Val Armstrong had to be institutionalized."

Christina was the only seventh-grader with courage. She thought it was because of her island upbringing. She was granite, Christina of the Isle. Any other day, she would have retorted, "*Your* son had to be institutionalized, too, you know, Mrs. Shevvington. Your genes are nothing to brag about, either. You only said that to be mean."

But today she could not worry about Robbie, or his sister Val. For she could not get her mind off fire. She saw the flames on which they would roast hot dogs and the coals over which they would toast marshmallows. Vaguely she heard Vicki take over the picnic organization, after it was agreed that Robbie was too stupid; remotely she saw Robbie creep back to his seat. Gretch and Vicki discussed the menu. Suddenly it seemed very important to arrange for the bonfire. What if Vicki and Gretch forgot about the beach fire?

Christina interrupted. "First of all," she said urgently, "we'll need a huge fire. We should start gathering driftwood right now for the bonfire."

"A fire comes first?" repeated Mrs. Shevvington. Her f's and her s's hissed and curled like snakes. *A ffffire comesssss ffffirsssssst.* "How interesting, Christina. You have a special interest in fire, don't you?"

Christina nodded. "I love fire," she agreed. "Our bonfire should have flames up to the sky." She imagined craggy boulders, the bonfire thrusting among them, framed against the sky and the sea. She smiled to herself.

Mrs. Shevvington's eyes grew like puddles in a flood. *"Fffflames up to the ssssky."* she repeated. She turned to the class. "Say it with me," she told them, and they said it with her, like some horrible rhyme: *A ffffire comesssss ffffirsssssst . . . Fffflames up to the ssssky . . . Chhhrrrisssssstina lovesssss fffffire. . . .*

Mrs. Shevvington's eyes glittered like flecks of mica on rocks. In her furry voice, rasping like a cat's tongue on soft skin, she whispered, "There have been several suspicious fires in town lately, haven't there, class?"

Chapter 5

As a hiker in the woods checks herself for ticks, for the rest of the school day Christina searched herself continually for matches. She would never again wear clothes with pockets. She would stop carrying a purse. That would foil them.

The nerve of them! Sneaking into Christina's room, touching her clothes, fingering her pockets, stuffing her handbag, starting rumors!

And they'll laugh, she thought, because I knew all along and never could convince anybody. Every terrible thing that happened they weaseled out of because they could use their own son to blame it on! That bonfire last winter, when my whole wardrobe was burned in the snow — when everybody blamed me and said I was going island-mad. It was them, I know it was them.

Twice now — at least — the Shevvingtons had skulked through Christina's room, opened her drawers, handled her clothing, played tricks with fire and matches.

They got Anya by working on her fears, she thought. They won't do it that way with me. They won't try to make *me* afraid. They'll use rumor. They'll arrange my world so that other people become afraid of me.

At the end of the day, Robbie, slinking down the hall like her shadow, crept up behind her. His fingers touched her like falling ice cubes. "Robbie," snapped Christina, "if you hadn't scared me out there — "

"Listen," hissed Robbie.

"Stop whispering. You sound like a snake. Nothing but s's."

Robbie said, "I'm going to visit my sister Val in the institution. You know, the mental home where Mr. and Mrs. Shevvington talked my parents into putting her? The social worker has to visit a bunch of patients there this afternoon, and he said he'd take me along tomorrow after school. You want to come?"

Val, Val, who was crimson and blue.

Last winter, being punished for something she had not done, Christina had been confined alone in Schooner Inne. And that day, peeking into the empty guest rooms that ringed the tilting balcony, she understood why Mr. and Mrs. Shevvington owned a guest house, but did not advertise nor accept guests. Each room was a victim. No flesh and blood would occupy those rooms. They were already occupied.

With ghosts.

The Shevvingtons had even furnished the rooms to match. That was one of their hobbies: admiring their guest rooms, cherishing the memories of their collection of empty girls.

Anya had been number 8; the room meant for her had been fragile like lace, its carpets and cushions streaked with silver and gray — like storm clouds.

Anya had been saved. Christina and Blake had accomplished that.

But Robbie Armstrong's sister, Val, whom the Shevvingtons had chosen the year before — Val had been lost.

Number 7 was Val. Carpet blue as the sea in summer, walls rich violet, like sunset. Dark like a crimson flower in a crystal vase. This was the living Val: Val before the Shevvingtons. And now Val was mindless on a narrow cot in a quiet hospital.

Or was she mindless? Would she have clues? Would she have knowledge? Would she be able to say to Christina, from the fragments of her left in the real world, *This is how to stop the Shevvingtons?*

Room 8, meant for Anya's ghost — stormy and fallen — could be redecorated. It could become Christina's, a room of fire and islands.

Seventeen days were enough.

The minute school was out, everybody converged on Vicki's aunt's beach to study the grounds and make the important decisions. Most of the girls stood around arguing about who would bring the volleyball net and who would supply the radios and cassette players. Most of the boys scoured the beach for logs, pieces of smashed boat, steps off dock ladders, and other debris. Christina forgot Mrs. Shevvington. She loved being outdoors. Anything to do with the beach and the sea was home to Christina.

Christina and Jonah climbed over seaweed-slippery rocks, dragging wood, until the pile was taller than any of them. "Now that," said Christina, surveying the mountain of wood, "will make a real fire."

"Ssssshhhhhh!" said Jonah. He looked around uneasily. "Don't talk so loud, you dumbo," he whispered.

"Why not?"

"Didn't you see Mrs. Shevvington looking at you? Her eyes stuck to you like chewing gum, Chrissie. There may be only seventeen more days till the end of the school year," said Jonah, "but there's next year to worry about, too. Eighth grade. Think of all they could plan over the summer, Chrissie. Be careful."

Eighth grade. Room 8.

Did it mean something? Was it fate?

"The Shevvingtons don't scare me anymore," she said, which was a lie. "Besides, they won't be here next year. He's getting a job in Chicago, and they're putting Schooner Inne on the market." She looked down at the sand at her feet. She was foot-doodling. She often wrote her initials in the sand. But these were not initials. They were —

"Leaving?" repeated Jonah. He frowned. "But they have such a perfect setup here. The town adores them. They can get away with anything. Why would they leave?"

Candle flames. She had drawn fire. Was Mrs. Shevvington right? Who had drawn those English book doodles? The memory of the candle in the coffee can came back to her. Her own urgent voice saying fire had to come first.

Christina erased her sand marks. Her leg was shaking, as if she had just fallen or nearly had an accident. "Who cares?" she said. "They're going." Her head filled with candles and arson, with slippery cliffs and tumbling rocks.

Gretch was promising to bring a badminton set.

"Be sure to buy extra birdies," ordered Vicki. Vicki had a small notebook in which she was writing down everybody's promises. "See, Robbie," she said, "this is how it's done. When your hidden leadership qualities rise up, be sure to bring a notebook along."

This is what they had learned in seventh grade: how to taunt each other. Mrs. Shevvington treated the seventh-graders like pets. Dogs to be kicked — like Robbie. Dogs to be put on a leash — like Vicki. Vicki would do anything Mrs. Shevvington told her to.

Jennie said eagerly that she had a shiny new croquet set; she would bring her croquet set.

"Nobody wants to play croquet," said Vicki scornfully, "it's slow and pointless. Don't bring your old croquet set."

The delight vanished from Jennie's eyes. Shame replaced it. Jennie hung her head and scuffled her old sneakers in the sand.

Vicki and her best friend Gretch were "in." This was a phenomenon Christina had read about, but never experienced till this year, as the island had so few children. Seventh-graders angled for the chance to share a table with Vicki and Gretch. Vicki and Gretch were given extra desserts. Their opinions were sought and their jokes laughed at.

Now Jennie was the joke.

Fat, ugly Katy stepped up close to the important notebook. "I'll bring the marshmallows," she offered. "And I can cut plenty of green twigs to toast them on. We have lots of good bushes on our property."

Vicki smiled. She touched her own silk-smooth hair, admired her own slender ankles. "How suitable, Katy," she said, in the smooth, vicious voice she had learned from Mrs. Shevvington. "Marshmallows match your face."

Christina lost her temper. "I'll give *you* a marshmallow face!" she yelled. She hit Vicki.

Jonah pulled Christina off. "Don't give her a bloody lip," he said, "or you'll be in trouble again.

Less than three weeks to go, Chrissie. Stay good!"

"*I* don't get into trouble!" said Christina. How could her only ally talk like that? Jonah knew the truth; had always known the truth. "The Shevvingtons force me into it."

"Oh ho!" said Vicki. "Now you're going to blame poor Mr. and Mrs. Shevvington because you hit me. I'll tell you something, Christina Romney. Not everybody believes that the Shevvingtons' son did all the stuff you said he did." Vicki covered her swelling mouth with a manicured hand. "Like that time your entire winter wardrobe burned in a bonfire in the snow? You can't blame that on their son, Christina. We know better." Vicki raised her voice to reach her audience. "You're an island girl. They're all half crazy. You set that fire yourself."

The sea crept wetly around their sneakers, slurping at the dry land. The seventh grade watched Christina. It seemed to her that she was alone, and they were together; she was small and thin, and they were a crowd. A mob.

The force of their bodies and faces and eyes and voices rolled over her like a great drowning wave. Now they were a single creature: the enemy. A group to push her backward into Candle Cove and watch, laughing, while the tide came in over her broken bones.

Christina ran.

She had never done such a thing before. She was the fighter, the one who never gave up. Alone she ran, over the cliffs, among the craggy boulders, past the millionaires' mansions. Anything to get away, to be safe.

Her greatest fear in life was that she would be alone: without friends.

I should have given my friends a chance to speak up, she thought miserably. I played into the Shevvingtons' hands again. They want me friendless and running. And they've got it.

With her fists she rubbed away the tears that rolled over her eyes like fog over the island. So many victims. So much pain. All caused by Mr. and Mrs. Shevvington — humiliating, manipulating, taunting.

"But it doesn't matter now," Christina said to the sea gulls who floated in the air currents above her. "They're leaving!" she yelled to the barn swallows who dipped and swerved over the green meadow grass. "It's over!"

Christina went on past the old wharf that had once protruded a quarter mile into the ocean and was nothing now but piers sticking up like the feet of drowning men. She ran all the way to the storm cottages.

Many years before, in 1938, a great hurricane crossed New England. When it was over, buildings had been tossed to the ground in splinters. Back then, summer people came for only a few weeks, so they didn't care about quality building techniques. After the hurricane, the cottage owners made walls of broken boards and nailed on roofs that leaked and swayed.

The storm cottages looked as if they had been built with bent nails by a beginning Girl Scout troop. They tilted, with crazy stairs and mismatched windows. Some had plumbing and some didn't. Some had electricity and some didn't. It was hard to believe they were now worth hundreds of thousands of dollars because they were ocean-front.

Today, the storm cottages were still closed for the winter, shutters fastened over the windows.

Christina opened the shutters to the window on the sagging front porch of her favorite storm cottage. She eased the window up, and slipped inside. The storm cottage was painted white: ceilings, walls, doors, and even floors. The furniture was winter-draped in white sheets. A crack of sun came through the window Christina had opened, like a huge golden pencil.

Christina tiptoed through. In the funny old kitchen there were no counters, just a beaten-up table. The bathroom had a stand-up shower crammed in the corner, but the water was turned off. Upstairs a miniature bedroom held a bed with bare metal springs. Christina lay down and it was as comfortable as you would expect metal springs to be.

She knew these summer people. They came in August. And they did not rent it out the rest of the time. She could use the storm cottage for her hideout these last seventeen days. Actually, day seventeen was nearly over. Sixteen days, then. Who would hide out with me? she wondered.

Michael and Benjamin Jaye were the only other island children at Schooner Inne now.

On Burning Fog, Christina and Michael had been good friends, but the mainland pulled them apart. Michael was such a good athlete that he had already moved up the social ladder, and was important, because everybody knew he would be captain of everything one day, winning games against old rivals. Michael would laugh at her if she suggested a hideaway and Christina had been laughed at enough today.

Benjamin was out of the question. Benj was a sophomore, two years and six months older than Christina. If she told Benj about the storm cottage, the two years and six months between them would seem like a century. "Chrissie, that's trespassing," he would say in his heavy, slow, islander's voice.

"Not really," Christina would argue. "I've always done it. Besides, it's just a storm cottage. Practically public property."

Slowly a frown would materialize on Benj's forehead. Benj did everything slowly. "Christina," he would say reprovingly. He probably wouldn't stop her, and he probably wouldn't tell, because he wanted her to help him raise money for Disney World, but he certainly wouldn't hide out with her.

That left Jonah. But he was being poopy. Don't

fight, don't start things. Why share a hideaway with him?

She let her mind drift over Blake, pretending she could live here with him. Handsome, perfect Blake. Anya's boyfriend, however. Anya's rescuer, too. Blake had taken Anya away from the Shevvingtons, stashing her with some relative of his in the city while he finished up at boarding school.

The winter before, Christina had had such a crush on Blake! The crush had left her panting and trembling, dizzy and excited. Blake, of course, had not noticed. Eighteen-year-olds did not pay attention to the emotions of thirteen-year-olds. But Christina knew how love felt now, and Jonah did not inspire love. Jonah was just Jonah.

She sighed. Blake would be too busy driving his sports car and dressing in his catalog Maine clothing to bother with games in a storm cottage.

Christina checked the kitchen drawer. (There was only one drawer in the whole cottage.) Cheap forks, knives, and spoons; a spatula, a steak knife, can opener, and screwdriver. On a shelf were dented pots, ancient plastic plates, and a lemonade pitcher. Christina peeked under the sink. One squirt of dish soap, one stained sponge, and a box of kitchen matches.

I could have a cookout, thought Christina. No. People would see the smoke and investigate. Besides, then Benji would be right. It's one thing to creep in and out. It's another thing entirely to cook a hamburger in the fireplace.

Christina set the kitchen table for one and pretended to have pancakes, bacon, orange juice, and grapefruit halves with extra spoonfuls of sugar. I'm thirteen and playing house, she thought. This is so silly. In seventh grade, you're supposed to grow up, not down.

She put everything away exactly as she had found it.

Her bad moods never lasted long and this one was gone. Pleased with her hideaway, Christina decided to go make friends with the seventh grade again. She slid out the window, tucked the shutter in, and ran back down the cliffs.

Far away, in the cupola of Schooner Inne, sun glinted off a pair of binoculars.

Chapter 6

"This," said Robbie to Mr. O'Neil, the social worker, "is my cousin."

Christina tried to look like an Armstrong cousin. She had had a bad day in school and was rather hoping the afternoon trip to the mental institution would be a nice ride.

"Her name is Iris," added Robbie.

Iris? Christina wished she could have chosen her own fake name. If I could pick, she thought, it would be a name soft and beautiful. Now she was stuck with Iris. Still, it was fun to be a different person for an afternoon. Christina filled her head with Iris-type thoughts.

The social worker was big but limp. Shaking hands with him was like holding a wet sneaker. Mr. O'Neill drove slumped over the steering wheel and talked slow; even his cheeks drooped. How could a visit from this lump cheer anybody up?

He also asked too many questions. Christina knew nothing about Robbie's family. What was she supposed to say when he asked was Iris related by blood to the Armstrongs?

"No," said Robbie, "she's on my mother's side. She's a Murch."

Iris Murch? thought Christina. I can't stand this.

The social worker said, "Robbie, next time you might want to drive up with the Shevvingtons. They visit your sister every week. They're such fine people. Why, Val is practically catatonic; she hardly ever speaks; she's almost unreachable. Yet week after week Mr. and Mrs. Shevvington are there to encourage and comfort." He shook his big, loose head, like a cow shaking away flies. "What fine people," he repeated.

Week after week . . . the Shevvingtons appearing by Val's bed . . . creeping up like rodents in the dark . . . smiling in front of the staff, and gloating when they were alone with Val.

Christina imagined Mrs. Shevvington rocking with silent laughter, looking down at Val. Val, huddled under the pitiful protection of a hospital blanket, hiding from the very people who had put her in that prison. Of course Val will never get well, thought Christina. Not when the Shevvingtons come every week to renew her terror.

"They'll be so glad Val's cousin is visiting," added the social worker. "They'll want to meet you, Iris. Where do you go to school, anyway?"

Robbie said quickly, "Her parents teach her at home. You've heard of that. Home schooling. They don't approve of public schools. Or private schools, either."

The social worker said, "How fascinating, Iris. I would love to discuss that with your parents. Are they in town, too?"

"No," said Christina firmly. "Where is this hospital, anyway? Are we almost there? Do you think we could turn on the radio?" She hissed in Robbie's ear, "You dodo. What if he tells the Shevvingtons about me?"

Robbie said loudly, "Don't introduce Iris to the Shevvingtons. Her parents hate anybody that teaches school. They had very bad experiences when they were young. Her parents will never let Iris visit Val again if you mention school principals."

"What a fascinating neurosis," said Mr. O'Neill. "I promise, Iris. I can see you have a difficult life, and I don't want to add to it."

They traveled on, Christina making desperate meaningless conversation with Robbie about the baseball season. Nerves made Christina laugh as if she, too, were insane. The social worker watched in his rearview mirror, trying to identify *her* neurosis.

Suddenly, at a turn in the road, a high iron fence jumped up from the fields and flowers. Wire was woven among the black spikes, making the fence impassable from either side. A small white sign read "Shoreline Institute for the Mentally Troubled. Check in at gate. Visitors by pass only."

A guard stood in a little cubicle, swinging car gates open by pressing a button. He wrote down all their names. Iris Murch had just become real.

Mr. O'Neill said he would be visiting patients in another hall; Robbie and Iris could be with Val for half an hour, and then they were to wait for him in the Visitors' Lounge where, he assured them, a color television would keep them happy and occupied.

They parked.

Silent, empty cars glistened in the sun.

From the buildings came no sound; on the grass nobody walked. And yet there must be patients living behind each pane of glass.

They entered a wide lobby with polished floors and a smiling receptionist in a white uniform. "Doesn't it look like a Fat Farm," whispered Robbie, "where you pay a fortune to eat nothing and get massages?" But the hall doors were keyed; you could not get in or out without an attendant. The attendant on Val's hall was a man in white: white shirt, pants, socks, and shoes, as if he intended to blend in with the white walls and the white sheets. Christina worried about all these confused patients with no way to exit. "What do you do if there's a fire?" she said uneasily.

"Don't you think about that," said the attendant, patting her. "It's all arranged." He smiled at Christina. The teeth were Mrs. Shevvington's — wrinkled, dried corn on the cob. Christina shuddered. The attendant smiled even wider. Whispering, as if it were study hall, he breathed, "And what is your name?"

Patients' rooms stretched on either side, but there was no talk, no laughter, no radios, no yelling. If she looked in the rooms would they be like the guest rooms at Schooner Inne — occupied only by ghosts?

"My name is Iris," she whispered back.

In the first room, a man sat in a chair, looking at nothing, mouth hanging open, no sound coming out.

"They drug them," whispered Robbie. "That way the staff doesn't have to do anything."

Christina and Robbie walked slower, as if they too had been drugged and were sliding into a silent world.

"Here is your room," whispered the attendant. He took Christina's arm, as if he were about to lock her in. His hand was thick and inhuman, like a rubber glove filled with sand.

Robbie betrayed me! thought Christina, dizzy with shock. He and the Shevvingtons planned this. Robbie is going to have me admitted as Iris Murch. Nobody will ever see Christina Romney again. The attendant and the social worker are part of it. They didn't need eighteen days! They just needed one afternoon. And Robbie.

Christina tried to free herself but the attendant's grip had hardened like cement. She swung fear-wide eyes toward Robbie, but he was staring at his shoes. The attendant's lips never covered his yellow teeth. His smile stayed on and on, like a frozen frame in a movie.

If I can break free, she thought, I can run down the hall. But I have no key to let myself out. A patient's window? No. The glass is lined with wire. Even if I got into the yard, the fence has no toe-holds. There's no way over.

She had a vision of her future: white walls, television with the sound turned off, attendants with triumphant smiles.

"Chrissie, relax," muttered Robbie. "It's not that bad. Val just lies there. What's the matter? You look as if you're having a breakdown yourself."

He had called her Chrissie, not Iris. She whirled. The attendant was back at the other end of the hall, keying himself out.

I fell into paranoia, thought Christina. I thought *They* were after me, all of *Them*. I thought *They* had a conspiracy against me.

How easy it was, then, to go crazy. All you had to do was think about it, and you began to fall toward it, the tilting floor of your own mind sliding you into a crack that would smash shut.

Val was exceptionally pretty.

Christina had expected someone beaten and bruised. Someone on whom the Shevvingtons' handiwork would show.

But the girl sitting cross-legged in the center of the neatly made bed had big brown eyes, tan skin, long lashes, and a wide firm mouth. She wore khaki pants and a cotton sweater, white with horizontal khaki stripes. Val looked like a girl who danced and partied; whose laughter was a shout of glee.

But Val did not blink. Her huge eyes just sat there. When Robbie and Christina crossed the room, the eyes did not follow them. The eyes did not see; needed no tears. Mrs. Shevvington's eyes, thought Christina. That's how the Shevvingtons got inside her. Through the eyes.

Robbie sat beside his sister, and the bed sank down, making her slender body tip against him. "Val?" he said. "I've brought you a friend. Her name is — " Robbie stopped, not knowing which name to use.

"I'm Anya's friend, from Burning Fog Isle," said Christina softly. "Do you remember Anya? You two used to be in school together."

Val got lower and lower in the bed, as if assuming a fetal position. She spoke in a voice so light it felt like a draft. *"Anya!"* Like air escaping from a balloon. *"Anya is next."*

"No. Anya is safe. Anya got away."

There was a conversation between them, one which Robbie was not part of. Val's eyes cleared, and she made her first blink. It took a great effort, as if her lids scraped and ached. *"Anya is safe?"*

"Anya is safe," said Christina firmly. "I saved her. Now she's living in the city with friends. She won't be back for a long time."

"I won't be back for a long time, either," whispered Val.

"Come back," said Christina urgently. "I need

you. Come back now, Val. Because *I'm* next."

Val's eyes opened even wider. She seemed to suck Christina in through her pupils. She leaned toward Christina. Her fingers grappled with Christina's dangling hair, gathering it in her hands like a harvest. "Then what are you doing here? The Shevvingtons might come!" She never raised her voice. As if the Shevvingtons' ears were pressed to cracks.

"I live with them," said Christina. "I have to board at Schooner Inne. Like Anya."

"They'll get you," said Val. Suddenly her voice was normal. As if having the Shevvingtons win were also normal.

Christina shook her head. "No, they won't. I know their plan."

"It doesn't help to know their plan. They get the other adults on their side. They get your parents and your teachers. They get psychiatrists. They make up lies. They corner you. They crowd you."

Val's huge eyes stared into a white corner of her white room, as if seeing a white rat there, trapped, caught, destroyed.

"If you're next, and you know it," whispered Val, "you must run." She lay back on her bed. Suddenly she was limp as a wet dishrag. Just clothes lying on the bedcovers, with no body inside them.

"Come back!" said Christina authoritatively.

But Val did not come back.

Robbie talked.

Christina talked.

482

But Val was not there. She was gone. Lost perhaps in her own head. Or floating in the room.

Or perhaps her soul lived in Number 7 at Schooner Inne. Only her flesh was in this institution. Attendants dressed an empty body in this cotton sweater and khaki pants. Val was trapped forever in a room of crimson and blue that stared into the tides of the mind.

"Half hour's up," said the attendant cheerily. He looked pleased to see Val lying on the bed like a dead person. "She's always like that," he confided. "We prop her up to take food."

Christina's hair separated with horror: the silver and gold standing apart from the brown. The attendant said, "What interesting hair," and without asking he touched it. She leaped away from him, into the hall.

Val's doe eyes fixed on the white corner and the white floor.

"Let's watch TV in the lounge," said Robbie. The attendant keyed them into the lounge. What a slick, shiny room it was. All its furniture could be scrubbed. There was no personality in it, as if mops and detergents had been used to scour away any trace of humankind. The television was twice the size of most, and the people in the soap opera more life-size than the silent patients in their rooms.

Robbie hissed, "Lie down. Roll over. Hide."

"What am I, a hound dog?" said Christina.

Robbie kicked her. "The Shevvingtons are here!" he hissed.

Christina lay down, rolled over, and tried to hide behind a couch. But this was not a place where hiding was allowed. No drapes hung to the floor, no skirts surrounded chairs, no doors jutted out. In the corners of the room, video cameras scanned for missing patients.

Robbie ran to the door of the lounge to keep the Shevvingtons from coming in. "Hi, Mrs. Shevvington," he called out. "I just visited Val. She's the same as ever. How are you?"

"My goodness, Robbie, you're in a lively mood today," said Mrs. Shevvington. "I suppose it's the thought of finishing seventh grade up in only a few days, isn't it?" She laughed merrily. No doubt for the benefit of other people listening: a psychiatrist or parents.

I am in a mental institution hiding behind a see-through couch, pretending to be Iris Murch, thought Christina. This really is lunatic. If they see me . . .

Even underneath the couch was clean. This place was remarkable. Somebody must mop upside down.

The social worker's floppy voice said, "Well, Robbie, where's your cousin? We need to be leaving."

"Cousin?" repeated Mrs. Shevvington. Her voice folded around him like a blanket. "Why, Robbie, who is that? I don't recall meeting any of your family except your parents."

Christina drew into a tuck, like Val, whimpering, praying not to be caught.

"I guess she's still with Val," said Robbie brightly. "Let's find her."

Three pairs of feet passed the lounge door. Mr. Shevvington's shoes were black and gleaming. Mrs. Shevvington's were red with heels like stabbing knives. Robbie had on dirty and torn sneakers. Christina's palm left a sweaty handprint on the linoleum.

In the front hall she heard Mr. O'Neill chatting with the receptionist. She got up and sauntered out, wondering who was watching the cameras and what they thought and what they would do. "Hi, Mr. O'Neill. I'll wait for you in the car," she said. He was too nerdy to sense anything strange.

Out in the sunshine, Christina nearly danced across the smooth golf-green grass. I'm free, I'm safe! But that might look crazed. So she walked sedately to the car.

Strewn over the backseat were matches. The tools of an arsonist. The joy of a child insane with the love of fire. "Poor little Christina," the Shevvingtons would say. "See how she crept into the mental home. A plea, of course. Crying out for help. Saying, lock me up before I set fire to something or hurt somebody! Poor little dear. So demented she can't even use her real name."

Christina gathered the matches desperately. There were so many she could hardly hold them in her cupped hands. Stooping, slithering, she rushed among the parked cars to the Shevvingtons' van.

It was locked.

She could not get rid of the matches.

They would find her — they knew they would — they were on their way. They would bring witnesses — it was just as Val had predicted — it didn't matter that she knew the plan. They would still win — she would be caught clutching the matches to her heart!

Val had known, Val had said *run*!

The car next to the Shevvingtons was unlocked. Christina ripped open the back door, threw the matches in, and shoveled them beneath the driver's seat.

Panting, she leaped back to the social worker's car, where she lay curled on the backseat, hidden from the windows and eyes of the Institute.

How did the Shevvingtons plan so easily?

What ally did the Shevvingtons have, that Christina did not know about? Was it Michael? Was it Benj? Was it Jonah?

Chapter 7

The air was hot and heavy and full of omens.

Not a leaf stirred. Not a hair on Christina's head lifted.

The air did not want to be breathed. When Christina filled her lungs, the air objected, lying thick inside her, making her cough.

"An electrical storm coming," said Jonah uneasily.

They were standing on the top of the cliffs. Rocks above them, rocks below them. The Atlantic was between tides and merely lapped at its boundaries instead of fighting or fleeing them. Seaweed lay like sickness on the surface.

The sky turned strange colors, as if becoming ill.

Christina held her hands up to the heavens.

"Don't do that," said Jonah. "You look —"

He broke off. Christina turned to look at him, her eyes huge in her face, her separate colors of hair tangled above her head like —

"Snakes," said Jonah, shivering. "You look like

someone from a Greek myth, like some ancient woman spying on the gods on Olympus."

Christina laughed. But her laugh, too, was ancient, as if her mind and body had been scooped up by another time, another power.

Jonah tried to talk to her about school, about himself. Christina did not listen to him. She floated at the cliff edge. I'm ready to leave the world, she thought. Where would I be going if I went?

"We'd better go inside," said Jonah. His nervousness was as palpable as the coming storm. "If lightning strikes, it'll strike here. We're higher than anything."

She would not go. She could imagine herself, outlined against the bruised sky: the long wild skirt, the slender ankles below, the upstretched hands, and the tangled mane of hair. Christina wanted summer people and painters and photographers to see her and immortalize her. She wanted to be strange and different and weird.

"Come in!" cried Jonah.

The sky split open. A sheet of silver sliced into the sea like javelins thrown by angry gods.

Jonah grabbed her hand and yanked her toward the big green doors of Schooner Inne.

"I want to watch the lightning," whispered Christina. She could feel the electricity in her hair. The electricity came in her own three colors.

Jonah shoved her ahead of him.

"I want to *be* the lightning!" she cried.

He bundled her in the door. "We'll watch from

the window," he said, and the sky went crazy. Lightning, rain, and wind burst forth.

Jonah slammed the door behind them.

Christina pressed her palms against the door as if to embrace the weather.

Jonah said shakily, "Chrissie, you're too much for me. I think maybe when the storm's over, I'll just go on home."

She came down to earth in a hurry. She was just a seventh-grade girl with a boy she liked. "Don't go, Jonah. I'm sorry I went off with Robbie yesterday instead of you. And you're wrong to think there's something between Benj and me. Except Burning Fog. He's my brother."

Jonah kept furniture between them like a shield. "You made me think of Anya," he said. His voice shook. "Remember how she went crazy last winter? That's how you looked out there, trying to hold hands with the lightning."

"Oh, Jonah, I was not. Don't exaggerate. I just like weather. That's what it is to be an island girl. You're one with the weather."

"But you're not on the island now," he said.

"I am always on the island," said Christina. What made me say that? she wondered. It will scare him more. Why do I want to scare him? She made her eyes glitter to match her lightning-rod hair, and Jonah shivered, and went home.

She was alone in the sea captain's house, alone in the rooms furnished for the bride who flung herself to the rocks all those years ago. She felt the sea calling her name; felt the lightning clapping its hands — crying — *Christina . . . Christina. . . .*

The syllables of her name shivered through the house, like Jonah leaving. Like leaves falling. *Chhhhrissssss . . .* said the house.

"Shhh!" said Christina.

Chhhhrrissssss . . . said the house.

It was upstairs. She stood at the bottom of the steps, staring up into the dizzying circle of tipping white balconies. Gripping the banister she went up, step by step. "Who's calling me?" she said loudly.

The carpet muffled her steps.

The emptiness in the house smothered her heartbeat.

Chhhhrrisssss . . . said the house.

Above her the floor creaked.

"Who's there?" cried Christina Romney.

Beyond the cupola windows, lightning lit the sky. Thunder crashed. The tide began to change, and the ocean began to sing. From everywhere, from nowhere, the world whispered, *Chhhhrrisssss. . . .*

She stood on the second floor.

She ripped open the door to Anya's room, that room of silver and gray, of fragile lace and airspun gauze.

It was gone.

The room was on fire.

Curls of flame and gleaming angry coals cried her name.

It became my room, thought Christina. I knew

it would happen. Val knew it would happen. They have me. A room of fire and islands. I was falling into this room even while Jonah was standing there. I'll never get out. This is the other world I knew was waiting for me.

Christina . . . said the voice beyond the walls, behind the fires . . . *Christina . . . stay here.* . . .

If I can get out of the room, thought Christina, if I can take a step backward, I can save myself.

She tried to breathe, but the air in the house was as thick and smothery as the air outside. She turned. She fell. She crawled toward the stairs, toward the opening — any opening — anything at all. The banisters were white prison bars, the stairway descended . . . but the voice stayed upstairs.

"Dialing the emergency number?" said Mrs. Shevvington, in a voice as thick as mud. Her heavy hands closed on Christina's thin shoulders and moved her away from the telephone.

"Fire," mumbled Christina. "There's a fire upstairs."

"Is there?" Mrs. Shevvington's smile was a crack in the cold, congealed oatmeal of her face. "A fire that you set, Christina? We have your fingerprints, you know," she said very softly. "On that tin can you put that candle in." Her voice was air, without form and texture. "The one you like to light in your bedroom." The voice crawled on Christina's skin.

"The one you took downstairs, and tried to hide behind the geraniums."

The house had turned silent. No voices anywhere.

Mr. Shevvington stood behind his wife, stiff as a mannequin, his fine tailored suit just hanging there, as if he had stepped out for a while, leaving his flesh behind. His eyes glowed like coals of blue ice.

The hottest fires are blue, not yellow. He's going to set fire to me, she thought.

"What a wharf rat you are, Christina," remarked Mrs. Shevvington. "Good for nothing. Destructive behavior whenever you think nobody is looking."

"There is no fire," said Mr. Shevvington, and his voice laughed like a little brook in the spring, tumbling over smooth rocks. "Come, Christina. Let's look."

He dragged her up the stairs. He said, "You've been complaining about your little attic room, Christina. You've been telling the children at school that criminals have better housing than you do. If only you had confided in us — why, we would have moved you immediately. But we're moving you now, Christina."

He propelled her into room number 8. She tried to get free. He was as strong as Michael. She could not twist loose. She was the kitten, on her way to the vet's, to be put down.

Where are the boys? thought Christina. Why aren't they home yet? I need them. I need Benj.

"Michael and Benjamin are both staying at friends' houses for the night," said Mrs. Shevvington. "What a shame that you have no friends, Christina. Nobody ever asks you to spend the night."

She was in Room 8. They were blocking the doorway. She was trapped. Mrs. Shevvington's thick body and Mr. Shevvington's striped suit filled the only exit.

Chhhhrisssstina . . . said the voice beyond the walls. *Chhhhrisssstina* . . . it cried from behind the fires . . . *stay here* . . .

"A cold fire?" she said, confused. She stretched out her hands to warm them in front of the flickering flames. But the fire stayed cold and metallic. Behind it was a wall of foggy sea, painted with seawater itself, and a suggestion of an island: a mere whiff of island. Seagulls and twisted pines beckoned. *Chhhhrisssstina* . . . said the voice beyond the walls. *Chhhhrisssstina* . . . *stay here* . . .

"Home," whispered Mrs. Shevvington. "This is home."

"Home," repeated Christina. "This is home."

Mrs. Shevvington sat on the pretty bed, sinking in the soft mattress. She took Christina in her lap, as so often she had held Dolly. "It's nice to be home at last, isn't it, Christina, darling?"

Christina nodded.

"You'll sleep well here, won't you Christina, dear?"

Christina nodded.

"Among the fire and islands," said Mrs. Shevvington, like a lullaby. "The sea keeps count, you know. It wants one of you."

"Me," said Christina. "It can have me."

Mrs. Shevvington rocked her and rocked her. "It will," said Mrs. Shevvington. "It will."

Chapter 8

In the night, the sea tried to crumble the foundation of the house.

Down in the cove, down among the rocks, the sea fingered every crevice, washed into every crack. The tide rose, and the sea shouldered its way into the cliff, calling, *Chhhrrrrissssssteeeennnaaahh.*

She heard it break into the house, she heard it filling the cellar, she heard it lapping up the stairs, calling her name.

A foghorn blew deep and throbbingly out at sea.

Half of her woke up and half of her slid between cracks, like the sea. She did not know where she was. In a boat? On Burning Fog Isle? In her attic bedroom?

She sat up. The room around her slowly came into dark, nightlike focus. It was guest room number 8. She was alone in the house with the voices and the sea and the Shevvingtons.

Wake up all the way, she ordered herself. Or else you'll wake in the morning and be part of the room

. . . like the girls before you. The room and the Shevvingtons will own you. Like Val in the mental hospital, you'll be a body for strangers to dress, drug, and prop in front of a television . . . while you, Christina, drift on a painted sea to a fiery isle. . . .

She dragged herself out of the drug of fear.

Had it been easier for Val to let herself sift like flour into insanity? Had Val tired of fighting, she thought, just as you have tired of keeping your eyes open?

She had never slept on the second floor before. The house creaked differently; the ocean was louder. But oh, so distinct! So clear! A voice like a solo in a concert.

Chhhrrrrissssssteeennnaaahh . . . sang the ocean.

The creak, like the sea, came nearer.

The creak gathered rhythm, and volume, and creaked on into guest room number 8.

The door moved.

No, she told herself. It didn't move. It was open like that before, wasn't it?

She could actually hear the water in the house. The ocean had come for her. Just as Anya had foretold. *The sea, Chrissie, the sea wants one of us.* And last night Christina had promised Mrs. Shevvington — it can have me, Mrs. Shevvington!

Something moved behind the door.

Something that breathed and waited and reached.

She could not look; not even she, Christina, granite of the Isle. She closed her eyes while her lungs jerked for air and her skin shivered with fear.

And into the soft fog of the room came the ocean, crying, *Chhhrrrrisssssssteeennnaaahh*; crying, *here I am, move over, I've come for you.*

It came swaying. Crawling.

Christina whimpered, and the tears flowed down her cheeks, and she thought: Tears are saltwater; soon I will be all tears — all saltwater — vanished into the ocean.

It got into the bed with her.

Its fingers closed around her skin.

Christina's scream of horror pierced the silent night. It cut through the plaster walls and through the cracks of doors and through the white forest of tilting rails on tilting balconies.

The hand of the ocean covered Christina's mouth and the ocean murmured, "It's just me. Val. I ran away from the Institute. I've been hiding in the room next door. I've been calling your name all night, Christina, so you'd come and find me. Instead you've gone and screamed, and now the Shevvingtons will come in to see what is the matter and they'll know I'm here."

Christina was as flat as one of the sheets on her bed. She thought she would probably never speak again, or think, or stand up. Val added proudly, "I've been so clever. I got out of the Institute, and nobody saw me. Even with all their cameras and bed checks and supervisors, nobody saw."

Christina waited for her scream to bring the Shevvingtons.

But it did not.

She knew they had heard the scream. People in Utah had probably heard the scream. Her hair was damp from the sweat of terror and the pillow damp from the tears of fear. Why had the Shevvingtons not come running?

And then she remembered. These were the Shevvingtons. She was always expecting them to be like regular grown-ups, even after all this time. To protect and to worry. But they never protected. Never worried. No. The Shevvingtons planned and gloated instead.

"Don't worry," she said to Val. "They want me to be afraid. They are probably awake and happy because of that scream." She thought of their smiles: Mr. Shevvington's, smooth and hidden in the dark; Mrs. Shevvington's, yellow and curled at his side.

And I, she thought, am no longer half here. I am all here. "Thank you, Val," she whispered, hugging the other girl. "I nearly slipped into the crack. You saved me."

She turned on the tiny lamp by the bedside table.

In the half light, fire and smoke seemed to creep out of the cracks of the walls. For a moment she was ready to run, ready to scream *Fire!*, to save Val as she had once saved Dolly.

It's just paint, she thought. Anya fell into the changing posters of the sea that Mrs. Shevvington put in her room. I will fall into the mural they've painted on the wall. This afternoon I panicked. I was expecting fire so it became fire.

I must remember that. Things become what you expect them to become. But I am granite. Nothing can shatter me.

Christina lay back on the pillow again, comforted.

"Now hide me somewhere," whispered Val.

"Why can't you go home? I haven't met your mother and father, but Robbie is nice. Just explain that you're better and you can live at home now."

"You don't understand. They think the Shevvingtons know best. The Institute has probably already telephoned them. And all they would do is call an ambulance and send me back."

A year ago, Christina would never have believed that. Now she believed.

"I can't hide here, either." Val's voice was breath, without tone. "The Shevvingtons chose the Institute. They'd love driving me back there. Shutting the gates. Closing the glass. Smiling sadly when I tried to explain."

The house creaked.

Val whimpered.

Even when there are no footsteps, thought Christina, in this house you hear them. You hear the ghosts of these rooms, all the souls trying to get free of the Shevvingtons.

Outside the ocean spit water against the cliffs, but it did not call her name. Had it been Val whispering *Christina*? Or the ocean? And why wasn't it talking now? Was the ocean just resting between tides?

Between victims?

In the morning, thought Christina, I will go to the hardware store and buy a gallon of paint. I will paint over these walls. I will paint away the fire and the fog. I will say to the Shevvingtons, "It's my room and I like it plain white." With a paintbrush I will end the nightmare.

She imagined herself flicking paint in their eyes if they argued.

She imagined them taking the tin can with the candle and the fingerprints to the police, and telling them of arson; imagined the ambulance coming for her as well as for Val. Imagined the Shevvingtons saying to her mother and father, You tried — but sometimes mental illness seizes a child no matter how well intentioned the parents; nobody knows better than we; are we not suffering the very same catastrophe that you are? Our only son locked up just as your only daughter must be? Be brave, like us, and say good-bye to the Christina you once knew.

"The storm cottage," breathed Christina. "Val, that's where you can hide! Nobody will look there. The summer people don't come till August." Christina slid out of the bed. She pulled on jeans and yanked her sweatshirt over her head.

"Step where I step," instructed Christina in the softest voice she had. "Skip stairs where I skip."

Val said, "Shouldn't we wait till the sun comes up?"

Christina shook her head. "People might see us," she whispered.

Down, down they went: ghosts on the run.

As they went lower and lower, Christina smelled the tide. For a moment she could not take the last step off the stairs, for fear she would tumble into the sea. It was right here — right in the house!

Val said, "The cellar is full of water. I know because I tried to hide there. It chased me up the stairs."

The snick of the front door lock seemed loud as a cannon. They waited, but the Shevvingtons' bedroom door did not open.

They slid out, and eased the door shut behind them.

The stars in the sky trembled.

The waves in the ocean fluttered.

They scuttled over rocks and sand, past deserted docks, and silent parked cars.

"I know what happened," said Christina, disgusted with herself. Why, oh, why did she let herself yarn? Michael was right; Christina would stretch any story at all. The cannon strength of the tides had broken through the cellar passage, that was all. It was open again. The flimsy cement layer the Shevvingtons had used to block up their son's creepy entrance had burst.

"Honestly," said Christina to Val, "I'm such a

dodo bird. I make such a big deal out of every little thing."

The horizon glowed pink. The sun edged toward Maine. They had barely gotten past the wharf when the first lobsterman pulled up in his truck, stomped down the dock, started the engine on his boat.

Silent as seabirds they crept around the closed cottages.

"This is perfect," said Christina happily. "You'll be safe here, Val. Nobody can find you here."

In a window high in Schooner Inne, the first ray of sun glinted off a pair of binoculars.

Chapter 9

Christina had always wanted to stay up all night. Every time on Burning Fog Isle when she had a friend spending the night, she begged her parents to let them stay up all night, and her parents always said no.

But it was not as much fun as she had expected.

In school the next day, she was dizzy with sleepiness; her eyelids closed relentlessly. When her brain dredged for information, it found only grit.

She worried continually about Val, sleeping on bare metal springs in a vacant house. Was Val stable enough, well enough for such a night? Was it even safe for anybody to stay alone like that? Should Christina call Mr. and Mrs. Armstrong and tell them? Should Christina tell Robbie? Or Benj? Or her own mother and father?

But the Shevvingtons must have an ally she had not identified. What if the ally was Robbie? And when she said, "I have Val!" what if his mouth went thin and evil like Mrs. Shevvington's . . . his eyes hot and yellow like theirs?

As for Benj, last night when she could have used his granite, he had been elsewhere. At some meeting for Band, working on fund-raisers. Oh, sure, he said he wanted her help, but when push came to shove, he got all stuttery and embarrassed and said he couldn't bring a seventh-grader to the meeting. "I mean, girls like Astrid and Megan are going to be on the committee," he said helplessly. Astrid and Megan were impressive, exciting seniors. Once they had been best friends with Anya. But when Anya began to collapse, Astrid and Megan vanished. They weren't going to hang around with a failure. Christina would just as soon kick Astrid and Megan in the shins as work with them. "That's why you can't come," Benj had said at last. "You act like a seventh-grader, too."

I do not act like a seventh-grader! thought Christina resentfully, walking down middle school halls, passing middle school classrooms. Who saved Val, anyway?

But oh, how Christina wanted to lean on somebody. How she wanted a partner! Or at least some advice.

From some unknown source Val had acquired a surge of strength. But breaking out of the Institute, hitchhiking to the village, creeping into Schooner Inne, hiding from the Shevvingtons . . . all Val's resources were used up.

Now Val expected Christina to accomplish every-thing else — bring food and news and company. Find a way to make her freedom last. Save Val from going back. Prove that Val was well again. Prove, in fact, that she had never been ill to start with. That it was all the Shevvingtons' contrivance.

Christina did not have the slightest idea how to do any of that.

If only she had gotten a full night's rest. Then perhaps she could think clearly. As it was, all her thoughts were blurred.

In school it was Safety Week. Christina tried to open her eyes and concentrate on Safety. The Fire Department gave an assembly talk about safety with matches, lawnmowers, and barbecues.

Nobody in seventh grade wanted to be safe. What was exciting about safety? Everybody wanted to be in danger. In history they talked about ter-rorism and how it was sweeping the world. Jonah said, "I like terrorism. It's exciting to get on a plane and wonder if you'll be hijacked and end up a pris-oner." Everybody agreed that was much more ex-citing than getting salted nuts for a snack.

In Art they had to make posters about safety, and in English Mrs. Shevvington made them write slogans for the posters. Christina was too tired even to hang onto a crayon, let along design something. "We're too old for this," she complained. "Elemen-tary school kids have to make posters, but seventh-graders have outgrown it."

"Outgrown safety?" said Mrs. Shevvington. "How interesting, Christina. I shall bear that in mind."

"Yeah," said Gretch, "you should see what she's doing in woodworking. She's making a fire."

Mrs. Shevvington's little eyes flared. She turned her whole body, like a vehicle, and her flat oatmeal face fastened on Christina. "Making fires?" she repeated.

"We're all making summer fires," said Christina.

"But only yours," smirked Vicki, "has flames."

For Father's Day, the seventh-graders were painting plywood cut-outs to be placed in the empty fireplace for decoration during the summer. Most kids were doing geraniums or cats. Christina, however, thought a summer fire should be a fire, and hers was bigger than anybody's, with curling flames she had cut on the jigsaw. She had chosen metallic paint — bronze and gold with flecks that glittered.

"Oh, you know her fire obsession, Mrs. Shevvington," said Gretch. "You were the one who told us about it. Remember how she wrote essays over the winter about fire? About how she'd like to burn all her sweaters because she was so sick of them? Well, you should see how much she loves Woodworking. She can play with fire all — "

Christina was too tired to think. "You shut up!" she yelled. "Or I'll burn *you*!"

The room went silent.

The hum of fans and the whir of traffic invaded the room, like crawling insects. The eyes of the classroom rotated and fixed on Christina. Her threat seemed to hang in the room like loops of crepe paper, flaming, touching Gretchen.

Christina lifted her hands as if she could cut off the rays of their stares with her flat palms. Her lids scraped mercilessly over her dried-out eyes. Being so sleepy made her nervous and twitchy.

Am I really twitching? thought Christina. Is my cheek jerking like Robbie's? Are my hands knotting? Do I look insane? Or is it just inside my head where the twitching and the panting is going on?

"Christina," said Mrs. Shevvington. Her voice was silken now, drawing across Christina's cheek like a veil. "How queer you sound, my dear. First you don't care about Safety." Her voice curled like smoke and the room seemed to fog up.

Like the wall in bedroom number 8, Christina thought. I meant to buy paint today. Paint over the fire and islands. But instead I have to get food for Val.

"Then, Christina, dear, you tell us that only little children should worry about Safety?" The voice crept like a cat, playing with that word *safety*, mocking it, tossing it around like a dead mouse.

"Then you play with fire," whispered Mrs. Shevvington, her voice a wind that flickered flames. The classroom shivered. Even Jonah shivered. "And finally, Christina . . ." She spoke like the sea. *Chhhhrrissssteeenah*, she hissed. " . . . you threaten your classmates?"

Christina tried to wake up. She was falling into

a trap; she knew it, she could see the steel teeth of the jaws of the trap, but she could not run.

"*Chhhhrrissssteeenah!*" said Mrs. Shevvington, wet like tides, "what is that I see on your desk?"

The mass of eyes swerved and followed the thick, stubby, pointing finger. In her morning stupor, Christina had forgotten to bring her books to school, so the desktop was empty: just a rectangle of blonde wood with a groove for a pencil. Christina lowered her head, although she was so tired she was afraid she would drop down onto the desk and sleep: through school, or through life.

The desk was not empty.

Lying on the edge was a tiny box of matches, the kind with a little drawer, that Christina had used for bureaus for her dolls' bedrooms when she had had a dollhouse. The red tip of a single match stuck out of the tiny drawer.

Mrs. Shevvington gasped, and clutched her chest.

The seventh grade gasped, and covered their mouths.

"Yesterday on the playing field, matchbooks fell out of her jacket pocket," said Vicki.

"It's not mine," said Christina. She pushed the matchbox away, and it fell on the floor. The mass of eyes tilted to see the floor. She was no longer in a room with twenty-five thirteen-year-olds; they were just eyes. Eyes that peeked and peered.

"Stop staring at me!" Christina cried out.

The eyes turned away, full of pity, saying in eye

language, *poor Christina . . . poor Christina . . . poor sick Christina.*

Mrs. Shevvington knelt beside Christina's desk. Her oatmeal face was close to Christina's; her tiny yellow teeth near enough to bite. Her hand was so fat, the flesh grew over her rings, and her thick, bitten nails pressed jaggedy half moons into Christina's kneecap. Christina nearly gagged.

"You feel sick, don't you, Christina? What kind of sickness is it, Christina? Sickness of the heart? Or — sickness of the mind, my dear?" Her voice oozed like a jellyfish.

"It's sickness from cafeteria food," said Jonah loudly. "They served last week's tunafish."

"I had that," said Katy. "It was disgusting. I practically threw up."

Jonah and Katy batted words back and forth, like a ball over a volley net, and the eyes stopped staring, and Mrs. Shevvington stopped kneeling, and finally, finally, class was over.

Christina felt as fragile as spun glass. If somebody pushes me, she thought, I'll shatter.

Walking down the halls with the others, she tried to make herself small and safe. *What if a fire starts? They'll say that I —*

Somebody touched her. Christina leaped as if attacked by a nest of wasps. Gretch and Vicki snickered. "It's only your old lobsterman," they said.

It was Benj. She could not imagine what he was doing in this hallway. High school did not share corridors with middle school. Benj seemed out of breath, almost frantic. Had the Shevvingtons hurt Benj, too? I should be an owl, she thought, so I can swivel my head in all directions. I can't keep track of the Shevvingtons.

"You were in bed when I got home from our meeting," Benj said, "so I didn't get to tell you about it. The fund-raising committee," he added, because she looked so blank, "for Disney World. And guess what?" His eyes were fever-bright.

I have to feed Val, she thought, and paint the wall, and stay awake, and keep away from matches. "What?" she said dimly.

His voice was still as the surface of a pond. "I'm chairman," Benj told her.

School did not interest Benj and had little to do with his life. He had never joined anything except Band, never played a sport, never attended a show. It was Michael for whom the games and activities of school were lifeblood. For Benj only the sea mattered; only Burning Fog Isle, and his own boat.

Something in Christina awoke. Off to the side of her own problems, she remembered his. "You're chairman," Christina repeated. "Benj!" She hugged him. "I'm so proud of you."

He let out the puff of air he had been holding onto, and he grinned. "I've never done anything like this before, Chrissie," he confided. "I don't really know where to start. But I told everybody your ideas. The walk-a-thon. Car washes. Bake sales. But mostly the chowder-thon. Everybody said it was the best idea they'd ever heard. Even Astrid and Megan thought it was the best idea they'd ever heard. And they nominated *me* chairman!"

Vicki and Gretch snickered. Vicki said, "They just couldn't find a sucker to do it except you, Benjamin."

Christina backed up and jammed her shoe heel down toward the bare toes peeking out of Vicki's sandals.

"You missed," said Vicki sweetly.

Mrs. Shevvington caught up to them. "Why, Benjamin," she said, "what are you doing in the middle school wing? You know we can't have older, wilder boys around the younger children."

Vicki and Gretch giggled. "Older and wilder?" repeated Gretch scornfully, stroking her seal-smooth brown hair.

Mrs. Shevvington laughed a civilized little laugh. "Of course, you're right, girls. How silly of me. Benjamin may be older, but he's too dull to be wild. He couldn't corrupt a clam."

Threats filled Christina's head: terrible things to say and do to Mrs. Shevvington and Vicki and Gretch. I hate them! she thought. They can flatten anybody. All they need is bad words and good timing.

But Benjamin Jaye surprised her. He hardly heard Mrs. Shevvington. He certainly hadn't heard Vicki and Gretch; those two girls meant nothing to him; never had; never would.

Benj took Christina's waist in his two big workman's hands and lifted her into the air. He swung her in a circle the way he would have swung his baby sister Dolly.

It was sheer athletic exuberence. Benjamin was overflowing with pride in himself: For the first time ever, he was stretching himself — doing more — reaching out — getting ready to pull something off: something that mattered.

Christina laughed, sharing his joy.

When he set her down she hugged him a second time and looked up into his face to admire his happiness. He looked down to share it with her and the world changed.

The halls vanished.

Mrs. Shevvington evaporated.

Vicki and Gretch were silent wraiths.

Jonah and Robbie were gone as if they had never been.

Benjamin's hands left her waist and found her hair. He separated the silver from the gold, the gold from the chocolate brown. He twined his fingers in her strange mass of tangled hair and tangled it more. He bent forward. His lips touched her forehead and seemed to hover there, as if all their lives had been waiting for this moment: waiting to be together.

Benj said, "The sophomore dance is Friday night." His voice was husky and muffled.

Christina thought, He has never asked anybody to go to a dance. He has never even thought of asking anybody to go to a dance.

"Will you go with me?" said Benj.

Chapter 10

"Christina," breathed Katy, awestruck and proud to be Christina's friend. Her plump cheeks grew even fatter with her excited smile. "You're going to the *sophomore* dance? With Benjamin Jaye? The one whose muscles split open the sleeves of his T-shirts?"

Christina paraded in front of the seventh-grade girls. I am the only one, she thought, going to a high school dance. Even Vicki and Gretch are nobodies compared to me. Christina's head sang songs of triumph. Her feet danced rhythms of conquering.

"He's just a smelly old lobsterman," said Vicki contemptuously. "Who would want to go anywhere with Old Benj?"

"Besides," said Gretch, giggling, "it's not a real date. Christina's practically his sister. Everybody's related to everybody on that silly island. A *real* date would be Benjamin asking a *real* person. Somebody from the mainland."

"But who from the mainland would go anywhere

with that dim old fisherman?" snickered Vicki.

"Here's what their conversation will be," said Gretch. "Christina will babble about fires and islands. Benj will grunt. Christina will babble about safety posters and woodworking class. Benj will grunt." Gretch and Vicki grunted at each other, laughing hysterically.

"Don't hit them," said Jonah in an undertone. "Chrissie, get a grip on yourself. Mrs. Shevvington is watching. Don't hit Vicki or Gretch."

"Hit them?" said Christina gaily. "I hardly even hear them. They're just little seventh-graders. I'm the one going to a high school dance." She began dancing with Jonah, gripping his hand, swinging him back, yanking herself in, taking up the entire hall in her exuberance.

Jonah let her dance him like a puppet. Then he said hesitantly, "But they're right, aren't they? You are just going as island friends, aren't you?"

Christina could feel the separate colors of her hair dazzling in the sun's rays. She felt herself giving off heat — sparkling from behind her eyes. She danced away from Jonah, off by herself, wearing the gown of her golden hair. I am on fire, she thought. I might even decide to fall in love.

The seventh-graders stared after her. The girls were half envious and half afraid. They could not imagine going anywhere with a real live sixteen-year-old boy.

Vicki whispered, "You know what I bet?"

"What?" said the seventh-grade girls. They wondered how did Christina suddenly get so much older than they were? What did Christina have to offer that they did not?

"I bet Christina's going to be a wharf rat."

"No, she won't," said Jonah.

"You always defend her," said Gretch. "Your opinion doesn't count."

Jonah wanted to run after Christina and warn her, but he didn't want to be teased by Vicki and Gretch. He hated being teased. Hated the way Vicki and Gretch could flick words around like the tip of a whip.

Nor could he stay among these girls any longer. Like some great ugly hen, Mrs. Shevvington was spreading her filthy wings over her brood. The girls were clucking like her; scratching in the dirt like her. Jonah felt as if any moment the girls would start pecking Christina. They wanted to say vicious things; he could feel their eagerness to repeat anything Mrs. Shevvington said.

"What is a wharf rat, anyway?" asked Katy.

"A girl," said Mrs. Shevvington, "who works in factories and has babies before she's sixteen."

Jonah fled.

"A girl who loses all her teeth and doesn't get false ones," said Vicki, loudly, so the words would follow Jonah and sink into his vision. "Like that girl who pumps gas at the town dock and eats ten jelly doughnuts at a time. She's only seventeen. That's a wharf rat."

Katy said desperately, "I don't think that would

happen to Christina. She has plans. She's going to amount to something." Down the hall Christina Romney danced alone, the ceiling lights turning her hair to spun gold, and then to threads of silver.

"What about Anya?" countered Gretchen. "She was supposed to graduate first in her class, and what happened? She dropped out of high school last winter to work at the laundromat. That was her big starry future. Folding other people's underwear."

"I am afraid," said Mrs. Shevvington sadly, "that all too often that's what happens to island girls. All they can do is work at the cannery, canning fish."

Vicki laughed. "Benj can catch 'em," she snickered. "Christina can can 'em."

"We can certainly hope Christina does not fall into the same grim future as those examples," said Mrs. Shevvington. "You girls must keep an eye on her."

All their eyes were on her. She was dancing back toward them now, and they had no idea what they would say to her, or think of her.

"That's what school is all about," said Mrs. Shevvington softly. "Forming a community to help one another. Poor Christina is in a time of trouble. This appalling obsession with fire is becoming quite an emotional problem."

Katy remembered the woman on the dock — only seventeen years old! Could that happen to small, slim, brave Christina? Mrs. Shevvington knew about these things. And Mrs. Shevvington said . . .

At lunch, although she was starving, Christina ate nothing. She took food from the cold line — a sandwich, a yogurt, an apple. Talking brightly to Jonah, she removed each piece of food to her lap, wrapped it into a napkin without looking, and slid it carefully into her bookbag. There, she thought proudly. Food for Val.

"Look out for the Shevvingtons," muttered Jonah. "I know you think you've seen everything they can do, but they're crafty. They're going to turn all the girls against you. You've got to pay attention, Chrissie."

Christina thought of all she had accomplished lately: getting into the Institute as Iris Murch, making friends with Val, smuggling Val into the storm cottage, and all the while telling Benj how to raise money, and having him fall in love with her. It was amazing how much strength you got just from knowing that a boy adored you. You could take on the world when a boy ached for you. The Shevvingtons. Hah! Small potatoes. Hardly worth a thought, let alone panic. "Jonah, I'm smarter."

Jonah's face curled: nose, lips, even cheeks, making a big, dumb, seventh-grade face. "Don't be so cocky."

"You're just jealous, Jonah, because I'm going out with Benjamin."

"Oh, it's going out now, is it? You're dating now, huh? Fine. Date him. See if I care." Jonah crumpled his brown lunch bag, threw it violently into a trash can, and stomped away.

In woodworking, Christina painted her summer fire.

"What color is fire anyway?" she muttered to herself. She struck a match and studied the flame, how it was yellow, blue, white. The flame from the match was not much to get excited about. "I want a fiercer fire," she told the teacher. She mixed scarlet and orange into her yellow, until the tips of the flames glittered savagely.

When she turned from admiring her work, Mr. Shevvington was standing behind her. "Christina?" he said. The word floated like a leaf, staying aloft. As concerned principal, Mr. Shevvington talked with the woodworking teacher about poor Christina — about how the administration was worried. Was Christina, perhaps, a bit unnatural in her interest in fire? A bit . . . not to exaggerate . . . but . . . a bit *dangerous*?

Christina set her summer fire against the wall to dry. He didn't scare her. She was full of philosophy and love. She was protected by the colors of her hair, by Benj's crush, by her own isle, far out at sea, waiting for her to come home.

Mr. Shevvington's big sad eyes caught the eyes of the class. He tilted his elegant head to the side, pitying Christina. The class, like sunflowers worshiping, tilted with him, growing sad, full of pity.

Mr. Shevvington shook his head slowly. Once.

The class shook its head slowly. Once. Like a decision: a decree.

She's crazy. She's not one of us. Keep your eyes on her.

Christina stared into her summer fire, thinking of Val.

After school, Christina slung her bookbag over her shoulder, careful not to squash Val's sandwich, and headed for the storm cottage. She was scarcely out the door when Robbie cornered her. "Christina!" he hissed in her ear. "Something terrible has happened."

"What?"

He cupped his hands around his lips and breathed in her ear. "Val is missing! My parents took me out of class fifth period to ask if I knew anything. They think she's run away, but I think the Shevvingtons have done away with her."

If she told Robbie that Val was fine, enjoying a storm cottage and freedom, Robbie would tell his parents, Mr. and Mrs. Armstrong would call an ambulance, and Val would be locked up in a hurry. "Robbie," she said nervously, wondering what kind of an actress she would be, "that's so scary. I'm so sorry." Should I drop a clue? she thought.

Benjamin arrived beside them. He elbowed Robbie out of the way. "I have to go to work," he said to Christina.

She nodded.

"But you can walk with me to the gas station," he said.

She nodded again.

Robbie flattened himself against the wall, looking miserable and helpless. Christina had an unworthy thought: Val had chosen to go to a stranger for help, not her own brother. Even lost, Val had known it was Christina who was made of granite. I'm granite of the Isle, thought Christina, and the whole middle school is watching Benj and me. She loved being the center of their attention. She paraded a little more.

Jonah and Robbie fell in step with them. Christina knew they were waiting for her to join them, talk to them, solve their problems for them. She said nothing. It was powerful: being silent when people wanted you to talk.

"Benj gave you his silence for your fourteenth birthday," teased Jonah. "Now he'll be with one who knows how to talk, Chrissie, and you'll be the silent Maine fisherman."

Benjamin ignored Jonah as too young and scrawny to count. "Astrid and Megan said they'd be happy to work with you," he said to Christina.

Robbie and Jonah faded away, like sails slipping from the shore. She felt herself stepping away from the entire seventh grade, moving up several years in several minutes.

For Benj's sake, she would not hold it against Astrid and Megan that they had abandoned Anya.

Perhaps they couldn't help it. Perhaps there were extenuating circumstances. Anyway, somebody as mature as Christina could forgive that sort of thing. She took Benj's hand and swung it.

"I got a B on an English paragraph today," he told her shyly.

She could not recall Benjamin Jaye ever mentioning an academic subject. Benj filled desk space, but he didn't actually do schoolwork. "That's wonderful," she said. "What was the paragraph about?"

Benjamin talked for several minutes as they walked down the blocks to his gas station. Why, he always had things to say, thought Christina. There just wasn't anybody listening!

At the gas station, however, Benj was the youngest. This changed him. His feet as well as his tongue stumbled. The other men grinned at Christina and looked knowingly at the clasped hands. Benjamin dropped her hand quickly to grip a toolbox instead.

"Little young, isn't she?" said an oil-stained man.

"I'm fourteen," said Christina with dignity.

The men all laughed, and Benj blushed. "Goodbye," he said, without looking at her. But she felt his heat.

He can't look at me, she thought. He's combustible: He'd catch fire. "Bye, Benj," she whispered, running off, escaping from the same fire: the fire that would consume them both. This is like when I had a crush on Blake! she thought, forgetting what pain that had brought her, remembering only the intense wonderful burning of love.

She meant to follow the shoreline to the storm cottage and get the food to Val. But she spotted Vicki and Gretch shopping in the boutiques that were beginning to open up for the tourist season. She went in another direction, and there, up the alley, was Robbie Armstrong coming toward her. She'd already talked to Robbie.

She ran again, taking the corners at full speed, bumping into tourists, and dashing between city cars. At the Town Hall she ducked in the lower entrance. There were public bathrooms and a drinking fountain; she would waste a little time there until the coast was clear and she could wend her way to the storm cottage and Val.

Across from the water fountain was an office whose sign read TOWN PERSONNEL. Christina frowned slightly. She considered the word "personnel" and what it meant. Then she walked in. Behind a counter made of rows of filing cabinets sat a gray-haired secretary. "Hello," said Christina.

The secretary smiled blankly. She seemed the kind of person who smiled well, but otherwise did nothing. Easy to con. "Um," began Christina, her head full of possibilities but none clear enough to surface. "Um," she said again. "There's going to be a surprise party," she said finally. "For the Shevvingtons. Do you know them? He's the principal and she teaches seventh-grade English."

"Oh, of course I know him. Such a fine man. I heard he's leaving our school system, though! What a loss to the town."

"A terrible loss," agreed Christina. "And the seventh grade is giving them a surprise good-bye party."

"How sweet! I didn't know children were still so sweet in this day and age."

"Well, they are," said Christina, who was not. "And what we want is guests from towns where the Shevvingtons used to teach. Before they came to Maine. So . . . um . . . I need a list of addresses. And it has to be a secret. Or the party won't be any fun. Promise?"

"I promise!" said the secretary gaily, and got right into the spirit of the thing, digging out addresses of schools where Mr. Shevvington had been principal before, and the names of the people who had written him recommendations. Mr. Shevvington had been in Louisiana and Pennsylvania, Oregon and New Jersey.

Christina slid the addresses into her bookbag. I've got it! she exulted. I've got a way to find out what they did before. I can locate the girls before Val! I can find out whose ghosts are locked into the first six guest rooms. I'm going to win. I'll save Val and not only that, I'll be saving all the girls who are out there, all unknowing, in the next town.

She said to the secretary, "This is so nice of you."

"I'd love to come to the party," said the secretary shyly.

"I'll send you an invitation," promised Christina. Party, she thought, hah! It's going to be a hanging.

Chapter 11

The long hills of Maine rippled like a Chinese dragon.

The sky grew dark. Fog bulged on the oceantop like the dragon's discarded skin; empty; ready to swallow victims.

Christina felt the sea dragon on her right side, curling forward over the waves. She felt the land dragon on her left, leaning through the trees and over the village.

She watched her feet instead, seeing her white sneakers grow wet as she wound among the rocks. She did not dare go on the upper path because summer people had come for the weekend, and they would leap forward the way summer people did, screaming, "What are you doing on my property!" Summer people were always frantic. They were always afraid of trespassers. They were always crying out, "I'll sue you!" instead of just getting a tan.

Christina scrambled among the smaller rocks below the seawall, exposed by the tide, where the dead horseshoe crabs lay among the dank seaweed and the barnacles scraped her skin.

Out at sea the wind increased. It took the fog in its arms and flung it toward Christina. It touched her bare arms and fondled her bare cheeks.

When she was below the storm cottage, she picked her way up the boulders to the rickety porch. The fog chased her ankles. She tilted open the shutter. "Val?" she hissed. She slid into the living room. The fog tried to follow. The wind came through the crack with her, lifting the white sheets on the furniture. The white walls waved, and the white floor shivered. But nobody answered.

"Val?" whispered Christina again.

How strange the house smelled. She paused in the whiteness of the rooms, sniffing. The smell was oily and cruel. It smelled of cities and gutters.

Something primitive, ancient and evil, crept up Christina's spine. The smell entered her nose and mouth, walked through her insides, and the entire world — all her flesh and all her soul — stank of the evil of it.

"*Val!*" she shouted.

What was the smell?

Had it sucked Val up?

She ran from room to room, and the smell ran with her. Every time her foot touched the floor she thought her sneaker sole might be eaten by acid.

Every breath she took, she thought her lungs would decay. *"Val! Where are you? Are you all right? I brought food!"*

The cottage was empty.

No one lay on the bare metal springs of the ugly old cots.

No one sat at the white porcelain table or opened the single drawer in the kitchen.

Val was gone.

Christina ran back to her window entrance.

The wind had thrown the shutter back and it was stuck fast.

She pushed and pulled at it, but its handles were on the outside. She ran to the other windows but they, too, were fastened from the outside. The smell grew thicker and stronger as if it were growing up from the cellar. Its appetite had increased. It liked little girls.

She flung herself into the tiny kitchen, and jumped up onto the counter. The tiny window over the old deep sink did not open. It never had, it never would. She jumped back down.

On the table — the tiny kitchen table — stood an old coffee can.

Inside the can tilted an old candle.

The candle was burning.

It was the can the Shevvingtons had left in her bedroom, the one she had tried to hide behind the geraniums. The one which had her fingerprints.

My fingerprints are on everything in this house,

thought Christina. And that smell — it's gasoline. This house is ready to burn.

From the depths of memory she heard Anya's voice. (Anya last fall, when the Shevvingtons began eating at her sanity.) "No, Chrissie," Anya had said, her hair a cloud of spun black glass. "The Shevvingtons will not destroy you. *You will destroy yourself.*"

Christina did not dare blow the flame out. There were enough gas fumes to light the kitchen. She wet her fingertips and squashed the flame. Racing back into the living room, she kicked the shutter open. The bottom hinge broke. It was no secret now; anybody could tell the storm cottage had been broken into.

And she knew, grimly, who would do the telling. The Shevvingtons.

And she knew who would produce the fingerprints for comparison. The Shevvingtons.

And she knew who would say, *But didn't we tell you she was nothing but a wharf rat?*

How had they known? How had they found out? Christina had told nobody!

She went out the window. The world was invisible. The fog was as thick as the inside of an envelope. The ocean she could not see chewed on the rocks she could not locate.

It was Anya's ocean; Anya had always said that at times like this, the sea sounded like a coffin being dragged over broken glass.

Whose coffin? thought Christina.

Mine?

Val's?

She ran, and the fog ran with her, engulfing her feet, swallowing the tips of her own fingers. She stumbled, but fog was no cushion. Rocks and barnacles ripped her skin. She cut between summer people's houses. The wet soggy branches of forsythia whipped her cheeks, and the heavy perfume of lilacs slapped her face. She slid on the grass and stained her clothes. At last she came out on the road, among headlights of cars, like dim yellow baskets.

Val, where are you? thought Christina. Are you safe? Did you go home? What happened?

She came into the village again and here the fog had come in soft and gray and cozy. Summer people were laughing at being lost only a few feet from each other. Natives were irritated and hoping it would sweep away soon.

Jonah was right, she thought. I got cocky. I was so sure of myself, so proud. He kept saying, *Pay attention, they're after you.* But would I listen to Jonah? No, because he's just in seventh grade and seventh-graders bore me.

A queer, horrible worry made her stop and look in her bookbag. She sat on a bench for tourists. Red geraniums nodded at her from out of the fog. She took out the sandwich. She took out the yogurt. She took out the apple. She took out her arithmetic book and her history book.

And yes.

There, beneath everything, caught in a seam, a lump so small only police fingers would have found it, was a box of matches.

Her hair was wet from the fog. No separate colors sprang from her head: no silver and gold, no rich chocolate-brown. Her hair was just a soggy mass, no different from anybody else's in the rain.

Nothing will save me, thought Christina Romney.

There will be a fire. The town will say that I set it. There will be fingerprints. The town will say I put them there. There will be a matchbox. The town will say I took it with me. They have forgotten the past. The memory of the village has been sealed up also.

They will catch me.

Mr. Shevvington's eyes will be soft and gray, like spring rain.

Mrs. Shevvington will nod her head like a guillotine in slow motion.

And the town will whisper, *We always knew she was just a wharf rat.*

Chapter 12

The fog began whispering. The whisper was thick and snuffly and damp. *"The alone,"* it breathed. *"The alone."*

It was the voice of Christina's fears: that one day she would be alone . . . all alone . . . the world would end . . . while she wandered . . . her breathing the only breathing on earth . . . her footsteps the only footsteps on earth. *The alone.*

Mattresses of fog disappeared when she walked through them.

The alone, repeated the world.

Fear struck Christina's lungs, and she breathed in the fog itself, lungs heaving as if she were in a track race. The fog sat in her lungs like a wet towel, suffocating her.

And now the fog murmured *Chhhrrrissssteee-nnnaaaaaaaahhhh,* and she knew it had come for her; it was going to wrap its wet arms around her; it would take her —

"I was afraid of *the alone*," said Val clearly, and

now Christina could see her: slim and damply pretty, blending with the tourists. "The storm cottage," said Val, clinging to Christina, her fingers like tree toads plastered to Christina's arms. "It was so full of *alone*. I was alone, it was alone, the sea was alone, the sheets on the chairs were alone. Christina, I couldn't bear it."

Christina tried to peel Val off but Val was too afraid of *the alone* to let go. Her fingers are just fingers, Christina told herself, not toads.

"The Shevvingtons called the fog in," said Val. "I heard them. They were in the storm cottage and they called to the fog, and the fog answered and obeyed."

Christina shuddered convulsively. She could imagine their arms, their curled fingers, their furry voices. "The fog was coming in anyway, Val," said Christina. "They weren't calling it. They don't have special powers."

"Of course they do," said Val. "I knew once the fog came in, the alone would have me, and the Shevvingtons would have me and it would be over. They stood on the rocks outside the storm cottage and held their hands up to the ocean, laughing, and the ocean laughed with them, and all together they cried, '*Fog. Fog. Fog.*' "

I knew they were in the storm cottage, thought Christina. I knew they were the ones who spilled . . .

Her thoughts bumped into a terrible wall. A wall of sharp spikes and knife-edged wire. A wall of Evil.

Gasoline. Matches. Val.

"No," said Christina, as if to stop Evil with a syllable. "The Shevvingtons are terrible people, but setting fire to the storm cottage while you were in it? Even the Shevvingtons wouldn't —"

"Yes, they would," said Val. "I'm starving, Christina. Did you bring me anything to eat?"

Christina handed over the sandwich. Val tore off the wrapper and ate savagely. Christina pictured the sandwich still whole lying in Val's stomach.

I told Benj to believe in Evil, thought Christina, but here I am facing Evil, and I don't believe. People don't really do things like that. Not just for the fun of it. Because there's no reason except entertainment. There's no money, no power, no status. "But why?" whispered Christina. "Why would they plan that?"

"Because there aren't enough days left," said Val. "You keep outwitting them, Christina. That's dumb. If you would just be dumb yourself, they wouldn't care about getting you, too. They were gloating, because they could get both of us forever. They said it would be a pleasant finale to a difficult year. That was their word. Pleasant. They said it would be pleasant to wrap things up. Meaning you. Do you have anything else to eat?"

Christina gave her the apple. I bet she eats the core, too, thought Christina, and she was right.

Christina's head throbbed hideously. So this is what a real headache is, she thought. It bites from the inside. It chews on your eyes and your brain and the hearing parts of your ears.

"We have to call the fire department before the gasoline catches," she said dully. "Or they'll blame me." Christina started crying. She thought of the storm cottage, and the innocent summer people whose place would go up in flames, and all because — as Benj would have been the first to tell her — she had trespassed for the fun of it. "They'll blame me anyway. I'll be the one calling the fire department, and my fingerprints are all over the place." Christina could not imagine what her mother and father and Benj and Jonah and Vicki and Gretch and everybody else on earth would have to say.

And then she could imagine.

Perfectly.

Wharf rat, they would say, their pointing fingers jabbing into her chest. Wharf rat, wharf rat, wharf rat!

Val shook her head. "Chrissie, I didn't have anything else to do waiting for you to come back, so I scrubbed everything you had touched. And you carried the coffee can and the candle away with you." Val grubbed in the bookbag, hoping for more to eat, and found the yogurt. She used two bent fingers for a spoon and slurped it up. She said, "Anyhow, while they summoned the fog, I slid out the cellar window."

"I'm impressed, Val. I thought you'd be insane."

"I was for a while. The alone really got to me. But you're here now. I'm leaning on you, and I'm fine. Where are you going to hide me now?"

Christina knew more or less where they were,

but the fog that had hidden Val from Christina's sight could hide listeners and enemies, too: the Shevvingtons need stand only a few yards away and they, too, would be swallowed in the thick gray fog.

The passage to the sea, thought Christina. The cliff passage where the Shevvingtons' horrible insane son slipped back and forth unseen so he could terrorize Anya. The sea opened it up again. I heard it crash through last night.

Generations ago, the sea captain had built in that strange location, where the high tide coming into Candle Cove made the house shake with every thundering wave. Nobody knew why he chose that cliff edge. And then Christina had found out why: He must have been smuggling something in or out his hidden hole. You could reach it only at low tide. At high tide, it was covered by water. How well she knew that cellar. The mold that grew on the walls; the smell of the tide lodged in the cracks; the cold, watery drafts that slid around your ankles. She remembered how the horrible passage tilted into the water, and she had once been forced down it, while the *thing*, the unknowable, rubbery, inhuman thing, had laughed madly from above. The thing that was the Shevvingtons' son.

She could imagine herself in that passage again — and the Shevvingtons cementing it up on both sides while she was trying to hide Val there.

No, the cliff passage was not a possibility.

"I can't go back to the storm cottage," quavered

Val. She shuddered and grabbed Christina's hand. "The alone would get me."

Christina could not loosen Val's grip. She had the impression that if Val did not hang onto her, Val would tip over. Val was literally, as well as mentally, unbalanced.

The full horror of it struck Christina. Val *needed* the care and the help of professionals. She needed the love and the knowledge of people who helped the mentally distraught. She probably needed her mother. It couldn't be good for Val to be by herself, surrounded by white sheets and booming tides, wondering if *the alone* was going to get her.

The fog began to curl back away from the coast, as if the gods of the sea — of the Shevvingtons — were peeling it away. They could see twenty feet ahead of them, and then a hundred feet.

The Atlantic burbled and chuckled like a nursery school playgroup.

Far out on the horizon, a fire blazed. Gaudy strips of flame pierced the fog. Glowing embers of ship or house. Burning Fog Isle, up to its old tricks with the prism of fog and sun.

I want to go home, thought Christina. I want my mother. I want my father. I want everything the way it used to be, all safe and cozy.

She could telephone her parents. "Mommy, remember how Anya almost lost her mind, and the year before, Robbie's sister Val did lose hers and had to be put away? Val ran away from the Institute and came to me because I went there under a false name to visit her because I needed information against the Shevvingtons. The Shevvingtons know that I know about them, and they have very little time to destroy me. They are planning to set fire to the storm cottage where I've been hiding Val, and they will make it look as if I did it. They've been putting matches and candles everywhere I go. They are going to blame me for arson, Mommy! I'll be a wharf rat before I'm even in high school."

And her parents would say — as they wept — "No nice, kind adult like dear Mr. Shevvington would do that. It must be something about the way we brought her up, out here on this island, without a normal twentieth-century social life; it must be our fault. Christina really did do it herself."

And yet . . . if Christina did *not* tell, Val might slip into the alone, and never come out.

Chapter 13

"*Stay here?*" cried Val. "Oh, no, Chrissie, no, I — "

"Here," said Christina firmly.

"Impossible," breathed Val. "I'll go insane."

They giggled desperately. Room 7 swirled around them, crimson and dark violet, crystal clear and dusk-quiet.

"I'll be in and out," promised Christina.

"But Chrissie." Val was gasping for breath. "Chrissie, it's their plan." Her voice became softer, tinier. "For me to come here. I can feel it. *The Shevvingtons know.*"

"They do not know. And you can get away with it, Val, I know you can. The first rule of hiding something is to put it right out in the open where it belongs. Like the best place to hide a car is a big parking lot, not a backyard."

"This room isn't big."

"It's yours, though, Val. It was decorated for you."

"It's my shell. You said so yourself."

"You'll find yourself in here, Val. You'll go back to being the old Val."

Val's laugh was high and broken, like the top of an electric keyboard, losing its current. "My ghost lives here. *The alone* lives here."

"The Shevvingtons'll be at school during the day. You can eat and go to the bathroom and watch television. And if there are cookies gone or something — why, three teenagers eat here, anyway. What do they expect? Besides, they'd never think to look for you here, Val. They'd expect you to run as far from them as you could."

The sun had moved over Schooner Inne to the west, town-facing side of the house. Room 7 looked out on an ocean not blue, nor green, but kitten-gray. Soft, fuzzy, wet gray. The sky dissolved like aspirin in a glass, and you could not tell the horizon from the ocean.

"It's too bleak," Val whispered. "I've always been afraid of the ocean. It's so noisy. It yells at me. Calls my name." Val pulled the window shades down and yanked the crimson curtains shut.

"You shouldn't do that," said Christina. "That's evidence. If they look in this guest room, and they will, because they gloat every day, they'll see the curtains have been moved."

"They look in here every day? You put me on purpose in a room the Shevvingtons look in every day?"

Christina twitched the curtains back and yanked

the shade up again. Against the aspirin sky, a dark thundercloud began to form.

"Chrissie, don't do that. I can't have an open window where things can look in at me. That cloud is pointing straight at me."

"There's nothing out there but cliff and air," said Christina. "The only thing that could look at you is a sea gull."

"They called the fog," said Val. "They could call a sea gull. They could come as sea gulls. They could float in on the tide, like *the alone*. Like the fog."

"Don't be ridiculous," said Christina. "Get a grip on yourself."

Val laughed again. It sounded like a tourist, somebody from a pickup truck throwing a glass bottle against the sidewalk. Tourists loved to break glass.

Will this break Val? thought Christina. But there isn't anyplace else. I can't take her back to the storm cottage. The Shevvingtons —

— *were planning even now to set fire to the storm cottage.* Where they expected Val to be. They had to be stopped. "Remember my rules," said Christina fiercely to Val, and she ran back down the stairs.

In the dim half-light of the front hall, with the forest of white-carved banisters curling above her, she began dialing the phone. Nine, one, one. Her fingers shook. The phone seemed remarkably heavy.

Above her, on the middle landing, Val leaned over the railing. "I'm dizzy, Chrissie," she muttered. "It's dizzy up here." If Val fainted, she'd do a swan dive down the stairs.

"Emergency," said a solid, sure voice. The kind of voice that knew how to do things with hoses and ladders and horrors. It had a heavy Maine accent: almost an island voice. A voice whose twang spelled comfort and safety to Christina Romney.

"I need help," said Christina, and the moment she admitted it, her own voice broke and she burst into tears.

"I'm here," said the voice, "don't panic. Tell me where you are and what the emergency is."

On the upstairs balcony, Val began sobbing in harmony with her. It was eerie, like weeping through stereo speakers. "There isn't a fire yet," said Christina, struggling to control the sobs. I can't break down, she thought, I've been so strong so far. "I was playing house in a summer cottage. A storm cottage up the shore. I know I shouldn't have been there. But when I went up today, somebody had splashed gasoline all over the house. I think they're going to set fire to it." Did she dare tell the good twanging Maine voice that the Shevvingtons were going to set the fire? The principal everybody loved versus the mad little island girl whose pockets were stuffed with matches? "Please — please — " What am I saying *please* for? wondered Christina as she said it. Please save me? Please save Val? Please end this?

The voice was slow and easy. It coaxed Christina to give her name and location, the address of the storm cottage, the number of times she had played in the house.

Val crept down the carpeted stairs, sidled up to Christina, and stood with her head pressed against Christina's thick hair, soaking up equal comfort from the voice inside the phone. "Go back upstairs and hide," hissed Christina.

Val shook her head. "Too scary up there."

A few moments later they heard sirens, but the voice kept on talking. "You're a good brave girl, Christina," said the voice. "You did the right thing. I'm a friend of your parents, did you know that? I'm Jimmy Gardner; I went to high school with your mom. I'm in the fire department. Volunteer, of course. My real job's running the cannery."

The cannery. Wharf rats. Empty shells.

"Now you stay on the phone with me. I had somebody get on another line and call your school. Mr. Shevvington is coming right down to be with you. He'll be kind and understanding. He's a fine man."

Christina began laughing.

"Don't get hysterical on me," said Mr. Gardner. "You've been calm so far. You probably prevented arson. We had some trouble with that last year in empty houses, and we certainly don't want it again this year." He paused, but Christina had nothing to say.

The front door to Schooner Inne opened.

Val leaped backwards, falling into the parlor with the cold fire.

Mr. Shevvington filled the hall. Today's three-piece suit was a deep, rich, navy blue. One of the colors of Val's room. Had he seen Val? Did he already know? Would he tell Mr. Gardner to send an ambulance for Val as well?

Mr. Shevvington took the phone out of Christina's hands. "I'm here, Jim," he said into the receiver. "Good of you to handle her so gently. Poor Christina often does not entirely understand what is going on."

His mad blue eyes rotated in his head as if they had come unattached. He was not only insane-mad; right now he was furious-mad. His fingers dug into Christina like lobster claws until she cried out in pain. In sympathy, Val moaned behind the parlor door.

The phone mumbled.

"Your wife is what?" repeated Mr. Shevvington into the phone. "Your wife is the personnel secretary?"

Christina went limp. It was easy to forget what a small town this was; how everybody knew everybody, or was married to somebody's cousin, or had been to school with somebody.

"And Christina was in the personnel office getting addresses of my previous schools? For a surprise party?" Mr. Shevvington's lips began to curl back away from his teeth. They drew out into a horrible lifted oval, so all his teeth pointed at her.

He began bending over her, bringing his twisted face closer and closer to hers. Christina shrank back against the flocked wallpaper. Through the crack of the door Val's single brown eye watched in horror.

"But your wife asked other seventh-graders and there was no surprise party planned?" Mr. Shevvington straightened up. The lips closed again and then folded over, making several smiles — a whole series of smiles — like evil plans. "Why, Jim, how thoughtful of you to become concerned. And of course, you are so intuitive, you and your dear wife . . . yes . . . poor Christina . . . you're absolutely right, these island children are ingrown . . . warped . . . a sort of wharf rat mentality . . . frightening in certain ways . . . thank you for telling me . . . my wife and I will certainly bear this in mind."

He hung up.

The storm cottage was safe.

But Christina and Val were not.

Chapter 14

Christina could hear the double breathing. Her own shallow and moist; Val's quick and dry. It seemed impossible that Mr. Shevvington did not hear both girls.

It was on Christina alone that his hands tightened, and his fury mounted.

She tried to get the telephone back, to call 911 again.

"And what would you say?" asked Mr. Shevvington sweetly. "Dear Mr. Gardner, I think Mr. Shevvington is annoyed with me! Please send help."

Christina bit him.

It was the most disgusting thing she had ever done in her life. Even the time two summers ago when Michael dared her to eat a jellyfish raw from the beach, and she did, it had not been so disgusting. She was the one who screamed, not Mr. Shevvington. He yanked his hand back and stared at her.

"I'm rabid," Christina told him. "You'll need shots. Right in the stomach. Hundreds of them."

The doorbell rang.

Mr. Shevvington looked at his watch and muttered to himself. Quickly he wrapped her tooth marks in his handkerchief. He always wore a lovely silk hanky whose tips decorated his lapel pocket. The crimson and royal-blue paisley seemed stolen from Val's room. "It's a potential buyer," he mumbled. "A couple coming to look at the Inne."

Christina smiled. "I'll be sure to tell them what it's really like here."

But when the door opened, before Mr. Shevvington could go to answer it, Robbie and his mother peeked into the front hall. Christina squeaked. Behind her door Val swallowed as loud as an engine. The thunderstorm that had been brewing between the island and the coast, broke. Rain came down in sweeping torrents. Val could lie down and groan now and nobody would hear, thought Christina. They would still see, however.

"Come in, come in," said Mr. Shevvington testily, worried now about his wallpaper and his carpet getting wet.

Mrs. Armstrong looked like Val, but haggard — the way Val's grandmother ought to look. The Shevvingtons did that, thought Christina. They aged her, when they chose Val to ruin.

"We haven't found a trace of Val. Can you think of anyplace else to look?"

Mr. Shevvington put his good arm around her shoulder, protectively cradling his bitten hand. "Poor, poor Genevieve," he said.

So that was her name. It was a good name for her. Gentle and old.

Genevieve wept. Not the lumpy crying of Christina's panic with Mr. Gardner. Nor the homesick tears that had drenched her pillow at the beginning of the school year. But old tears, as if she were recycling them from a previous disaster.

Val won't be able to stand this, thought Christina. She'll come out from behind the door. I would, too, in her place. Her mother needs her. Anyway, any institution would be less risky than the Shevvingtons.

"My father's driving around town," Robbie said. "He thinks maybe he'll find her hitchhiking."

"Poor, poor Alan," said Mr. Shevvington. His eyes were half hidden under folded lids, as if he were resting in there, swinging in a hammock, enjoying himself.

Why, he has two extra victims I didn't even know about, realized Christina. He uses their first names to make them littler, younger. Because that's what he's reduced them to: They're hardly more than seventh-graders themselves. Genevieve and Alan. Not Mr. and Mrs. Armstrong. Not grown-ups.

One good thing: Val was only a few feet away. Either she would surrender or she wouldn't. The choice was no longer Christina's.

"They've explained to us," said Val's mother sadly, "that Val has to spend her life at the Institute. We have to get her back there."

"Her *life!*" cried Christina. "She's only seventeen."

Robbie shrugged. "There's no other answer."

"There has to be another answer," said Christina.

"Robbie, let's go, honey," said his mother, sagging. "I don't know why we came here, really. Except we've been everywhere else."

"I'll walk you to your car," said Mr. Shevvington, opening the door again. The rain was even heavier. He hoisted a huge British umbrella and held it over Mrs. Armstrong.

"Oh, Arnold, you're so kind," she wept. She leaned on him as they went down the granite steps, crossed Breakneck Hill Road, and stopped at the old economy-model Ford.

Christina jerked Val out from behind the parlor door. "Run upstairs!" she hissed. "If they're showing the house to buyers, they'll look everywhere. Hide in your room."

Val wouldn't budge. "They'll look there, too, Chrissie. Did you hear what my mother said? My own mother? She is going to lock me up forever. And I'm only seventeen."

"The Shevvingtons probably told an all-new set of stories about you. Probably convinced the whole staff whatever it is is true. We'll get you away. *Just hurry up the stairs.*"

Val was thin from her hospital stay. Her skinny little legs churned up the long staircase.

As thin as Dolly, thought Christina, or as Anya

when she was at her most faded. Perhaps food and energy is the real key to keeping sane. So I'll be sure to have a big dinner. Plenty of roast beef.

Knowing Mrs. Shevvington they would be having eggplant lasagne instead. Ugh.

Mr. Shevvington came back in. Gently he shook the umbrella. Gracefully he closed it, setting it to drain in the elegant Chinese vase the sea captain had brought back from his voyages to the Orient. Mr. Shevvington's smile peaked and valleyed on his face like the crest of a wave. Christina moved down the hall, to a place where she had several choices: kitchen, back door, stairs. "So, Christina of the Isle," he said softly, "where is our little Valerie?"

"Val? I haven't even met her. She's been in an institution since I came on the mainland, remember?"

The evil inside Mr. Shevvington glowed. She could see it through his skin: lanterns of it. If she touched his glow, would it be hot or cold? Would it, once touched, pass into her body, too, like an electrical current? Turning even Christina of the Isle into someone evil?

Upstairs a door snicked shut. Mr. Shevvington did not appear to hear it. The hand she had bitten came toward her. The paisley silk kerchief dangled on it like a flag over a coffin. The blue eyes fell down, as if unhinged, and the lobster claw fingers caught the fabric of Christina's shirt.

Christina did not dare leave Val alone — but she could not stay here, either.

Val was on her own.

Christina tore loose. She burst out the door into the pouring rain and ran to the gas station. The rain soaked her. The thunder jarred her joints. Lightning bristled in the sky like rocket launches. I'll get Benjamin, she thought. He's safe, he's strong. I'll tell him, he'll know what to do.

With the confusing abruptness of summer storms, the rain moved on up the coast to attack other towns. The sun came back out, the ocean turned blue-green again, and the road surfaces steamed. Christina sprinted through puddles and splashed herself with mud. I probably look about ten years old, she thought. And I still have teary-red eyes. What will Benjamin think of me?

It was the first time in her life she had really wondered what a boy would think of her looks. Or cared.

Christina ran through the empty lot behind the gas station. Tall weeds brushed her legs. A small white butterfly fled from her thrashing feet. Behind the garage was a car storage yard, fenced like a prison. Barbed wire curled on top. Far above, in the suddenly blue sky, was a bird, floating.

Benjamin! Benjamin!

She planned to fling herself on him, tell him everything, stand still while he solved it.

But Benjamin was surrounded by tourists, expecting him to fix their cars. All her island training rose up: She must not look demented in front of tourists. They were lifeblood; they were money. She slowed, donning her "Welcome, Tourist" face.

How pleased Benjamin was to see her. Why, even as disheveled as she was, she had only to walk up, and his face lit up in a smile so handsome, so fine, that she wanted to keep it for her very own. A smile he'd kept secret for just this: a girl.

I'm the girl, marveled Christina. She stood in the shade of a maple tree, behind a wreck recently towed in by the state police. She was glad she was turning fourteen soon. Thirteen seemed too young for love. Her parents would not like it.

"Be with you in a minute," said Benj. "I have to change the belts on this car."

How impatient the tourists were. Christina had a fine eye for tourists. Before she was two years old, she could tell a tourist from an islander. Now she preferred finer divisions. Boston or New York? Michigan or Mississippi? She murmured the question to Benj. "I don't divide them that way," he said.

"How do you divide them?" she asked.

"Dragged and undragged."

Christina pictured a fisherman's net hauled along the ocean floor, gathering scallops and tourists. But she did not understand.

"The ones who want to come on vacation, and the ones who are dragged," explained Benj.

Christina checked them out. Sure enough, the man wanted to be on vacation and the woman did not. The wife would have liked to be back in whatever city she came from, making money, being important. Her husband just wanted to be sailing. Well, it was possible to combine these things on the coast of Maine. Christina almost said to them, "Want to buy an inn?"

"Yep," said Benjamin, actually laughing out loud. "Dragged and undragged. Like school." (Benj was definitely dragged to school.)

"Think Disney World," said Christina.

Benjamin, hands black with oil, coveralls stained, cheek smeared, smiled again. His smile lit her heart like a match. "Think sophomore dance," he said.

And so she told Benj nothing.

For it dawned on Christina that she did not know Benjamin Jaye at all. Who would have guessed that his heart was full of romance and his soul yearned for love? She would have said his heart beat only for fishing; that his soul never noticed anything, except whether it was low tide.

Perhaps nobody knows anybody, thought Christina.

It was a terrifying thought: like *the alone*. That you could know people well, and know them again the following year, and then know them more . . . and yet remain strangers forever.

Chapter 15

Christina sat on the open back of the garage's pickup truck, swinging her feet above the pavement, waiting for Benj. Her feet were bare and dusty in her narrow leather sandals. In the stiff breeze, her thin skirt swirled and unswirled around her legs like pink cotton candy spun onto the white paper cylinder.

"That little girl looks like the figurehead on a sailing ship," said the tourist woman to her husband.

Christina liked that, and kept her chin high, bending her small wrists into the air as if she were a prow, cutting through the Atlantic. Finally there was a moment of quiet at the garage, and Benj perched on the edge of the truck with her. His legs dangled, too, but he did not swing them. Benj was not a swinger, not of legs and not of life. She said, "My mother's coming in on Frankie's boat tomorrow. We'll go shopping for a dress for the dance."

Benj said, "I don't know what I should wear."

"What's everybody else wearing?" asked Christina immediately.

Benj smiled slightly. "Chrissie Romney," he said, "I didn't think you cared what anybody else did."

"For clothes I do. If you go to a dance in the wrong things you won't have any fun, that's all. What did the other boys say they were wearing?"

"They didn't say."

"Ask them."

Benj shrugged. "I don't want to talk about dumb things like that."

"I'll ask, then. Who shall I ask? I don't know any other sophomores."

"But you did ask your parents if it's all right, didn't you?" said Benj anxiously.

"Of course. They think it's neat." Christina smiled at him, and to her surprise he ducked his head, staring at the mess of car parts and broken tools and pieces off things that leaned against the side of the garage. We're flirting, she thought. I bet no other seventh-grade girl is practicing to flirt right now. It's because I'm so mature. It's my island granite. And after all, he's only two years and a few months older.

She was seized by joy. She jumped up into the bed of the pickup, with its corrugated metal bottom, and began dancing. "Dance with me," she commanded him, but of course he didn't. He told her to stop, because she looked weird, you weren't supposed to dance in trucks.

Christina stopped. But not because you weren't

supposed to dance in trucks. Because a short, heavy man with a thick, bristly beard and a big barrel chest was coming toward her. He waved in a friendly way. He said, "Christina? Say, I'm glad to meet you."

Christina was normally very friendly to strangers. She loved strangers. But this was no tourist; she who knew her tourists knew he was a local. But unknown to her. She felt a strange quiver of suspicion. Why had he parked, blocking the garage? Why was he striding over like this? Who —?

"Jim Gardner," he said, a smile peeking out from behind the beard. There was too much hair over the smile to tell if it was a real smile or a fake smile: It was just a flash of teeth. He stuck his hand out. He had a huge hand, much bigger than he should have had for his body. The hand gave Christina the creeps, and when she shook it, the hot dry skin felt like a reptile's. He hung onto her too long, as if he planned on keeping her. "Hi, Benj," he said in a familiar way.

"Jim," nodded Benj.

The man turned immediately away from Benjamin. His face was eye level to her dancing legs. "Christina, honey, I wonder if you and I could have a little talk. About the Shevvingtons. About the storm cottage."

Benj swung around to look Christina in the eyes. She was above him, too, in the truckbed. "What storm cottage?" said Benj, frowning.

It made her so mad! The Shevvingtons weren't coming after her themselves; they were sending Another Authority. Someone nobody questioned, even Benjamin Jaye. He was already prepared to assume Christina was in the wrong. "My storm cottage," she said brightly, "the one I sneak into sometimes. I told Mr. Gardner about it. There's nothing more to say. I won't trespass any more." Christina hated to apologize. The worst sentence in English was "I'm sorry." She forced herself to spit it out, even though she wasn't sorry and would never be sorry. "I'm sorry." She did not sound sorry. She sounded as if she would like to throw dirt in their faces. Her parents would never let her get away with that tone of voice, but Mr. Gardner and Benj didn't know what to do about it.

Christina backed up against the cab of the truck, leaned on the rusting red paint, and folded her arms over her chest.

"Christina, you have to believe I'm your friend in this," said Mr. Gardner. He took hold of the side of the truck. His smile came back and stayed beneath the beard, little bits of white tooth sticking out, as if his teeth weren't attached, merely sprinkled into the beard.

He's here to take me away! she thought. The Shevvingtons said I was insane. A crazy wharf rat. Plays with matches. "You think I need a friend right now?" she said nervously.

He vaulted up into the truck with her and came

closer, slowly, as if she were dangerous.

She held up her hands, flat, like a barricade. "Don't touch me."

"Chrissie," said Benj blankly, "what's going on? Nobody's going to touch you. What are you afraid of? Mr. Gardner's an old friend of your parents'."

The air was humid, and the world hummed.

"All we need is a little talk, Chrissie," said Mr. Gardner in a slow, soothing voice. An attendant's voice. A white-uniformed guard's voice. It oiled its way across the truck, even as his shoes slid across the truck, getting closer and closer. His hands were out, too, ready to grab her wrists. He had his car parked like that to block her escape. Probably his car had no handles on the inside. Probably once she was in that car, she was in it forever.

Like Val.

At seventeen, her own mother agreeing to shut her up forever. Forever. Forever. Christina backed into the far corner. It was not a large truck. There was not much corner. "Leave me alone."

"I have to talk to you, Christina," he said. His voice was silky, like all enclosures, like all traps.

Christina. Child of wind and sand, tides and isles. "No, don't lock me up!" she screamed. "I can't stand it!" She jumped over the edge of the truck, landing lightly on her sandals. Benj circled the truck to grab her. Mr. Gardner jumped off after her.

"I'm your parents' friend!" shouted Mr. Gardner, coming after her. "Don't be afraid of me."

She had never run so fast. She had not known

she was capable of running so fast. She reached the sidewalk and saw the Shevvingtons' van at the other end of the street. They had blocked her off. They were on all sides.

The only sounds on earth were the smacking of Christina's sandals on pavement and the heaving of her lungs. In silence the Shevvingtons lunged for her, in silence Mr. Gardner chased her, in silence Benjamin tried to cut her off.

In the west, the sun chose an angle that was piercing and harsh. Christina's hair was on fire with it, melting. She felt the heat, felt her separate colors, and then — no color at all. They've come for me and taken my color, thought Christina. I'll be white, like the sheets in the storm cottage and the uniforms at the Institute.

Her feet slapped the pavement. Wharf, rat, wharf, rat, wharf, rat, wharf, said the rhythm of her running.

Up Breakneck Hill she ran; through the thick green doors of Schooner Inne; into the cold silent house where Evil lived. She bolted the doors behind her, so nobody could get in: nobody, no matter how many keys they carried and how well they called the fog.

She took the stairs two at a time. She flung open the door to her bedroom: the guest room of fire and isles. It was empty. She flung open the door to guest room number 7: the room of Val, of crimson and violet. It was empty. Empty in the closet, empty under the bed, empty in the blanket chest, empty behind the curtains. "Val!" screamed Christina. "Val, where are you? We have to go!"

She ran up to the third floor to her old room, with its peeling paint and its single dark window. It was empty. The mattress was stripped. The posters were gone. The lamp had no bulb. "Val! Val!" shrieked Christina. "They're coming! We have to go!"

She looked in the boys' room. She looked in the room that Dolly and Anya had once shared. She looked in the cupola.

Empty. Empty. Empty.

Like our souls, thought Christina. Like all the girls before us.

She ran down the stairs, ran down and down and down among the forest of white banisters, while the house whispered, *Chhhhhrrrrissssssstina! Chhhhrrrrissssssstina!* The tide slammed against the foundations and the house rocked. Her heart and soul rocked with it, shaken inside her ribs, thrown against her hope. She ran through the hall, she tore through the kitchen, she ripped open the cellar door. "Val, where are you?"

Brown hair emerged from the floor. Insane brown eyes stared out of pale, scared skin.

"Val?" whispered Christina.

But it was not Val. It had fingers like Val, and bones like Val, and skin like Val, but there was no person inside it. Its eyes flew around like small birds.

"It's me," whispered Christina.

Val slithered out like an animal and crawled up to Christina, making little whimpery noises. Her touch was clammy and damp, like frogs.

"*The alone*," said Val. "The alone got me."

Christina could feel *the alone*. It was under the house, hot and panting. It was up the stairs, crouching and sucking. It was in the air, ghostly and sightless.

FffffFFFFFF*FFFFFF*, said the house.

FffffFFFFFF*FFFFFF*, said the sea.

I am granite of the Isle, she reminded herself. I am Christina Romney and I am afraid of nothing. "I'm here now. You're not alone." I'm lying, she thought. When I first came here, Mr. Shevvington wanted me to make a list of all the things I am afraid of. For his Fear Files. I remember Anya filled it out. But I wouldn't do it. I didn't want him to know what I'm afraid of. But he knew anyway. He knew before I ever got to Schooner Inne.

Val's eyes widened.

"I am not afraid," said Christina. But she was afraid. She was afraid of being alone, and unloved, and unwanted. She was afraid of falling backward, of the Shevvingtons' plans.

Val's eyes grew wider still: holes for Christina to fall in. "I will always be alone," she said. Her voice was dead and lost.

"No," said Christina loudly. She felt that the louder they talked, the more she could scare off *the alone*. "Come back, Val. You're not alone. I'm here." She dragged Val into the kitchen but she could go no further. She felt as if she had dragged Val a hundred miles.

They fell into chairs at the table. The room had the thick, dull heat of closed-up rooms in summer. The only cheerful spot in the entire dreary kitchen was a bowl of oranges in the center of the table. Christina lifted one as if it were a leaden weight. "Here. Let's have an orange." She knew they should be running. The Shevvingtons, Mr. Gardner, and Benj were on their way, closing in. But she could not move. She was sapped of energy. Is this what a maple tree feels like when they tap its juices? she thought. Is the tree tired and its leaves droopy and then rooted forever to one place and can never move on?

Val stared at the round, bright fruits as if they were unknown to her; as if they grew on other planets, in other eons. "No, thank you," she said.

Trees can't move on anyway, thought Christina. I'm definitely going insane. But I have to get Val out of *the alone* first.

Christina felt it: *The alone* came up from the cellar on the sea wind, full of damp and decay. It touched her bare ankles and crept up her bare legs. She tried to brush it off, like insects, and it swarmed around her jackhammering head, like wasps.

I'm half here, she thought. Like being half in the water. My tide is rising. Or is it ebbing? Where is the rest of me? Drowning?

"I'll peel one for you," Christina offered. She dug her fingernails into the orange peel, and the air suddenly smelled of citrus: It was a sharp, tangy, good smell. It killed off *the alone* that was lingering by their shoulders, touching their hair. "Doesn't it smell wonderful?" said Christina, holding it up, wafting it around like incense.

A smile touched Val's lips. "It smells like Christmas." She touched the orange skin lightly with one finger, exploring memories. "And all the things I don't have anymore," she said sadly.

"But they'll come back now, Val," said Christina. "You'll be well and everything good will be yours."

Val laughed. Her laugh was bright and brittle. It had a crack in it, like an old piece of pottery. She looked at Christina as an ancient crone looks at innocence. "No," said Val. "I think when you've lost childhood, you've lost it forever."

Chapter 16

"Chrissie," said Val. Her lovely eyes were half hidden by falling lids almost transparent: The tiny veins were maps of blue.

You can see right through her, thought Christina. "What, Val?" She felt like taking a nap. Or two naps. She had never been so tired in her life. She wondered if her eyes looked like Val's. How did sleep restore eyelids?

Val leaned forward, so limp and exhausted she folded down over the table and the orange peels. "They know I'm here."

"Who knows?"

"The Shevvingtons."

"They do not! If they knew, they'd turn you in."

Val shook her head. "Cats don't always kill the mouse, you know. Sometimes they catch it in their teeth and shake it around, and drop it, and let it run a few feet, and then catch it again."

Christina's big, old house and barn on the island had a dozen cats, and perhaps a thousand mice. She knew cats and mice. She said, "Did the Shevvingtons see you in here, Val?"

"No. But they laughed. The way they did each time they visited me at the Shoreline Institute. Gloating. Knowing."

In the hot, still, musty house Christina began shivering.

"Mrs. Shevvington purrs," said Val.

The house closed in on them like an envelope, sealing them in with the stickiness of Mrs. Shevvington.

"I lay under the bed in my room," said Val, "and the bedcovers draped down so low I was completely hidden. They stood in the doorway and laughed like leopards. Furry and spotted. Then they went downstairs and lit a fire in the fireplace. I got out from under the bed and I ran into your room Christina."

"Which of my rooms?"

"The attic."

"There's no place to hide in there."

"There's a blanket chest. I got in there and shut the lid on myself."

"You could have suffocated!"

"It doesn't close that tight. I checked first. Anyway, the Shevvingtons were showing the Inne to a couple who wanted to buy it and when they got up to the second balcony, they looked in the empty room that Anya and Dolly used to have, and they looked in the room that Michael and Benj share — but they stood outside your door, Chrissie, and they laughed, and they said to the couple, 'This is just like the other rooms, but we haven't cleaned it out yet. There are things in it we're going to throw away.' "

The girls looked at each other.

Things in it the Shevvingtons were going to throw away.

"Us," whispered Val.

As if they had not listened to earlier, softer, warnings, the tide began slamming against the house. It pounded and pounded, like fists on wood. "When I was in the cellar," Val whispered, "the house called your name, Chrissie. I think they'll throw you away first."

Christina's head throbbed. She could no longer tell if the noise was the tide, or the world, or her own brain. I need earplugs, she thought. Unless all the noise is really me, in which case I need an ice-cream scoop, to scoop it all out of my head.

What a weird idea. Perhaps this was the way people went insane. They decided they didn't want the insides of their heads anymore and scooped it out like ice cream and let it all melt.

She was going in and out of her mind like a cartoon character caught in a revolving door. Briefly Christina swung into her mind and her mind rushed on, dumping her somewhere else.

Chhhhhrrrrrrissssssstina, said the house.

Come, Chhhhrrrrrissssssstina.

Crazy, thought Christina. I'm going crazy.

She stood up and walked away, as if crazy were a destination: a seat at the kitchen table, a place you could vacate if you just picked yourself up and walked off.

Suddenly the pounding took on form and meaning.

Christina rolled her eyes and heaved a sigh of disgust. It wasn't the tide. It was Benj and Mr. Shevvington, and probably that Mr. Gardner. Pounding on the doors, yelling her name. "I forgot I bolted the doors on the inside. Val, you have to hide."

"There's no point in hiding. They know I'm here."

"They think you're in the bedrooms. Go back to the cellar. They'll never look there."

"I can't go back in the cellar. *The alone* will get me."

"There's no such thing as the alone. It won't get you. Take an orange with you." Christina bundled Val toward the cellar door.

"But what about that Mr. Gardner?" cried Val. "What if they take you away and I'm still in the cellar? What if I'm trapped down there forever? Chrissie, you can't do this to me. They're taking you, I can feel them taking you. You —"

"Don't be silly," said Christina, opening the cellar door.

Val staggered down the steps, into the seaweed-slick dark. "No," she whimpered, clinging to the splintery wooden rail with her left hand. With her right hand, she clung to Christina. "You come down here with me," she said, and her fingers wrapped and crawled up Christina to find a better grip.

"I can't. I have to save us. I have to let them in."

"That won't save us! That's how they'll get us. Chrissie, let me back up. Into the light. Into the world. I can't stay down here."

Christina peeled Val off and backed up the steps. "Ssssshhh. Don't make any noise."

The cellar made its own noises. Whispering, folding, creaking noises. Noises that slunk forward and crept through their legs. In the dark, among the spiderwebs and the abandoned, moldy boxes of things nobody wanted, Val inched her way to the furnace. It heated water even in the summer. She leaned on it, soaking up its warmth like an infant trying to find a mother substitute.

"You okay?" said Christina. "Can I shut the door now?"

Val laughed insanely.

Christina Romney shut the door.

"She's one of them," Val told the furnace. "She's part of it all. She wants me down here. With *the alone.*"

The shadows closed in.

Val's mind shut down.

The furnace chuckled to itself.

Chapter 17

Christina was on the wharf, waiting for her mother to come in on Frankie's boat. It was a clear day: The sea was sparkling glass. Christina felt as if she could see through the curving horizon of ocean all the way to Burning Fog Isle. She loved the wharf: the stacks of lobster traps, the lapping water, the clacking of ropes and chains against flagpoles and masts.

Benj stood as solid as the wooden pilings on which the wharf was built. "Chrissie, what is all this about? Mr. Gardner wouldn't tell me. The Shevvingtons wouldn't tell me. And now you won't tell me, either."

She could not tell him.

The night had been so long. There had been storms, and every streak of lightning and every boom of thunder seemed to call her name. The ocean had raged, hurling itself against the cliff, the waves reaching for Schooner Inne like drowning sailors trying to get out of the water.

She had not slept. She had lain in her warm bed, in her room of fire and islands, and thought of Val, alone in the darkness of the cellar.

At two in the morning she got up. She slid out of bed, slid out of her room, slid toward the stairs — only to find Mr. Shevvington standing there, still in his suit, as if he never undressed, as if he had come that way: tailored and pinstriped and perfect, like a Ken doll you zipped back into its carrying case when you were done playing with him. "Going somewhere, Christina?" said Mr. Shevvington, and he laughed.

"I'm getting a drink of water," she said with dignity.

"The bathroom is the other way," said Mr. Shevvington, smiling, enjoying himself.

Did the Shevvingtons know about *the alone*, creeping up, swarming around their ankles, trying to pull Christina and Val both underwater, to drown in the ocean of their minds? They must. Perhaps *they* were the alone.

She had gotten a drink of water. And stood in the bathroom and wept, because she could not check on Val. Could not tiptoe down and cuddle her in the dark, in the endless night.

I'm wrong, Christina had thought, lying in bed again. I shut her up for no reason. I can't save Val from anything. I'm only making it worse.

She tried to imagine spending an entire night down there in that cellar.

* * *

"Talk to me, Christina!" said Benjamin on the way to the dock to meet Christina's mother the next morning.

She laughed. It was a queer, shaky laugh, because she had had no sleep to back it up. "That's good coming from you," she teased, "who only started talking last week."

Christina stared at Schooner Inne, where she had learned about Evil. The glass in the high cupola caught the morning sun and blinded her. She decided to test Benj. See if he could understand. "Think of Anya," she said to him, picking her words carefully. "The Shevvingtons chose Anya as a victim. They attacked her in every way. Humiliating her, setting her up, terrifying her, undermining her courage. She began to lose her mind. And then her looks, her character, her grades. That's evil, Benj. It's the Shevvingtons' hobby. And with me, with Val, they —"

"Christina, stop it! Anya was trying too hard. She got too nervous to stay in school and she dropped out for a while. It happens to a lot of kids. They take a little rest and they're fine. There is no evil, Chrissie, no plot."

Christina was exhausted and desperate. But Benjamin Jaye was furious. Every bone, every muscle was tight and full of anger. "The reason you've had problems with Mr. and Mrs. Shevvington is your bad attitude, Chrissie. You made up your mind from the beginning not to get along. The very first day in September when we got off Frankie's boat, you were spoiling for a fight. And when spooky things happened, you blamed them on the Shevvingtons. I thought you were making everything up. When we found out about the Shevvingtons' insane son, and that you were right, we apologized, Chrissie. But you still wanted the Shevvingtons to be evil. Evil, evil, evil! That's all we heard from you." Benj took a breath. His lungs filled, his T-shirt stretched, his big shoulders lifted and stayed there. "Christina, some people are dumb and some are mean and some lose their minds, but nobody is evil."

He wants the world to be like himself, thought Christina. Solid and secure and comprehensible. He wants a perfect match: engines that work, tides that change, people who are reliable. Once I thought the world was like that. I thought all parents were like my parents: perfect and loving. I thought all teachers were like my teacher on the Isle: good and kind. I thought all grown-ups could be trusted.

On land and sea, motors roared. Sea gulls screamed and dipped. Benj let out his breath. Like a summer person he stared at the sea and the eternal waves, hoping the rhythm of the world would ease his tension.

Frankie's boat was visible. Her mother would be standing by the rail, hungry to see Christina. Frankie's nasty dog Rindge was barking; his tourist-scaring yap crossed the waves ahead of the boat.

She remembered her grand idea of telephoning all those principals to get the names of girls who had had nervous breakdowns while the Shevvingtons were there. But the personnel secretary — married to that Mr. Gardner — had alerted the Shevvingtons, who doubtless had alerted their allies back in Louisiana and Oregon and Pennsylvania and New Jersey. Christina would never know.

And even if she did get the names, none of those families of the past would blame the Shevvingtons, either.

That was the whole key — make it be the girl's fault. Make her be weak, or stupid, or nervous, or uncooperative.

Never use words like Evil.

People could not accept the presence of Evil. They had to laugh, or shrug. Walk away, or look elsewhere.

Look at Benj, furious with her for not trusting him, and then when she trusted him and told him what was happening, he got even more furious with her for making it up.

My mother will be exactly the same, thought Christina. She wants to talk about buying a dance dress. About summer coming, and her restaurant on the Isle, and how Daddy is repairing the tennis courts, and how summer people are trespassing on the bird nesting preserve again this year. I am alone in the battle.

Unless . . .

Christina was suddenly shot through with hope.

Little crystals of hope tumbled through her mind like fireworks in a distant sky.

. . . unless I can get hold of the briefcase! The one where they keep the Fear Files: the folders with our photographs on them: the only part left of the girls who are in rooms 1 through 6.

I've tried before . . . but I can try again. You can always try again. That's what I am. Granite of the Isle.

The wharf came to life. People waiting for Frankie's boat emerged from cars and off benches. They brought packages to carry to Burning Fog and waved to their friends coming in. The sea gulls screamed for sandwich crusts and the last of the popcorn.

A horn honked in the parking lot on the hill. It beat a tattoo until everybody on the wharf turned to look. "Chrissie!" came a shout. "Hey, Benj! It's me, Anya!" Anya — who had left Schooner Inne so fragile she hardly breathed on her own? Anya — who without Blake would have folded like paper, shut in the envelope of her mind?

Today's Anya danced over the sunburned rocks, tripping down the long, steep wooden steps. Light as a cloud, Anya came to rest against Christina and Benj. "Chrissie," she said, cuddling. "It's wonderful to see you. I've missed you so, living with Blake's aunt in the city. But it gave me time to calm down."

"And be free of the Shevvingtons," said Christina.

Anya's chuckle hit the waves and the waves

tossed it back. "I'm healed, Chrissie. I can hardly wait to be home." She breathed in a great lungful of restorative sea air.

"What healed you?" said Christina.

"Blake's aunt. She made me finish my senior year after all. Did you know you can go to night school, with adults, and still get your credits? And she said the most calming thing is to read how other people stayed calm, so she made me read ancient books of truth: Plato, Isaiah, Marcus Aurelius."

Christina could not imagine choosing a "calming" book. She liked her books packed with action and excitement, preferably murders and chases.

"I need to go to Burning Fog, Chrissie. I need to smell it and see it and walk it!" She was the island princess again, sea spray misting her hair like diamonds. "Here's Frankie's boat! Here's your mother. Oh, Christina, I'm so glad to be going home." She whirled around, shading her eyes against the bright sun, calling upward, "Blake! Hurry!"

Blake was here! Blake, whom Christina had adored with all her strength and mind and soul. Her heart soared, carried by Anya's high, happy voice.

"See, Christina," said Benj. "Nothing evil touched Anya. She just needed a rest. It's true what they say about island girls. There's something about all that isolation. It touches each of you when you get to the mainland. It's harder for you."

He rambled on about Anya and Dolly and Christina. But Christina had forgotten Benj. Forgotten the Shevvingtons. Forgotten evil.

Like a catalog advertisement — windblown hair, fine physique, excellent clothing — Blake leaned against the shining red triangle of his sports car. The car was nothing but an accessory: his was the beauty. When he descended the steps, he was taking over the world. He radiated exciting plans.

Christina yearned to run up to him, fling herself upon him, tell him that he had just lit up the world. But she held herself still. If she touched Blake, she would turn hot and gasping with love. And what would she do with all that love? Blake was not hers. He was Anya's. And even if he were not, she was — rounding off — only fourteen to his eighteen. He would have no use for her puppy love.

"Christina," said Blake, holding out his arms. In his mouth the world was perfection and romance.

"Hi, Blake," she said, not moving. Without permission, her heart took off anyway, thundering down the road to love. In a one-second daydream, Blake forgot Anya, begged Christina to love him, took her to Paris, asked her to marry him.

"No hug?" teased Blake, hugging her anyway. "I've missed you, kid. What a senior year I've endured — Anya off with my aunt in one town, you here at home, and me at that ridiculous boarding school." He grinned. "But I triumphed. Graduated with honors and went back to claim Anya. Knight in shining armor that I am."

Next to this conqueror, how quaint, how dull Benj was.

I am granite, Christina reminded herself.

But she was not. She was Silly Putty.

Frankie's boat docked. Ropes were tossed, mail carried off. Rindge barked like an attack dog. Christina's mother leaped into the huddle of Anya, Blake, Christina, and Benj. Hugging them separately and then all together, she cried, "What a pleasure! How is everybody?"

They all claimed to be "Very well, thank you." They kissed, hugged, said how their parents were, how the weather had been, when graduation was. How well-named was "small talk." This group had no lack of "large" topics: they could talk of Evil, Jealousy, or Nervous Breakdowns, but no, they said how blue the sky was.

"Guess what we're off to do," said Mrs. Romney to Anya and Blake. "Dress shopping." She giggled. "Benj and Christina are going to the sophomore dance together next Friday."

Anya shrieked joyously, the way girls do when romance appears. Blake grinned and shook hands with Benj, who remained solid and silent.

"A landmark occasion," said Mrs. Romney. "My daughter's first dance. I'm so excited."

Benj did not look the least bit excited, but nobody expected him to.

Her mother rattled off department store and dress shop names. "Mother," protested Christina, "some of those are miles away."

"This is an all-day expedition," said Mrs. Romney. "We have to find the perfect dress and you can't do that in a minute."

Frankie leaned on the whistle of his boat. Tourists scrambled on. Groceries, dry cleaning, engine parts, new screen windows were carried aboard. Anya cried, "Good-bye everybody!" She and Blake, holding hands, dashed gracefully onto the boat.

Christina ached to be that hand. To be tightly clasped by Blake.

How could life be so unfair? The only two escaped victims of the Shevvingtons — Anya and Blake — were vanishing again, without admitting the war was still on. What did they think of Christina still living with the Shevvingtons? Did Anya choose not to remember what had really happened to her? Did she, too, think that it had been her own imagination and weakness? Did she think Evil was disposed of forever?

The wind increased. A deep, cruel cloud covered the horizon. The ocean stopped laughing. It slapped the cliffs with its usual anger. On top of Breakneck Hill, Schooner Inne stood alone: its white-clapboard bulk perched on the very edge, ready to tumble off the cliff.

Christina's mother ran up the steep stairs toward the parked cars. She always had energy to spare. "Come on," she cried to Christina and Benj. "Benj, do you want to come shopping with us?"

Benjamin Jaye touched Christina's hair. She could feel her colors. He was touching the gold. He wound her hair around his wrists, binding himself to her by golden ropes. "I'm not going, but get a pretty dress," he said.

She saw that he loved her as a faithful, uncomprehending dog would love her. That he would adore, accept her flaws, and be hers.

For a terrible moment, he seemed nothing but a burden. She wanted to run or fly. To skim away like the terns fluttering so close to the waves. Motionless, Christina stood on the wharf, while her mother and Benjamin Jaye ascended. The bones on her face seemed truly carved of granite. She had been quarried from Burning Fog's deep abandoned pools.

In the cupola of Schooner Inne, sun glinted off a pair of binoculars.

Chapter 18

The afternoon had a cycle.

Mrs. Romney would say, "Darling, that dress looks perfect. I love the neckline."

Christina would say, "Mother, you know what?"

"What, dear? Do you think we want larger flower patterns, like this, like splashy watercolors? Or tiny flower patterns, like this one, sort of Early American?"

How, in the petite section of the dress shop, surrounded by linen and cotton, rayon and blends, was Christina to talk about Evil? She would say, "I'm not sure I want any flowers on the dress at all, Mother. I'm not that much of a flower person." I'm granite, she thought. But none of the dresses looked right for granite.

"Mother," she tried again, "the Shevvingtons are being really awful."

"I know you don't get along, dear, but there are only a few days till school is out. In fact, let's count up so you can start ticking the hours off. Next year they'll be gone, and we'll have better arrangements. I feel terrible that you've had such a difficult year, but you have to remember poor Mr. and Mrs. Shevvington have had a grim year also. Imagine struggling for twenty-five years to bring up your son, and you think at last he's managing on his own — even if it is just a furnished room a few blocks away above a coffee shop — still, you have hope — and what do you learn? He's completely crazy and trying to torment the very young girls you have under your own protection." Mrs. Romney shook her head. "I feel so sorry for them, Chrissie. It breaks my heart. It's every parent's nightmare, that her own child will turn out wrong."

"But Mother, they really are terrible people. I just can't get through to you. The Shevvingtons..." but her voice dwindled away. Even to Christina, it no longer seemed possible. This was Maine. The United States. America. Pine woods and crashing seas. Blue skies and loving mother.

Instead of Evil, they talked of Benj, and whether he was romantic and what this dance would lead to. She saw that her mother misunderstood. Her mother thought this was For Eternity. . . . The Future. . . . True Love. All it was was a dance, and Benj was asking the girl he knew best.

"Nonsense," said her mother. "I've seen plenty of boys in love and that one's in love. Now tell me everything. Absolutely everything."

But of course her mother did not mean that at all. Her mother did not want to hear that the Shevvingtons were stuffing her pockets with match books to prove she was a wharf rat. Her mother wanted to hear that Benj had swept her away, kissed her by candlelight.

"Let's go for ice cream," said Christina. "Butterscotch sauce on buttercrunch ice cream, just what you like."

"I love when you remember details," said her mother happily. "We're so close, you and I."

Through the countryside they drove. The road passed between two wide meadows. "Look!" cried her mother, slowing. Three bright blue dots fluttering across the grass. Indigo blue: the color of postcards from the Mediterranean. "Bluebirds," whispered her mother reverently. "I haven't seen a bluebird in years. Chrissie, that's when you know God's in his heaven and all's right with the world. When you see bluebirds again."

Christina could think of several arguments against this. All's *not* right with the world, she thought. I don't know how things will ever be right in Val's world again. I don't even know what world Val will have.

"Mommy, have you heard anything about Val?" she asked.

"Everybody's still searching for her, I guess. She was in Anya's class, I think. A jinxed group if there ever was one. Just one nervous breakdown after another."

"Did you ever think it was — well — planned?"

said Christina. "That somebody made all those things happen on purpose?"

"Don't be silly," said her mother, and quickly drove to another dress shop. Like Benj, her mother wanted only a pretty world, where bluebirds danced in green grass.

The dress they finally found was stark, blinding white. Its shoulders were narrow, laced with tiny ribbons. It had no waist, but fell straight, doubling up at the thighs in pleats and runs of ribbon. "What a twenties' flapper would wear to communion," giggled her mother. "Wild but pure."

If I wore this dress to the storm cottage, thought Christina, you could not tell me apart from the walls and the floors.

"Let's go to the hairdresser," said her mother.

Christina had never had her hair professionally done. It was so tangly, long and thick, there had never seemed any point. Her mother simply trimmed it straight across when it needed it. Their timing was perfect. The mall stylist had an opening just as they walked in.

He washed her hair. The sweet perfume of the conditioner wafted around Christina like mist. He divided her hair into its separate colors, setting them in long, twisting curls. "Banana curls, your grandmother would call those," said her mother. The stylist lifted the gold into a separate section, catching it with a ribbon and letting it fall: a bouquet of golden locks on a silver sea.

When she looked in a mirror she could not see herself. An island nymph sparkled back: a sprite, formed not of earth or flesh, but a swimmer in the sea. Around her, shoppers paused and stared. Other hairdressers, other customers, stood still. She felt all of their eyes, as if they had no bodies: only eyes. Eyes. Eyes.

I am separate, thought Christina, like my hair. I am not one with the world. When I need help, no one will come. No one will recognize me.

Her mother had to rush to catch Frankie's last run back to the Isle. Dropping Christina off in front of Schooner Inne, she barely even stopped the car. "Say hello to the Shevvingtons for me," she cried. Christina's heart answered, *Say hello to Blake for me!* But aloud she called after her mother, "Say hello to Daddy." Her mother drove down Breakneck Hill, honking madly to signal Frankie not to leave without her. Frankie waved his baseball cap in acknowledgment.

Time stopped.

They turned into a photograph: an old, sepia-colored photo in which they would stand forever: Frankie waving a baseball cap, her mother opening a car door. She wanted to scream, *Wait for me!* Wanted to run down there, leap into Eternity with them, and be saved.

But Frankie lowered his cap. Her mother dashed down the wharf steps.

Christina slipped inside the Inne and ran up the

stairs, dress box in hand, and on up to the cupola for the best view of the boat returning to Burning Fog. As she rose up the stairs in the old sea captain's house, a sick feeling rose with her, engulfing her like rising tide. Her mother would never return for her. Or, if her mother returned, Christina would not know. They were parting — minds and souls — forever.

The stairs went on and on. Flight after flight after flight. She seemed to climb into the sky. Into other worlds. Outside the ocean whispered, FfffFFFFFFFFFF. It whispered inside her head, tangling in her hair like seaweed.

FfffFFFFFFFFFF, said the house.

FffffFFFFFFFFFF, said the sea.

Christina clung to the curly banisters. She was wading in seawater. Tides yanked her under. Her head spun. Her hair blinded her. The house smelled of low tides and rotting fish.

Chhhhhrrrissssssstinahh, whispered the sea.

Chhhhhrrrissssssstinahh, whispered the house.

She dropped the dress box. She fell to her knees. The sea sucked her down like mud. Dark, thick, oily mud. "Hello, Christina," whispered the house, in a voice as furry as a leopard's. It wrapped its arms around her. Christina and the sea washed into the empty guest room.

How tired she was from all that shopping. How she yearned to lie down. Perhaps she, like Val, would lie down forever. She would rest and not talk. Sleep and not think.

The bed was soft and welcoming.

Chhhhhrrrisssssssstinahh, whispered the world.

She felt herself turning white and formless, like the furniture in the storm cottage, shapeless beneath the sheets. She was no longer separate from the world, but one with it. Sinking into it by losing her grip on it. She thought of her hair, of its separate colors, but she could no longer feel them. She thought of Blake, but could no longer remember what he looked like. Thought of Benj, but he did not matter.

"Here I am," she said to the house and the sea.

When her eyes closed, she knew she would never open them. She lacked the desire. She would stay deep inside herself, where all was known, all was safe.

She thought of Christina Romney, but even Christina Romney did not seem to matter. She was a person, but the person was not Chrissie Romney, nearly fourteen, end of seventh grade, Maine, USA, the World. She was someone else, floating through time and weather.

Someone ancient and new.

Someone at war and at peace.

"Here I am," she said to the house and the sea.

She lay quietly in the inside of her mind. It was not muddy dark at all, but soft and rocking, like a hammock in the shade.

Outside in the hall, the brass numbers on each guest room door winked and went out like candles.

There was a creaking and a sighing, like the footsteps of ghosts.

I am a shell, thought Christina.

She did not mind. It was safe and easy, being a shell. No insides to worry about.

"I'll stay," she said to the house and sea.

Chapter 19

"Today's the seventh-grade picnic," said Michael at breakfast.

Mrs. Shevvington had made runny poached eggs. Michael and Benj liked them that way, but Christina did not. But today it didn't matter. Christina had not gotten up. Benj had gone into her bedroom and told her it was time for school. Michael had gone in to say it was time for breakfast. But Christina just lay there.

Mr. Shevvington said, "What a shame. Since Christina won't be in school, she cannot attend the picnic in the evening. For of course the school rule is that you cannot participate in after-school activities if you choose to skip school by day."

"Won't be in school?" said Benj. "Of course she'll be in school. I'll go drag her out of bed."

"She needs her rest," said Mrs. Shevvington. She smiled at her egg and stabbed the little yellow mound with her fork. Yellow yolk spurted over the egg white and ran into the toast. Mrs. Shevvington cut a little square of bread and sopped up the egg yolk with it. It was the kind of thing that made Christina gag. "After the way Christina has been acting," said Mrs. Shevvington, "running away from Mr. Gardner, locking us out of our own house, playing with candles and matches — well! — you know, at the very least, the girl is overtired."

"Overtired?" repeated Mr. Shevvington. His eyebrows reached into his forehead and hid beneath his long, silvery hair. "It's certainly more than that, my dear. We do not wish to frighten her parents unnecessarily. But there is a strong similarity between the mental collapse Anya suffered and what is happening to Christina. Of course, Christina's is so much more serious. So much more dangerous. I have spoken to school and fire department officials and everyone agrees that there is a strong possibility that Christina is the one who — "

"There is not!" shouted Benjamin. He threw his plate across the room. He stared at the plate, broken in two large and several tiny pieces. At the egg on the wall and the flight pattern of yellow across the floor. He had never before in his life thrown anything in a rage.

Mrs. Shevvington smiled at him. "You knew what Mr. Shevvington was going to say, though, didn't you, Benjamin? You cannot deny the thought has passed through your own mind. That Christina's affection for fire borders on the insane. Look at you, making excuses for her, hiding matches from her, snuffing out candles for her."

"She says *you* hid the matches," Benj said.

In the voice of a sad angel, Mrs. Shevvington said, "Benj, Benj. And you believe her? Hers is a true case of paranoia, of believing the world is after her. Here it is the end of the school year. Christina has been studying so hard for exams. It's a struggle for all you island children to keep up with the mainlanders. And poor Christina is desperate to catch up to girls like Gretchen and Vicki. Jealousy eats away at the soul, you know, Benjamin. Poor Christina has the acid of jealousy rusting her heart."

"She's dying to go to the picnic," he said. "And besides, we have a Band Committee meeting today right after school. She has to come."

The Shevvingtons regarded him silently. The silence built, and became a space in the room, something Benjamin could hardly see through, or think past. His mind fumbled to understand what was going on. There were questions to ask; questions to ask Christina; but he did not know what they were, and the thick, hanging silence of the room stilled his tongue.

"And I think it's time you accepted your part of the blame, Benjamin," said Mrs. Shevvington.

"My part of the blame?" repeated Benj. The woman put her arm on his. It felt as sticky as suction cups. He had the creepiest sense that she was attaching herself.

"You demanded that the poor child try to keep up with seniors like Megan and Astrid, Benjamin! Was that not an act of cruelty on your part?"

Benjamin was taken aback.

"And then — you asked her to your sophomore dance. You — age sixteen! Inviting a child, forcing her to try to be sophisticated and adult almost overnight."

"She said yes," Benj defended himself.

"Of course she said yes! You're older and exciting and intriguing. How could she turn you down? Nevertheless, look what all this combined pressure forced her into, Benjamin!"

He was flattered, in a sickening way, to be called exciting and intriguing.

"Coaxing her to do this, pushing her to do that!" Mrs. Shevvington shook her head, appalled. "When you knew — better than any of us — how fragile Christina is! Then purposely adding pressure — *pressure! Pressure!* Demands — *demands! Demands!* On a thirteen-year-old, Benjamin!"

Benjamin mumbled something, ashamed. Michael shifted his weight around on his chair, looking at nobody, as if afraid of infection through eye contact.

"I am shocked, aren't you, that her parents didn't mind?" said Mr. Shevvington. His voice was as cold as glaciers. "Had it been up to us, Benjamin, you may be sure we would have put a stop to your behavior."

"What do you have to say for yourself, Benjamin?" said Mrs. Shevvington softly, forgivingly.

"I guess I used bad judgment," he said helplessly.

"At least you admit it. Although it's too late to

help Christina now. The only decent thing for you to do, Benjamin, is to let the poor child rest. Leave her alone. Completely alone."

Benjamin swirled the orange juice in his glass without drinking it. Michael tore his toast up into little shreds, as if planning to feed ducks.

Mrs. Shevvington said to her husband. "It's a continual surprise to me that a little girl's own parents have so little concern for her emotional well-being."

"At least she'll sleep," said Mr. Shevvington. "Probably the only rest she'll have before the truth comes out."

"What truth?" said Michael nervously.

The house creaked.

Steps above them bent and shuffled.

"She's getting up!" cried Benj, and he ran out of the kitchen, to the bottom of the stairs, looking up. Nobody was there. He ran on up the stairs, taking them two at a time, barreling open the half-closed door to Christina's room. But she was still motionless under the white sheet, as if laid out in a funeral home.

Benj said, "Chrissie, you've got to get up. Pull yourself together!" He wet his lips. He started to say, *I'm here, I love you, I'll stick by you*. But Mrs. Shevvington came into the room, and he could not say words like that in front of witnesses. He was not sure he could say words like that at all.

He meant to give her a hand; haul her bodily out of the bed, prop her on her feet. But how eerily still she lay. He could not bring himself to grab her fingers and pull. She hardly seemed like Christina — more like a shell from which Christina had fled. He caught himself hunching down, peering nervously around, as if Christina's ghost were being prepared in the air above his head, were floating by.

Mrs. Shevvington crossed the room, passed the bed, and reached behind the draperies to find the cord. She pulled them shut slowly, as if closing a lid. The room was dark now, all natural light extinguished. Christina, who gave off light herself, from her golden hair and her shining personality, was dark also. The colors of her hair were meaningless.

Mr. Shevvington emerged silently from behind Benj, as if he had not used his feet to climb, but glided up. "Now, Benjamin. Cheer up. You have a big band meeting today after school for the Disney trip. You've received permission, remember. And you have to put together the fund-raisers."

"Christina was going to work on that," said Benj numbly.

"What a shame," said Mr. Shevvington sadly. "But the senior girls can easily handle it without her."

From the hallway below, Michael yelled, "Come on, Benj, we'll be late."

Benjamin backed onto the balcony. The Shevvingtons came out with him. "Don't worry about her," said Mrs. Shevvington gently. "We all make mistakes. It was a serious one you made with Christina, but as for the fires, you know Benjamin, that was her own choice. So don't feel too bad. And I'll come home at lunch to check on her."

They shut the door to Christina's room.

Down the curling stairs they went, down, and down, and down. Benjamin had the queerest sensation that he was sinking into the bowels of the earth, that he was going down flight after flight after flight. The house whispered and folded around him, its darkness coming up the cracks, crawling upward, seeking light.

He remembered once he had gotten silly on his lobster boat, playing games with Michael, knocking them both overboard. They were both fine swimmers, but it was a long, long way to shore. The boat lazily motored on; the boys swam after it. Swam, and swam, and swam, while the boat teasingly circled out of reach. The boys grew colder, their strokes shorter, their lungs tired. The sea seemed to laugh, tossing waves over their eyes, throwing seaweed over their faces, yanking their feet down.

He felt as if the house were in control of him, as the sea had been once. That he was as close to drowning now as he had been that terrible day.

With relief he reached ground level, followed Michael to the door, stared out into a real world, with real cars and noise and people.

Behind him Mr. and Mrs. Shevvington paused to enfold each other. It was not a hug. It was a wrapping of one around the other. They spread each other's evil and lived on it.

The day was hot. In the parlors and sitting rooms of the old mansion, curtains blew softly in the sea breeze. "The next owners will probably replace all these old drapes," remarked Mrs. Shevvington. "What a shame. They're so historic." She picked up a sheaf of seventh-grade papers, corrected, ready to return, and walked out the door. Mr. Shevvington cradled in his arms the briefcase Christina had so wanted to steal. His fingers lingered on the smooth, supple leather as if stroking a loved one.

The great green doors were shut fast.

Christina was alone.

A shaft of gaudy yellow sunshine, golden as Christina's hair had once been, shot from the cupola glass above to the guest room doors below. Like diamonds, the brass number 8 glittered. Tiny rainbows — shattered pieces of Christina — danced on the balcony walls. Then the sun passed on, the rainbows vanished, and all was quiet.

Christina was gone.

Chapter 20

Seventh-graders splashed down the hallways like waterfalls tumbling. They bubbled and pushed and chattered and laughed. It was an end-of-the-year sound. A we're-almost-free sound. A summer-soon sound.

It ceased at the door to Mrs. Shevvington's English room.

But Mrs. Shevvington amazed them. She was laughing and light herself. She actually joked. She even said they would do no work today, but would be reading a play aloud. She had chosen a play in which there were enough parts to go around for the entire class.

There was one empty seat.

Jonah said, "Where's Christina?"

Mrs. Shevvington said, "She's been feeling a little run-down lately. She decided to sleep in instead of coming to school today."

The class was shocked. They exchanged glances. The picnic wouldn't be any fun without Christina.

Even for Vicki and Gretch it wouldn't be; the whole seventh grade revolved around Christina.

Jonah said slowly, "I can't believe Christina wouldn't be in school today. She knows as well as any of us that if she doesn't attend classes she can't come to the picnic."

"I'm not sure the picnic is quite as important to Christina as it is to you children," said Mrs. Shevvington kindly. "You must remember how homesick these island children become, how desperate she is to get back to Burning Fog."

"But she planned the picnic," said Katy. "She planned the games and she got the grocery store to donate chocolate bars, graham crackers, and marshmallows for the S'mores."

"She got the Sailing Shop to donate prizes," said Gretch suddenly.

"And the Gift Shoppe," said another girl.

Mrs. Shevvington said, "Open your play scripts please. Vicki, I am casting you as Lady Roxbury. In this play, you are a very elegant and beautiful Englishwoman. Can you imitate an English accent, Vicki?"

Jonah said, "I'm going to check on Christina."

Mrs. Shevvington stared at him. Her black pebble eyes glittered. Her thick fingers dripped blood red polish. She took one step toward Jonah. The class flinched. She took another step.

Jonah said, "I want to be sure nothing has happened to Christina."

" 'Happened to Christina'?" repeated Mrs. Shevvington. "What on earth do you mean by that, Jonah?"

Jonah stood up. How scrawny he looked. Mrs. Shevvington was solid as a small refrigerator, or a stacked washer/dryer. Jonah was all dangling bones and uncoordinated joints. "The way things happened to Anya, Mrs. Shevvington."

Her eyebrows flattened.

"The way things happened to Dolly," said Jonah. He was losing his voice; her eyes were freezing him over like ice on a pond. "The way things happened to Val," he whispered.

Mrs. Shevvington's eyes were gone. Her lids closed over them like cracked tan paper shades.

The class shivered.

She opened her eyes and snagged Jonah on them.

"Sit down, Jonah," breathed Katy. "Or things will happen to you."

Mrs. Shevvington's little yellow corn teeth showed. "Katy, Katy. Such imagination. What a shame you are not able to demonstrate it in your homework. Jonah is welcome to check on Christina, of course. But that would be skipping school. He would not be able to attend the picnic either."

"Then Christina and I will have a separate picnic," said Jonah.

Mrs. Shevvington laughed. "Christina is in love with Benjamin, who is sixteen. And also in love with Blake, who is eighteen. Do you think she will even notice a little boy like you attempting to 'save' her?"

Her laugh rattled around like pebbles thrown into a tin bucket.

Jonah flushed.

Vicki and Gretch giggled. "At least you have a brain, Jonah," said Vicki. "Benjamin doesn't. You could offer Chrissie your brain."

"She likes muscles," said Gretch, "and Jonah doesn't have any of those."

"Run along, Jonah," said Mrs. Shevvington. "You may certainly come back to school and report what you find. We'll all be so interested."

Behind Jonah, between the snickering girls, Robbie stood up. He was even scrawnier than Jonah and much shorter, not having started his growth at all. He looked about nine. He said, "I'm going with you Jonah."

Vicki and Gretch burst into gales of laughter. "What a team!" snickered Gretch. "Gosh, I hope when I'm in trouble, I get rescued by men like these."

Mrs. Shevvington's birdseed teeth vanished, as if she had swallowed them herself. "Let's not tease, girls. It's painful to be an adolescent boy with nothing to offer. Let's not make it worse."

The door to the English room creaked.

Slowly, as if the hinges had grown together, it began opening.

The door cried out, rustily, as if it hurt.

The children froze, staring.

Mrs. Shevvington seemed to swell and bloat.

Slowly the door ate its way into the classroom. Gently it tapped the far wall. It shivered against the plaster.

A ray of sun walked across the classroom from the window to the door, like a golden ghost.

Standing in the shaft of light was a tangle of silver and gold: the tri-colored hair of Christina Romney.

She looked at the class. She looked at Robbie and at Jonah, standing up for her. She looked at Vicki and Gretch, laughing at them all. She looked at Mrs. Shevvington. Without a sound . . . slowly, as if wound up . . . she entered the room. She raised her small chin and pointed her small nose forward. "I came to get you, Mrs. Shevvington," said Christina Romney. In her hand she held a sheaf of grayish-white papers: Xeroxed copies. She tapped them against her open palm.

Gretch and Vicki tittered.

Jonah and Robbie sank back into their seats.

Mrs. Shevvington looked like a dead fish on the sand, filled with her own poisons. "You're late, Christina," she whispered, hissing.

"But not too late," said Christina Romney.

"Go to the office. Mr. Shevvington will take care of you."

Christina's soft eyebrows rose like Roman arches, carved on stone. Her chin lifted higher, like a goddess of the sea. "No."

The class gasped. Nobody said "No" to Mrs. Shevvington.

"I beg your pardon?" said Mrs. Shevvington.

"No," repeated Christina softly. "I have to look at you first. You destroyed so many of us, and you nearly destroyed me. I need to look at you first and know that you are just an ordinary person."

"Go to the office!" said Mrs. Shevvington. Her voice was thick.

The sun glittered on Christina's hair. It divided into separate, living creatures, like silver snakes, or sable ribbons. "Val heard you laughing in the night," said Christina. "You shouldn't have laughed. It woke her up."

Mrs. Shevvington's slick tongue wet her mean little lips. She laughed again, but this time it was queer and bubbly, like froth rising on a milk shake.

"Val remembered, long long ago, when you first befriended her, when you first started eating away at her like acid, that you kept a file on her. She remembered that you had copies. And she found them. In the cellar. Damp and moldy, Mrs. Shevvington, but they have the truth in them. The truth about Emily and Wendy, Margaret and Jessica. And all your other victims. Their photographs, your notes, what happened to them, how you did it."

"Who are Jessica and Emily and all?" said Gretch.

"Shells," said Christina.

"My sister?" cried Robbie. "Christina, is Val all right?"

"No," said Christina, "but she's better. She came for me. She woke me. She dressed me. She was the only one who knew how, because she had been there. She had swung in the same hammock."

"Hammock?" said Vicki and Gretch together. "Christina, do you have any idea how weird you sound?"

"Come, Christina," said Mrs. Shevvington. "You and I will go down to the office. You need sedation. Mr. Shevvington and I will help you."

"I will go to the office with you," said Christina. "But I am using the phone there. To end all the terrible things you have been doing."

"Excuse me?" said Mrs. Shevvington, pasting a smile on her oatmeal face.

"No," said Christina, slowly shaking her head back and forth. The silver locks slid over the gold and tangled with the brown. "I will not excuse you. The law will not excuse you. Parents will not excuse you."

"She *has* flipped out," whispered Vicki. "You were right, Mrs. Shevvington. Christina is gone-zo." Vicki and Gretch snickered.

The froth on Mrs. Shevvington's lips spilled over.

"Being crazy is rather pleasant," said Christina, "once they soften it with drugs or sleep. Like a hammock. You just swing quietly in the shade of your mind."

Mrs. Shevvington seemed to rock back and forth, like a swing.

"And Val," said Robbie, "is Val still in the shade?"

"No," said Christina. "She is back."

Mrs. Shevvington licked the froth from her mouth. "Come, my child of the Isle," she said. "We

600

will go read your silly little papers together. And if you call the police, that is fine with me. It's about time they put a stop to your fire-setting and your match-collecting."

They entered the hallway of the middle school together.

Jonah and Robbie tried to follow.

"I think not," said Mrs. Shevvington, closing the door of the seventh-grade English room behind her. She and Christina walked down the long, wide corridors, where no teacher stood, no student passed, no janitor cleaned. Alone, they walked.

"You made a fatal error, Christina," said Mrs. Shevvington. Her smile widened, as if the smile planned to slit her face, as if it were a parasite turning on its own body. "You wanted to gloat. I sympathize. I enjoy gloating." The smile ate like acid into the oatmeal complexion, until Mrs. Shevvington's face vanished and nothing was there but a yellow slit of triumph. *Val is not safe,* said Mrs. Shevvington. Laughing, she whispered, "And neither, my fair island girl, are you."

Chapter 21

They were too far from the seventh-grade class for her to scream for Robbie or Jonah. Too far from the high school halls to scream for Michael or Benjamin Jaye. They were in the front lobby, by the school offices, where only parents and teachers went willingly.

Mrs. Shevvington stumped on. It was like the evening they went for ice cream, and she struggled in Michael's grip like a kitten dragged to the vet.

Jonah knew this would happen, thought Christina. He told me I was getting cocky. But I had to show off. I had to sashay in there, so the seventh grade would know. I was playing games. But this isn't a game. Don't *I* know that best? But even so, I kept playing games, thinking I would win.

The grown-ups always win.

In lock-step Mrs. Shevvington and Christina entered the outer office. Filing cabinet drawers were half open while secretaries pretended to look things up. A gym coach without a class lounged on the counter and a big kid getting suspended slouched against the wall.

The staff glanced up. "Oh! Mrs. Shevvington!" they said, ignoring Christina. "Mr. Shevvington just left! Poor little Val showed up after all this time!"

Christina cried out.

"Mr. Shevvington was so sweet to her," put in the file clerk, not answering her ringing phone. "Val was so strange. You would not have believed the accusations she made. The poor child. A clinical case of paranoia if I ever saw one. Just like on soap operas. And she comes from such a nice family, too."

"She was supposed to stay at the Inne," mumbled Christina. "Where she'd be safe."

The gym coach slapped the counter with his huge flat hand. "You're the one who was hiding Val?" he demanded. "You're one of those island girls, aren't you? The one who plays with matches and tried to set a storm cottage on fire. I heard about you. Kids like you shouldn't be allowed in the school system with regular kids."

Christina ripped loose from Mrs. Shevvington and tried to bolt. The gym coach caught Christina's elbows and pinned her to the wall. "This has been some year!" he said to Mrs. Shevvington. "I bet you guys are sorry you ever transferred to Maine. We've handed you more crazies than the rest of the country has in a generation!"

Mrs. Shevvington smiled. There was a puffiness to her now: a contentment. "So true," said Mrs.

Shevvington. "You might call the ambulance for Christina. She must be sedated."

Christina remembered the quiet of the guest room, the painted isles, and the foggy mind. I'll be back there in a minute, she thought. Or in the Institute. And I won't know, or care. I'll be a shell again. What made Val come here? What made either of us come here? Did the Shevvingtons pull us in with their evil or did something in us want to be defeated?

Christina felt herself fading like a sheet in the storm cottage, drifting into mists of mindlessness. Perhaps you had to participate in your own ending. You had to allow it to happen.

"Mr. Shevvington was going to call Val's parents from Schooner Inne," said the file clerk, "for privacy. He always puts the child first, you know. No matter how undeserving. He drove Val back there."

"Did my husband have his briefcase?" asked Mrs. Shevvington.

"Why, yes," said the typist, "I believe he went back into the office to get it. He had Val in one hand and the briefcase in the other."

The coach released Christina's arms. Defeat was so complete that she went limp and sagged to the floor. He knelt beside her. "I'd better get her a glass of water."

The typist said, "I'll call the nurse."

"No need," said Mrs. Shevvington, retrieving the pile of papers that had slipped out of Christina's hands.

"She might be ill," protested the coach. "Sometimes when my students act weird out on the field, it turns out to be heatstroke or something."

"The ambulance is coming. Some things are better left to trained paramedics."

Christina was not ill. She was faking. She leaped to her feet, shoving Mrs. Shevvington against the door. She raced out of the office, skidding on waxy floors toward the front doors. "Stop her!" cried Mrs. Shevvington. "She's dangerous."

Gym coach, secretary, and teacher lurched after Christina.

The big kid getting suspended yawned, stretched, and stuck his feet out. "Oh, sorry," he said pleasantly, when they tripped over him and knocked into each other, bottling up their own exit.

Through the lobby, out the doors, down the wide granite steps, Christina tried to soak granite through her shoes; she would need it all. She heard them coming after her, but the women were wearing narrow skirts and high heels; the coach made kids exercise but rarely exercised himself; Christina was too fleet of foot for them.

Across the wide green expanse of campus she ran. The coach tried to catch her, but Mrs. Shevvington didn't bother. She headed for her car. Christina swerved through the trees, cutting through the opening in the fence. Mrs. Shevvington started her engine. Christina burst out onto the sidewalk, ran down School Street, heading for town. Mrs. Shevvington, driving in the most ordinary way, without unseemly haste, could go forty miles an hour. The woman turned onto the School Street and accelerated.

Christina, sobbing for breath, ran up a side street, crossed two backyards, ducked down a driveway, and came out behind the laundromat. Through the laundromat, between the clattering washers and the steamy dryers, she went. Anya had worked here. Mindlessly folding other people's underwear. Don't let them catch me! prayed Christina.

She crossed Seaside Avenue, and jumped up onto the sidewalk just as Mrs. Shevvington drove across Seaside. She's not trying to catch me, thought Christina. She's going straight to Schooner Inne.

Christina came out at the bottom of Breakneck Hill. Mrs. Shevvington came out at the top and parked in front of Schooner Inne. She unlocked the huge green door, let herself in, and shut it behind her.

I have to get Val, thought Christina. I did this. This is my fault. How did it happen?

Christina stepped over the cliff. She had come up these rocks, but never gone down. Tide was out. The mudflats were slimy and pockmarked. She climbed carefully down the treacherous crags and outcroppings. She had to drop down into the mud. It sucked her in almost to the knees. She tugged her right foot free, and it came out black with slime. Slogging across the flats, mud sucking at her feet, Christina stayed next to the cliffs. No windows in

Schooner Inne could see a person at the bottom of the cliff. In some places the mud had dried and she walked on top. In some places there was water a foot deep, or even two feet, and she waded, or fell in.

She made her way around a jutting stone with sharp edges, and there, hidden in a cleft, was the entrance to the cellar passage the old sea captain had used for smuggling. They would not be expecting her to arrive this way. They would look for her by road, by door, but not by cellar. Tearing her hands, ripping her clothes, she finally got up to the opening. The opening she and Dolly had found so tantalizing—had fallen out of, and nearly been swallowed by the tide while the Shevvingtons' insane son laughed joyfully above.

Christina tiptoed up the splintery wooden cellar steps. How many horrible sounds had she heard in this black hole? How many times had she been cornered here? But today it was her secret entry. Creeping up from the cellar — as the Shevvingtons' son had done in his time — she would slip unnoticed into the house, as Mr. and Mrs. Shevvington watched for her from the doors and windows, and silently she and Val would go back to the sea. Just as she had done with Dolly! They would sail back to the Isle and be safe. Somehow Christina would make all the parents believe her.

Her heart was thudding painfully. Her feet slid muddily inside her own shoes. Pressing her ear against the door that opened into the kitchen, she listened for the silence that would mean she could ease herself inside the house.

"Christina's here," said Mr. Shevvington, laughing. "Open the door, Valerie dear, and let her in."

The kitchen door opened and Christina fell onto the linoleum. Val, whimpering, crowded up against her.

Mr. Shevvington laughed and laughed. The laughter whipped him back and forth, like a flag in the wind. "Come," he said gaily. "Follow me."

The girls followed as if on leashes.

"What's happening?" said Christina. She was crying. All her pain, all her dangerous effort — and for what?

"We thought you'd enjoy watching your so-called proof burn up," said Mrs. Shevvington. "We have files on you, Christina, dear, and on Val of course. On Anya and Dolly. But there are other names. Emily. Margaret. Jessica. Wendy. And oh, so many more! And it will continue, of course. We will never stop."

The wind from the sea came up the cellar passage and tossed the kitchen door back and forth, in a wet, ghostly, low-tide way.

"But we have learned a little something from you, Christina," said Mr. Shevvington. "I just want you to know that first. You taught us not to write anything down and not to save it. So when you're in your little cot, swallowing your little pills, watching your little television, you remember how generous you were to us. Helping us out."

"And giving us," said Mrs. Shevvington, beaming, "such an exciting year. Christina, you were a worthy opponent. I have truly enjoyed bringing you down."

Christina halted at the door to the parlor. "Come on, Val," she said, trying not to let her voice shake, "let's just go out the front door."

"You cannot get out the front door, my dear," said Mrs. Shevvington. "Or any other door. There are bolts, as you well know. There is no exit from this house, Christina, darling. And the windows, too, are locked. The only way out is through the cellar. And what good would that do you? Because the tide is rising."

The tide whiffled and puffed between the cliffs. The sound of the sea blowing out its birthday candles. Candle Cove.

"You and Dolly managed it once, my dear. Late last winter. And you survived. But I doubt if you would be so lucky again." Mrs. Shevvington laughed. "Would you like to light the fire, Christina, dear? Since you so enjoy playing with matches? Would you like to see yourself go up in smoke?"

Val shivered up against Christina like a draft. "It's my fault," she said, weeping on Christina. "I thought I was doing the right thing. I wanted the whole town to see how terrible they are, so I thought I would start with the school and the teachers and tell them out loud what the Shevvingtons have been doing. But they thought I was crazy."

We *were* crazy, thought Christina, to believe for

a single moment that we could beat Authority. People are dogs on leashes. They follow the biggest and the strongest, not the small and weak. "It's all right," said Christina, patting Val. To the Shevvingtons she said, "What are you going to do with us after you burn all those papers?"

Mr. Shevvington laughed. "Christina, you know better," he chided gently. "We won't do anything to you. Your own families, your own neighbors, perhaps your own boyfriend, will do things to you. Get you psychiatrists, medications, institutional care. This is America, the end of the twentieth century. We don't take care of our mentally deranged at home. We hospitalize them. Otherwise they would upset us." His voice was like old velvet: soft, but cracked.

The girls were pushed into the parlor.

Mr. Shevvington picked one file out of his bulging briefcase. From his jacket pocket he took a slim, gold-trimmed fountain pen. In neat black ink he added a brief notation. Then he handed the file to Christina.

It was her own. Dated the first day of school, the past September. On that day they had chosen her, had opened her file. And the new writing was today's date.

This day in May, before she was fourteen, before she went to the dance, before she had her first date, before she danced in her innocent white dress — Christina Romney's file would close.

Mr. and Mrs. Shevvington lit a real fire in the fireplace with the sea-green mantel. The mantel arched over the cold stone. The fire caught. While Christina clung to her own file, Mr. Shevvington drew another from his beloved briefcase. "Jessica," he said lovingly to his wife.

"Jessica," she nodded, and they smiled, remembering. They crumpled all the evidence of Jessica — perhaps all that Jessica was or ever would be now — and tossed it onto the fire, smiling, smiling, smiling. The fire flickered and smiled back, like an ally. Like an old friend.

The day was hot. Mrs. Shevvington crossed the parlor with its dark flocked walls and pushed aside the thick ancient curtains, with their linings as ancient and rotten as her own mind. She thrust open the window.

The curtains swayed in the breeze.

The scent of roses, wisteria vines, and sea grass reached their noses; the perfumes of Christina's world. Of her own space on this earth. Of Burning Fog Isle.

Come to me! thought Christina. Come save me. I am Christina of the Isle, and I need you.

Sea wind raced over the waves, lifting them into great curls, like fingers of the dead.

Sea wind separated the three colors of her hair: again, she was silver and gold and sable.

Sea wind coursed through the dry, old house. It

came in through the cellar passage, and passed through the kitchen, and crept into the hallways, invisibly swirling and twisting.

It entered every room, looking for a way out.

Jessica burst into flames.

Mrs. Shevvington added Emily.

The wind kicked the parlor door open.

The door slammed against the wall, as if an angry ghost had stormed in.

The Shevvingtons turned, alarmed. But nothing was there. "For a minute, I thought Christina had found a way out," laughed Mr. Shevvington. He tossed crunched-up remains of Emily into the fire.

Nothing visible had been added to the room.

But the wind had come: Christina's wind, of the Isle.

Chapter 22

Sea wind reached into the shallow fireplace. It lifted the crumpled, flaming balls of paper that were Jessica and Emily. There was no grate, no screen. The wind hurled the smouldering proof across the room into the dry, silken, old drapes.

The curtains caught fire in the blink of an eye. They turned silver and gold and then immediately were nothing but black char, falling to the floor.

The green-flocked wallpaper caught fire.

The intricate, creamy wooden molding around the windows caught fire.

The old spindled tables and elegant varnished chairs caught fire.

Val screamed. Christina and Val backed into the hall. Mr. and Mrs. Shevvington came right after them. Mr. Shevvington said calmly to his wife, "Just shut the door, my dear. Stopping the draft will stop the fire."

Christina grabbed Val's hand and they ran up

the stairs. Up, up, and up, to the only place left to go, to the cupola.

But the parlor door was as old as the curtains, and it no longer met at the edges. Flames licked through the cracks like long yellow tongues. The fire ran ahead of the wind, snatching curtains and furniture, old walls and ancient beams.

The parlor was consumed.

The fire reached for the hall.

More! cried the house, which the Shevvingtons had wired to whisper names and evil thoughts.

More! cried the wind, which the Shevvingtons had caused to whistle through tiny holes and frighten fragile Anya.

More! cried the sea, whose tides the Shevvingtons had used to swallow Dolly.

Christina coughed.

Val choked.

Down below, Mr. Shevvington said, "Just unlock the front door my dear, and we'll go next door and be safe. What a pity the girls forgot elementary safety rules. Anybody knows that fire and smoke rise."

Val was fastening herself so tightly to Christina that it was like wearing another layer of extremely heavy clothing. Christina reached the final step. With scrabbling fingers she struggled to find the latches that would release the cupola windows. They opened outward to a narrow wooden ledge where once there had been a widow's walk. Christina had been out there once. But the latches were too tight for her to budge. Or else they, too, were locked. Christina's small fingers were the right size to get under the little latches, but too small to have enough force to open them.

"The fire will burn the floor out from under our feet," sobbed Val.

Below them, Mr. Shevvington said, "Open the bolt, my dear."

"I'm trying," said Mrs. Shevvington. "I can't see it. There's too much smoke."

Christina could not see her latches either in the dark swirls. "Hold your breath, Val," she muttered. Her lungs seared with pain, from the hot smoke or from needing another fresh breath. But she did not breathe. She fought with the latch. "I can't get it," she said to Val.

"We're going to burn to death," whispered Val.

Downstairs, Mrs. Shevvington screamed, "I got the bolt out. But where are the keys? We have to get the lock, too! Give me your keys!"

"No, we're not," said Christina. She kicked in the window. Glass spattered out into the air and shot through the sky. Glass, and only glass, leaped over the roof and fell below on the rocks of Candle Cove. High tide thundered in to meet it. The spray of waves met the spray of falling glass and no eye could tell one from the other.

Christina stepped out onto the ledge, dragging Val with her. "It's over for me now," said Christina dully. "I might as well step off into Candle Cove."

"What do you mean?" cried Val sucking in wonderful clean ocean air, laughing in the blue sky. "We got out! You did it, Christina! We're going to be all right. Look, somebody's already reported the fire. I hear sirens. We're so high up I bet we can see the firehouse doors open. Yes — here comes the first truck! They'll take us down the ladder."

Great heat rose up the stairwell, as if in a huge, stepped chimney. Wreaths of smoke danced around the two girls. Under their feet they could feel the temperature increasing. Val danced lightly on the narrow wooden shelf.

In the road fire engines gleamed scarlet, with the brightness that only fire engines have. Two kinds of sirens screamed. Tourists yanked cars halfway onto sidewalks and children turned to see where the fire engines were going.

Christina and Val could see the whole village, the whole school complex. Christina thought of the seventh grade, and what they would think of her. Of Jonah and Benjamin, of Anya and Blake, but most of all, of her mother and father.

"The Shevvingtons will tell everybody I lit the fire," said Christina. "The Shevvingtons will say I did this. They'll have all their terrible stories to back it up. Nobody will believe me. Not ever."

The first shining truck came out of the narrow roads above Breakneck Hill Road. Breakneck Hill was named for a little boy who a hundred years before had ridden a bike down it, and lost control. I'm in control now, thought Christina. But I never will be again. The Shevvingtons have won.

A ladder wound off the top of the immense truck, like some enormous chain necklace. On the pavement, firemen began yanking on huge protective yellow and black suits. Val screamed and yelled and waved as if it were a Halloween parade.

"You go first," said Christina, as the fireman began coming up the ladder toward them.

She stood alone on the ledge, her hair blowing in the wind from Burning Fog Isle. Under her feet, the ancient wood crackled and burned. For Christina, the worst nightmare had come true. She was alone, friendless, and lost. Forever, and ever, and ever.

Chapter 23

It was a very tiny airplane.

From where Christina stood, between Mr. Gardner and Mrs. Gardner, it looked like a paper airplane a seventh-grader might throw across the room when the teacher wasn't looking.

"I thought my parents would come in on Frankie's boat," she said.

"Certainly not," said Mr. Gardner. "Not when it's this much of an emergency. They chartered a plane." He picked Christina up, as if she were three or four years old, instead of nearly fourteen. He hugged her hard and said, "They love you, Christina. They'll be here in a minute."

"You see, Christina," said the fire chief, standing behind Mr. Gardner, "the only fingerprints we found at the storm cottage were Mrs. Shevvington's. That made us wonder. Why had she trespassed? It's one thing for a little girl like you to slip into a locked summer house — but the seventh-grade teacher? And then both Robbie and Jonah came to us, telling us that they were pretty sure that Mrs. Shevvington was stuffing your purse and pockets with matches. That was such a sick and frightening image. I couldn't get it out of my mind."

"And," said Mrs. Gardner, the personnel secretary, "I made those telephone calls, Christina. I adored the Shevvingtons. I admit it. I thought they were wonderful. Loving, caring, generous. But I reached people in Oregon, in Louisiana, and in Pennsylvania, with stories like Val's. Like Anya's. Like yours. You were absolutely right, Christina. It was their hobby. The way some couples collect antiques or refinish cars, the Shevvingtons like to destroy."

"And when they were trying to label you a wharf rat," said Mr. Gardner, "even saying your mother and father were — why, we've known your family forever, Christina. It was impossible. Why would they say things like that? What was the point? I kept turning it over in my mind."

"We were slow figuring it out," said Mrs. Gardner. She rubbed Christina's back, comforting her. "We didn't want to admit that we had brought into our community a man and a woman who were genuine sadists. People who would start rumors for the joy of seeing the damage." She suddenly clung to Christina's shoulder, as if even Mrs. Gardner needed to hang onto the granite that was Christina Romney. "We began to see," said Mrs. Gardner, "that of course if you like to hurt people, you would choose a child who can't fight back. And in this town,

619

you would choose an island child, whose parents are not there to see. And you would choose the sweet ones, because where would the pleasure be in hurting the nasty kids? The fun is the emptying of a soul everybody loves, not a soul everybody loathes."

The fun, thought Christina.

Their final moment had not been fun.

"I feel terrible that you had to go through so much torture, Christina," said Mr. Gardner, "before we did our part in stopping the Shevvingtons. All the same, I wish it hadn't ended like that."

Everybody turned involuntarily, to look back across the cove and the village at the cliff where once a huge white sea captain's house had stood. Schooner Inne was gone. No sooner had Val and Christina been scooped off the cupola than flames shot from every window and the entire building turned black and collapsed. Nobody could have gotten out.

"We got a video," said another fireman. "What a shot! You girls will want to see that."

Christina did not think so. She remembered the screams from beneath her feet, when flames took the carpet under Mrs. Shevvington's heels, when the woman ran from room to room screaming, "Where are my keys?" When flames melted the doorknob under Mr. Shevvington's hand, and he jerked back, screaming, "Get the keys!"

The fireman said to Christina, "You'll be fantastic on that film footage. The way you stood on that ledge, your hair blowing in the wind, looking for all the world like the figurehead of some ancient sailing ship, pointing toward justice and port."

The tiny plane landed, bounced, slowed down, and taxied toward them. Christina freed herself from the Gardners and ran toward her mother and father. The little door opened and out popped her mother, holding out her arms, crying her daughter's name. And then her father, shouting, "Christina!" The plane motor cut the syllables of her name up into sections, and vibrated them across the pavement.

And then she was safe, wrapped in her family.

They held the seventh-grade picnic anyway. The school board said it would frighten the children to have to think about what Mr. and Mrs. Shevvington were really like, and it was best to have them think about three-legged races and watermelon seed-spitting contests instead. "We don't want our little boys and girls to have any knowledge of evil," said the man who had hired the Shevvingtons.

Christina thought that was silly. The more knowledge you had of evil, the better you could combat it. How could anybody learn from what she had been through if nobody would admit it had happened? Out there somewhere, in another state, in another village, another thirteen-year-old girl might come face to face with evil for the first time. She had to know what to do, how to tell the world.

The smell of wet towels and bathing suits filled the air. They had a lip-sync contest and a Frisbee toss. They had corn on the cob and blueberry cobbler. Parents stood around laughing, teachers sat cross-legged swatting gnats, and neighbors looked yearningly at the games, wishing they were children again.

Christina's parents could not stop hugging her, holding her, telling her how wonderful she was. "You triumphed," said her father. "You won."

"And without us," said her mother sadly. "We didn't believe you. I will never forgive myself that we didn't believe you."

Mr. and Mrs. Armstrong were awkward with Val. Christina could imagine why. How would it feel to know you had put the opinion of the high school principal ahead of the word of your daughter? How would it feel to know that your child had spent a year under lock, key, and tranquilizers because you did not believe in her?

Close, thought Christina. I came so close.

Blake came, and Anya, and they, too, hugged her and said how proud they were of her courage. Christina was surprised to find that a hug from Blake was only a hug; it did not take away her senses and fling her into crazy love. It was just two arms.

And when they walked away, she thought, I was the one with courage. Not Blake. He could have come back weekends from his boarding school. He could have spoken up for me after the thing with the cliff. But he was afraid he would sound dumb, and people would think he made it all up. So he said nothing.

She took a marshmallow when her father offered her one, and poked a green twig through it.

There were many marshmallow-roasting techniques. Some people liked to get their marshmallow an even, light tan all over, and some liked to set it on fire, and some liked it to start dripping down the stick so you could lick it up, tongue-burning hot and crispy black on the outside.

Like Schooner Inne.

They had brought forth what they said was Mr. and Mrs. Shevvington. It was teeth, actually, and belt buckles, and bones.

When Anya had been afraid of the poster of the sea, she had thought she could see the hands of the drowned reaching up through the waves. The sea wants one of us! she had cried.

The sea had two now. By its wind and tide, it had set its own fires to take the Shevvingtons.

I was afraid, she thought. More afraid than Blake or Benj could ever know. And nobody believed me. But I was born in the arms of Good, and I am made of granite, and if I had let them go — Anya and Dolly and Val — I would have been Evil myself.

There is Evil in silence.

But there is no silence at a seventh-grade picnic.

Rock music jarred Christina awake. Throbbing, strumming guitars, drums, and electric keyboards.

The seventh grade was dancing without her. Everybody was dancing. Summer people and townspeople, firemen and teachers, parents and children.

The music screamed; the tide slapped; the sun set.

Her father and mother danced; Mr. and Mrs. Gardner danced; Mr. and Mrs. Armstrong danced. Blake danced with Anya and then he danced with Val.

It's primitive, thought Christina. Like ancient warriors by the sea, we are having our funeral celebration for the death of Evil among us.

Benjamin and Jonah came toward her, one from the sea and one from the land. One with broad shoulders and strong arms, one with long skinny legs and a long skinny smile.

The boys hardly saw each other. They had eyes only for Christina of the Isle. And, at the same time, they said, "Chrissie? Let's dance." Each held out a hand. The silver and gold of Christina's strange hair divided, and tangled, and told her secrets.

She remembered all that was to come: the sophomore dance, the fund-raising for the band trip to Disney World, the ferry on which Jonah could come, the lobster boat she could go out on with Benjamin. Summer on Burning Fog. The roses that bloomed among the rocks and the cats that had kittens in the barns.

"Oh, yes," said Christina Romney. "There is so much to dance for."

And she took both hands.

About the Author

Caroline B. Cooney lives in a small seacoast village in Connecticut. She writes every day and then goes for a long walk down the beach to figure out what she's going to write the following day. She's written over fifty books for young people including *The Party's Over*; the acclaimed *The Face on the Milk Carton* quartet; *Flight #116 Is Down*, which won the 1994 Golden Sower Award for Young Adults, the 1995 Rebecca Caudill Young Readers' Book Award, and was selected as an ALA Recommended Book for the Reluctant Young Adult Reader; *Flash Fire*; *Emergency Room*; *The Stranger*; and *Twins*. *Wanted!* and *The Terrorist* were both 1998 ALA Quick Picks for Reluctant Young Adult Readers.

Ms. Cooney reads as much as possible and has three grown children.

Other Caroline B. Cooney
Paperbacks you will enjoy:

Flight 116 Is Down

The Terrorist

Mummy

Hush Little Baby

Emergency Room

Wanted!

Twins